To my wife, Jenny, and our boys, plus the doctors and nurses who have helped me in my darkest hours, of which there have been far too many!

Tim Brightwell

A New Beginning

Austin Macauley Publishers
LONDON * CAMBRIDGE * NEW YORK * SHARJAH

Copyright © Tim Brightwell 2021

The right of Tim Brightwell to be identified as author of this work has been asserted by the author in accordance with section 77 and 78 of the Copyright, Designs and Patents Act 1988.

All rights reserved. No part of this publication may be reproduced, stored in a retrieval system, or transmitted in any form or by any means, electronic, mechanical, photocopying, recording, or otherwise, without the prior permission of the publishers.

Any person who commits any unauthorised act in relation to this publication may be liable to criminal prosecution and civil claims for damages.

This is a work of fiction. Names, characters, businesses, places, events, locales, and incidents are either the products of the author's imagination or used in a fictitious manner. Any resemblance to actual persons, living or dead, or actual events is purely coincidental.

A CIP catalogue record for this title is available from the British Library.

ISBN 9781528916097 (Paperback)
ISBN 9781528919067 (ePub e-book)

www.austinmacauley.com

First Published 2021
Austin Macauley Publishers Ltd®
1 Canada Square
Canary Wharf
London
E14 5AA

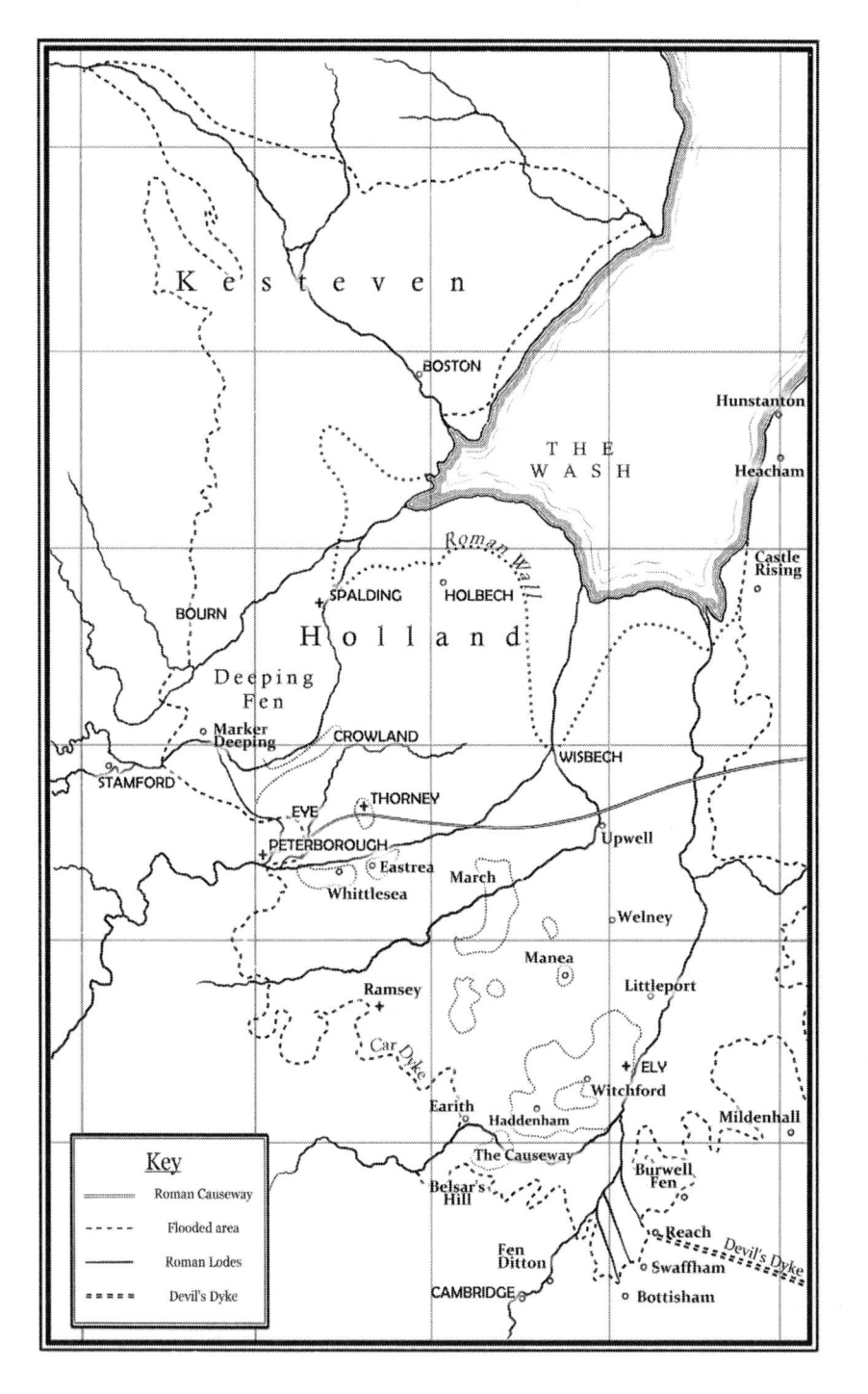

Map to "CAMP OF REFUGE" showing the islands in the flooded landscape which form the basis for the books.

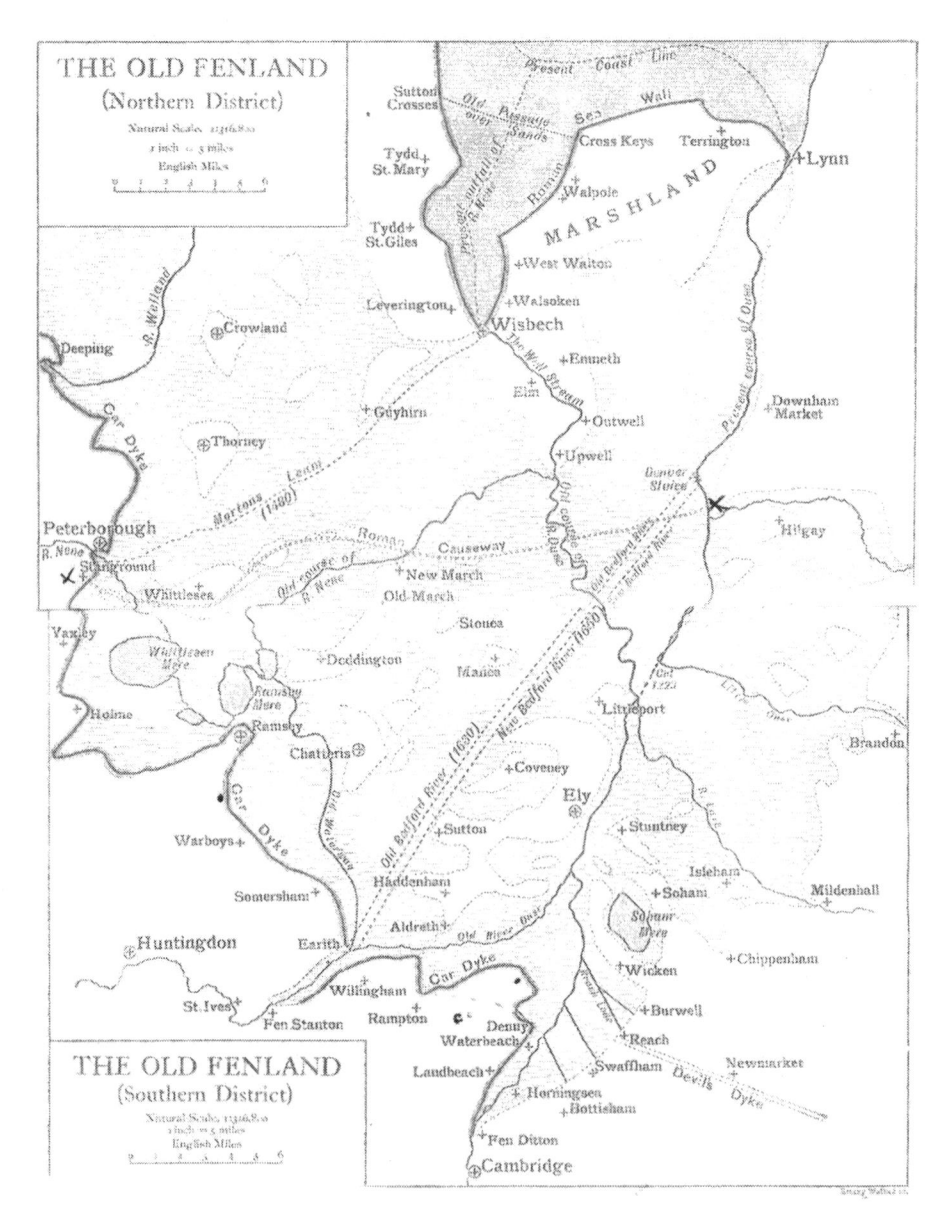

This map shows the rivers dug to drain the fenland in the 15th and 17th centuries, the causeway and the Lodes of Bottisham, Reach, Burwell and Swaffam, plus Car Dyke were achieved by the Romans. Much other work was done through the ages before we reached where we are today.

Chapter 1
A New Beginning
1066

Leofric's story with Hereward the Wake, leaders of the Saxon Fightback.

Setting the Scene

Summer at our cell in Spalding, Lincolnshire.
 Summer in the flood lands and the Fens of the Isle of Ely, near Cambridge.
 The sun shone through the reeds to greet another day, the river Glen looked calm and quite normal for this time of year as it flowed towards joining the river Welland, the reeds were rustling and swaying in the wind. It was a beautiful day, one on which you could only feel glad to be alive.
 My thoughts were, however, elsewhere, as I wrestled with the problems of the future of our kingdom. The freedom and contentment of our Anglo-Saxon population was ever with me at this time.
 Another day dawned, one of rumour and intrigue, the question on our minds, were the Normans going to arrive or not, and if they did what was going to happen.
 The word was that they would destroy much of our Abbey, if we tried to defend it, and murder and replace our abbot with one of their own, let alone what they would do to the local population if there was any resistance.

King of Northumbria

The man who, along with the King of Norway, tried to topple King Harold.
 Earl Tostig, brother of King Harold, was deposed as King of Northumbria in October,1065, he took refuge in Flanders that year and became one of the first to champion William the Conqueror.
 In the middle of 1066, he raided the Isle of Wight with a large number of soldiers and went on to ravage parts of Sussex. This was why Harold waited for William on the Isle, he thought William would land at the same spot Earl Tostig had. It clearly was not a good place to land as you only had to march a short distance, then you would have to get onto ships again and sail to the mainland itself.
 He then went on to raid the North of Lincolnshire but was sent packing by Earl Eadwine, Edwin, and Morkere, better known as Morcar, he then sought

refuge in Scotland with King Malcolm. Edwin and Morcar were sons of Alfgar, brothers in law to King Harold.

Stamford Bridge and King Harold

Harold had other problems, challenges to his throne in the north of England. A huge fight with the Vikings at Stamford Bridge took place.

Earl Tostig enlisted the aid of Harrold Hadrada, King of Norway. With him and his troops, he invaded Yorkshire and camped at Stamford Bridge, eight miles east of York. Our King Harold and his men fought well and won. Tostig and Harrold both died in the battle on the 25th September. 1066.

Harold was then told William had landed at Pevensey Bay, on the south coast, as Harold had told his ships to stand down, there was no opposition.

William took over the area unopposed, wiping out villages in his way as he went, mainly to cause Harold to react sooner rather than later as he would not have time to recover from the Stamford Bridge battles. He brought 700 ships, and 14,000 men with him, 2000 horse as cavalry. This alone, was a huge undertaking, just imagine!

Harold paused for three days in London on his return, he then went to fight William. William sent an envoy to speak to Harold and offered to fight him by himself thereby saving their armies.

Harold refused, and on 13th October 1066, they were just eight miles apart.

On Saturday 14th October 1066, the fighting began. At Battle, eight miles from Hastings, Harold had the high ground, on Senlac Hill. William had bows and arrows, that could, and did, kill men easily at eighty to one hundred metres distant. William had cavalry and charged the English lines, Harold's men formed a great shield wall to hold them off which they did very well by all accounts. After hours of attacks, Williams's men were getting nowhere.

Suddenly, a whole group of William's men began to run from the fight, apparently Harold's men thought they were fleeing, though I suspect it was merely a ploy, so they followed, and in rode Williams's cavalry to begin slaughtering all in the English lines.

Harold chose to not use his horses in battle, if he had, he might not have lost, he rode to the fight and fought on foot. His men stood little chance against the well drilled cavalry, then the infantry finished the English (Anglo-Saxons) off.

Before this Harold was struck by a stray arrow in the eye, he soon died of his wounds, another story tells us that William sent in a death squad to kill him, who really knows?

It was 6th January 1066; when he died, he had been king for only 281 days. He became one of our most talked of kings, due to the battle, one can only wonder what he might have achieved if he had had the chance of a long and fruitful life!

William thought he would be offered to become king straight away, this did not happen, so he travelled along the coast to Dover, killing those who opposed him, he followed the line of north Kent to London. He was forced away from the bridge into London.

The Normans crossed the Thames at Wallingford and followed the road to Beckhampstead, 25 miles from the city, there the English leaders met him, submitted to him, and offered him to become King of England.

On 25th December 1066, he was crowned at Westminster, William the First.

He might have expected everyone to submit to him, they did not, he had many years of fighting to come. William had the Tower of London built and began taking over his new country.

The Viking Age was over, we were forced to look to France and Rome now. William spent most of the rest of his life in Normandy and died in 1087.

It is interesting to note that the Normans were originally Vikings who fought any opposition and colonised the Normandy area, they settled with acceptance from the French king. He had no choice at the time, as he was weak, they adopted their laws and language. They did fight and take other areas of France, and many other lands on their way to the crusades, hence, "Normandy", men from the north.

Following the dreadful events at Hastings where our King Harold had been killed by the Normans, William had moved about "settling" each district with his own lord and abbot where applicable.

Our own abbot had told us that this was a Norman takeover and to make no mistake they would be here. This area of marsh, rivers, islands and reeds was the last to be settled as it was so inhospitable, but settled in the Norman way it would be, we had no doubt, this did not bode well!

The remaining Saxons were terrified, even dead Saxons were having their tombs smashed, the living were demoralized.

We heard stories, we hoped were wrong but they centred on the, we hoped false lines, that our York minster was gone in flames and every religious house and church and chapel were destroyed and plundered right across the country, they were intent on wiping us from the face of the earth, if we stood in their way.

Pavefactus est Populus. The people were terrified.

Frithric, Abbot of St Albans, was evicted and replaced by a man called Paul, a Norman monk, he was helped by Archbishop Lanfranc to build the great church of St Albans.

It is said some of the ruins of Verulam, the Roman city, were used to build this 548-foot-long place of worship, Roman bricks are visible in the arches of the transept. It seems that this Paul brought all his friends and relations from Normandy, many of these people were ignorant but they were given farms and woods and property in general formerly owned by the Anglo-Saxon/English.

Frithric was fond of saying *Libera Nos Domine*, Good lord deliver us, but we received no help from above! Another line he uttered frequently was, *Deus Noster Refugium* God is our refuge, though this seemed to little avail.

Chapter 2

Reed-gatherer near Ely *circa r* 1880-90 but it could have been taken any time
throughout the ages
The dog went by the name of Blake.
Photo: Camb. Antiq. Soc.

Exploring the Floodland!

I looked around for places to hide, tiny pieces of land surrounded by thick reed beds that nobody who did not live here would know about, I was busily making note of them in the back of my mind…….just in case a fast exit was needed to a good hiding place.

Training Future Soldiers

I, Leofric Bartholomew, and some friends, were part of a group of local young blokes, who had formed an unofficial group of defenders against the Norman onslaught. We called ourselves the "Boston Defenders" after one of the lads who was born in Boston; we thought it was a grand title! We were forty in number, to begin with. The number rose, very quickly, even before we had experienced any fighting! Hatred towards the invaders of our peaceful land was rife.

I was a novice from Thorney abbey, set on an island in the midst of the waters that surrounded the area, I seemed to get enough time to run the group, so mainly on the grounds that nobody else had put up their hand to do the job I took it on!

Was I a mug? Not sure yet, though I must admit I enjoyed getting everyone together and it was always good fun, we all had a laugh! Plus the fact that we felt we were doing something positive in relation to making a stand against the enemy, attempting to fight back! At this point it was mainly talk, we were just doing something positive in the very negative world that surrounded us. There seemed to be no talk of fighting back, we had to try and do something, surely?

We trained several times a week, using the same methods we watched the local force carry out, though our swords were only pieces of wood, we used short broad hunting knives and used shields to protect ourselves, the knives were concealed under the skirts of our garments, tied to our girdles.

I must admit we got carried away with this fighting/training at times. To build our leg muscles we ran in the shallow fen, we raced until we were exhausted, then lay on an island laughing at ourselves, we carried logs of different sizes over longer and longer distances to build our muscles.

At times, we carried a long pole as the quickest way to travel the fens was to launch yourself across the waterways that were not too far across, poles were left permanently at certain places to aid folk in general. The general way to get through the flood lands/marshlands was by horse or boat in areas too deep.

Stilts were used by some people as you could go where you needed, we all became experts with these, had long and drawn out mock fights. Our shoulder and arm muscles developed quickly, we had our own poles hidden away as you were never sure as to where and when they might be needed, the lower end of these poles consisted of heavy iron with spikes of nails sticking out of them to not only give us grip in the water/mud but to use in defence if necessary.

Our main method of fighting was with our bows and arrows, when we had any time it was used in practising firing, a lot of dinners were provided after our efforts as we improved, the use of short lances was becoming more and more important, especially when planning to attack from our flat-bottomed boats.

More importantly, on horseback, we got very wet in rushing onto land in mock attack mode. Arrows slung across our shoulders, knives, bows, poles at the ready and lances. We were beginning to put on a show of strength, impressing even ourselves.

In short, we thought, we were very strong and fit, as at that time, we did not know what lay in the future, we hoped we were prepared for all eventualities, or at least some of them! We lacked confidence of a battle of any sort, there was only one way of achieving that state of mind, get amongst the fighting as soon as possible, we must aim for that first moment and build from there!

We only knew of the perilous state of our country and that we would fight to the end to protect our way of life, and our families, if we could. Our parents knew little of what we did in our spare time.

Leofric Bartholomew-myself!

I did not actually get as much spare time as I used to, my responsibilities were increasing at the cell, as I was a novice at Thorney abbey, I had been moved to the succursal cell, or dependent house, at Spalding, which was bang in the middle of the Lincolnshire fenlands at this time.

These fens tended to grow and shrink in area depending on the amount of rainfall we had during the winter months in and around the thirteen counties that emptied their rain through their rivers into our fen area. Spalding was not far out of the flood lands at this time.

The Cell/Our Religious House

We had six friars, three novices, three lay brothers and four hinds, it was founded in 1052 by a prior Hurbert, he was a sub prior of Crowland/Thorney Abbeys.

The building was made of stone, brick, and rubble, it was very strong but the upper part was of wood with a few round headed arches with short mullions, they were evidence of the chapel and where the hall was used as chapter, refectory and a great many other things.

Away from the chapel was a bell tower, built in the same way, the top part had open arches, the old bell was on view as was the ponderous mallet which was the clapper. It was moated and gated. The wood was the only real problem as that could be set on fire much too easily, thereby setting alight the rest of the building inside which was of course wood as well, clearly, not enough thought had been put into the entire construction of this building. Nothing could be done about that now.

We all felt quite secure, until the Norman invasion. We had fought off two attacks from the Danes in the past, with the help of men from Spalding. It was moated, though the drawbridge was not very large.

Chapter 3

Abbot of Caen

The enemy installed Lanfranc of Bec, as primate of our kingdom. Most Saxon abbots and priors were evicted and replaced by French or Italians, a few stayed, subject on submission to William.

Most of these people spoke no English, it was the most insulting thing that could happen in these religiously charged times. Nothing from the pulpit or confessional could be understood, many of the clergy were instructed to only confer in French or Latin. Most of them could do no other!

The people leading the country had cut themselves off from its population, considering themselves far superior. We would make them pay, sooner or later, somehow!

It was said that Aldred, archbishop of York, had placed the crown on Williams head, as he did Harold's, and that he had rebuked William for wrong doing, murdering so many civilians causing so much pain and suffering, burning towns and villages. He sadly passed away due to stress and sorrow on 11th September 1069. He could not stand to see his country torn apart, his own kin murdered.

The Norman age had begun, or had it! Really?

Spalding

This was great in the summer, but with the dreadful winter winds coming in from the wash, it brought snow, ice and rain, it was as a result very cold, worse than a little further inland at Thorney, or maybe it just felt that way.

I had made my way from Thorney by boat to the nearest dry land towards Crowland abbey, there were a number of heron making their dreadful startled noise when they were disturbed. We were also delighted to see the wonderful coloured flash of a kingfisher flying by. Squabbling ducks were everywhere fighting over food or a drake, pidgeon were fighting in the trees along the edge of the water making a lot of noise. Everything seemed to be fighting these days.

This was a lovely scene, the waterways were a beautiful place to live, even the noise of the breeze going through the reed beds was quite special, relaxing in its own way.

You could almost believe no war existed amongst us in our land.

It did exist, however, and we would all have our lives turned upside down, very soon!

When I was dropped off on dry land, I began to make my way through the vast forests of elder, willow and reeds, they never seemed to end. The tops of the willows caught the breeze on this early morning, little snaps of blue sky fought their way through with a welcome shot of warmth, though the air was not cold.

I thought that going cross country may have been easier for me than taking the road which was not at all direct, this was not so as even for me it was hard going. I regarded myself as being quite fit, at least at the beginning of this trip.

The pole was proving a great help, as I could get a good distance with a little run up to help get me over the fen ditches, though the reeds held me back at times. I must admit, I soon became wet and muddy, it did not matter how hard I tried to stay clear of all water and mud it began to cling to me.

However, I knew there was a quite large river that may or may not be full at this time of year, at times it tended to fill or drain, it went by the name of Cat water, I could perhaps clean myself of the mud, before going on my way.

Every now and then, the breeze produced an unusual sound, I had to stop to make sure it was not perhaps some Normans waiting somewhere near me to cause trouble, I was being very careful these days, who was around the next corner?

I could hear some splashing up ahead of me and wondered what was causing it, quite a lot of crashing noise in the reeds going on too.

A lot of noise was coming towards me, splashing water and crashing reeds, I crouched to the ground, didn't know what else to do, it became so loud, suddenly a huge stag appeared in front of me and stood very still. His eyes were bright and shining, as he gazed in my direction, if he could make out what I was, he did not seem to mind, another came crashing through the reeds and reared up when he noticed the other had stopped.

I had no way of transporting these animals, so no use for food, even if I could subdue one so I just kept my position and watched, the larger one snorted several times reared up and stormed off followed by the other. There were others I could hear moving in my general direction, so I kept my place and saw a few more, nothing to match either of the first two though, what beautiful animals. What a lovely land we lived in!

There was a track on the other side of the water which led to Crowland abbey, my destination for the rest of today and tonight. I carried some papers for abbot Adhelm, a good friend and frequent visitor to our Abbot Rudgang at Thorney, I was given the impression that advice on what we may expect if, more likely when, the Normans came.

I looked either way as far as I could see, not that that was very far, and listened for anything that might be approaching.

I then took a few steps backwards, prepared my pole, ran towards the water and took a leap, planted the pole towards the middle of the said water.

It was much deeper than I had expected, the first section of the pole disappeared into bog leaving me with not much to propel myself to the other side, with a rather large splash I found myself desperately trying to get out of this very cold, muddy and wet situation. I would like to think I moved on from this with some sort of dignity but sadly I didn't.

Very wet and rather unhappily, I progressed along the side of the track, glad to see the paperwork was alright as it was in a sealed leather bag around my neck.

It was about four miles from Thorney to Crowland in a straight line, quite a few more if you went by track, the idea being safer and possible quicker going through the fen. I think I will stick to the track in future!

There was a gravel ridge up and out of the fen near here, much dry ground for those in need, towards the end of it was my destination, Crowland abbey.

As I sat in the sun, I could hear a group of horses approaching, sounded like quite a lot of people. This was not normal as only the abbey was along this track, I fell to my knees and lay behind a bed of reeds.

As the first horse appeared, the dreaded thought that this was the first of the Norman invasion came into my mind. The men were all wearing battle gear and were talking in a language I did not understand, so it appeared I was thinking along the right lines.

This was not good, I had my knife and pole to defend myself, but was lacking any experience, or confidence, come to that, and there was nobody with me. I would just have to stay hidden, no matter what, and hope nobody would see me.

Chapter 4

My group of Fen fighters, known as "The Boston Defenders".

All of the Defenders would be with their families, which was not ideal, as I could not get a message to them to prepare for the worst, the worst being our force of fathers fighting would not be of any use against the fearsome and very well drilled Normans.

The main body of horse had now passed, I estimated their number to be between forty and fifty, the dust they caused in the air was really bad, they were on a mission without a doubt. I hoped I was wrong in thinking the worst not just for the abbey but the people of Spalding and my cell who had been nothing but supportive in their dealings with us at the abbey and cell.

The original Boston Defenders:

Edgar Kenulph.scout.	Wulfric the Black. leader/trainer.
William Ryce scout.	Guthrum. leader/trainer.
Matthew Upton Cynesige scout.	Titus Frithric.arrow/spearman
Wilfrith Meginhard scout.	Iggy Hubert.arrow/spearman
Walter Reynold scout.	Cedric Wybert.arrow/spearman
Warinus Bassingbourn scout.	Ralph of Spalding.arrow/spearman
Richard Hokyton group Leader.	Thurston. Ralph of the Dyke.
Nicholas Bacon group Leader.	Kenelm Withlag.
Peter Ganning group Leader.	Hodge The Miller.
Thomas Eltisle group Leader.	Colin Rush.

*Leofric (myself) Bartholomew. elected Leader.	Prithee.
Cedric (The Fen) Wenoth. Leader. My No.2.	Old Gaffers Son.
Xanda Garrod, (brave spearman) Brown.	Goodman Hodge.
Simeon Ellison-expert with the sword.	Hob the Carpenter.
Athelred Dexter. Camp/hut maker.	Godeine Gille.
Edric Dickenson. Fireman.	Herman Duti.
Leofric Dorsey. Fireman.	Leofwine.
Aart Dwerryhouse. Eel trapper.	Hugo the Priest.
Acton Dickman. Arrow man.	Outi.
Aiken Eads. Arrow man.	Leofric. The Deacon.

Aiden Edgar Camp/Hut Maker

Alton Endicott. Fisherman
Zac Fishman. Fireman
Holt Franklyn. Fisherman
Manton Espenson. Arrow man
Montgomery Haggard. Eel trapper
Rand Hampton. Butcher 1
Rice Cyneric, Camp/Hutmaker
Ripley Kersey. From Boston…
Roan Hunnisett, Arrow Man
Roe Leofwine. Camp/Hutmaker
Rowan Meginhard. Doctor 1
Roweson Ledford. Camp/Hutmaker
Ware Jernigan. Butcher 2
Whitney Cynebald. Doctor 2
Wilbur Hathaway. Camp/Hutmaker
Wilfrid Eoforwine
Winchell Millhouse. Camp/Hutmaker
Woodrow Huxtable

Tait Hambleton
Tedman Martinson
Wynchell Marley
Zack Brightcard
Xander Brightcard (our only brothers).

The Girvii

Gopal Girvii Aescwine. Wife's name, Rahmullah
Vitt Hal Biotmonap, Leader of the Girvii.
Vin Girvii Eadgifri,
Star Girvii Osiac,
Bikassim Girvii Sunningfu,
Gopal Girvii Grendel,
Andi Girvii Hanaper, Wife's name, Haddof
Rizal Girvii Ecgfrith, Wife's Name, Waiyawut.

Six Iceni/Romano Britons

Arthfael,
Bricius,
Sextilius,
Their leader :Vercingetorix, (King over Warriors)
Seisyll,
Toutorix

Soldiers to Begin the Fight Back!
The Girvii

These men came highly recommended by Tonbert, King of the Girvii, he felt they could represent his people, of the old English tribe, well in battle. We would no doubt need people like them if we were going to make any mark at all against the Norman invader. Some of my men thought they would be difficult to work with; they were soon proved wrong!

They were very disciplined and exceptionally strong, not only that but they mucked in with the rest of us with any job, at any time. Their enthusiasm and commitment were infectious.

They had fled and fought the Romans, then the Angles from the north, then the Saxons from the south in the 5th century. They eventually found peace in the wilds of the fens, lost to all, for a long time! Their peace was ruined by these new invaders from across the sea, so they decided to join with the Anglo-Saxons and fight, yet again, for their freedom, land and solitude.

Iceni

These men had joined us, or offered to join us before we had even laid plans for this adventure. They were hardy men from Norfolk and had been trained to a high standard by their King. Their men had fought against the Romans long ago and kept a small force on standby when the enemy had left to protect themselves against possible foes appearing. They had done so in the form of the Normans and felt they must try and protect themselves and their way of life.

Chapter 5

Attack on Crowland

I began to walk back towards Crowland, the horses had gone from view, so I was back to the peace and quiet of the fens.

Not for long the peace as I could hear much shouting and the odd sound of commands in the air, so I decided to move a little quicker. The great abbey appeared as I rounded the last corner in the track, it seemed to take in the whole sky for a moment.

Much commotion was happening at the front of the abbey. A line of horses at the entrance and a lot of shouting, other horses were going around the sides of the walls, presumable to enter by the back gate.

I had heard of the Normans taking lads of my age and training them to fight, they were left with no choice, punished if they did not do as they were told. They were indoctrinated in the Norman way so there was no way I was going to be taken by these dreadful killers whose sole purpose was to take over all walks of life, even the way we speak. So much for the abbey and its staff, all lost without so much as a fight. I must try and warn Spalding of what to expect, things were dire, indeed!

I ran across the track, feeling much safer behind thick beds of reed, made my way over water I had not seen before, small islands, deep ditches to leap over, this was quite tiring but I felt better as the sound of the takeover began to fade.

It was lucky I was not there as I had planned, that was as close as I ever wanted to be to the Normans. My resolve to fight these people became stronger and stronger from this point. I would not be told what to do or how to do it by people I did not know or respect, couldn't understand what they said either, come to that!

It was time for food, so I sat and ate some meat I had brought with me. I could still hear the noise, made me feel useless, I could not help in any way.

I never wanted to feel this way again. I would resist this takeover with all my being, I feared for the good abbot and all else at the abbey.

I began to sadly leave the gravel ridge that the abbey was built on, more and more waterway/fen appeared in front of me, it would be a challenge to make it through to my succursal cell at Spalding before night time.

Some small pathways could be seen going, more or less, in the right direction, so I decided to take one. Back into the mud and water again!

Some people said I had a good sense of direction, it really was of no use here as there was nothing but bog, reed bed and more bog or even stream or river mingled with the odd island, a usual fen area! No hills to climb to see where you were. A tree helped if you could find one, to climb and get a good view over the reed beds.

Before Spalding, there was the great moated house that was once the home of earl Leofric, it was now inhabited by a relative of William himself, said to be a nephew, he went by the name of William Wadard.

The house was built of stone, it was battlemented and moated, built to withstand a siege, in these times it was essential to have this kind of mansion if you held power among the people and indeed expected to keep this hold over the area. Regular raids from the continent were not welcome and would happen so when you built a place you needed to take the view that some inevitable would happen. You needed to be secure!

This was very impressive, as all the stone had to be brought many miles to construct the build. To dig the moat must have been a massive undertaking as well.

All around this house had been cleared of trees and reeds, most of the land around had been drained to flow away from the house to a large mere, the rest was brought to create the deep moat to protect the household/garrison within.

A trumpet blasted, startling me out of the thought process I was in, the gate opened, and out came a number of horses, all the men riding were dressed to fight, I did not expect there to be any organised resistance, one could only hope the cell would have time to at least do something, though I supposed they could only delay the inevitable, we were a spent force it seemed at this time.

I Was Never One to Be Written Off!

I struggled for what seemed an age, I was making for the river Welland which runs through Spalding, then into the wash.

A massive flock of sea birds came in off the wash, all making alarming noises, something was disturbing them. Dread filled me as it was possible the Normans in their boats coming up river via the wash.

Just before Spalding there was a crossing point, so I slowly made my way there, at least I thought that I was going in that direction, time would tell.

As I came close to where I thought the river was, I could hear the sound of horses and men chattering, there was a track near the river, this must be the one I needed. Lots of noise splashing in the water filled my ears, though I could hear men's voices, their language I could not understand, it must be Norman/French so I huddled down in the reeds and waited for the horses to go by.

I was not at all sure what the raiders might do to me, but from what I had heard it would not be pleasant, they would kill all who opposed them, even men who were just of fighting age as they would be enemy of the future!

Any group of men would be challenged and killed on the spot if they were thought to be plotting, or able, to fight. If a particular leader of the enemy took a dislike to you, you were as good as dead!

Getting the Boston Boys Together

I decided I needed to start rounding up my group of friends, we needed to talk about proposals to defend ourselves and maybe talk to our families and see what the defence force could do to protect our homes and villages. Quite an amount of this area was flooded at times. Spalding was built on dry land for the most part though some parts flooded at times, it was in general a good area for growing food.

There were signs of fighting, or at least a skirmish, on the outskirts of the town I discovered on my approach.

I eventually reached the river Welland, on the opposite bank was our cell, our ferry boat was moored under the walls of the house but there was nobody to row over, it appeared. It was getting dark so I thought I had better sort of swim, I say sort of swim as we muddled our way over waterways, our feet doing most of the pushing us across.

There was a hard bottom to this section of river, as we had gone through the water so many times at this point. I threw over my pole and jumped in. It was not long enough to help me get over to the other side on this occasion,

The water was very cold, but at least it would get some of the mud that had accumulated from the ditches off my cloths, parts of me smelt more than a little rank.

I reached the far bank and pulled myself out of the water, pulled off the outer layer of clothing I had on and stamped my feet. I rushed over to the main gate and knocked. After quite a long wait, a slow shuffling of feet could be heard, and some moaning, my return was not being greeted by all I feared.

One of the other novices pulled back the lock and opened the gate. Joffrid smiled a greeting when he realised it was me, asked me straight away what I had seen about the state of the country away from the walls of protection, he then lowered the small, but effective, drawbridge to let me enter.

When in, I helped pull up the bridge and locked the great iron studded doors. I said a few words regarding the Normans and said I would rather explain to everyone so he had better wait until after our meal, I crossed the cloistered court and ascended the stairs.

Everyone was in pensive mood, dulled by events outside in the country, things were made worse by the news I gave. I talked to father Adhelm but all listened at the door to his room, he asked me to tell of good tidings but I was afraid there were none to tell.

He thought that the Lord Abbot might have gained the kings peace, I explained that I had heard no such thing from anywhere. We were indeed alone!

The Enemy Would Probably Be Amongst Us Soon

We thought the leader would be a William Wadard, already mentioned as the local Norman thug, who had quickly become known as "the devil of the fens". His group of enemy soldiers would be first to approach/attack us we had no doubt!

Chapter 6

Leaving the Cell to the Enemy

The thinking was to disband the cell altogether, we could not hope to defend it against armed assault, the strength of the enemy was too great, those who could would return to their families and leave it to its fate.

Enemy Approaching

We heard shouting slightly up river, ran to the small windows that looked that way and could see two boats approaching, filled with the enemy, we assumed. As they came nearer and you could make out about twenty soldiers in each boat, crouching, you could make out shields along the outside of the boats, they had swords in one hand, ready to fight if needed. They were clad in mail, what appeared to be spears lay in the boats.

They landed and were at the gates in what seemed a moment, they called, in very bad English, for the gates to be opened and the drawbridge to be lowered. They were intent on taking over! We delayed and ran for anything we valued to take with us, quickly said our goodbyes, and left by the back gate.

This was going to be a huge wrench for the older folk, they would probably have nowhere to go, we simple had no choice, to leave or die a painful death was no choice at all!

To fight and die would be no help to anyone, to leave and train to fight as our group intended was the best, and only, way forward. It was our intention to trap small groups of the enemy and to wipe them out, we may even find other groups of Anglo-Saxons ready to fight and become a force to be reckoned with.

We were all of us sad people, some had spent a huge tract of our lives here, some like me had not but we all felt it a special place and that we had spent some special years there.

These were grim times, we were having to learn some hard facts, we were being taken over in every walk of life, we could not challenge them in small numbers, disorganised and not of fighting fitness.

We did, however, have a chance of fighting them in small numbers at set points in the waterways, marshes and fens amidst the islands we knew so well. Plus the ones we did not know at present.

At least it would be some kind of resistance. We were determined to give them some pain. How any of this would work out in the months, or years, ahead, only time would tell!

I and another novice, Cedric Wenoth, set about a plan to collect our band of "Bostonians" together, so that if things began to look bad for the majority of the people of Spalding we would, if we got the chance to talk with all families, discuss what we proposed, and go and fight the evil Normans in our own back yard. We also collected our Girvii and Iceni men at this time.

The local force of men from the Spalding area who had put up a fight had erected a barrier over the main track into town but were unable to hold off the invaders as all their houses and families were threatened with burning and death, not much option really.

"Hit and Run" Brigade

So it was decided that we would take most of the arms of the Spalding unit of fighting men, collect all those "Bostonians" including Girvii and Iceni "warriors", as they preferred to be known, who had heard of our plans and go and live as a hit and run unit in the wilds of the fens.

That was our plan to begin with and it sounded good at the time.

By this time a large part of the town was in the hands of the Normans, they did not waste time, they were in particular looking for young men who could fight, either they would kill them or take them into their ranks and force them to fight alongside themselves, if they didn't they were told they would be tortured or their families would suffer. No one doubted them!

Cedric and I told all to gather a few clothes and some food and make for a particular point just outside the town, we would try and meet together at a set time on a set day or those who got there soonest to just get away from the track and set up camp and wait for everyone else.

We were all getting exited, the rest of our families were not, who knows when, or indeed if, we would meet again? These were dark times.

We all promised to try and keep in touch, all too soon the time came to leave, so we bade all farewell, and under the cover of darkness left our hometown/area most of us had known all our short lives and set off on the adventure of a lifetime.

Nobody knew, where it would lead us or what we may be forced to do to survive but we swore we would not give an inch of our countryside to our foe without a fight, how many of us would outlive this adventure nobody knew, as many said, it was in the lap of the gods! We just hoped the gods were on our side.

Chapter 7

Though we were not trying die, we were dying to try and force these men from overseas back to their homeland. These islands were special to us and we would not give up without a considerable fight, to the death if necessary! All of us were prepared for this end if it came.

When they took control of Spalding, there were not many seventeen to eighteen-year olds, most were in our forty strong force, which was now seventy-seven, and seemed to be growing all the time, the rest had been sent to areas where there was no sign of trouble to avoid being taken by force to fight against us on pain of having their families/homes destroyed. These were not decent people.

Their Standards Were Inhuman

Some of our women folk were "interfered" with and in general treated badly. This made our hatred much worse.

I was a little concerned our number maybe too many to begin this fight back, we were simple not used to command. Wait and see was the decision of Cedric and myself! Time would tell. If it was deemed better we might break into two groups, wait and see was the order given.

The Leaders

We had left the town in groups of ten to try and avoid attention, Cedric took a group out to the left, Wulfric took another near the track, I took ten the opposite side of the track and Guthrum led another further out, Richard Hokyton, Peter Ganning, Thomas Eltisle Vitt Hal Girvii Biomonap, Nicholas Bacon and Vercingetorix took the other groups.

We split one of the groups into two lots of five as we felt we had nine leaders and thought giving them all a chance would be good to prove themselves. We made slow progress through the firm reeds but we did not want anyone to hear so we kept this up for quite some distance, where there was deeper water it slowed us more. We all thought we had too many leaders but it worked for now, kept us all closer to each other which was of the utmost importance. We had to yet realise who was good at leading with orders or training under orders, this alone was not easy. It was a new world for us all and we had much to learn.

Wulfrics group carried on for some time, they didn't realise we had all stopped, we thought this quite funny. On a serious note, we decided we must never lose touch with a group of us again as it could have been fatal for them.

Just ten men could have been spotted by the enemy and easily killed off, all of us quite close together would be a much more difficult matter for them to contend with.

Eventually, the group to our right decided we had reached the point where we were due to meet the others, so we all, this side of the track, joined them and made our way to the main track which we had to cross to get to the tree at the arranged meeting point.

As we came near, we could hear horses approaching from our left, Spalding, we all froze where we stood and crouched on the ground or in the water, very low as we were quite near the track. Luck was with us as the reeds were thick.

French Speaking!

A lot of a strange speaking tongue could be heard, Cedric murmured to me that the shouts were in French, rushing horses crashing now along the track, sped by us at a good speed, it really was quite exciting. As the dust settled we all stood, made our way to the road, crossed and joined up with the whole group. Our first taste of the enemy!

We congratulated each other on keeping quiet, it could have become a major hassle for us if we had been discovered. Many of us dead or injured before we had done any good at all, possible all rounded up and forced to fight for the enemy, what a nightmare thought. We were simple not ready for action yet, not by any means!

We had made it to the River Glen, Cedric, (the fen) grumbled that it was going to be too muddy to cross here, they would all get filthy and smell of mud and bog for ages. He crossed as we all did eventually, when told the option may be being seen by the enemy at a guarded bridge crossing and having to fight a battle we did not want, we all washed most of the mud away in the water.

Once across, we thought it time to feed so we lost ourselves in a wooded area just above the water line, nice to dry out in the sun, near some trees, and peel off the remaining mud that had caked itself to our clothes.

Obviously, the Normans were intent on moving rapidly through the area and taking over. We had better get ourselves trained into using the weapons we had been given very quickly we all decided.

We were near the hamlet of Gosberton now, one of the lads, Simeon Ellison, had a relative living there, so the leaders decided to visit to hear what these people had to say about the takeover of our land. Though they offered us food, we knew they could not afford to feed us, so we respectfully thanked them and went on our way.

The comments regarding the enemy were unprintable, the stories doing the rounds were getting worse by the moment, it seemed. A nice warm greeting from them cheered us all up no end, the small things in life really matter at times like these we decided. We told them nothing of our plans, we did feel a little odd just now, all out on our own for the very first time, no family home to go back to, though we could if we wanted. Some of us were finding the change in our circumstances a lot more difficult to come to terms with than they had thought. Cedric and I had to almost act like parents to begin with, though everyone eventually got into the spirit of what we were aiming for.

Chapter 8

Training to Fight

We had to try and find some area away from anybody else. No people, no cattle, no farms, no villages, no enemy, nothing but somewhere where we could not be heard in training. We would have to try and be as silent as possible. Wulfric claimed to know of such a place, so after we had fed ourselves we followed him. We had to avoid any regularly used waterways, you could quite easily see where locals had come through to fish or just to get from A to B.

He took us towards the wash, there was a place we found with a few islands but mainly reed beds, pretty thick at this time of year, so it looked good, we could base ourselves here for a time we thought, without being seen or heard.

We kept in our groups and decided to see if we could get on some islands and make some sort of camp near each other for protection, if needed, we thought we would be all right to light small fires at night and maybe catch some fish or wildfowl to eat. After a few hours, we had finished the covers under which we were going to sleep, to keep the rain off, and were settled so food was on the agenda.

Some things had been put together in the rush to leave our homes, knives to cut reeds and willow in particular, to strip the bark and make traps for fish, especially eels, we had three main trappers, Aart Dwerryhouse, Montgomery Haggard, and Gopal Girvii Grendel, they were simply superb at getting these fish. We had two bait fishermen in Alton Endicott and Holt Franklyn. They were a staple, food wise, for most of us. Some got busy with these. Others went to use their gift of being a very good shot with bow and arrow to help feed us with gulls, ducks and pidgeon etc. The four best shots for this were Aiken Eads and Roan Hunnisett, Acton Dickman and Manton Espenson. Bricius, of the Iceni, was a great hunter as well. Several other lads went along to receive training from the best marksmen. It was not just being a good shot with an arrow that helped get food for our table, you had to learn to stalk the animal you were after, whether it is fish, rabbit, seagull, deer, boar, pidgeon etc. Training took place on a daily basis.

Other important tasks such as wood gathering for the fires were implemented. Edric Dickenson, Leofric Dorsey and Hugh Fishman took care of this most days, they had fires going very quickly and somehow never seemed to run out of wood supplies. We joked, they were magicians at finding the supplies we needed so badly, so often.

It began to rain, so our small low reed huts, which were mainly roof, were in use from this time, dotted around the islands, a larger one was put quite low to the ground so no one could see it where we could feed ourselves and talk quietly about how hard we had to train before we were able to take on a fight of any kind. If anything we were over cautious about the noise we made which was a good thing! It tended to carry a little over the water though it was muffled by the reed beds, we were almost in another world it seemed to us all, far from any enemy, far from anything!

Food

Coarse Bread and gruel, just like home! Food in general was carried on horseback as stores.

Our two cooks, plus helpers, were busy with a couple of metal box "things", they became christened the "things" as nobody came up with a better reference, that would produce some kind of coarse bread if left over the embers of a fire.

I was not sure anyone thought they would work, but after a few attempts, it really did produce something that looked like bread, you got used to the taste! It was acquired, but it filled a gap when you were waiting for a main meal. We had some hungry men in our ranks.

Another staple was gruel, the best way to describe it would be to call it thin porridge, it was made by boiling grouts, crushed grain of various cereals, in water or milk, and mixing oatmeal with cold water to a paste, boil for ten minutes, add salt to taste, flour or millet gruel. We often referred to it as internal heating as it was a good way to start a cold and wet day!

When in season, we had wild fruit, pears, quinces, strawberries, raspberries and red currants.

We grew wheat, barley, oats and rye, plus pulses as a nation. Beans and peas grew well. We bought various foods as and when needed along the way, wheat and barley, etc.

In season on the fruit side we had apples, plums, berries and nuts. From small gardens people grew onions, turnips and carrots.

Our use of herbs consisted of coriander and dill, they were used a lot, along with honey to sweeten.

Beef was eaten a lot these days, pork was the most popular, as pigs grew fast and there was not much wastage. Sheep were bred for meat and wool as were goats, plus, their milk, chicken was a key source of protein. rabbits, deer, pigeon and wild boar, were every day food alongside the fish.

If any of us lived by the sea, or inland waterways, it provided porpoise and sturgeon, swan mussels and oysters, cockles, lobsters and crab. What did not get eaten straight away was salted down or smoked to great effect, it tasted great and lasted a long time.

Ale was the everyday drink as water was unsafe, mead was consumed by the elite! Wine was also imported for these people. Even the children drank ale, normally weakened.

Salt was mined in Worcestershire and taken from the salterns at Wainfleet, Lincolnshire, among other places for flavouring food.

Plums were often made into alcohol, as were apples and cherries, barley was part of our staple diet, it was ground to make bread and fermented to make ale. Other food grown: garlic, cabbage, beetroot and parsnips.

Camp Building

Our camp builder's/hut makers were Athelred Dexter, Aiden Edgar, Rice Cyneric, Roe Leofwine, Roweson Ledford, Winchell Millhouse, Tedman Martinson, and Vitt Hal. It became amazing just how fast they could build something out of nothing. The huts did not need to be disguised as normally we found a place in the middle of nowhere to camp. There was plenty of clear space here and around the fenland, waterways in general.

Cedric and I must prepare for our first ambush/skirmish with our foe, we could not afford to lose as our confidence would wane and we may not recover. I sent out men back and over to the main track to see if there were points where the track became wider, to see if we had room to be able to manage space to fight the enemy, with bows and arrows, then swords, if needed.

It took a lot of energy to achieve this in a few hours, so we decided to crash soon after, said our good nights to the other "islanders" and settled down for the night.

It was weird for us all, away from everything and everyone we knew. We all knew we had no choice, so it was exciting, training in the early mornings, some food, then training, then food, then talk of where we should go first and talk of tactics in a fight, then if there was still light in the sky yet more training, how to react in an open area of fen or in a built-up area of housing. Each would present different problems and we would have to deal with them at a moment's notice or perish trying!

Trying to consider all options, mock attacks from all directions, not knowing where or when they were coming from. A few injuries were inflicted though nothing serious which was good.

One of the lads knew a little of how to treat wounds, so we were careful not to get carried away with our fights, though you could get carried away quite easily in the heat of the moment. It had become my job to lead from the front as an example to all. I found this difficult to deal with, Cedric and I had to have all the answers to everything. We tried and I like to think that at this time we succeeded. The other leaders began to take the strain as time went along so we progressed as a group.

We considered we were now expert with bow and arrow, our arms had become used to the swords though we muffled the edges with quite thick layers of reed and willow to muffle the sounds made by our training, we made short lances of willow which were surprisingly effective.

One of our major innovations were the stilts we made of strong willow or anything else that would do, if we could goad the enemy into a particular fen area we could attack them through the water. We could move so fast through the mud/water we were confident we could defeat anyone the enemy cared to throw at us! These were of course no use in the deeper sections of the waterways.

We organised major mock fights against all of us. It was a joke to start with but as we became better we used tactics such as sending in four men to entice ten from another angle to fight. What a mess it made but we became expert and confident that we could take on anyone.

Willow were everywhere so we could make some up anytime, the same for arrows and bows, though other wood was used at times, some better, some not so good. Fighting on the water put us at a major advantage over the enemy, we could move so quickly, so much faster than the enemy, who we hoped had no experience of such action! Though we realised they may learn quite quickly as we would use them as often as possible.

Group Leaders

We kept the leaders of each group, as they were selected at the start of this adventure into the unknown so I led one, Cedric (the fen), Wenoth led two, Wulfric the Black led three, Richard Hokyton led four, Guthrum led five, Nicholas Bacon led six, Peter Ganning led seven, Thomas Eltisle led eight and Vitt Hal Biomonap led the Girvii. Vercingetorix led his five men of the Iceni.

It was decided that we would keep a check on how we all fared as time went by, if another leader emerged as we progressed we would change as we thought best.

If leaders were changed, nobody was to feel let down as the only thing that mattered was our welfare and ultimate success, we would be working side by side for one another, not competing against each other. I was thinking of making less leaders in the long run, it worked for now, though it seemed clumsy. It worked now, so why change it!

The only problem in our lives was our enemy and our task was to inflict as much damage as we could on these dreadful people who were taking over our lives and country, very much against our wishes.

We began to talk of where we should seek our first skirmish, could not call it a proposed battle as we did not have the numbers yet, we hoped we might grow as a unit as we went on our way, time would tell. We all knew we had a long way to go if we were going to make any impression on the enemy.

We needed somewhere where we could be easily under the cover of reed beds, but with an open space to fight, overlooking a track which was used by the Normans on a regular basis. As we had decided to go towards Boston where Ripley Kersey and Cedric came from we asked them to think of such a place. There were many such places they could take us to so we began to pack what we needed and set off in our groups, leaving a considerable gap between each so as to not make too much noise in any one place.

Up for a Fight!

We looked a war like bunch, I was pleased to note, packs strapped to our backs, swords to our sides, the odd lance as used by a particular member of each squad, arrows strapped to our backs. We were all organised to fight a particular part of any one battle, one lance, three bow and arrow etc. and we kept in a line in number up to the ten, or five as the case maybe. Each fight was going to be organised by how many men we were up against, two groups of ten would go to the front and hide in reeds, trees etc. another group would be in the middle and the last one would fight from the rear, hopefully trapping the enemy and destroying them. The other lads would watch as best they could, and learn.

The number of men in the fight would alter as to how many enemies we were fighting against. As a plan it sounded all right, only time would tell. We would adapt and adjust if and when needed.

No prisoners were to be taken, we simple could not keep them. This was fighting to the death!

We passed the main track to Boston, along the banks of the river Welland, there were huge patches of fen as always, some quite deep, some not, a great many reed beds, good and thick which made it an ideal training ground.

We trained and trained, setting our groups up quickly, it soon became second nature, to trot along in fen or on the banks of a river, to move quietly and quickly to a set point. To have another group attack without any kind of notice.

We trained to get all of our gear by us in complete darkness ready for immediate action, lots of fumbling to begin with, expert when finished.

Chapter 9

To all intents and purposes Cedric and I thought we were ready to test our battle readiness, all of the leaders of the groups thought so too. They had talked among themselves and made a unanimous decision, these decisions were always made as a group as we all relied on each other.

So, We Were Fit to go!

We talked of where we could meet the enemy, how to catch them by surprise, how much clear open land, without reed beds, would be needed, all sorts of questions, all sorts of answers.

We knew we could only attack small groups but we also knew we could make a dent in the confidence of the Normans. They would become wary, probably more difficult to beat but we were sure we could fight and win, on a small scale to begin with, who could tell where it would end?

Nothing Ventured, Nothing Gained!

There was a small settlement near a track, Ripley Kersey told us, Cedric and Ripley knew the area well, quite near the Welland, so we identified a clearing in quite a large reed bed near the main track and settled down to await our fate!

This clearing seemed to be used on a regular basis so it appeared to be a good choice, there was a main pathway leading from one end to the other with a few smaller ones off to different places. The main track would be from Spalding to Boston along the coast line.

We decided to set some of the men in place for a fight, Guthrums group at the far end and others at points along the edge of the track, taking care to not put men opposite each other so we were clear of each other's arrows, we arranged to only fire arrows between certain points from each side though we knew in the heat of battle things might be difficult, we would have to learn as we progressed.

This alone was going to be hard to get right. I felt sure we would quickly pick this up as we went along.

I could only feel pride in all the men as we took our places in the reed beds. Confidence was high, we were fit and strong and ready to start taking our revenge on the dreaded foe.

We all settled into our positions and luckily had already decided that we would let some people, if they were locals, go by just to make sure we were not in view from any direction, clearly only if they were Anglo-Saxons or friendly.

Some children could be heard shouting and some grown up commands to them to keep out of the water, eight people came into view, four parents and four youngsters, and oh dear, a dog. It came crashing through the reeds, was having a great time attacking the youngsters.

We did not really want to be found out at all, we had clothes on that disguised us better in the reeds, though this would not help with the dog as it would detect our scent, any information as to our whereabouts may have been passed on to the enemy even if not on purpose by these or any other people that came upon us at a later date so we were very relieved when one of the parents hauled the poor dog to his side and put some rope around his neck. Presumable, they had trouble with the animal getting lost in this part of their journey before. So with doggy under strict control they continued on their way and we heaved a sigh of relief and settled back into our quite comfortable positions.

Ready for the Next Drama, I Hoped!
First Blood

We could hear horses coming from Spalding and as they came nearer the language was without question not local, so we prepared for our first action. We did not have time to become frightened, as the first horse with rider appeared, followed in quick succession by three more. When they were about in the centre of the clearing our arrows flew into them, arrow after arrow.

I think they were dispatched many times over. They all four crashed to the ground with heavy thuds as they hit it, the horses reared and being alarmed they flew off into any direction as long as it was away from this place.

All of us made our way into the clearing and congratulated each other, clearing up all the evidence began immediately. All arrows retrieved, all swords etc. pulled off the Normans, a spot of scavenging was common place as the enemy had better fighting gear than most of our men, bodies pulled away into the fen and weighted down. Hopefully they would not be discovered for some time which would give us time to get well clear. Some of their clothes were quite thick so we took them as well, might need them especially on a cold or wet night, waste not was the order of the day!

The horses had settled a little way in various directions, they all had packs on them, we found some lovely food here and the odd blanket which was much appreciated by all, though it did not go far! We kept these horses to use as pack animals or for us to ride if we needed. Also very useful for practicing at horse riding during fighting training sessions.

The next task was to decide where we should go now, we had to make sure it was far from here as Normans were not kind to those who took up arms against them.

Rowan Meginhard came forward and said he knew of a place not unlike this one quite a few miles away so after talking amongst ourselves for a time we set off in our groups until night began to fall. We sent out our scouts to find islands well covered by reeds, willows, elders or whatever and well away from anything so we could kill and cook something before sleep took us all, it had been a hard and stressful day and we were all pretty exhausted.

The land here was covered in sedge, willow, alda and guilder rose. The fen, bog myrtle and of course reed beds en masse. It was quite a mix of colour this time of the year.

Though we had done very little, apart from sending some arrows into the enemy, our lives to this time had been dedicated to those moments of killing the enemy, a lot of pressure on us all, though we did not like to admit it.

Psychologically it was the most important thing we had achieved yet as a force.

We had begun the fightback at last! All of us knew we had an awful lot to do to make any impression on the enemy.

All of us settled on a few islands and began to get food as we were hungry now.

Fish were easily caught, some ducks went down well and a lot of eggs were eaten as we quietly spoke of how we felt.

Chapter 10

An Anti-Climax!

None of us felt great to be honest, to kill someone was an awful thing to have to do. There was no choice, kill or be killed. Times were hard at this time in the history of our country. To train, to fight, to kill or be killed, that was our reality. Unless of course we gave in, learned the French language, accepted we were a lessor race, and let our lives be dominated by these soldiers. This was unacceptable to us all. We needed to be battle hardened and carry on with our quest. To build from here was our only option!

A great many Anglo-Saxons and others were at least attempting to slow the onslaught, most were dying in the process. We all felt we had no option but to keep trying, or to get wiped from the face of the earth.

We were encouraged by our first skirmish, it certainly was not a battle but we had emerged victorious, even if we had somewhat "over killed" a few Normans by putting goodness knows how many arrows into them. Looking back it gave a number of the lads confidence to do just that, first arrows shot into the enemy. This was not the same as shooting targets.

It was a symbolic moment for us all, even those who had just watched.

Early the next morning we woke to a wonderful bright sunny day, with a decent wind rustling through the very dense reed beds. We felt reborn to a certain extent, it was a new world for us all. The experience against the enemy had changed us all, in the long term for the better, I hoped. All of us coped in a different manner with this, it was surprisingly hard!

We washed, caught fish, or rather Alton Endicott did, Holt Franklyn did well too, sent more arrows at birds to get our breakfast, just watching Acton Dickman and Manton Espenson at work made you hungry, some of the lads got some wood and cooked and ate the wonderful food that was provided for us by our wonderful water land. The Iceni and Girvii all took part as groups to see who could get the most food, then the most wood etc. Making it a competition made everyone try harder and achieve the result more quickly, in this case an earlier dinner.

I always had a few of the lads wandering around wherever we camped, just to see what was about the locality. Houses, parish's, stock pens, people, especially those damned Normans. Normally the enemy were nowhere to be seen in the fens and that suited us fine at the moment.

Hodge the miller was one of these "wanderers", he returned with news of some deer not too far away.

Three of us decided to go with him in search of this possible addition to our food. We approached some woods and at the edge there were four of the beauties just waiting for us.

We made sure we were down wind of them and crept very slowly behind one of the trees and quickly aimed and fired in one stroke, Acton Dickman got the first and I got the second. We had shot them, just behind their front legs, straight into their hearts, instantly dead! It wasn't a difficult shot but I was very pleased I had not missed as that would have been a bad show, we rushed out to claim our winnings.

The two of us hung them on branches and bled them, then gutted them and rather messily took the husks back to camp. When we got back, I was pleased to see everyone was training with their weapons, it showed the dedication we would need to make our mark in this war. We needed to be ready to fight at all times whether we wanted to or not.

Everyone was overjoyed to see such a huge amount of meat added to our food chest, the animals had a different view, no doubt! But we quickly washed and skinned them and cut them into steaks, rather large ones they were. A lot would be eaten today and tomorrow, the rest would be salted down and smoked to make it last as long as possible. Our butcher was a chap called Rand Hampton, he was a very busy man, cutting carcasses, smoking meat and fish. He was training Ware Jerrigan as his number two, this was to make sure we had back up if Rand became injured, or ill. We had other men to assist with preparation of the food, etc. the Girvii ladies helped no end as well.

Things looked a lot better from then on, we fought each other most of that day, eventually we tired, more wood collecting was needed for the fires followed by much talk of the future.

Where to go from here? Should we cut back south and stay in the water lands or go north. Should we just run from this area completely as the Normans might find their dead men and swarm the area with their men trying to find the killers! That was what we were now I reminded all. It sounded strange even to me. To the enemy we were just killers who needed to be brought to justice. Their justice, not ours, I hasten to add! We viewed ourselves as freedom fighters, nothing more or less!

The Isle

We had heard talk of a huge Anglo-Saxon stand being possibly made at what had become known as the Camp of Refuge, on the Isle of Ely. We discussed this until very late that night, eventually turning in in the early hours. Maybe we could join up with the force there.

Eventually, feeling very well fed and moaning a little from our training pains, we decided to turn in. Some would be stiff in the morning though it would soon wear off, no doubt.

When we were ready to move out in the morning, we decided to head for the town of Boston, there were one of two settlements in between us and the town. Cedric/the Fen, Wenoth, he got this title as he seemed to always talk of the beloved land where he had grown up, knew the area well and some of the families were known to him, so that would be good. Hopefully we could gather news of troop movements and all else as the grape vine was good, news travelled fast, even in these wild parts of the country.

We walked away from the track to Sutterton and Algarkirk, Cedric went on ahead to see if people were here that were known to him, they were but they came to meet us in the bush so as to not be seen by neighbours and talked about in the future when it could be dangerous. Everyone was being cautious, as word had spread of the killing of some Norman soldiers; they asked if we knew anything about it. We made a good job of saying we had nothing to do with any fighting, but that we were quite pleased somebody was picking up the mantle of fighting back against the enemy!

We were unsettled by the uproar caused by our slaying of the Normans, the soldiers were coming from all directions, it seemed, to maybe beat someone senseless to try and find clues about the men who had killed them, or raiding houses and smashing them and generally being a mob of thugs against Saxons and Britons alike. We said our farewells and began to move out. All of us were unsettled by the news of the beatings but we expected that to happen, sooner or later. It was an added pressure on our shoulders but what could we do? The answer was to just carry on as we were!

Chapter 11

'Fen slodgers', early nineteenth century. A decent representation of the men of the area at any time throughout the centuries.

Still in our groups, apart from each other for safety, we moved slowly through the fen, much preferring to walk the watery fen and through dense woodland than on the paths, where it was easy to pick up that seventy-seven lads had passed any particular way, this was all thought through sensibly. Any tracking would be difficult, if we instilled this into our force now we hoped it would stick with them all the time.

After some miles of trekking, we picked out a small settlement ahead, Cedric Wenoth knew one of the families so he went ahead to see if all was clear and if we would be welcomed.

We sat and waited for some time, he re-appeared and said they would like to meet us so just the leaders followed. At the back of their premises, was a walled in area so we settled in to talk with these people.

They kindly offered us some drink and as we drank, the man of the house said how much he appreciated Cedric calling, and had we heard of the killing of the Norman soldiers? He looked at us in an odd way and said we had better take care to stay unseen as everybody in the area would be suspected of this deed and a small group of men together would probably be killed on sight just on suspicion of being able to do such a thing. He added that these were dark days.

He looked at Cedric in an accusing manner. I changed the subject very quickly to ramble about the weather, some days fine, some the opposite etc. and that seemed to alter the man's thinking, he merely agreed with me. I also explained that we were passing through to get some work we had been promised in Boston as we had need of money.

We sat and talked, mainly about the blasted Normans for quite a time, then said our thank you and left. As we did so, the man gently chided Cedric about taking great care with any exploits he, or we, might get up to. I felt pretty sure he realised the killings were down to us, he gave us a great wave and smile, and wished us the very best!

He added to be very careful, again, in these dangerous times.

Norman Take Over, Increased Tax

We considered later what was said, talk was of the takeover of a number of large houses by the Normans, and their estates. It was just as we had feared, our people were scared and I did not blame them at all. Orders had been coming to them to surrender an ever-larger amount of the food they produced to these dreadful people as tax. How could these families survive, what sort of future did they have? None at all, was my view. At best, they had a very difficult future, at worst they simple had no future at all, that was the overall view.

The head of the household said there were patrols going to and from Spalding on a regular basis so we had better be prepared to avoid them by staying clear of the main pathways and keeping in small numbers.

We bade them farewell and took to small tracks each side of the pathway to Boston, we had one man moving near to the side of the track so he could let us know if Normans were in sight, coming or going. If there were he would make signal with his hands as to how many or he would blow on his horn to alert us of a small number we thought we might attack as we were confident we could easily take them by surprise.

This was not really effective, as at times our man could be out of sight, we could only try. We decided to put three men at the front and two at the rear and we felt much more confident from that point onwards!

All of us hit a long stretch of open track which was clear to begin with but as we went along six horses appeared at the far end, with French riders in uniform. Our men quickly signalled and we, as quietly as possible, made our way to the edge of the fen/trees at the trackside.

Guthrums lads at the front waited until all six were covered by our group and shot arrow into the back two, the front two were shot leaving the middle two to us, again no drama as we took them completely by surprise, dead or dying as soon as the arrows were loosed. I watched the lads to see how they behaved against the dead enemy, silly really, but everyone was respectful and had a certain regret at this situation. I wondered how the Normans would have disposed of our bodies had this event turned out differently! I expect our corpses would have been taken to town, stripped, displayed and left to rot in some dreadful manner to warn others to not take up arms against them!

Athelred Dexter checked to make sure they were dispatched and quickly pulled those that were still on their horses off the path, Athelred always made sure they were dead, his family had been murdered, his mother raped, so he had no bother in finishing off these soldiers, "they are animals", he often said. Those who had fallen straight away we dragged away from the small battle area.

It was decided that we would keep the horses, if only to carry spare clothes we had "acquired" and lances etc. after taking any food packed for ourselves, and taking jackets, shoes etc. that would be useful.

We would build up the number of animals we needed as we went along, we would ride on and off them when we wanted. We would train to use them in battle as our enemy did! This would make us a much more fearsome fighting unit I felt sure.

While it was very exciting, we all felt bad that we felt we had to kill these Normans. However, they left us with no choice, we had to remind ourselves, kill or be killed was the order of the day.

We travelled in deeper fen/bog areas now so the horses could not be seen from the track. The reed bed "forest" here was immense and easy to get lost to all in if you were not careful so we kept close tabs on each other.

The area was cleared as much as possible, so it appeared no one had been there, marched about a mile, and decided we had better settle down, eat what food we had and find somewhere, as usual, well hidden in the fen, to talk tactics or just talk and to spend the night.

Though we could view our success with fighting as we were, we knew word would eventually reach the higher ranks of the Norman command and they would seek answers as to why some of their soldiers were disappearing and that things would not remain as they were, it all seemed too easy and we knew it would not remain so!

We had not met any soldiers head to head yet, we would delay that as long as we could, as we knew what a test that would be, we would train more the following morning.

Sword fighting was a different kind of test to firing arrows and we had much to learn!

Binding Wounds

We also trained two of our men to bind wounds that we might have, they were Rowan Meginhard and Whitney Eoforwine, one of the packs we had taken from the horses had material to bind wounds and some ruff smelling sticky stuff that we recognised was used to try and keep infection out of wounds and help them heal more quickly.

The morning came, it was damp, cloudy and pretty grim! All of us were a little subdued. We ate early and began training as planned, we kept the noise to a minimum, which was difficult in itself but went through our phases with bow and arrow, our short lances and swords at the ready. Horses crashing through the watery fen were not silent either!

Chapter 12

'The Nearest Way Out Is the Farthest Way Home'. This Victorian portrayal of the fens in the mid-18th century is less fanciful and more realistic than might appear!it could represent the area any time throughout the centuries, but having said that most of the fen area during the time the books are set had a great deal more depth of water.It does however give a decent impression of the shallow areas.

Being Tracked

We were stopped in our tracks, as the guard, scout, we had left near the path where we had the fight came in very quickly and told us to hush everything as a lot of horses, plus riders of course, had begun running up and down the path, doubtless looking for their comrades.

A very quick change of plan was needed. We decided to very smartly move out in single file, away from the area, out into the deepest fen area, if needed, where we could hopefully not be traced.

It was cold and the water was really deep in places but we trudged along as best we could. The deeper the water the better we felt as we would surely lose the enemy if followed.

Mile after mile we went, though it seemed much more. We were now getting tired so we stopped to eat the leftovers from our main meal as we sat on a quite large island in the reeds. As all was soundless in the lovely fen we thought we ought to replenish our fish stocks so we set out some rods of wood and began fishing. I also thought fishing might stop the lads worrying about the enemy for a time.

Duck and seagull began to join our mobile larder via our skill with bow and arrow. Aart Dwerryhouse had a field day with his skill for trapping eels, I had never seen anything like the amount he brought in.

This took our minds off the fact that the Normans were beginning to stir against us, we felt rather like seasoned veterans' now. Being followed was something we were not used to and we did not like it much! We would have to get used to it, if we liked it or not was of no consequence. All of us knew we had to fight therefore we would be chased at some point!

We heard nothing more, so we moved to some nearby islands where we were closer to each other than before and began the process of making our reed covers over where we were going to sleep, or maybe just rest, there was a lot to think about and chat amongst ourselves over the fight and what we should do in the near future.

Light rain fell from the almost see through clouds which made matters a little worse, the winds began to stir the reed beds and we settled for the night!

The Normans had lost ten men, though this was nothing to them. They knew enough to see how uprisings against them had begun in the past and they knew they needed to crush any such thing as soon as possible, they would be angry to stamp us out if they could find us.

From our point of view, we needed to train more with all our weapons, our scouts at front and back needed to get back to us more quickly so we could plan our fighting better, not that they had let us down, we could not always rely on surprise, they may well be ready for us sometime in the future, we tried to plan for every eventuality.

Myself, Cedric, Wulfric, Guthum and Richard, Vitt Hal, Vercingetorix, Nicholas, Peter and Thomas, the leaders, got together and talked of getting better with our training, hopefully getting the scouts to react faster, putting out three instead of two, to think for themselves and to get that thinking right first time, it was so important!

They were our first line of defence or attack so it was vital they understood this and made their position count. Everyone had to know their place in any battle formation and stick to it. There was very little to learn at this time, but as we hopefully grew into a major fighting force these same principles would hold true. Stay as you were instructed, or ordered, however you chose to look at it, but do it none the less!

We had not been caught in a trap yet by the enemy, it's something I feared, especially the first time. We would lose men but we would emerge stronger and much more confident I had no doubt!

In the heat of battle things would become confused but we had to train when we fought to have men spare at our backs to protect us and a couple each end. This made sense to us all, it gave us more confidence, everybody was throwing their ideas into the ring. Some seemed a bit daft but we talked them through to make sure everyone's ideas were not just overlooked, the better we performed as a group of leaders the better battle group we would make.

We wanted nobody to feel left out, Cedric and I were very determined on this point. Disgruntled members of our force were no good!

All of us felt settled here for a few days, so we stayed as we must have escaped the Normans again.

Meal time again, it was quite a job cooking food, we tried to filter the smoke from rising as a mass, we had become quite good at it but we were helped by the weather being clouded by mist on this occasion. Eels were very good food and easy to catch. They lasted well when smoked or just salted down, we caught them in traps made of willow and on our lines, we did not have to pluck the fish so they were popular from that point of view as well.

Someone suggested we find the holes in the mud in which the eels lived, push a stick into the bed of the fen, put some line with bait on it outside and see if we could catch anything overnight. This proved very effective, breakfast was waiting for us in the morning, great idea, fast food in the 11th century! Skinning animals was easy as well, especially large ones.

To be honest, we began to get bored, Peter Ganning pointed out that it was a pretty bad thing for any armed force, so we aimed to get back on our way to Boston, Lincolnshire.

The going was tough as we wanted to stay clear of all pathways so we pushed the reeds apart and stumbled along in the fen, pretty boggy, smelly and deep in places, this was making our leg muscles very strong so the side effect was good.

We would outrun our enemy as tough fen men if nothing else, not running from them, chasing them away, we hoped. This should help us no end sometime in the future.

We were fully fledged fen men now. Rough, tough and ready to fight and win any war! Or so we confidently hoped. Time would tell on that one.

Just to mingle with our people would be good again, we mainly wanted to get news of what was happening in the country in general. Where there were groups of our foe and how big these groups were, how much were they interfering with everyday Anglo-Saxon life and that of the Britons too, come to that.

They were good fighters, we had heard some had joined the fight on the Isle of Ely with some of the commanders that had fought with King Harold at Hastings, an ever-larger group of soldiers were heading in that direction too. Tonbert, King of the Girvii, was on the Isle as well.

Maybe, if we became good enough, we could add our strength to this endeavour, that would be an adventure to hopefully tell our children. Quite some way in the future that might be we thought! Still, we could dream! Without dreams and ambition life would surely be meaningless. Our immediate ambition was clouded by fighting and ridding this land of the enemy, hopefully normal life would resume following these dreadful acts! We had so much to do before any kind of peace could possibly be established.

We came across another settlement, of a few houses near the largest path, so I said I wanted to approach some of the people just to see how things were in general. Cedric came with me.

Everyone else stayed out of sight, as I knocked on the door of the first house, an old gentleman answered it, surprised to see anyone this early in the morning, he invited me in and offered me a hot drink. There was an old lady making some bread for the day ahead and a good smelling pie of some sort nearing the cooked stage.

This was a lovely setting, it made me realise what we had given up to fight. We were of course fighting for this very situation, for our people to live as they were and for us to do so too.

I left Cedric in charge, though, he thought Guthrum should have a go, even if it was just in title, on reflection, I had agreed.

Chapter 13

I explained that I was on my way to Boston to buy some goods from the market to take back to Spalding. All the talk was of the damned Normans and the chaos they were creating, overtaxing everyone for everything, what a disaster, where was it all going to end!

Then they asked if we had seen or heard anything regarding the killing of some soldiers, we denied hearing about this but added that it was good to hear some of us were fighting back, they agreed but were worried about possible reprisals from the French.

This is something we had all spoken of and were quite concerned about but what could we do, were we to just give up all of our lands and way of life. I think not! Certainly not yet, as we had not offered any real organised resistance, we could not judge what we might achieve if we did not even try and fight.

We said our goodbye to this fine couple, during my years of fighting, I often thought of them, in that peaceful setting I envied them their life and I hoped it continued for many years to come. This was what we were fighting for, the right to live in peace as we pleased. We may have been a war like race in the past but now we were settled and happy. We needed to become a war like race again, well drilled and trained to the hilt, on a huge scale if we were going to live as we wanted.

Boston

We made our way back to the lads and we went on our way towards Boston, pleased to be greeted by new stand in leader, Guthrum, no less, he was complete with a broad grin. Who would have thought it, Guthrum leading an Anglo-Saxon force against the invader of our land! Come to think of it who would have thought I would be doing so but here I was! I still found this leading very difficult!

Keeping out of sight for the most part, only in groups of five or ten so nobody thought anything of it, our pack horses with our gear always stayed approximately in the middle of us all, further away from the track to be unseen, as we went along so we could retrieve our fighting equipment quickly at any time.

We had left the river Glen behind us a long time ago, so our next river would be the Witham, the main body of Boston was on the far side of this, and some way inland. The ground was low and boggy; the water was not very deep so we made good time and we passed a settlement called Frampton, a tiny place inhabited by farm workers, very cosy and tidy.

While I was occupied with the couple in the house I visited, Richard Hoykton decided the group needed to practice our fighting some more, he thought some of the lads could be much better than they appeared, more practice was the name of the game and as I encouraged all the men to come up with ideas, they went along with his idea as we might get into a fight with a larger number of the enemy at any time.

On returning to the force, I said news of the Normans was rife and not good so we continued on our way close to the coastline, better for our larder, fish wise, as any food we had carried with us had quickly dwindled. We took deer and boar as we found them. Some of the pack animals became a little overloaded.

As we were training, two groups went up ahead and hid in bush/trees and ambushed us as we approached. They had hidden well and as we slowly came upon some of them we were attacked by some of the other group as well. We fought them off, as we continued we were circled by all remaining men. This could have been difficult as an ambush situation which might well work out in the future so it was sensible to practice, it was hard to fight a bunch of well-armed fit men even though they were on our side.

No doubt about it, we were all getting much better at this game, good thinking by the leaders, well executed by all the men. Wulfric the Black and Guthrum had set it up, they were getting better, as leaders, all the time.

We found a patch of well-hidden ground at a point where the river met the wash, the tide was in so we thought we would see if we could catch some fish. Keeping in our groups we thought we would see who could catch the most. A bit of competition was no bad thing and I thought the groups had grown together, so keeping them that way would be good for each other, making the group tighter could only be good for each member of it, to rely on each other for safety and food.

Fishing

Cedrics group were into the fish first, they had baited up quickly and were generally more organised, they had six good size fish before one of my group got our first. Richards lads got four, we got three more and coming in last at this point was Nicholas with just a couple.

The rest of the lads were doing very well, so soon it was time to think of cooking and eating our fresh catch, they were good size fish and they cooked quickly and were consumed even more quickly!

We kept catching, it was so easy. The "Iceni six" as they had become known were the best fishing group as a whole, they caught a huge amount. The lads lit the fires some way off in some dense thickets of scrub so hopefully we would not let the smoke be seen. Tait Hambleton, helped by Warinus Bassingbourn, cooked, several more helped.

An evening well spent amidst much laughing and good fun! We placed extra guards all around us to make sure we were not discovered. As always, they were changed frequently, so no one felt left out or went hungry.

Ripley Kersey talked of possible fighting in town, this would be much more difficult than our experience to date, maybe house to house, a different world than our water land. It would be exciting or dreadful, depending on how we fared, we were quite sure we would learn a lot quickly, that was most important.

Ripley talked of the different clear spaces that would be good to catch the Normans and do some major damage, then make our way out of town through the small streets that were abundant. He knew of many ways to confuse the enemy regarding their exit from any tight spots they may find themselves in.

It was decided we would leave men at street corners leading off the main streets to cause as much mayhem as possible on our exit from town, they would fire arrows into any following enemy which should have the desired effect, to cause confusion and slow them down, giving our main body of men the chance to get well clear.

We would need to scout the exit tracks and arrange to meet after any fighting at a certain spot after the main battle.

All of us would go into town in small numbers and pick some part that was quite open so we could aim our arrows with certainty and get our quarry, we were all of us good enough to get targets within the distances we would need to kill off enemy without getting any "locals", we hoped, then leave………rather fast!

A sound plan, catching the enemy unawares was imperative.

It sounded simple enough, we would need to hide our equipment and clothes and spare food and bedding, and leave our horses guarded, much of our fighting equipment would have to stay, though we felt rather naked without it all. We had not been separated since we began this enterprise. Having it with us made us all feel more secure.

Chapter 14

Destination Boston

In fact we would take in only what we needed to fight with at any one time, perhaps swords and bows and arrows. They could be hidden under our coats in a way that they could not be picked out easily by eye.

We were very conscious of the lumps on our backs, with cloaks over the top of our arrows, but we carried on regardless! The arrows were not above our shoulder height, we secured them lower down our backs so they did not stand out. Nobody challenged us, though there were Normans milling around the side streets in small numbers.

So, having cleared away as much evidence of the fact that we had been there as we could, fire embers etc. we set off on the track to Boston. We made a point of clearing as much as we could of our camp sites so they could not be easily followed by enemy scouts.

We entered the town from the south. All agreed to meet back at camp as it was such a good spot for food and cover to sleep by mid-afternoon.

As we approached the main path, we listened for any trace of anyone on it, as there was not, we set off in groups of ten, as we seemed in the clear, especially from an enemy view point, a few locals wandered about the track.

This was a market town, but we had little money, so we would need to stay out of peoples view as much as possible, as we would perhaps be expected to buy provisions etc. we did not want to raise suspicions by just standing around on streets.

Men of fighting age, loitering in batches, would be asking for trouble from the Normans.

As two of our number lived here for some years we took their advice on places to look.

Boston

It was a busy town with a quite large population. There were quite a number of groups of horses, the riders seemed to be all Normans, going around in groups, or sitting in public houses, having consumed amounts of alcohol, and making plenty of noise so it was easy to note where they were.

The French language rolled over the square, it could clearly be heard. This was something we hoped we could change. To be rid of the French and the sound of their talk!

Our understanding of these people was that they were very disciplined soldiers, this must have been a group off duty. In this, we may have been lucky, only time would tell.

We had entered the town via the Skirbeck area, on the Spalding road, it was lovely and still along the water's edge though there was quite a wind blowing into town, it was quite cloudy, but as the wind moved the clouds, there were patches of sunshine beaming through to greet us all.

Nobody took any notice of us, still in our groups, we crossed the bridge and over the river. We passed some lanes, then on our left was an open space. There were quite a few people about here, none seemed to look up as we passed.

We passed the Assemble Rooms and onto the edge of the huge market square, or Market Place, as it was officially known.

My group scouted around to find where the French were staying, they had taken over some buildings with rooms and had men stationed by them in chairs, they were the worse for ale so we did not think they would be trouble.

I suppose if they did not fear anyone and had not been attacked then they would not worry about being caught off guard.

At this time in England they very much had the upper hand, nobody to challenge them, so they thought. It was up to us to change their thinking!

Having thought that it would be foolish to think they would be a walkover in a fight. Our group scout at this time, Wilfrith Meginhard, was not at ease with our fighting in any built-up area, I couldn't quite make out why, perhaps because he was born and brought up in a fen, possible he just didn't like built up areas, question mark over his comments, time would tell, hopefully giving me the answers!

I saw and had a few words with other members of our force, as to where we had been so as not to double up and waste our time. We all made a mental map of tracks out of the town and as the day was getting on began to make our way back to our base, trying to stay a good distance from anyone of our group we saw doing the same thing.

When we all arrived back, we went through what we had seen and considered our options. We could fairly easily take out quite a few of the enemy, then as the fighting group backed out a retreat we could trap more and fight house to house, this would also make the enemy unsure how many men were waiting for them hidden, but more important would slow down their pursuit of us, therefore making it safer for the majority of our men to get clear.

Our attack would happen quite early in the evening, as we could hide more easily and they would not find it easy to follow. They would not know the size of our force either so that would be an advantage, surprise was very important, as always.

We noted tracks leading out of town, three small lanes between houses to our right coming out of town then onto Furtherend Lane, several others that led straight onto fields that would eventually place us in the right area to make for the track to our hidden camp. It was important for each group to know how to get back the most direct way if we were chased and forced to split up.

We returned to our "base" and set about feeding ourselves again, there were many pidgeon about that evening, a large number of them became dinner. Acton Dickman, in particular with his spectacular arrow shooting got most of the flying type of food this time while sitting in the trees, the pidgeon that is, not Acton, and fish filled our stomachs as well.

I thought, not for the first time, what a team we had become, living and fighting in unison. What an adventure! Hopefully it was never going to be a disaster! Though that was always a possibility. The odds were stacked against us. Could we really make the difference Cedric and I were thinking of?

I spoke to all that evening regarding my pleasure at working with all of what I called "my men", and said I was always there if anyone needed to talk about anything, any suggestions as well would be welcome regarding our force, in our training, battle plans etc.

We prepared for the night in usual fashion, using covers for us to sleep under, and slept well. The sky that night was beautifully open to the stars, it was a sight that fascinated me, the leaders often moaned at me for commenting on it as often as I did. It was just me,

I Explained, Interested in Everything and Everyone Except If You Were a Norman!!

The dawn chorus woke us, as always, the birds were really going for it, the beautiful clear noise was a wonder from the trees and the sky it seemed today. A slight warm breeze touched our cheeks as we rose looking forward to a very exciting days' work. We all knew it could turn out badly for some of us but we were still very excited. The thinking was that injuries always happened to someone else, never oneself! So we were all in a pretty confident mood which is where we needed to be, after all!

We did some training most of that day to keep our minds off the attack which would take place probable early evening, some of the men fished.

This would be a real test for us. We knew we would set the cat amongst the pidgeon, as it were, not pidgeon to eat this time! There would be consequences, perhaps far and wide. All of us would simply have to live with them whatever they may be.

The Normans were not known for putting up with people who fought back against them. We would have to be careful afterwards, we planned to move quickly out of the area, hoping we had no injured to contend with that would slow us down, and hopefully, no dead.

We approached the town in groups of ten, our own store of arrows were fixed further down our backs than normal so they were disguised and covered by jackets or cloaks. Some crossed the river to come in from the opposite direction as ourselves, hopefully we could cause as much mayhem as possible and in the madness cause some real damage to the enemy. Some real fightback was needed and we were going to start it!

Chapter 15

The Boston Defenders Take on the Enemy in Boston!

We entered the centre, there were a great many people about, selling and buying goods of all sorts from the market. Quite a few groups of enemy soldiers.

I signalled for us all to gather loosely at one end where the greatest density was and simple threw open our coats and fire at will at anyone in Norman uniform.

We placed our arrows in our bows and listened to the familiar twang of our bows letting loose death on our enemy, the whoosh as the arrows let go of their energy, the cries of the enemy who received them, or not, for those who were dead where they stood!

Mayhem ensued, lots of soldiers falling to the ground, we fired and fired. Others came to their aid, they died or were injured too, Cedric cried out that other troops were getting together and preparing to attack us on horseback. The locals were running for cover, everywhere and anywhere, as long as it was out of the line of fire, or horses, complete with the enemy on their backs that were trying to get to us. It was a crazy sight to experience!

We fired at them, they fired back, I was amazed at how many we had mown down in such a short space of time. We quickly began to fall back as a group into the housing as we had planned, along the track to the site where we were staying at camp, quite a number of miles away, down river from here. Guthrum led this main group out of town.

We crossed the bridge again and ran down the Spalding road, passing West road.

Surprise Had Again Been With Us and we had used It Well!

Several groups of ten of our men were left in the street where we exited, just long enough to stay and give them more of a bloody nose as they chased us, then ten more at the next gap between the houses, etc. This would slow down their pursuit of us.

I stayed with the last group near the outskirts of town, we made sure all of our lads were clear before waiting for the remains of the group that were chasing us. We stayed a little too long and had a mad rush to get clear, leaving just a couple of enemy stumbling around trying to find us and get revenge on losing so many of their comrades. We suffered more injuries here which was not good!

We made it, out into the darkness, having finished off many enemies, dead and injured. At this point I knew of twenty of our men who were hurt, not too badly though, they may not agree with my diagnosis! As clearly the pain they were in showed. We had slowed them down a huge amount by leaving men on the tracks leaving town. They were clearly not confident with not knowing what lay around the next corner, or in fact the next doorway!

All of us rushed over the fields to get as far as possible out of the area with the aid of the night, which was thankfully dark by this time. We reached our horses, those who had them, and moved out at a slow canter, as we could not see far ahead of us. Some of the men were not yet confident on horseback so they ran by our sides. We did not yet have the full complement of animals anyway.

When we reached our camp, we were all very excited at our success, goodness knows how many we had killed or injured. The men, we referred to them as "doctors" they were, I was afraid, far from being that, became busy sealing and dressing the wounds, that's Rowen and Whitney, as they were untrained at this, they were doing a pretty good job. I thought then that we must get more men trained in at least trying to repair any damage caused by our fighting, We needed everyone fighting fit, quite literally. We had not lost anyone because we had fired more and more arrows, not stopping, very rapidly, therefore not allowing the enemy time to organise to fight back, by the time they had some soldiers on horseback to attack we were gone, leaving men on corners and in doorways to slow them further. Those who followed on horseback were easy to pick off with arrows.

Surprise was our main aid and we knew we would never have that again, they would seek to make examples of us all, we discussed moving much further into the waterways and fenland and decided to move right away from here, rather quickly!

Cedric (the fen) Wenoth, was a fen man at heart, he had lived his early years in the fens but had moved to be near family in Boston and his father for work, he became known as "the fen" as he referred to them so often. I have probable mentioned this before, it just amuses me as to how people get a nick name that seemed to stick forever. It became accepted and it certainly stuck in his case.

He stayed behind to see his family and keep an eye on what the Normans did after our attack, this may be important in the long term in relation to what we did after such a fight in the future. We returned to camp overnight and had arranged to leave a mark as to where we had gone the following morning by one of the trees we stayed near, so he could follow easily, maybe not easily but follow he did.

When he rejoined us he said many soldiers had begun breaking houses apart to try and find the men responsible for killing so many of their soldiers, as we had left no evidence of our staying in the town as we had not done so, they could find nothing.

Then they took a number of men as prisoners and began to torture them in the centre of the market place. This was the last thing any of us wanted to hear but in our hearts we knew this would happen sometime.

It must have been dreadful for the families concerned, we felt for them. We had talked about this sort of thing to some of the Boston people. They said they would continue to support us no matter what which was a very brave decision!

The Normans eventually decided we had not been staying here, we had just come along and decided to cause as much damage as possible, so, come first light they would try and trace exactly where we had gone. They sent out their scouts to try and find which track away from Boston we had taken, as we had left little mark it took them some time.

If there was reward going, and they were offering a lot of money for information, staying here and wasting time torturing people was nothing but a waste of time! Some of the enemy enjoyed inflicting torment on our folk, mind you, some saw it as part of their job to inflict pain on us.

Boats

We stayed that night at the camp and from first light we prepared to move out, we crossed the river just inland from the estuary and headed along the coast.

We spent a good part of the day repairing injuries to some of the force

Not far along this track we began to make out small boats at the water's edge, some were pulled out onto the bank, so we had to watch out we did not make noise, as the owners of these boats may be close by and if they were, as we suspected, Normans, then they would be very angry with us to say the least!

I had meant to think those last few words, but I had murmured them enough for Cedric to hear, I had to explain I was joking, their entire existence was dominated by the need to catch and kill every last one of us I knew very well. That is just the enemy in our area, we had not become national enemy number one yet. I found the stress of what we did each day a little much at times, I tried to cope by treating it as a game, though it was far from that!

When you considered we were a pretty small band of Anglo-Saxons trying to get the men of our country mobilised, get them all angry enough to train and take these enemy on in battle, we had fought hard to gain this land but we had become lazy in peace time, as a result we were being made to suffer at the hands of this enemy.

A small start to change our whole world! All the leaders believed we really could make that difference, to show all we could take on the enemy and win!

There was a camp close by, we could easily pick out the fires, some way inland so they would be no bother, only if they had left guards very nearby would we have a problem.

We found it very odd to find they had left nobody to protect them so we were alright for the time being.

The Boston Deeps

Many smaller boats appeared and we could see what they were here for. Large troop ships appeared out of the gloom if you looked hard enough, stationed along the Boston Deeps, these were small flat-bottomed boats and had been used to ferry men ashore.

We wondered what bother we could cause these men and their small boats. Talking quietly, we wondered if we could perhaps set fire to them. Then it struck us that maybe if we could load some of the small boats with wood we may be able to attach them to just some of the troop carriers in the Deeps and set them alight.

This was what we decided to do, we were as silent as we could possibly be as we placed the small burning boats so the wind was in the right direction to help the fire jump from the small boats to the large ones. We would need to move fast and make no sound if at all possible.

All of us felt sure we could have some fun with these fires. The problem was going to be the soldiers, just how many were there, and were they up for a fight?

Not many were near the fires just inland from where we were. All of us thought we would set some on fire to see how many enemies appeared out of the gloom, if we could deal with them we would be all right, after all there was only a few fires in view at the time.

Burning Troop Boats

The boats were filled with any wood we could find close by and we tied these small rowing boats to the large ones, which were much larger than we were used to.

Richard was first off with two of his men, quietly mumbling that the tide was fast, we would need to be careful, I took out another rowing boat with two men on the oars, Thomas took another, and Wulfric took the last one that was close to us. The two lads who were with me, Henry Garrod and Simeon Ellison were pretty good with the oars, so we made good speed. All of us were involved by now. Time to light the fires!

Fire in the Ships

The troops nearby were beginning to move, they were camped not far away after all. They were left as guards though they had not done much of a job, they were busily getting their gear together to either move out or just make sure the ships were alright.

They started out in our direction so we quickly finished lighting our fires and moved out ourselves, keeping just a little distance away, as we could fire into the soldiers if they tried to put the flames out.

The Reaction

They were slow to react to the fires but as soon as they realised what was going on they began shouting, men running everywhere. It was comical, as they panicked and thought about putting out the flames, before all in front of them was destroyed.

Wulfric and Guthrum stood next to Acton Dickman and Aiken Eads, readied themselves to fire arrows into the enemy, along with most of the others, except the injured. I hushed the men to not fire until I gave the word so we could disable as many as possible in one go, catching them by surprise.

When they were all crowded around the edge of the wash, we let our arrows loose, they were very effective, I had to admit to myself. We let another batch loose and as they had not left any guard we moved in for the kill, swords at the ready.

We were not really very prepared for hand to hand fighting but we had little choice. Luck was with us again as these enemy soldiers had been "taking of the ale", they were off duty, I suppose. Not that that was an excuse for too much drinking to excess, they were lazy with their swords, so our fighting looked better than it really was.

Simeon Ellison was knocking any Frenchie to bits and pieces, he was really good. Outstanding was a better word I thought on reflection. Woodrow Huxtable was not far behind as a master swordsman, others were watching as best they could in the melee that surrounded us all.

Wilfrith Meginhard and Walter Reynold were making a name for themselves too. We all wanted to be the best, a healthy consideration, I thought it bode well for the future! For all of us to be as good as the best, and for the best to be very good!

Chapter 16

That Was a Challenge!

I didn't really have time to consider much more of the fight, as I was quickly dragged into the fray as an enemy soldier tried to hack off my right arm.

I leapt out of the way, only just in time, pulled up my sword to hit his, he stumbled to my right. I brought my sword up and attacked his side, I caught him and he stumbled out of the fight, for the time being at least!

Two more enemy replaced him, came straight at me, head on, these were angry men. No time to think, I slashed at the one who was about one pace nearer with huge might, knocked his sword out of the way and fairly launched myself towards the other one.

His sword was aimed at my chest, I pulled up mine below his and knocked it skywards, still in his hand, I quickly aimed mine at his chest, he surprised me by turning sideways to me, I could not stop so I passed him by. I felt a total idiot in the moment that followed!

I turned quickly to see he was about to run me through. No time to think, I leapt to one side, and ran him through the chest, as I pushed into him he just came onto my sword.

Another one bites the dust, I thought. That was a win, though it was hard fought.

My mind was on thinking of training each group to try and back up each other as fighting progressed, we must train better, plan each attack as best we could, I was thinking.

My thinking was quickly interrupted by another cry out loud from a Norman trying to kill me, very quick thought, must concentrate only on fighting in a fight!! Nothing else. I kept telling everyone else just that, I must train myself quickly to do the same though this was easier said than done.

This fellow was another chap on the large side, much taller than myself. Where do they get all these big lads from? What are they feeding them on? Two other Normans stood aside to let him through to get to me, I wish they hadn't bothered!

Phew! Here we go again, I brushed his sword aside as he tried to cut me in two, jumped out of reach to give myself a second to consider how best to attack the fellow. Was he all strength and no thought? I was only confident of the fact that I would soon see! Nothing else as he truly towered over me.

Before I had time to take a breath, he rushed at me again, we clashed very loudly, you could clearly hear above the noise of the fight.

As our swords went to one side, my sword was above his so I was fastest to get mine back into action, I struck him in his left arm/shoulder. The cut went pretty deep, he yelled even louder than before as he tried to get me anywhere he could as his sword arm came back to the fight.

He missed me completely, in his anger he wasn't thinking straight and he followed his arm to the ground, he didn't quite fall over, he went close enough to give me all the time needed to cut into his side.

He staggered a little, not sure whether to continue, and struggled to get his sword arm ready to have yet another go at me.

He was not looking good at all at this point, but give him his due he threw all his weight into his next action. I very neatly, though I say so myself, leapt to one side, crouched and followed my sword towards his chest. He was surprised as I thrust it into his chest and he ran onto my weapon as I pushed it into him to finish the fight.

He was gone, I tried to pull my weapon from his body, it was difficult and before I could do so another enemy was upon me. I continued to try and retrieve my beloved sword and was suddenly pushed to one side.

I had no idea who had done this, it turned out to be one of the men from my group who had seen my predicament and come to help. To save me from injury, would perhaps be better put, as looking back, I was in dire trouble in those moments. A sword fight could change in a split second and it was scary stuff.

He took this new fellow and hit his sword out of harm's way, followed by a mighty strike into the man's neck.

That would teach him, a little late, to not go into battle with his gorget (neck protector) not in place! Most of these men were not in full armour thankfully. Time only for a smile as my hero attacked another enemy, I pulled my sword out of the big chap and carried on myself.

This was still going on all along the line of the fight. It was illuminated by the huge fire in the ships. I am sure we all had great shadows, dancing all over the place, this must have been interesting during the fight. No time to stop and look, never mind! We had a lot else to concentrate on at this time, so we did!

A couple of our men were injured and a group of their friends were protecting them by forming a protective wall around them. This was disrupting the fight along its line for other Saxons but it came good before long I was glad to note.

That might not be in any fighters manual, but it was good to see, working together for each other.

That is the way any country should operate let alone an armed force! Working together for the benefit of all.

All else was returning to silence as my men finished the enemy off. After a time, all finished and it was time to leave! I genuinely look back on these actions in a state of horror but at the time we simple had no option!

We watched for a few minutes as the flames took hold of these mighty ships, the heat coming off them was immense so we moved back from the edge of the wash quite a way. They would be quickly devoured and sink. Another good job done.

A couple of the leaders came over to me and suggested we burn as many as we can, we had after all, rid ourselves of our enemy. That is the ones who were closest.

I quickly thought, why not?

Let's create an inferno on the water, so that was what we set out to do. Same process as before, fill the small rowing boats with wood, take them out to the ships, attach them to the ships and set them alight. It sounded almost too easy! All of us set to work, grabbing all the driftwood on the bank and any other we could lay our hands on and place it in the little boats, get them out and fixed to the larger ones and set them alight as quickly as possible. Job just about done! All of us watched in wonder as the fires took hold very quickly.

As we turned away from the boats, we could hear some shouting coming from not too far off inland.

Chapter 17

Inferno on the Wash
Ship Burning/Fighting

Two of our scouts came running in, looking pretty agitated, to inform us of a very large contingent of the enemy approaching rather quickly.

Obviously the troops that had been carried by these ships had not gone very far away and they had been roused by the fires that their scouts would have seen, suddenly staying and lighting the other ships was not such a good idea. We could, however, not turn back the clock. There were so many we couldn't possible take them on, so what to do was the question?

Cedric and I called the leaders over, hopefully to think and think fast. The tide was running, did we have time to get to one or two of the ships, get on board, and somehow, get it moving out into the wash, any other ideas?

We quickly clambered aboard the rowing boats that we had not burned, I would like to say that this was forward thinking but it was only luck! And got to the nearest ship we might escape in.

We suddenly thought that we must take the ones nearest the main exit channel, so we rowed some more to get to the very last two from the shore. We jumped on board, knew we had major problems from the start as we had never taken out a ship of any size. These were desperate actions in desperate times!

I asked if anyone knew what to do next. In desperation, two of the scouts jumped forward, one on the other ship, they said some relatives had taken them out a number of times onto the sea. Thank goodness for relatives I thought.

William Rice had been instructed for a time, the other, Edgar Kenulph, talked a lot, I just hoped he knew what he talked about!

Sails up Check

I called out for someone to pull in the anchor and turned into the main flow of water which we hoped would take us away, the whole area seemed alight, it was truly spectacular, smoke and flames engulfed the whole place.

There was a huge amount of noise from the bank now as the enemy realised what a mess we had made of their fleet and probable their futures. Their superiors would not be impressed to say the least.

Enemy soldiers ran about everywhere on the shore, they could do nothing about the burning and sinking ships but they could, they hoped, get the perpetrators of this crime, as they would no doubt see it. We saw it somewhat differently. Waves of arrows were sent towards us to no avail. Our shields giving us the protection needed.

Cedric had told all to set alight any small boats, so the enemy had to swim, or put the fires out if they could, to get to the remaining ships. This would give us a little time in which to try and get away.

In retrospect, we would have been much better to move on quickly after destroying a few of their ships and getting well away to fight another day. At fighting we knew about rather than sailing these huge ships into the unknown. This could end badly!

Sails up and we were away, the oars were huge and heavy and cumbersome to begin with, the strongest men were put to work and not stop,..... ever. What were we going to do, just where this was going to end I had no idea!!

We had to get as far away from any other enemy ships as we could to have any chance of surviving the attack we would certainly have to defend at some point.

That is, of course, if we were caught. Did we have even a chance of getting away, I really had no idea at this time!

There were several ships we didn't destroy and I knew the Normans would not be far behind us.

Edgar and William were doing great things so far, trying to organise the sails and the rowing etc. so we went over to them to say well done and congratulate them.

They didn't even notice us to begin with, they were so engrossed in getting this ship rowing hard and using the wind in our sails, and the other one, sailing as well as possible. I was really proud of all our lads, I mean men, they were certainly not lads any more, and I should credit that to them, at the very least.

Plenty of French exclamations could be heard across the wash, they were still some way off back in the smoke that engulfed the wash now so we must be making good speed, hopefully that would continue while I discussed a plan to get back on land, somehow, without being chased and attacked.

This was going to be difficult though, my head was already churning over a few ideas. Cedric and I put our heads together again!

Much thinking, but not much else, I had to admit. Play it by ear, said Cedric, we both smiled at each other, the two of us being useless on water. We often use this comment today when faced with a problem and end up laughing uncontrollable.

Our speed was really good considering we did not really know what we were doing, Edgar Kenulph not only talked the talk! We were very glad to see he knew what he was talking about. My admiration was apparent. I asked him how long he thought he could keep up the speed and stay away from the following enemy. Of course, he hadn't a clue, what a daft question!

The wind was quite good and going in the right direction. I instructed everyone to see if they could see any rivers flowing from the land into the wash, that maybe offered an escape route?

It was very hard to make anything out at present, so we continued to go with the wind. The ship suddenly veered towards the middle of the wash, away from the bank. It must be a tributary to the wash, though it was not very strong, its flow interrupting our passage with both ships.

We tried to get back to this place but the following enemy were catching quite fast, so we continued and hoped we would soon find another river, hoping the next one might be larger, with a stronger flow.

Tait Hambleton was one of the men at the front of the ship, he called out that he could hear rushing water, well, maybe not rushing, something interfering with our progress, the sound of the water hitting our boat changed, we began moving out into the wash, we feared another fight with all those very angry enemy.

We thought we must take a very fast look at this. It may be just the chance we needed to get out of the wash and away up a river. I took a real chance and called to the man at the rudder to alter course at a moment's notice.

That moment came very quickly, as we could hear the water hitting the boat from another direction, we turned to the left as I shouted.

The first section was deep but now it became shallower quickly. I called to try and stay in the middle of the flow. This was difficult, especially as the wind was now in the wrong direction.

What to do? We tried to make the lads row harder, we were not good at this, in this large ship it was difficult. Practice made perfect, as my father used to say, the trouble was we had no time at all to get any practice. We needed to be good at rowing now, and steering come to that! We needed to be sailors and we were far from being that.

In this reasonable small river, as it entered the wash, it would have helped if we knew what we were doing, trouble was, we really didn't, nor did the men in our other ship.

Panic took over. We frantically shouted for all to paddle harder to try and progress up river so we would be out of sight from the following enemy, eventually we made progress against the river flow. I heaved a sigh of relief and I decided we should see if we could find land, out of this blasted water.

This was easier said than done, after much manic paddling from the rowers, we had returned to the middle of the river, we even managed to get up a little speed. There was a cry of "land ahead" from Roan Hunnisett at the front of the ship, so we just aimed our ship in that direction and hoped things would come out alright. I called out to the other ship to follow us, at least we would be together, wherever this trip ended!

Lady luck was with us again as after a few minutes, we crashed into the bank of the river.

We all leapt over the sides and scrambled onto dry land. All of us were very wet and cold, the other lads in the other ship followed on quite quickly.

We listened for the approaching enemy, keeping very silent.

All too soon the cries from the ships approached us from behind the smoke, they kept quite away from the banks of the wash, staying towards the middle of the main flow.

This could be their big mistake! If they continued out there, the chance was that they may well just miss us altogether.

They must be thinking that we will stay towards the middle of the flow, for the sake of safety staying in the deepest water, they didn't realise we were landlubbers and were right out of our depth, quite literally!

They sailed past us, we all had laughter in our eyes, but not on our lips! This was a very silent tribute to lady luck. We began looking for somewhere to hide, and maybe find somewhere where we could defend ourselves against a very angry bunch of enemies, if they ever found us! Surely they must eventually realise we had vanished up one of the rivers that ran into the wash.

They carried on out of earshot so we became a little more relaxed. I gave the order to try and pull the ships out of sight from the wash and disguise them with branches of trees and bushes. We had to push them back out towards the wash, then bring them back in near the middle of the river, then find a corner of the river, where some trees had created an overhang over the water, tie them in, and cover them both until hidden. I do not think any of us really expected to use these boats ever again as was my first thought but at least the enemy would have trouble finding where we had landed, thereby getting no idea where we might have gone and giving us time to get well away from the area.

We nearly lost Alton Enddicott and Auden Edgar to the wash as the water nearly carried them away during this work, the current was really strong and as a result dangerous. It probable became stronger as the tide in the wash receded.

Our ability to keep afloat was not too good! We must practice and become used to keeping ropes and perhaps a large lump of wood to throw at our men if they got into distress on any water. We were too few to start this fight back and we could not afford to lose any men so cheaply!

I was thinking perhaps of getting away from this part of England, across the wash, to Norfolk, then onto the Isle. This might be a better way than going across country, though all that land that would have Normans looking out for us everywhere we went.

What to do now was the question, the enemy would be after us full on. They would not just be going up and down the wash looking for signs of our passing, not many of that force would be on the ships, plenty more would be trying to find out where we had landed, if we had landed, by combing the land around here to find our tracks or indeed the ships we had taken.

They would have probable sent for more troops as we had caused so much bother now, they must get us finished off, killed. We had embarrassed them no end and killed many of their forces, therefore we must be made to pay the ultimate price, with our lives!

Our version of what we had achieved so far was somewhat different.

Chapter 18

Nearby Stabling and a Camp

We heard noise, men speaking nearby, of the Norman variety we thought, so having calmed down, we went towards the sound, making sure to make no noise ourselves. Maybe, just maybe, they had some horses we could take! Their accents were broken English/French so they were not friendly fighters.

There was quite a large camp here, nestled in the reed beds, on dry ground, which we found very strange, there were some stabled horses to one side on open ground. It looked as though these soldiers were trying to hide from the Saxons or Girvii, maybe the Normans as well?

No uniform was being worn, as far as we could tell, we could not tell who they were. Anyway we needed horses, fast, so we had a look at how many men were here and decided we would attack and take their animals. We were desperate men and we would not be taking no for an answer!

Maybe they were deserters from the Norman ranks, who knows, we did not have time to find out for sure! Maybe they were a special group set up to try and find us and kill us off! We simple did not have time to find out, they seemed heavily armed and we needed horses to get clear of the following enemy. One option, attack and take their animals! We could hardly enter negotiations and bid for them, they may not have listened !!

We would try and attack from four sides at the same time, as we practised before, the camp was not that large so we set up in our different groups ready to go. I sent out the other groups, it wouldn't take long to get ready to attack.

Nicholas Bacon was opposite where my group was, Peter Ganning to our right, Richard Hokton to our left Thomas Eltisle, the other leaders took charge of their men. Our Girvii and Iceni men thought it would be good to fight this as a group, so I agreed, they had worked harder than anyone else to prove themselves, I would continue to keep a good eye on them, they opened another point from which to attack. They hated the enemy even more than the rest of us, it appeared and were certainly not afraid to show it on the battlefield.

As we were waiting, some horses approached from outside the camp, about ten in number, we could just make them out as the light was still bad. They made for the largest covered area, making plenty of noise, no English language was heard, so they were enemy, a lot of shouting followed, everyone was woken from their slumber, they got very excited and began making for their roped horses.

I quickly changed plans, as we would have to attack straight away, we needed their animals, we needed to be away from here, and we were between the men and their horses.

With little choice, we attacked, caught them by complete surprise. It was quite a battle, close up with swords, our eyes were acclimatised to the near dark and fog which helped no end. At this point they were just turning from their fires so I was sure they could not see us properly.

We tried to kill them all off but there were just too many, all our other men joined in, it was a real job now to make sure we didn't get many of our force injured, or worse!

After much slaughter, we made huge inroads into this enemy. Some of them managed to get away which was not good at all, we may have to pay for that later, as was my usual thought at times like this.

Peter Ganning and his men managed to kill off as many enemies as we did which was very good going, as he came to the fight last.

His men always seemed to have more energy than the rest of us, maybe it was just the way he led his men? We would have to talk! Had I missed a trick, if I had we must all learn it, and quickly too! Maybe his group were just fitter than the rest of us.

None of us relished this killing, we all had problems coping with it. It was just a job in these very difficult times, we told ourselves, to kill or be killed. The options were not good! As expected the Girvii and Iceni cleared any enemy near them with ease and skill. They quickly moved onto the next bunch. I was very pleased I had brought these men with us.

Much groaning from enemy wounded, a few of ours too, we were in a hurry now to get the animals and put as many miles between us and the enemy as we could.

Sadly, we left a few good men dead, said our goodbyes, pretty quickly, which seemed disrespectful, and prepared to move off. The dead would have understood, we told ourselves, much too risky to stay for more than a few minutes. If those angry enemy were on our tails, we needed to be away from here as soon as possible.

The horses were more than a bit jumpy to begin with but soon settled down as we went along, they quickly adjusted. Amazing animals these horses! There were a few too many, we took them all. You never know just when you might need a new nag! One may go lame or just be in a bad mood too often.

Those who were not horse "friendly" to begin with were now good horsemen, our rate of traveling was much improved so we quickly got under way.

The injured, and there were quite a few, had to put up with a lot of pain, being juggled around on horseback was not good. They knew we had no choice but to carry on and to grin and bear it, it was no good leaving them to the mercy of the enemy as they had none, they would be tortured and killed.

I thought there would be much scrub land and reed beds from here along the edge of the wash, lots of area in which to hide.

I was quickly proven right, as the track petered out, first to rough grassland, then trees, reed beds, and fresh water followed by the sea water in the wash. It was really wild.

We rode into the thick bush, trying to leave as little trace of our passing as we could. This was easier said than done, we went right to the end of nowhere, or so it seemed, on we walked for about a mile trying to clear all trace that we had passed this way. There really was nothing here, us and a lot of water and wild bush was all.

Perfect for what we needed, so we settled down to catch food and eat, after we had some rest.

Even at this point we were excited about our first battle, mainly with swords, though it had not lasted long it had been exciting. We realised at this point that we would perhaps never have the advantage of surprise again, we certainly gave them a bloody nose this time, they were unlikely to forget about us now, their command would be going crazy for our blood.

Mystery Group of Fighters

I was not at all sure just who this last group was, they may have been a Norman group working on a special mission, perhaps, we would never know. We all talked into the night, with our small fires to keep us warm. Very still and no noise, this place was more than a little weird. After the noise of battle we appreciated it so much more. Those soldiers had unsettled me, not knowing who they were was disturbing.

A lovely bright day followed, as we woke and prepared to look around us, to see how safe we were, and to see if we needed to run, then which way?

We split up into groups, to have a look around us before deciding which way to go from here. We needed to know if troops were following, if they were from which direction were they coming, knowledge was imperative.

My group travelled along the coast line, one went a little inland, the other groups went towards the Boston track. The tide was turning now, all the land where the water had been looked dirty grey in colour, this of course was quite normal to us, but it was such an expanse! Imagine how many miles the country must gain each time the tide went out! Extra land all around our island of Britain.

An interesting thought, pointless, but interesting. My mind was in relaxed mode, my thoughts wandering as they tended to at such times.

Chapter 19

There was quite a large fire ahead, judging from the smoke puffing into the sky. It could be a Norman camp or just a farmer burning scrub, or trees, one of the other groups should find out what that was about and report back.

We reached the allotted time to return to our "base", only to find one group there. The smoke was indeed from Norman soldiers, a pretty large group we were told, feeding themselves. We had no way of finding out what they were doing so we had to think they were after us and be very careful, indeed.

We assumed they were after us, they were probable preparing to enter this wilderness in groups to find out if we were here or had travelled through here to escape. They had enough soldiers to take London the lads thought. Time to move out of the area and fast!

So we all got our equipment together and moved out. We trotted our new horses as far as we could manage as a group, we used a main track, with extra scouts out to give us time to get clear of the track if needed, so we would not be delayed in our rush to exit the area. After many more miles we split back into groups of ten or twenty, off the road and out of sight.

We went around a parish called Benington. In peaceful times we would possible have looked and stayed for a time, chatted to the locals, etc. no time for pleasantries now! This did slow us quite a bit but we kept an eye on the track, as to what was coming and going, two large groups of horse passed us by, going at quite a speed along the coast.

I though I might well go into one of the alehouses where perhaps they might stay and find out what they were about, if anyone heard anything, they might just pick up some information, as we needed to be alert.

They might set up blocks across the tracks anywhere or begin to search areas off the main track if they suspected we had perhaps broken up as a group to hide into a community somewhere.

One such alehouse appeared ahead of us with a large section of land behind it, able to take many horses and men, so I signalled to all and met the leaders of each group, explained what I proposed, which was to enter the house and ask if any work was available. I was pleased they all agreed it was a good idea as we were very new to giving out orders to each other preferring to reach an idea through sensible conversation between us all.

So I set off, we were in no mad hurry now as we had got clear of the fighting area, we did need to be very careful as we had more than annoyed a lot of Norman officers by killing their men, and to date, at least, getting away with it.

Most of us had got away with it, some had not and they had paid heavily. Both Cedric and I had awful trouble dealing with our losses at times. The sense of never seeing some of our comrades/friends again was ever with us and was a heavy weight to carry.

I kept reminding myself, we were on a very difficult mission and nothing should take away from the ultimate prize, that of bringing down William the Conqueror and his not so merry men, not so merry in this area of England as we had begun the fightback by killing just a few of them! We all just hoped that we could impress upon the Anglo-Saxon race our need for getting back our instinct for fighting for our fair land!

There was quite a lot of rowdy noise coming from the building as I approached, entered and made my way to the table from which the ale was served, we had a small amount of money so I bought a pint, my first for a very long time.

My goodness, it tasted good. I struck up a conversation with the man serving, asked about work of any kind, cleaning, working with horses staying at their house, moving barrels, just anything as I was passing through and could do with some money, even keep and a dry place to put my head?

He said when things became less busy he would go and talk with the owner, I said my thanks and looked around for someone who was not talking to anyone, while listening to what the topic of the day was.

Chapter 20

Working at the Ale House

It appeared we had indeed set off a storm, most of the talk was of the daring raid on the Norman ships, they had not heard of our other exploits as yet.

The story was of the many "hundreds" of soldiers we had dispatched.

I suspected each time this story was told, the number was greater, but it did sound good, I hoped it would give confidence to others in the country, to follow our lead!

I sat near an old gentleman and introduced myself. He greeted me with an enthusiastic "hello", said his name was Ackerley Tadleigh and he lived and worked on a farm nearby, had done all his life as he loved the land, and a pint of good ale!

The Boston Deeps!

Though he was deeply troubled by these damned invaders who were demanding more and more of his bosses crops as payment for being allowed to exist, as a result he received less money himself, he thought he and his wife would survive all right.

He felt very sorry for the young folk with children, he said he did not know how they could survive.

Then he asked if I had heard of the brave lads who had burnt the Norman ships in the Boston Deeps, I said I had not as I had come down from the north, so he continued to tell me how many hundreds, possible thousands, of Normans had perished at Saxon hands and had their ships destroyed, burned and sunk.

He also told of the large group of enemy soldiers who had passed through, five of whom still remained at the back of this property, to look out for people passing by who might have been involved with this great deed, and to track and kill them.

Groups Were Being Left at Points Along the Way

This was of great interest to us, obviously, just what we wanted to know. Good information and a fine pint of ale. Life was getting better all the time! The day was looking up.

The owner came to our table and said he might well have some work for me, I said my thanks to the gentleman, and followed him to the rear of the pub. Pay would be difficult but if I started sorting out the empty barrels with the full ones and various crates he would prepare some food and we could talk, sounded good to me so I set to work. The ale was produced in a shed at the rear of the house.

It was easy, as I was so fit from our running, training and fighting that I soon had the job done. Nobody was about so I began sorting out his huge shed at the back of the alehouse, lots of wood cut for the fires in the evenings and winter so I stacked it in even piles and put the uncut wood neatly against the building, putting the saws and bill hooks all in one place, you could see where I had been. I moved the empty barrels to one side and stacked them.

The chap came out and was quite delighted by what he saw, neat yard and wood shed, clapped me on the back, thanked me for using my initiative and said to follow him to the kitchen as his wife had prepared a meal.

I felt bad as the lads were left to fend for themselves, I knew they could cope well, or so I told myself and hoped I was right.

The meal was lovely, lots of meat, vegetables and hot thick gravy, how I missed this home life, then came a pudding with pastry and apples…I could put up with this and live here.

Damn and forget the Normans! Maybe I could somehow forget these enemy, one thing was sure in my mind and that is they would never forget about us until we were a spent force, dead and buried! These were sobering thoughts.

The couple were chatty, obviously pleased to have someone else to talk to, Margaret even left the room to view what I had done in such a short space of time.

She was delighted too, everywhere I had been, neat and tidy, with a laugh she talked about adopting me before someone else did.

It was quite late when we had finished, I helped wash and clear away, only to be presented with another pint of ale, how could I refuse, I was just being sociable!

The Ale House

Their names were Simeon and Margaret Treton and they had taken over the business from his father, Thomas, whose father had built the building in the first place. The main topic of conversation was yet again of the burning of Norman ships and dead enemy soldiers.

About time we fought back, they both said, somebody had to start, now perhaps a real fight could begin. Someone must organise our forces and lead us out of the mess we were now in, even though it was more than a little late. Not too late perhaps!

Chapter 21

The Isle of Ely and Its History

When Rome had fallen and left Britons to fend for themselves, the incoming Anglo-Saxons had made the Britons fall back to this Isle for defence. Later, as the Saxons were assailed by the Danes and Norwegians and the whole host of Scandinavian pirates and rovers it was used again for the same reason.

The people sought exemption from the dreadful prospect of war. Elys early abbey had been destroyed by fire, the cities of Cambridge and Grantchester had suffered the same fate, Cambridge stood derelict for some three hundred years, after which it was rebuilt, Grantchester was never rebuilt as a city. It does make a lovely village on the meadows overlooking the river Cam though.

So the area suffered, as did the whole country, from these violent men. To fight against the dreaded Danish battle axes was to be delayed as long as possible, as well as all the other pirates, so the Camp of Refuge was ever used.

The Camp of Refuge

I mentioned I had heard of resistance going on in the Isle of Ely and wondered if I should see if we could lend a hand, I said my father and brothers had fought up north and had been forced to surrender or die. They went back to their farm, I left for adventure.

The couple thought there was going to be plenty of adventure to go around and hoped I found what I was looking for in these perilous times without getting caught or injured. They also said they had heard likewise of the Isle.

I excused myself and explained I felt the need to go for a walk before turning in for the night. I briskly walked to where the lads said they were going. I was alarmed at the noise they were making at the fireside and I told them off a little for not putting out a scout to make sure nobody was coming their way.

I need not have worried as Jordan Fantosme rushed up behind me, greeted me, and told me he had been following me for some time. I had tried to arrive unseen by my men.

They were getting good at this, I congratulated him and laughed. The force were finishing their food and chatting about nothing in particular, everything in general.

I told them of my experience at the ale house and thought it might be good to stay a few more days, they were quite pleased that news of our fighting had travelled so far so quickly but concerned that our foe was gathering strength to find us and wipe us out. We would need to lie low for a time, I suggested, and think what to do next and where to do it.

We had intended to have a hit and run policy, just attacking groups as, and if, the enemy appeared. This was always going to be difficult as we did not know how the Normans would react. It looked as though they were going to get very forceful straight away, I suppose we should have expected this.

We decided to lie low for a time, to try and drop off the scene as it were. The place where we were was not far from the coastline on the east coast of the North Sea so I suggested all of them took off to as protected a point as they could find and spend time training and practicing their use of arms, swords, axes, arrows and lances etc. while I learnt all I could from the public house and the five Normans that were staying there.

We would leave scouts out as always to give them time to hide if needed, we would use animal horns, by blowing into them, as always to alert of enemy on the way.

All agreed, they got the other groups together, and set off in an agreed direction, they were all in good spirits when they left, I wished them well, I felt alone and a little sad to see them go.

I had to laugh at myself, sad to see them go was a little dramatic! It was just that we had become so close as a group, living, planning and fighting together, and thinking of what the future held, the future of our country was perhaps in our very hands and it was so exciting!

We were almost living the dream, or nightmare. That depending on how you looked at it. Waking the Anglo-Saxon race from slumber, to fight back against the enemy, never to accept defeat! We all hoped we could make that difference. Was it just the confidence of youth? Only time would answer that. It was up to us to give it a try and see where it led! It would not be for the want of trying.

I made my way back to the track and the alehouse, and was greeted first by the old chap I had talked to on my arrival and then the owners of the establishment. A couple more ales went the same way as the others and I began chatting to anyone who would listen, though I was careful not to commit myself too heartily on any subject.

Quite a few talked of their hopes with the next seasons crops but were very upset by the Normans demands for a greater percentage of the money earned from this.

The local Norman was little more than a bully with a gang of crooks by his side whose place was to force the farmers to give up their percentage of crops in tax or money, they all felt sure these evil men kept a large proportion of that money/crops for themselves. These men were led by a man known as the "Devil of the Fens", said to be a nephew of William himself.

The stories regarding our fighting the Normans and destroying their ships were getting better and better. Tales of the many "thousands" of our enemies we had killed and the "entire" fleet we had destroyed, again, this was good for moral I thought. The hope was always that this would get us Anglo-Saxons fighting again, we must restore our pride and self-respect.

They may hear of the fighting before that sometime and they could make up all sorts of stories.

A loud thud on the door of the drinking room where we all sat startled everyone and in burst the five enemy soldiers from the field behind, demanding ale, the whole place went silent as they were served. The atmosphere turned sour and we hoped their ale did as well!!

They sat in a corner by a window and began jabbering away in French so we began talking again. Not another word was said regarding fighting, it was back to crops and rainfall and weed growth etc. Normal agricultural conversation that has taken place throughout the ages no doubt.

We did not know if they could understand anything we said but knew it was best to play safe.

I made my way over to where they were sitting to see if I could understand any of the words they were saying to each other, a few words were repeated a lot, 'damned enemy locals!' Among them.

They had apparently placed groups of about five soldiers up and down the track to try and find out where the Saxon fighters had gone, this helped a little, so I left it at that as they spoke too quickly, it was too much to try and understand.

The more drink they consumed, the faster they became with their stories. If I could find someone local who understood the language, it would be a great help. I decided I would have to work on that! If possible.

After a time, I went to my room, after saying good night to all, and drifted off to a very good night's sleep, aided by the ale, no doubt. This was novel, a room, no less, not sleeping in the open air for once!

Chapter 22

It seemed no time at all when there was a knock at the door, Margaret said it was time to eat breakfast before work began. This kitchen was amazing, it filled the whole place with the most amazing smell of cooking food. Everybody's day should begin like this, I said, she smiled and filled my dish. She said again it was good to have company and compliments!

I followed Simeon out the back door and asked what he had in mind workwise, the back roof of the shed needed some repairs so he asked if I was all right with heights.

I said I would give anything a go if it helped. We took two ladders to the back and climbed just to see what was needed, nails, wood, thatch, we quickly rounded up and began clearing away any old wood that needed replacing.

The job was done in a few short hours. The soldiers were preparing a meal for themselves, we shouted a greeting and they grunted and waved in return. I knew some Latin and French, though they would probable only speak in French, learned at the cell at Spalding and wondered if I dare approach them to get any information I could regarding their job of looking out for the men who had dared to fight them, us, in other words!

I talked to Simeon as we mended other parts of his buildings, and fed his geese, ducks and pigs.

He had a nice pidgeon loft as well. He was a hard worker and I respected him for that, he was more than a little miffed at having these "bloody Frenchies" on his land but he had no choice in the matter.

If he caused them trouble, he would be thrown out and his place burned to the ground so he had no option. Hopefully they would not stay long.

Things would soon return to normal I said with little confidence.

Mid-Day Came and We Were Called for Dinner

Pidgeon pie, just had loads of this, I felt like saying though it tasted much better in some pastry I had to admit, nice bit of gravy made it all the better! A spot of plum pudding followed, were they trying to get me to stay here forever?

We worked until dusk, nearly all the work done, Simeon said, so we stopped for some more ale, what a hard life! It certainly made getting back on the road an awful lot more difficult. A few more small jobs done, then off to bed.

The same knock on the door signalled breakfast. I will miss this I thought to myself! We were finished by eleven o clock and I said my farewells to two of the nicest people I had met. A good, decent, hardworking Anglo-Saxon couple.

Time to head off to meet the boys at work and play at the beach, hopefully nothing had gone wrong.

I headed off across the fields to the woods on the hill where we had stayed, from here you could see a long way but not quite far enough to see the sea. That would be in view from the next hill I thought. I made my way to the bottom of the little valley and crossed the track, glad to see there was nobody about.

I reached the top of the next hill and indeed the sea was in full view, as I ran to the bottom I was joined by our scout, Warinus Bassingbourn, who said he had seen nothing and nobody to date, should he return with me? I said he could come a little way but I would send someone out to replace him if he liked, it was best to be as safe as possible. He agreed, so he pushed his horse with mine and after a time I left him and I carried on.

I was nearly there when I was surprised by yet another scout, Wilfrith Meginhard, it was good to see they were taking security seriously without my pushing them.

Chapter 23

Training on the Beach

I was greeted with a pretty spectacular view of beach, the tide was out and it was a very sunny day, a few clouds and not much breeze. This view alone was worth fighting for, let alone the whole country, spectacular was the only way to describe it.

The sky met the sea on the horizon, the sun made it magic! Blue sky and waves in the distance. So different than our normal view, the heat from the sun made such a change. This heat, with the breeze, was so different than normal.

Some of the lads were mock fighting in the water, they looked tiny as they were so far off, others were in the dunes which were about six hills of dune deep along the coastline with a lot of grass holding them together, both scenes giving them great exercise which was the idea after all.

This made work so much more fun for everyone. Being physically fit led to being mentally fit also, I found, it was definitely a winning thing to do for us all.

Peter Ganning, I could just make out pushing his men harder and harder, perhaps they were just fitter than the rest of us, that was how they were more effective than the rest of us? I think congratulations were in order for him, all of us must step up our game, each group needs to be on a level par with each other.

Nicolas Bacons group were the ones in the dunes and they greeted me first, they were excited and exhausted from their games, of course, I mean training! Time for something to eat and a chat. I could see smoke coming from an area approximately 500 yards roughly north of where we were standing, there was a flat piece of sand, and they had made it into an outside eating space, between the dunes. This was so different than normal but it worked, made a nice change, mainly out of the wind as well. Fish were on the menu, I said about the superb food at the ale house, much to everyone's envy, and indeed the ale.

Our horses were paddocked nearby in the dunes and trees near to a stream so they had all the water they needed and some decent grass just a little inland.

The chaps out by the water's edge came in to hearty greetings, Thomas Eltisles group were soaked by the sea water but looked in great shape. Fit and ready for anything, or everything that was hurled at them, I hoped, as they may need to be!

Cedric Wenoths group had been quite deep in the water, they looked tired, pretty cold as well. It must have taken great strength to act fighting in such deep water, he reckoned it would pay off in the long term and I thought he was probable right.

I spoke of what the soldiers had said, making contact with them by using broken English, French with a few words of Latin, which was very useful. The teachers at the cell would have been impressed, though this was not exactly why they had taught me it in the first place.

One never knows when things might be useful in life as one of my tutors had told me at the cell.

It was interesting to note how much effort they were putting into catching us, making an example and they hoped, wiping us out. They had said they had put as many as one hundred, possibly two hundred men at arms into putting us down as soon as possible. They had spread out so thinly along the line of the track, I could not see how they hoped it would work. Ours was not to reason why? Maybe they were just hoping to get information regarding our whereabouts and then passing it on.

We Even Had a Price on Our Heads Now!

Money was offered to anyone who could help find us, we all thought it was funny that we were worth money now, dead or alive. It was an honour and we relished in it.

Each larger community along the way had a force of up to twenty men staying with them, they would be draining the food that was meant for everyone so they would not be popular wherever they stayed. Us Saxons and the Britons hated them to begin with, when they moved on they would be even more loathed, if that were possible.

We had passed a place called Old Leake to get to the peace and quiet of where we were now, the coast line was away from everything it seemed, the nearest settlement was Wrangle, just a few small houses where people worked the land, and no doubt fished a lot too, probable bartered at the nearest market for the other things they needed in their lives.

I bet it was very cold in the winter months as the sea breeze came in off the water, pretty much a hard life for all. They were nestled in by the lovely dunes though, which was some considerable compensation. A beautiful place for most of the year.

We considered killing off quite a few of these small groups of Norman soldiers. The trouble was with doing this we would be telling the enemy exactly where we were, so maybe not a good idea.

Chapter 24

Aim for the Camp of Refuge

It was decided that our main aim should be to see if we could join up with the men on the Isle of Ely, The Camp of Refuge, as it had become known. There were many miles and the wash between us and them so we had much to plan, just trying to evade the enemy was hard enough, getting our men through the countryside without a trace was difficult.

Then we would have to try and make contact with the leaders at Ely, get accepted, prove we were not the enemy in disguise, and get established on the Isle. A new part of the great Anglo-Saxon Army which we hoped to establish. We would try to reclaim our land! If we could not it would not be for the want of trying.

This was no easy task, we were all of us up for a fight and we would no doubt have to fight along the way to get to our destination. Then to begin planning and training our new forces, up and down the land, to coordinate battles to reclaim our beloved country.

We needed to find out where the Normans had placed their men if possible and make sure we avoided those places, though we would not be together in any more than ten or twenty so perhaps we would be alright, and we would not be travelling on the track at any time for the moment. Also to get the lay of the land in these parts would be good.

No fights would be possible as that would draw attention to us at that point. Our fish for food would need to be smoked, or just salted, we would catch as much as possible, any other meat would need the same treatment. It lasted well, though we would have to get some salt to brine it before smoking, I would see if I could get some from the alehouse the next day.

I left the boys catching fish, some had thought they had heard some boar grunting near the dunes at night so they would set off and see if they could find any to slaughter, a lot of meat on one of them, this might be good for us all. Seagulls would go down a treat as well, though there was not much meat on one of them unfortunately.

I called back at the alehouse and asked if I could buy some salt, they said if I cut some wood up for the winter fire I could have it for nothing so that's what I did. I took a large sack which would be fine, took it back to camp and began preparing the meat.

They did ask why I wanted such an awful lot of salt and I claimed I had relatives living along the coast, they used a lot to brine food for their family and they seemed to accept my explanation.

I was amazed when two of the lads, Manton Espenson and Walter Reynold, brought back a lovely large wild boar, they said there was a batch of them in the woods behind us. They went back to the woods with a couple of other men and brought back another six of the beauties. This was worthy of note maybe sometime in the future.

Another batch of fish appeared with some of my group which was good, some of our training was not wasted. I was concerned by the amount of smoke we were producing, hoping nobody would see or suspect our group was hiding here. There were few trees here to filter it whilst rising.

It was now afternoon and it would soon be getting dark so we continued with our tasks. We had left scouts out that changed every few hours to keep them sharp.

Four Normans

I was alarmed when one of our scouts said there were a number of people coming our way, he was about to rush back but they went off in a northern direction and did not seem to see the smoke, or if they did they were not bothered.

We were really startled when one of the other scouts rushed into camp and told us the group of Normans, four of the five, they assumed from the alehouse were on their way and appeared to have seen the smoke.

Our worst fears had materialised, we had to work quickly with no noise.

We dampened down the fires and sent one lad to tell the others out fishing on the beach to lay still and hope they were not spotted, or the soldiers might send for reinforcements before taking us on.

We hid in the dunes and could now hear the soldiers as they approached, we could not understand what they were saying so that did not help much, could hear the sand crunching under their feet, then they were upon us.

We all leapt up as one and fired, as per norm, arrow after arrow into them. They did not have time to react, one let an arrow go into the ground but that was all. Shooting arrows into fellow human beings was now part of a normal days work, letting them fly, watching men die. We were certainly not enjoying this at all, but getting used to it was a good start! To kill or be killed were the options, we all knew which we needed.

We buried them in the sand allowing extra depth to allow for the sand to maybe blow away for a time before anything was exposed.

All the men came into camp and we carefully talked about how lucky we were to have not got injured. We knew no word was sent out. Quickly we ate all we could and finished smoking the rest, put out the fires and prepared to leave.

Smoked boar tasted really good, maybe they tasted better than normal because of what they ate near the coastline, it being much different than normal grass. And yes I have to admit too much thinking on my part, again!

We knew now that Normans would soon be searching all around here to find their men and then any tracks we had left leaving the area. The game seemed to be upon us!

As it was our intention to go back towards the wash, we got some scrub, bushes, and began to clear our footsteps in the sand as we began to leave the area. The horse hoof marks were a real job to rub out, but we did that as well as best we could. The enemy soldier who was not with them, he had stayed behind to raise the alarm if they did not reappear, we assumed. We had no idea how long he would leave before doing something about his mates not returning so we worked quickly.

After a time, we thought we had cleared enough to hopefully get away, this was hard work as we kept slipping or falling in the sand as it was so fine.

I became very concerned about the other Norman near the alehouse. If we dispatched him, we would have a much greater amount of time to get away. For all we knew he could be on his way to find out where his friends had gone right now! We would be in a bad position from then on as he would doubtless tell his superiors, they would guess what had happened and send a major force to try and kill us off, once and for all!

So after much soul searching us leaders decided to go and finish the job and kill off this enemy. I unfortunately drew the short straw and decided to take Cedric with me, this was not something I was going to relish!

We both rode off, leaving Guthrum in charge, our horses moving quickly, almost as though they knew we were in a hurry to get this job done as soon as possible! It didn't take us long, we approached the field at the back of the alehouse, tied our horses. The Norman was not where he normally was, we heard a commotion at the rear of the house, and approached silently.

The French man was threatening the owner, apparently, he wanted to steal some money, the poor old chap was withering under this attack. I caught his wife out of the corner of my eye, creeping up behind the Norman with a large piece of wood. Clearly she was attempting to knock the enemy out of the contest. This was a good idea but as she prepared to knock him he saw her coming, raised his arm to deflect the wood, and hit her in the face.

My blood was boiling now as I ran forward with my sword drawn, he dropped the man, pulled out his sword and met me with an almighty clash. I was onto the next stroke with my blade before he had much chance to ready himself for defence.

He managed to protect himself, just! As I pulled back to go for a kill shot to his chest. He was fast, he moved just in time, I cussed myself for not being faster. He took a pace back and came at me with force and speed. I was ready, on autopilot, raging as the fury of the moment had taken hold, I turned his sword away and quickly plunged my weapon into his chest. Job done!

Land lady and lord saved in the nick of time. They were much too grateful, I was pleased as I did not like the idea of killing an enemy in cold blood, even though he was enemy, so we were all chuffed at the outcome, that is, except maybe the Norman!

We were told we must stay and take some ale, and, or food. We did explain we were in much too much of a hurry to stay any longer. We said we would take a rain check on it if that was all right, we would, hopefully be back. I said Cedric was a good friend, he had come to ride south with me.

We carried the body a long way to the rear of the alehouse, over in some woods, and dug a good deep hole for the Norman, so hopefully he would not be discovered, by animals or man.

Then we told the couple we were off and would no doubt see them sometime in the future, we hoped they would get no further trouble with any enemy and left two very happy people!

We told them to tell the enemy the soldiers had just left early one morning, possible deserting their army, they could do little about that as an explanation. Hopefully no beatings would be forthcoming. There was little else we could do.

Chapter 25

Joining up With the Rest of the Lads/Men

We took a last look over towards the camp from the hills, it was time to leave our seaside "camp" So we trudged off as quickly as we could, it would long stay in our memories as a very good place to be, a totally different setting than normal, away from the problems of today, if only for a short time.

The trouble was we were heading straight towards the biggest problems of our lives. Maybe not today but certainly over the next months or so, maybe even years. This was an exciting prospect for us all, though it could at times drag ones energy and confidence down. It could be a heavy burden to carry. The potential prize was immense and you may depend we were going for it!

That Was Our Job, We Reminded Ourselves!

We kept on the solid ground, inland of the land side of the dunes, some parts were a bit boggy so we had to go around them, we needed to leave as little evidence as possible of our passing through this part of our land, it was quite difficult as we moved fast, or as fast as possible. We had to pace our horses, set them to feed and water when needed, or they may well stop working with us.

Our scouts, Kenulph and Wilfrith, we added to their number to be safer as they were behind us and in front, making sure nobody was about to see or hear us. We put others either side of us too, Matthew Upton Cynesige was on our left and Walter Reynold was on our right, plus extra men. They were our eyes and ears! We knew we had set off a storm and a great deal of trouble was on the horizon, coming our way!

After several hours, we were thinking food and a decent rest, we were still growing boys, after all, hopefully we could find cover under some trees.

Not much to ask? It was proving quite difficult in this part of the countryside.

We decided to send Wilfrith a little further inland to see what was about from a cover point of view.

We trudged on, and on, and on. I, in particular, was tired though I tried to not show it, things were getting pretty bad. Even the weather had turned sour, gloomy and grey, rain on the way, yet again!

At last, we heard a dull call ahead, from Wilfriths horn, it was the sign he had said he would give if he had found somewhere, so we cheered up considerable.

All of us got to the place where we thought he would be and sat down to recover, just a little would help!

He joined us and said there were a good group of trees a few hundred yards on our right, over a small hill, good dense undergrowth as well in which to hide. He could not find evidence of people living nearby so it seemed a good bet, with a moan we rose again to very quietly make our way to these woods.

We caught up with our scout and followed him over the small hill, this indeed looked a good place to hide out, a woodland with no tracks, no people, no buildings and a small stream as well! With a sigh of relief we descended to the little valley floor near the stream.

The lads set about getting food and a good supply of wood for the fire. Huts were quickly constructed, mainly just low roof, enough to let us sleep easily in the dry, should it rain any more than it already was, we would be dry no matter what was thrown at us. The fires began to dry us out and cheer us up. Scout hides were established on all four hills around us, two men in each, well hidden, so we were secure, we hoped!

The cooks, we could call them that with some confidence now, prepared all food that was left, mainly smoked, and we ate it while waiting as the hunters gathered in all they could, plenty of deer and boar about, so again we ate well, rabbits a plenty, these were at least fast to cook. Soon great sides of cooked deer were cut away from the carcass to reveal yet more meat to cook and eat, the same with the boar. All of us regained our strength fast!

All had a good night's sleep and were reborn by the morning. Even the scouts were not disturbed.

Going Inland

We had crept through some tiny parishes, with what I regarded as charming names, Old Leake, Frithville, over Gipsey Bridge, onto Holland Fen, then onto an established track towards the old town of Sleaford. We kept to the track as much as possible as we had to put as much distance between us and the last fight, most of our belongings kept off the tracks and followed us to meet at set points along the way. We stopped at regular intervals to rest the horses, as well as ourselves, always finding a good hiding place in thick woodland or slight wolds, nothing looked untoward this way as we were set in our groups of not more than ten at any time.

We easily always found each other, it was rather like we were permanently attached, a group working together to the same end…fighting Normans.

There was a disturbance at a small hamlet called Anwick as we passed, quite a number of Norman soldiers were getting very busy trying to stop one set of locals fighting another, one of our groups looked set to interfere, attack the Normans and sort out the locals.

I rushed up to them and reminded them that we must try and keep out of the public eye, though I would have liked to smash our way into the Normans and sort out the rest, that I was afraid was not up to us, unless we wanted to tell the enemy where we were, and we certainly did not want to do that!

Sleaford

On we travelled and entered Sleaford, quite a busy market town, with some fine buildings. The main houses were now occupied by the enemy, as usual, this must have caused some dreadful trouble, upsetting the norm!

The original occupants thrown out and their land confiscated, if they objected too much they were slaughtered and or butchered in some way by our common "friends" the Normans.

We mingled on the outside of the busy market, watching and buying food we fancied and the odd drink, it was nice to feel almost normal for once. Not rushing around on horseback!

Some rowdy Normans began fighting over to our left, we shouldn't have interfered really but the odds were stacked against the few men who we thought were probable locals, about five to one, so we just thought we would make the odds a little more in favour of the locals.

We tied our horses and stood around the whole group, there was much shouting in very bad English, so I joined in and clouted the Norman who seemed to be in charge, he easily fell to the ground so I gave him a good kick, a mass punch up began, it was at least just fists, no time for anything else.

Henry Garrod launched himself at two of the Normans, he was a big bloke and he easily knocked them down. They got up quickly so he got a little miffed and sent them with his fists to the ground for good, knocked out.

Several more of our lads became involved, we all laid into them with great gusto! What a "common" punch up, great fun if you hated the guys you were punching and we all certainly did.

Athelred Dexter was damned strong, he soon showed that to several more enemy, putting them out of the game!

He was quite deceptive, as he was rather small and he did not speak very much, when he did it was important, if he needed to make a point and nobody listened, you needed to get out of his reach.

After they had given up or simple run off, there was much jeering from the crowd we had pulled, we were just laughing at each other on a job rather well done.

I told my lads that this was a lesson to them all of something never to do, ever! Under no circumstances should they ever do this kind of thing !! I realise that I had just told everyone earlier in the day to not get any attention drawn on us by doing this kind of thing, but when needs must! I for one was tired and annoyed and I took it out on these enemy which was something I should never have done. This was a very bad example to show my men and I would not forget it in a long time.

One of the lads brought to my attention that a group of Normans were on their way across the market, it was good that it was crowded as they were very slow making any headway on their animals.

Ok, chaps, it was time to leave this fine town, as quickly as we could, we ran to our horses and leapt on them.

We were off, and no mistake, a bit like the wind in these parts, flying off the sea as it did. There was much cheering from the market square, I bet the locals had not had so much to cheer about in a long time. Seeing some enemy being beaten was nothing but great fun! No risk to themselves.

As we reached the outskirts of the town, we slowed, caught up with each other, and laughed an awful lot, what bad boys we were!

The Normans were still in pursuit so we began to push our horses again, we were soon clear of the town, we broke up, some stayed on the track, two other groups went over fields and into woods, one went to the left.

The rest came with us. We had quickly talked about having a bit of fun with these enemy. We decided we would capture them and tie them up, hands and feet, and send off their horses, or take them with us, if we got the chance.

This would hopefully make the enemy think that we were not the same people who had caused them so much trouble by killing Normans and it would be a good laugh as well.

We had to catch them first, fun in itself. We quickly roped off gaps between trees and ditches and thought of ways to make the horses rear and throw off their mounts.

It did not take long, which was good, as we did not have much time, and as they were now split into groups chasing us, there were not many to catch in the group following us.

Eight horses came galloping in our direction, with Normans riding of course, they came towards the gap in the hedge. They were moving too fast to go through the gap we had roped off, they could not possibly make sure if it was clear or not, all hit the rope at such speed, six of them came straight off their animals, amidst mighty cries of pain and surprise as they hit the ground, the other two horses were rounded up by our lads and led to where the six were.

We pulled them off their mounts and tied them all up together. They did look silly, we gaged seven of them, left one able to cry for help from his comrades. They looked a sad bunch! We chased their horses away, kept a couple as they looked good, and said goodbye to the French! Their swords would be handy as well so they were taken.

Chapter 26

All of us travelled on our way, having met up again, the day dragged on, we looked for and found a large wooded area in which to spend the night. We were a good distance from Sleaford.

We crept into the low brush, trying to leave no trace of our passing by this point, it was very good cover, the horses were a little unsettled to begin with, we could see just a little light from above, this faded to almost nothing when we were in the woods proper, the tall trees blotted out most of the sky. The horses were left in some grass near a stream at the edge of this woodland before being brought near to where we were, the water nearby was called Cliff Beck.

We stayed in our groups of ten and settled quickly to sleep, left our scouts out, Kenulph and Wilfrith, in the direction we had come and sent out two more, Warinus and Richard ahead of us, just a little as I knew they were tired, into the woods. We all fell into a deep well-deserved sleep.

Peace Prevailed, at Least for the Moment!

I was really concerned now as the Normans would probably discover their men missing, even if they did not find them buried they might consider them killed by us and hidden, as before. We may have got a few days in which to make our partial escape, we needed more food and dense cover to be able to cook this food unnoticed by the outside world in general. We would have to see how large this wood was as soon as we woke. Our clothes were several layers thick and with the low brush keeping out the wind, it really was a good place to spend the night.

Woken by the dawn chorus, it was spectacular, it seemed every bird in the world had congregated above and around us and decided to celebrate the fact that we were there.

As leaders, we all met, a number of our best bowmen went out to get food as quickly as possible, we moved further into the woods to get an idea of where to go next, we met the two scouts who said they had not seen nor heard anything of note. I told them to go back to the group, come a little further into the woods and prepare fires ready to cook our meals, prepare and cook any bird or game they had managed to get but be careful as there may be people about, we must avoid anyone where possible, as always.

Universal hatred of the Normans was our defence, but if we were seen and this got talked of in the locality then a Norman spy, or a disgruntled local working for them, might hear and they would torture anyone they pleased to find out what was known, they would blind people, cut off their hands or legs, we all had to be careful. Talk was that William did not like killing people, as he would have to pay for such actions in the afterlife; he generally went for maiming his enemy, crippling their lives in some dreadful way. He seemed to think that killing people on a battlefield was a completely different matter which was more than a little strange.

We were not just worried for us but also for our people in general. We felt we were carrying the weight of our nation at times, just the group of us and that was a heavy load!

Most of the time, however, it was great, it was the right thing to do as it was the only thing to do right now!

The woods were huge we were very pleased to note so we made our way back to camp. Fires were burning with the smell of meat coming our way, it felt like a good day ahead! Several deer had been killed along with pidgeon a plenty so we ate very well, as usual.

We sent out new scouts to replace the existing ones who reported nothing untoward going on, such as troop movements, large or small so maybe the enemy had not organised itself as yet. It would take some time to get a force together and try and pick up our track to where we were, we felt confident.

We realised travelling along the edge of the coast would be very easy to track, so we would travel inland now. Our goal, the Isle of Ely, as before.

Just think what hundreds, maybe even thousands, of Anglo-Saxons and Britons would be able to achieve against Williams men. We had created a lot of trouble, involved them making perhaps hundreds of men available to track and try to kill us, just the group of us, we were causing havoc and it simple felt great.

Several of the lads were making new arrows with different wood, it would be interesting to fire them, hopefully into the enemy.

We invited all to talk of how they felt, what we should do now, where we should avoid, town wise, even some of the villages where Normans had settled, so we had to be careful to avoid settlements of any sort, to be as sure as we could of not being discovered.

Stories must now be rife of our small deeds of daring, no doubt having been exaggerated many times over, probable we would have killed thousands and sank fleets of ships. If it made our people feel better, then good, I say!

No matter what, we would carry on to the end, wherever, and whatever that may be.

We called in the scouts, cleared all evidence we could of our being here, got back into our groups and left. Further into the woods we went, very happy with the world in general. It was a majority decision to go the way we went, we all voted as a group as I felt this was of great importance to our moral, everyone had their say as usual.

We had become angry at being told what to do by the invaders of our land, it was important to talk, listen and learn from each other. In this way, I believed, we as a nation could win respect at the very least from the Normans. We may at least keep some of our land, I hoped at this time.

King Alfreds Wessex.

When King Alfred had defeated the Danes, he took a great part of England, Wessex, back from them under his control before going on to defeat them altogether, taking back all our land from the Danelaw, uniting England. Why could we not do a similar thing against the Normans.

Our ambition became greater as time went by and we became more successful.

The land was low and quite boggy in places as we went along but we made quite good time, the scout to our left came back to tell us of a place some way ahead that looked as if it had some sort of covering on it, it could be military he thought, so he and I went ahead to find out.
It turned out to be a large covered area indeed, we cautiously made our way closer, could not make out what it was doing here. A lot of smaller huts were now visible; some men were milling around in the early morning light, a great number of horses were penned in an area nearby.
It appeared they were training horses, many of them corralled up at one end of the enclosed land. We watched for a time as we needed to make sure they were Normans training horse for military use. We were all amazed at how quickly they had established this camp, they probable arranged such places as camps wherever they conquered just as soon as they could, so they could take over more quickly, their troops could get to their centres of control more quickly if they changed horses at set points around the countryside.
They were doing just that, so what to do? Not sure at this point, matters were going to get more than a bit angry in the following moments as the decision of what to do was taken out of our control.
A flash of uniform startled me, over to my left a large chap exited his hut building to greet the morning air, placing his coat over his shoulders, while we were watching him from over to our right someone called out, apparently to us. I did not understand what he said, but it was not friendly, and not in our language, so we turned and ran back to our group.
I called, not too loudly, for everyone to be ready to go further back into the woods. When I reached my group I explained what we had seen. We decided to make our way past the encampment with horses if we could carry on our journey without being seen.
This was not to be as noise on quite a large scale began coming from the camp, horses rearing as saddles were put on them, much shouting as the men prepared to come and fight. Word of our deeds had reached them we had no doubt, or perhaps they just fought any Saxon who dared to come close, who knows? We did not know how to fight in these cramped quarters so we could be

in trouble! I should point out that we had fought in woods before but that we were not happy doing so!

We would have to learn quickly if any of us were to survive, we may be outnumbered, my hope was that these were not regular soldiers. They may be a disorganised bunch of horse trainers, hoping to make the "big time."

They had probable been warned about us, or was I being big headed about our accomplishments to date. This could be possible, maybe they were after the reward for catching us, but what the hell. We were certainly not going to run, so fight we must!

We made the best of what cover we could find in the short amount of time we had before the rush of horses began to fill our ears, and indeed our sight as the enemy approached.

We kept to our groups of ten or twenty, I shouted for the men to not use too many arrows as we could hardly make more, thankfully, we did have a lot.

When they were nearly on us we stood as one and fired. We caught them by surprise and they fell easily, the horses kept running so we had to move all over the place, we fired again, same effect, bodies and horses everywhere.

Some of the Normans were swinging their swords at us now, I heard some cries of pain so they were hitting us to our group on my right, this was not good!

Then came some men running at us, I shouted to wait until they were close, then to fire at will, we must hit our targets with one arrow only if at all possible. I was impressed at the amount of enemy who had fallen. And still they came.

Was it mad to carry on fighting in a certain way? If I was losing so many men, I would change my attack, go around the back and sides and fight us on all quarters. We probable could not hold out for very long as they had no idea how many men we had. This was probable to our advantage. After all we may be just three or four strong. They were, it seemed, being led by someone who was clearly out of their depth.

Perhaps again, reward money was being offered, this could be clouding their decisions. They should have sent out for experienced soldiers, leaders of men, no less!

All of us Anglo-Saxons were very glad they did not do so!

Chapter 27

These are the remains of Burwell Castle, Cambridgeshire. Though this was not built at the time the books are set I have little doubt there was an earlier fortification on the ground.

The attack fell silent and what a relief, we quickly moved our injured a good few yards away, and met as a group, congratulated each other on our shooting, and wondered how long we might have before the next attack. We all knew we had lost men and were shocked by how we felt, a dreadful pain inside. We can feel bad later I said to all, we will avenge their deaths many times over, in fact we already had, so damn it, let's continue the fight and take it to the enemy. So we skirted the broken Normans laying in our path and made our way to the edge of the woods.

There were quite a number of men running around their camp, the group leaders met and we thought about wiping out this group altogether. No one left to tell the tale, could we do it? As always by doing so, we would slow the men looking for us therefore giving us the chance to get well clear of the area, hopefully long before the enemy knew of the battle.

The numbers were not in our favour, though we had put a lot out of action. We decided to send four men near their exit road to get any enemy that tried to escape. That done, we thought the best way to trap these men in their group of huts was to try and circle them and just pick them off one by one, they had no idea how many we were so that would be in our favour. Let's give it a go was the general thought so quickly that became the plan.

We stayed in groups of ten and readied ourselves, one sad fool tried to rush between two of the huts, I hit him high in the chest and he fell. Several more tried to move and were dead before they hit the ground, good shooting from the far side.

Then a general melee as soldiers ran towards their horses, they were dead, more went towards the main hut, they met the same end.

This went on for some time, some arrows were fired from the huts in our direction, did not disturb us one bit, we were in killing mode, and very unhappy at losing some of our men. Revenge was now the order of the day!

We confidently began moving towards the huts, bodies all around us, the door nearest us shot open, four men jumped out and were sent to hell very quickly. I looked in the door, clearly empty now, so signalled to all to move in slowly.

The group to my left opened their nearest hut door, two more stragglers put to death. All of us moved towards the main hut in the middle and surrounded it. I called to two men to support me as I went to this huts door. This was a little stupid I told all afterwards, we must support each other much better if we were going to keep causalities to a minimum.

Adrenaline took over and I was so pumped I could not stop myself. I dived in the door, shot off an arrow into a target, I mean the enemy. Both of the other lads rushed in after me and shot the two remaining soldiers with arrows.

We hoped that was it until we realised that a third of the building was shut off from us, some noise followed, footsteps, then some angry French men shouting.

A bow appeared, with some arms and a shot was loosed off towards us, we moved as soon as we saw the arm coming around the corner so it was wasted for them. We knew we could not take hostages where we were going so we had no choice but to kill or maim these men if we could, not nice, but they were the aggressor in these battles. They were the invader taking our lands.

We wanted nothing but peace and to be left to get on with our lives, several more of the lads came into the building to lend a hand, quickly I told them what the situation was.

One whispered to me that if we pushed the panels against the soldiers behind that would force them to come out, could be a problem as we had no idea how many men were there but the idea had merit and as nobody suggested anything else we thought we would give it a go.

I motioned for another eight men to join us, five to push the panels, the rest of us ready to fire into them, or prepare swords to fight them as they lost their cover. I motioned three, two, one go with my fingers and they rushed together and hit the panels.

No less than eight men roared out, or at least tried to, we struck them with killer shots. There was noise still behind the panels, some guys stuck there, one of our lads cried out in pain. I saw the flash of steel as he was stabbed by a sword. We were on them all and in a flash they were gone, four of the blighters, we were protecting each other, I felt great pride that we had done well. A couple of the lads took small injuries but nothing fatal.

No thought of possible danger, just do the job needed. All was not silent outside, some shouting, some wailing as a few more stragglers were mopped up in the hut opposite.

I called everyone together and proposed to go through each building nice and slowly, so we could be sure nobody escaped.

The hut next to us was similar, much the same problem, four more soldiers met their end in much the same way.

We came to the end hut, heard some noise, and approached the door, opened it to find panels nearly up to the door.

We were more than a little miffed by now, it was taking some time to clear the whole place and we wanted to be far away from here quickly.

I pondered what was the best thing to do, in fact, we all did.

I decided to rush in, push away the panel and smash the hell out of whatever or whoever was behind it. The biggest of us, there were four guys built like…well large! Ten of us were to follow, more in line if needed.

The big guys smashed their way in, much crashing, bashing and shouting. Not sure if it was wood or bones being crushed but in general all hell broke loose.

Those inside trying to get out, us trying to get in, a lot of sword play and not much room for it. One managed to get out alive, but not for long! A further seven were killed by sword. That was a rush, we all agreed as we dusted ourselves off, job done, good sword play. We appeared to have killed off all of the enemy at this particular point.

Chapter 28

We searched everywhere for any of the enemy left in one piece, found nobody, so decided we had cleared the enemy camp. Two more of our men were injured during this clearing.

Sky High Confidence!

There was no doubt at all in our minds that we were very lucky at finding such a soft target, let's hope our luck would continue for the future. This again was very good for our confidence. It was a building process, more fights, more wins, more confidence.

It was a learning curve we were on and we still had an awful long way to go! Fighting within a group of huts was different and we had caught on and learned more.

We quickly went through the huts to see if anything was of any use to us, some swords were very good so we swapped with the dead, arrows a plenty! Coats, hats, etc. We took some complete uniforms as well as they may be useful in the future if we disguised some of our men to infiltrate any enemy lines at some time. I must admit I had not thought about that use before. I was getting crafty in my planning, Cedric mentioned.

We wondered what we could do with the horses, as we knew it would be full of the enemy searching for us very soon, we decided to take those that looked the best and lead the rest off into the woods as they would be useful to the enemy chasing us. Our injured were going to be a problem, so what to do?

We took some branches off trees and lashed them together with rope and pulled our damaged comrades by horse though it slowed us down, those who were badly injured.

We would use some more animals as pack horses for supplies and carrying lances, spare clothing and food etc.

We were now a full complement of soldiers on horseback plus a train of pack horses. All of us looked the business! We were capable of being battle ready at all times, able to take an attack at any time and fight back at a moment's notice.

My commands were sounding better all the time, Cedric said to me later, I was feeling much more confident as time went by and I felt I was getting better at the task of leading. Just a few short years ago I would not dare say boo to a goose, as it were, I was quite shy and felt uneasy if I spoke. These days I cared only for the wellbeing of our men and the furtherance of our cause, neither of which were easy things to deal with at the best of times.

It was way out of my comfort zone to begin with and I had to be very strict with myself. My father used to say if you do not push yourself out of your comfort zone you will never know what you can achieve and he was right.

I sent six of the lads back into the woods to see how the injured were. Six dead. This felt dreadful, and eighteen more injured, not badly though, so they would tag along sitting on horseback. The number of men lost was only so low because we had not had to take on front line soldiers, those last soldiers surely shouldn't have taken us on in the first place but they did after all, attack us, leaving us with no choice.

Moving with many injured would slow us down but we were better off together, must look after the injured, apart from anything else better for moral for the whole group of Boston Defenders! To know you are going to be looked after if you get injured is a great comfort to a soldier. We were duty bound to help them all we could.

I organised the rest of our group to get any horse that had saddles and bridle and that appeared tame and get them ready to leave with us, some of them went into the woods to try and get any good saddles from the horses left by the enemy dead. Quite soon we had more than enough, this whole episode seemed too easy!

We had caused some major damage to our enemy and his takeover of this part of our land would have been slowed by our actions that day.

Having to take on so many enemies and winning so easily was so good for the force as a whole, we knew they were not front-line troops but still they must have had some training. It was as though a training fight had been set up for us to benefit. Both Cedric and I agreed that it seemed our destiny was set before us.

Some of these new horses were in a pretty bad mood as one lad was tossed off his saddle before he had had time to sit, another shot off in a nice straight line away from us at some speed. It looked good, not so when you considered the occupant had no idea what was going on or where he was going. I chased after him and eventually caught him just as he was about to enter a river.

It was quite wide, fast flowing and deep and if he had entered the water I doubted if we would have seen him again, maybe the horse but not him.

After some time we thought we were ready to get well away from here, all riders could just about get by.

Not very quickly but faster than walking and not sapping our energy!

We went to the woods and scraped some holes large enough to bury and say a few words over our fallen comrades.

Though we knew this would happen, it never prepares you for the extent grief gets to you. We all felt awful, we must never forget these brave men. We must turn away and fight more, but never forget.

As a unit, we had made a mess of a lot of Normans, we had fought against the odds in this latest battle and won, our practice at shooting arrows and keeping to orders and never turning to run was serving us well, we must look back at this fight and learn from it. Confidence was at a high and must be kept at all costs. The experience pushed us forward.

We all mounted and made off towards the track that was not far off now, or so we hoped. We could hear some movement ahead of us so we pulled off to the right of the track, behind some trees, we tied our horses and crept to the trackside. Six horses came around the corner in front of us, we moved into a ditch and prepared to shoot, again, it was too easy, they were not expecting anything, so they took the full power of our arrows. The full force of our fury.

One of these horse men had a dispatch bag with him so we took that and a very nice sword as well.

It was beautifully engraved, I claimed it first. Letters were in the bag, I would try and work out the Latin, or French later perhaps. Now we must ride fast and hard to stand any chance of avoiding very angry Normans. They would not appreciate our days' work.

They would now urge the force they had set up to get us killed off to do so more quickly. We would have to try and not be seen by anyone, anywhere for quite some time, we must get well away from here as soon as possible. Time was of the essence!

A disappearing act was needed before we could get back to fighting. We must only show our faces again when far away and ready to fight the good fight! Hopefully if we were careful not leaving tracks they would not be able to follow giving us time to get clear.

Our lead scout rushed back to us with the good news that the main track from south to north was not far ahead, obviously we had to go south towards the Isle. We wondered if we could ride along near the edge of it behind trees and not be seen. It was no use riding along the track as we would be too visible in the open, we would not have time to get clear and hidden if the enemy were about. I was sure if the enemy were not around this area now they damned soon would be!

By doing this, we would see what was coming and going, how many men were probable looking for us and in which direction they were going.

One of the men in my group, Walter Reynold, suggested we ride for a time in the wrong direction, north, cross the track, and come down in a southerly direction on the other side of the track making sure we cover our tracks as much as possible.

Though this might take a bit of time, we decided to do it as it might well save us a lot of time by confusing the enemy by sending them the wrong way.

This Was a Good Plan, We Hoped! It Was Worth a Try

We went about half a mile, found a dry piece of ground to leave no mark of our riding through and turned our horses to cross the track and head south again, before heading off we spent some time making sure evidence of our passing there was obliterated, that should give us a bit of time. We split the men into two groups, one each side of the track, with at least one horse in view at all times so we knew the other was all right.

The odd horse went along the track, which was a pain as we had to stop to not be seen or heard. It was decided to keep going into the night for as long as we could see. It had become nice open country as the moon rose but it quite soon became darker as clouds took over the sky and yes, the rain came with it!

We fumbled on for a few miles, but had to give up eventually as it was just too dark. The scout ahead of us came back and said there were some small hills on our right amongst trees. How he could manage to see I really don't know, but he assured me this was the case.

We led our horses, so as to make as little impression of our passing as possible, to the edge of these wolds, we could make out good tree growth so we proceeded to move into this place to camp, and yes, at last get some deserved rest. We were all exhausted. The excitement of the fighting and the aftermath of dead bodies, enemy and friend, had by now taken its toll on us. Plus the rush to get clear of that area.

We were not sure how long the Normans would give us, they would be very mad, when they found so many dead, they would surely be on our heels all too soon, and as for their horses we had taken, what a disaster for them!

It was quite warm in the hollow of these hills, no wind, so we just crashed. No food, just water, sleep and plenty of it!

Chapter 29

I arranged scouts to change every one and a half hours, at least some rest for them as well, having done my stint, then I crashed too. Sleep took us as we needed as much as was possible to give us the energy we would need to escape the wrath of the enemy.

Nothing happened that night, I was shaken awake by a scout as I had instructed, before first light, we woke everyone, pretty damned stiff, and quite a lot of moaning at being disturbed. I explained that we must get moving fast, so we did just that, no fuss, just move out!

No time for food or fires, or even conversation, just move to put as much distance between us and our fighting of yesterday as we could. Our "doctors" changed all bandages with good clean ones, even the injured were more cheerful, a good sign for the day that I knew would be gruelling, we would have to travel as many miles as possible in the shortest time to stand any chance of getting away from the enemy.

They would have blocked all tracks by now, in and out of a very large area with a huge amount of soldiers, that's what I would have expected at least. I always considered the worst-case scenario first, then whatever happened did not seem so bad.

Horses that became tired out were changed for the ones we had spare, as we travelled on our way.

A scout told us to keep extra quiet, as a pretty large troop movement was going along the track, from south to north, they may have been going up to find out what had happened at the horse camp, we had no way of finding out so we just kept tramping along our not too fast route, we had some good views of the area from here so we could tell if we were being followed.

They might not have found the battle ground yet, I suppose, still, it was better to move out as quickly as possible.

We moved on, passed several settlements between us and the track, life seemed to plod on for all, one town had a huge number of troops in it, we paused to take a drink, and saw they were moving south so not after us, or so we thought.

The lead scout came back to us and said he had found a nice woodland where we may be able to stay and get some food at long last, we had travelled a huge mileage, with the aid of our horses, I was pleased to note. I could not see us trying to move without them now.

He had found well, a small valley, with woods coming up each side, we should be able to cook on our open fires as usual, there was a low breeze that would disperse any cooking smoke, it seemed to whip along the tree line, once we had got a lot more food to eat that is, which was job number one!

There looked like plenty of rabbits about here, hopefully easy to catch our "larder" in the trees as our main cook described wood pidgeon and whatever else we could find to eat. Wild boar and deer were about so their numbers would dwindle while we were here.

We had got this down to a fine art by now, everyone knew what they were good at, whether it was collecting wood or kindling for fires, digging the fire pits, and latrine area, plucking and cleaning birds or animals, washing them, essential to have a stream nearby, washing ourselves was a good idea too! We did get to smell pretty ripe at times, what with training and moving around fast, we sweated an awful lot.

We laughed about it, but it was not that funny, we talked of killing the enemy with our odour, at times. We had to make sure our horses got plenty of water and access to grass all night if possible, it was something we had to consider each night. Those who were a good shot made their way to areas where they thought creatures to provide us with meat might be, it was a hard life, especially if you were one of the creatures we decided we needed to eat!

In no time at all things were cooking and smelling good. This was a good spot, indeed, we set about getting more food to cook and take with us, nobody seemed to live anywhere near here and the main track was several hills away.

We always kept our scouts out, we used eight normally, and they were very good at what they did, we always kept the eight out, at least, as that seemed the best to cover all areas, if we were near areas where people were we doubled the number, hopefully nobody could get near without us knowing. Nobody had done so to date, at least.

No people were near but I thought I would have a wander with most of the other leaders to have a better view of where we were, and to have a chat about what we had achieved so far etc. So I, Nicholas Bacon, Peter Ganning, Thomas Eltisle, Guthrum, Wulfric the Black, Cedric, Richard Hokyton and Vitt Hal Girvii, made our way out of camp to see how the scouts were, and just to chat in general. We included other "leaders" as time went on and men showed interest in making decisions and leading, it did encourage certain men to come forward. We felt we might need the next batch of leaders at any time, the future was perilous, who knew what was around the next corner? We may meet the biggest group of the enemy we had ever come across at any time and suffer dreadful losses, so we had to prepare for that possibility! Zack and Xander Brightcard joined us on this occasion.

Chapter 30

Wilfrith First

We knew roughly the area Wilfrith had set himself up in, so we went up the first hill, down and up again, making as little noise as possible, as it would be good if we could catch him out by creeping up on him without his knowledge. He was much better than us, he came up behind us and surprised us, scared the living daylights out of me for one!

We had a good laugh, he explained what he checked up on, which particular points he noted each time he scanned the other small valley. We could not fault him, so we left him to finish his meal, a good bloke was our Wilfrith, a man who took great pride in his work! He would not be beaten by friend or foe!

We talked of our fighting to date, we were all in agreement that we had been lucky so far, but to wipe out so many of the enemy and to have lost so few of our men was only good. Confidence was sky high and we must keep that up above all else. We must drill into the men that we had been lucky, their aiming and firing was very good but must get better and faster if possible. The men we may meet in the future would be battle hardened, front line fighters, the Normans knew we would be cock a hoop with our success to date. If they realised we were just one group, that is, we must never be over confident, that could get us all killed. Dead men were no good to any cause! There were already far too many dead Anglo-Saxon brothers to mourn, we needed no more.

We approached our next scout with more care, this was a Walter Reynold, I had not spoken with him very much, a quiet bloke, sat at the back, if you know what I mean, hopefully a deep thinker, therefore good at this job.

Would you believe it, he caught us out as well! These lads were good when you considered they had not been doing this very long, no prior experience what so ever. Much the same with all eight scouts. We chatted and encouraged them in the way they kept their eyes on the area and listened to every stick that broke in this place, they climbed trees to get a good look around, they seemed to be able to see in the darkness very well, any movement was considered, boar, deer, badger or human being in their area. They had to prove, enemy or what?

I had forgotten that one group had asked to put out maybe four other scouts to get some experience, we met them as we walked around our camp area.

Feeling very secure, we left them to go up the other side of our little valley and check the other scouts with much the same result, they were Matthew and William, also very much on the ball, complimenting them both, we returned to base after failing, yet again, to catch out the final two men.

All were talked to in this manner and congratulated on the jobs they were doing. We managed a good, long, deep, sleep and woke to the smell of more cooking. The lads realised we had spent quite a lot of the night with the scouts and had left us to get more rest, I was very proud of how close and caring as a group we were though I doubt if the Normans would agree with that sentiment!

It was their fault we were here, though, and because of the disgraceful way they treated us they were going to get more of the same.

The horses were well fed and watered now, they would have many miles in them before we would need to stop again.

We felt we needed to talk to all the men now, to see how they felt, who was doing a fine job and who was not, they were to come and talk privately to any of us if they needed too.

Did any of them think they needed more training, more fitness work? Anything. What plans should we be making regarding joining with Hereward on the Isle, which way to go to get there, we were a long way away, should we go by land, the easiest way, or surprise all and somehow get across the wash.

My own thoughts were to go across the wash, it would be wet, cold and very muddy but we might stand a better chance of success, much would depend on the weather, we would have to get a lot of small boats as well to carry us. The boats we had hidden in the river near the wash might come in handy, if they were still there. The horses would be a major problem, should we try and take them across or not? That would be the deciding factor as it may be too much hassle getting them over.

I had no doubt we could get some skerries, carrick's, just any flat-bottomed boats, pick a time when the tide was in and hope we were not being chased and row our way across the water, sounded easy! We would simply row to Norfolk, then go over land to the Isle. If we could confuse the enemy by doing this, by getting lost to them we could gain time and safety and not lose so many men as a result, hopefully.

We would all wait and see what opportunities were before us when we were ready to make a decision on that.

So we set our arrow producers to work. There were some nice willow and other wood around the stream where we camped. They lost a lot of branches, our short lances were produced here as well. These were very useful in battle at times.

There were a number of towns and parishes to get around, while we travelled, maybe some should go through in small groups of four or five and find out what the news was, we would have to send some around to carry our fighting gear with them, plus our mobile larder, we added to this as we went on our way if we came across deer or boar in particular, and the extra clothes we had taken we could wear so that would be no problem.

Thomas, Cedric and I then said we would go for a wander in the direction we were heading to see what was built there, if anything. We went towards the end of the little valley and over the ridge, it felt strange to be walking again, having left our horses to feed and water themselves.

It was too much of a problem to take them along with us as we would need to leave them to go through the built-up areas we found, if we tethered them, they would possible be stolen anyway, high value items, horses.

The main track was to our left and we could see it going through woods, settlements and over small hills southwards. It was a good view of the area in general, there were a few batches of houses along the roadside and what looked like a small town in the distance.

The plan was to make our way to the track and I thought if we found an alehouse we would go and find out if troop movements were being organised and how often this was happening, etc.

We met the track and travelled alongside it in the trees to give us cover to the nearest houses, these appeared to be run down farmworkers houses so we continued on our way.

There were quite large patches of grass, where sheep were feeding by the track side, it seemed quite an established business in this area, more than we had seen elsewhere.

We found an alehouse a little further along the track, this was quite a fine building, we entered, after making sure no troops were in residence, there were several people eating and more at the desk where the ale was served. We said our "good morning" to the owner and ordered some of his fine ale, direct from the table, which was much appreciated as we were quite dry having drank nothing since our first meal of the day.

It quickly loosened the tongue as well, I asked how trade was and was it effected by the Norman takeover, the chap said trade with the enemy was good, he had been forced to serve them, as they travelled up and down the track, but because they were here the locals mainly stayed away, which was not good. He had also been told to lower his prices to the enemy, again, not good.

But he said, had we heard of the daring attack on the huge stables used by the enemy, everyone was very excited by this, the blokes next to me joined in, they gave their support to whoever it was that had done this great deed. We were very surprised and disturbed that news had travelled so far so quickly. My mind was made up to travel much further away much more quickly from a battle area in the future avoiding contact with anyone!

To have wiped out this whole station must have been done by a huge and very well organised force, they all agreed. There was talk of other groups fighting back along the coast track too. I felt like shouting, it was us, but quickly thought better of it. The stories were getting better each time they were told I think. It would be nice to actually get some praise for our enterprise though that would have to wait.

We needed something to give us all confidence in our race, our fighting must be helping, we told ourselves later. It may even get people to join other groups and fight on other fronts up and down the country. One could but hope and dream!

I asked about troop movements, had they increased since the attack, had they heard anything at all changing since then. They said that things had changed very quickly, a huge troop came past here in the night, had passed by at first light so they must have moved in darkness, probable to the training camp. This was the second batch that we knew of, it was a bit scary. All these soldiers after us, we had set the cat amongst the pidgeon, no doubt about that!

We would have to travel with much more care in future, more scouts, more slowly, that did not suit us at all. We really needed to move fast, especially after a battle, and get away from an area as soon as possible.

Chapter 31

The rate we were going, we would have the entire Norman force in the country fighting us, though they were outnumbered 200 to one against our population they were a fearsome bunch of fighting men, that would not do at all. Our total Saxon fighting force was at present very small, just the odd group of disorganised men here and there around the country.

We must get to the Isle more quickly, if we were going to survive. Or think of some other plan, maybe break up as a group and find work on farms for a while until we could move again.

This was an idea that gained weight, the more I thought about it. The problem was that we were a large force, and it would be difficult for an area to digest without someone saying something to the wrong person and it getting back to the enemy.

After another ale, we sat and began talking in earnest about the economy in the area. This seemed to be a very live stock based farming community here, we had never seen so many animals, large farm estates, at least larger than we were used to, that were quite a distance from the track, the amount of people they employed was large and expanding, we had obviously met some people in the know as it were.

One of the chaps, a Geoffrey Leofwine, had bought a quite small farm some years ago and as land had come onto the market he had purchased well, he employed twenty people who lived on site, in houses he had had built. He grew more crops to feed his stock in the hard months of winter, as the number of animals he stocked increased. This was pretty enterprising we both thought, though it was common sense. You had to admire the drive and imagination of men like this. These men were the backbone of any nation and we needed them to make a strong Anglo-Saxon nation, not a Norman one!

Maybe there was a chance of seeing his business in the morning we asked, he was only too delighted to agree. We talked more about fighting the Normans as I, in particular, wanted his views on the takeover of our country!

He wasted no time in beating about the bush, his hatred was obvious, though they bought quite a lot of the animals he produced, they told him how much they were going to pay which was not much and he had no choice but to say yes. The Normans saw themselves as the owners of this land now and they would do as they thought fit as and when they wished!

The chap he was with, Roger Ogden, was his manager, invited us to stay the night at his house which we agreed to very quickly.

After some more idle chatting, we left for the farm, walked about a quarter of a mile, turned left off the track, walked some way through a group of trees, we saw some lights coming from the cottages where his staff lived, said goodnight to Geoffrey Leofwine and entered a cottage.

These were pretty small but cosy, we felt more than a little flaked out with the walking and the ale but before we slept we talked to our host about opposition to the Normans, was there any organised? If so, do they train together or organise to fight?

It turned out there was indeed a group, Geoffrey was the leader for this area, he had a group of twenty men, who met once a week to fight mock battles against each other, they were not very organised but hoped to take on more men and become a force to be reckoned with. We could add our training methods to theirs and make them much better. Twenty men was a beginning and you had to begin somewhere!

On that note, we said our goodnight and slept in a small room at the side of the cottage.

We talked together into the small hours and decided to talk with Geoffrey about maybe joining the group if we could find some work locally for a time, I had said to Cedric about my idea of us all staying for a time until the Normans gave up looking for us. To all intents and purposes we would disappear. This sounded a better idea the more we thought about it.

The Next Morning

We had an early start, as we had expected, two spare horses were brought for us to inspect Geoffrey's farm. He had a word with Roger who told of our conversation with him last night and we set off through the woods to begin with, he mentioned nothing, only regarding the farm.

He asked a lot regarding the Normans and our travelling through the area at this time, clearly trying to get an idea of what we were doing here.

About lunch time, I mentioned the force we had been told about. Clearly he was not amused Roger had told us anything but he relented after a time. He had no plans yet to attack anyone as he felt he was not ready. He asked again about the fighting at the horse training camp and elsewhere and had a job understanding why we claimed to have not heard much.

Cedric, Thomas and I had a word and agreed that we would tell him who we were and what we were doing in the area, this went against what we preached to all our men, but there was a time to tell and this was it!

We calmly spoke of our men at arms and that it was us that had destroyed the training camp near the woods. He was stunned to begin with, then laughed as he got off his horse to shake both our hands. There was much to talk about! He declared.

Chapter 32

At Geoffrey Leofwines House

We sat back at his house and described our action at the Norman camp, he demanded to know how many of the fights he had heard of were we responsible for and was amazed when we told him, it was so good just to talk to someone outside our group.

He said the word was out that we were the "Boston Defenders", and that we took no hostages, and were the bravest of the brave. I said to Cedric this was somewhat embarrassing but that is was no bad title, it was quite amusing when we thought about it later that day.

How the name had got out there we did not know at this time. Eventually we found out that one of the lads had left a note telling of us, how we were going to take the fight to the Normans, we discovered this much later.

Only four of us could write, so it was not that difficult to find the culprit. At the end of the day it mattered little! It really did sound a grand title! A grand title for a grand bunch of warriors! We had properly begun the fight against the invaders of our land and we would continue to do so.

We spoke of training his group, getting them fit, battle ready and above all confident to take on the enemy. We wondered if he knew farmers who could take any of us on, work wise, even for a small wage, we needed to keep out of public view and disappear for a time if that were possible.

He said he would have a word with those he trusted most, he was sure there would be something they could do that would help us, maybe not all, but some at least. It all sounded like the answer we were looking for.

We were not used to this type of farming at all, so we could all gain. It was very labour intensive. Any money earned would be welcome along the way as well. Extra ingredients for food were always useful.

Good as His Word

Geoffrey was as good at his word, he contacted his friends and they suggested a meeting at a nearby farm. They wanted to sound us out, make sure we were not planted by the Normans to catch them out. I could not blame them for that as the enemy would stoop to any low to catch us I felt sure.

So we agreed to start work right away, after I sent Thomas back to our camp to tell them what was going on. I started clearing a stream and an overgrown wooded area to be put down to grass for cattle. I first made sure I was not putting anyone out of work as I did not want anyone being disgruntled and telling the enemy, or anyone, come to that, that new staff had arrived in the area from nowhere. I felt sure they would add two and two and decide to investigate where a group of new staff had come from all at once into the same area.

It felt strange to be back in work again, though it had not been all that long since we left our area to fight, it was just that so much had happened in so short a time.

The boss, Geoffrey, returned and handed me a plate of meat for lunch, I had to ask him to stop treating me in any special way as I thought it might raise resentment with the other staff, he quickly agreed with me, and began chatting about the normal work in the fenland area/waterways.

It was so different than here, like another world, we had basket making, reeds for thatch, agriculture, fishing (eels in particular), wild fowling, a small number of cattle on patches of dry ground, etc. they had cattle, grass, grain, agriculture, they lived off boar, deer, rabbits and of course cattle, etc.

Then it was back to the inevitable topic on everyone's lips, the Normans, and training to fight them, so many risks, so much to gain. Much to lose if we were not careful but fight them we must, our self-respect was at stake, and much more, very much more!

Thomas returned, said all was well at camp, they would wait to hear from us regarding our next move. Tonight was the time the group of fighters met, so we both worked the rest of our day, cleared a lot of ground, though I say so myself, the stream had quite a few trout in it, they would make good variety to our diet at camp as it was generally meat at this time and not much else.

Geoffreys group.

After we had finished for the day, we went to Geoffrey's house, he was waiting with three of his workers at the front of the property. After greeting, we set off towards the farm next door to meet the whole group of fighters in training.

Twenty men awaited us, with bows, arrows and swords at the ready. Word had not got out about us being here, they were very surprised and amazed that we were, as a group, responsible for the fighting to date in Eastern England.

They all gathered around as we told of our exploits just in the hope of encouraging them to plot, plan, train and take the fight to the enemy. This would take some pressure off us. Where, they asked, were all the other Boston Defenders.

They found it hard to believe that they were in the hills behind where they lived, most of their talking together concerned our group. We were their heroes and we were living approximately a mile away and they had no idea! There was a lesson to be learned there somewhere. We both made it quite clear that nobody was to talk of us to anyone, ever, outside our company or theirs, not even to their families, a lot of money would change hands to get information regarding our whereabouts. A lot of people would also die, possible myself included. Idle talk could cost us all our lives!

Chapter 33

So we set about organising a fitness programme for them and us to join at a later date, made them into groups to challenge each other, a lot of horseback riding was to take place as practice made perfect. They were better than us on their animals, so we could learn which was going to be good. We set up distance racing to get them fitter, we had them running in quite deep water over long distances. In short we made them work hard and they responded well.

Young Ladies

A couple of the lads/men, Henry Garrod and Holt Franklyn started dating a couple of the young ladies that had begun coming to watch us train, they shouldn't have been allowed to come near us, but they just turned up one morning so the damage was done, They were sworn to secrecy.

I didn't really want this, as I thought it would take their attention away from the fighting we would have to do, but I couldn't in all honesty blame them, they were after all, very pretty and sensible young ladies, what could be more natural?

I hoped I wouldn't hear about them ever again! Nothing personal!

Lynelle Mordikai

Having said that, I had noticed the daughter of the farmer next door to Geoffrey Leofwine, Lynelle. She was the most beautiful women I had set eyes on, she never seemed to stop laughing when we were together, she made me laugh a lot, too, so I more than understood how my men felt. I longed for the next moment I could be with her. Life could be difficult to say the least. Just when, in life, to do what?

Us Saxons had no choice at the moment but to fight and possible die trying to save our nation! The ladies in our lives had to take a bit of a back seat. I think they understood, at least I hoped they did! Was I living by double standards, not wanting the lads to have lady friends, but it was alright if I did, sure as hell, I was! My feelings for this lady broke all the rules.

I honestly felt I could not be distracted from my main aim in life at the moment. Raising our nation from sleep, to fighting the good fight! Not that any fighting was in any way good but when you had no choice, you simple had to. Long term planning in our lives was very important, especially at our age at this time.

After a couple of weeks, we thought it would be sensible to put both groups together, a proper introduction. We both went back to camp for the night and agreed to bring all the force back with us the following morning.

At first light we rose, leaving behind four scouts, to protect our spare horses and property. We went in small groups of five or six horses at a time so we would not be noticed by anyone, anywhere, as a large number of men on horseback. This was a shame really as it was a sight to impress, with our fighting equipment at the ready. That could come later we decided.

On our return to the farm, much talking and laughter, as I introduced everyone, as bowmen, lancer, swordsmen etc. followed by their names. Several fires were lit and food cooked over them, a sort of huge early dinner/breakfast, a celebration of like-minded people with one aim in life. Also some of the women folk had made pies for us, great cooks, these ladies. A lot of ale was consumed, there would be some headaches in the morning no doubt!

It was time for an unwind and a party.

It was the first time in a long time that we had been sociable so it was really special, something we had missed without knowing it, being "civilised" with ones fellow Anglo-Saxon man! Cedric had a skin full of drink as well. He really didn't want to move in the morning.

We had to show all that we didn't do things like drink too much, so much it stopped us doing our jobs, so we stumbled through the day as best we could. What heroes we were, don't you think, eh? It was so good to relax with like-minded people with the same ambition and dreams.

We basically crashed out around the fires that night, the scouts were changed often so no one was left out of the get together, and began to wake at first light.

I was nursing a bad head myself, though I would never admit to it, the ale was stronger than we were used to, that was my excuse, anyway! I only had a couple of pints, honest!

A couple of the lads went off to get some rabbits, pidgeon, deer and anything that got in the way of an arrow basically that looked as if it had any meat on it and put it in the pot to start the day. Another couple headed for the river to see if they could get any fish as well, things were looking good! An amount of food was made available by Geoffrey, which was much appreciated.

Food over with, we got into groups, and set up areas to run off against each other. This went on for several hours.

The group of us leaders began talking to Geoffrey and his number two, Roger. They had decided to set this force up as a result of nothing happening regarding opposition to the enemy. They had been massively encouraged on hearing of our exploits but were not very confident of going into battle. Experience was what they needed and there was only one way to get that!

We explained how we had started going for "soft" targets and built up from there, we recognised we had a lot to learn, we emphasised, trying not to sound too big headed. This was important, as we needed them to fight, hopefully bringing an uprising in the near future, not just in this area, but the whole country. We didn't lack ambition, as I may have mentioned already!

They would need to scout far and wide and pick somewhere where they could mount an ambush, they would need to fight a great many miles from here so as to not bring the enemy back to their doorstep. It required a lot of thought and planning, we would be there for them as much as possible.

We fitted in some work most days between mock fights and fitness training, farming work still had to be done, crops could not be wasted, animals needed looking after. The enemy had expectations as to how much of their crop they could claim as taxation for living in "their England". Plus of course Geoffrey had to pay his staff and keep his family.

A good twenty-six of my men were living on farms now and working with the locals, who were by and large a good bunch. The rest stayed at our camp, way back in the wolds. We changed men around at some farms so they could get some experience of the work required, and to stop our men getting lazy in camp.

Time went by and we went on little trips to find a good place to set up an ambush, found several places of interest, which seemed to have a lot of horse movements between towns. We all decided on a particular place, nearly ten miles away, so began to plan. The game was afoot!

Some of us would ride cross country, some would go by road, the rest took a road slightly in the wrong direction and came back on themselves to meet in the woods nearby. This would disguise our tracks, so it did not appear as though one group of men on horseback was going in the same direction, ten horses here, ten horses there, seemed a good idea at the time. Nearly all of the Boston Boys came with us just for the experience.

We all met and decided to go further away from the track, the twenty newcomers took their horses to within a fifty feet of the track and climbed down from their horses.

Geoffrey and myself explained that it was best to get approximately six of the enemy for the first time, for no other reason than that was what we had done. We placed three men on each side of the track, then four, then three more, making sure they were not opposite each other as they may well shoot each other in the madness of combat.

Then we sat down to wait. Cedric pointed out that we didn't need to be here at all, it just gave these men confidence to begin their fightback against the foe! I said we would do our bit, even if it meant doing nothing on this occasion and left it at that.

We could see quite a distance, a couple of locals came by, then our quarry!

It was ten soldiers about to meet their match, they did this job very well, lightly cantering along, not a care in the world.

The lads waited until all were covered by our group and the arrows just flew into them, they all crashed to the ground. All of us were silent as we rushed onto the track and cleared the bodies off, the horses were rounded up and any travel gear, food etc. were taken as required, and let loose.

The bodies were buried in shallow graves, near some low bushes, then we ran back to our horses. When we arrived back at the place where the others were waiting we all cried out in victory, much laughing, it was such a relief to these new Anglo Saxon soldiers. They had started on our quest to reclaim our land, this England! Though they were shocked at killing men, it took time to get used to this and it was never easy.

It was of course no laughing matter at all. It was just all of that time, training, talking, training, talking and that was now over with.

Another armed force had begun to be established, it was that important Cedric and I felt. Geoffrey and Roger felt they were now established as a force, their confidence in their force going forward was in place. They would now plan and execute their own battles, hopefully.

Us or them, was the order of the day, hard facts, in a hard lifetime. I kept telling everyone to remember and not forget this fact! I reminded myself of these truths more often than I care to mention. The enemy were the aggressor, not us, we wanted to be left in peace. They wanted our land and they wanted us to pay them taxes for living here, what kind of joke was that!

It was still difficult to understand, kill or be killed, the dreaded invaders had much to answer for, turning our lives upside down was not good, changing our laws, ordering us about, changing our language, these were hard times indeed! They needed to be made to pay! We would not take this lightly.

We set off in our small groups and returned to the farm. Once we were all returned we talked of going out once more and settling some more scores, we wondered how long it would take for the enemy to respond.

Chapter 34

A Couple of Days!

Guthrum came to us from the track a couple of days later as he heard many horses going by on it, must have been several hundred, which was very unusual, any of us near the track stopped to look and listen, they were going at a real pace.

It turned out that they were seeking the men who had attacked their own and they were not happy!

Farms were being raided near the incident where they thought their soldiers had seemingly vanished to try and find clues, if any. People were being stopped in the area and questioned, beaten just for the hell of it. They found no evidence to help them, Threats were put out to us all in this area of the country, if anyone helped these men, us in other words, one could expect torture and death.

We felt very bad about all of this but the price was worth paying we convinced ourselves, the fight would go on, no matter what! It simple had to, there really was no option!

The men concentrated on their training, sword fighting and close combat. This was very important so we fought each other morning noon and night just to make sure we were the best we could possibly be. On horseback and on the ground we were good and no mistake. When we felt exhausted, we all made a point of fighting more, and more, to build up our strength, skill and ability. One could easily tell as we became better and better.

The Ale House

All of us sat, one evening, chatting over our ale very quietly, all the leaders and Geoffrey. We spoke of how we could maybe build a number of groups in this part of the country to fight the enemy and then extend the fighting groups all over the nation. I was saying that it was an exciting prospect, the thought of organised battles against the Normans up and down the country at the same time.

Our force could make a real difference, I said, and maybe even defeat the swine, that would be something to tell our grandchildren, providing of course we survived the fighting! Could we turn our dreams into reality? We all thought we could though it would take huge organisational skill to achieve that. It became our long-term plan, set in our minds.

Four horses came to the front of the building, very noisily, the riders leapt from them and more or less crashed through the front door, pushed their way through customers to the table where the beer was served and in pretty bad

English demanded four beers. The atmosphere turned sour again and we all hoped their ale did too, as before, they threw down some coin and drank.

Talk returned, somewhat subdued, but return it did, though everyone ceased to vent their anger against the Normans in our midst and elsewhere about the country.

I murmured to my friends that we should make our way towards the enemy and see if we could pick up a few ideas of what they were about. We did this, chatting as we went.

Roger understood a little French and I quite a bit of Latin from the abbey, so we may pick up a little here and there, though the Latin knowledge proved to be rather useless on this occasion as I expected.

They were saying how they were part of the group sent to find these men who were killing their soldiers, it had become clear to them that an organised rebellion was being arranged against them.

They had indeed linked all of our fighting to perhaps just one group, as we had feared. They were not as stupid as they sometimes appeared. We only got a few words but I think we added more than enough to make sense of what their conversation was about.

Estienne and Guiscard of the enemy force.

A possible 100/200 strong group of the enemy set up to destroy us! Led by a Estienne Enguerrand and Guiscard Onfroi. This was a frightening development and we would have to be double careful from now onwards if we were to survive!

This huge group of men, possible up to a couple of hundred in total, were sent to get us at all costs, it appeared they were under instruction to stop at nothing to gain their prize...us! They did not even want us dead or alive, they just wanted us dead! They muttered gleefully about getting a share of the reward.

They were to start at the far end of the little valley we were set in, break in and rubbish all buildings, houses and sheds in search of evidence of anything untoward going on, staff working on farms would need to have work and money coming onto the farm to justify them being here and being paid a wage.

Also, to see if men had family nearby, how had they obtained these jobs if they came from another area. To also seek out areas where we might be training. We left many tracks where we had regularly fought in the same area, we had set up fences for our horses to jump, all sorts of things would have to be changed very quickly if we were to survive here without a fight or being discovered or both!

I found it difficult to understand why the four fools were talking so freely but came to the conclusion that they thought we were all a bunch of very ignorant farm workers. We were not and we would take great delight in showing them.

They left and we quickly followed them out of the door, they on their way to find us, and us on our way to avoid them, I chuckled to myself, what a funny world we lived in?

Chapter 35

All of us went to Geoffrey's farm and set about organising the destruction of any evidence of our being there, we would have to work very hard, very quickly if we were going to disappear as it were.

We brought in the rest of our men from the hills at the back and worked until we dropped, cleared everything and disguised tracks made by our horses as best we could.

Now we had to think of the best way to distribute our group so we could not be found on farms, we had to hide somehow, if we were going to stay longer here, if we ran and the enemy discovered that we had been living with these people they would murder them all, no doubt about that, they would be wiped out, so we had a responsibility whether we liked it or not. We had to calm the situation somehow by making the enemy believe we had not been there at all, could we achieve that? that was the overriding question, could we provide an answer that would confound the enemy and relieve the pressure on the locals. It was a tall order, I can tell you and we were all of us unsure as to the outcome!

We wanted to continue to train and encourage their group of soldiers, the group of us leaders were openly talking of mounting an army to fight right across the nation if we could, what a thought that could become! To be rid of the Norman dictator was the overall plan. The ambition of youth knew no bounds, these thoughts dominated our joint conversations and thoughts so I repeat them here.

There were a lot of thick woods in this area, we decided to see if we could hide in small groups of perhaps not more than four in these places. I called in the scouts and the hunters who had sought our food about the area and asked them to describe any such places.

We pretty soon had a good number to choose from, gave each group an area in which to hunt for themselves, and began sending them off.

Geoffrey's men had some good ideas too. The men needed to be near water so they would not have to walk much in any open countryside to obtain it.

We had to take our camp apart, back in the hills, the rain covers under which we slept, all the evidence of our cooking and the remains of animals we had eaten, also the latrine we had dug had to be filled and disguised. All tracks had to be "lost" of our existence here which was surprisingly hard work.

We also had to inform everyone that the Normans were about to be with us and what to expect.

Eventually all clothes, fighting equipment and bedding were distributed so all were put into groups to disband and hide in the bush until told otherwise, we had made up a plan that I would keep very well-hidden of who was where, so I could keep a check on anyone I wished at any time.

No sooner had we said our goodbyes, and good luck, who approached the main gate way to the farm but the four Normans themselves.

They had come to inspect all paperwork and buildings and to check land, where possible, for their enemy, or traces of where they might have been. My first thought was for poor Lynelles family farm next door to Geoffreys.

To be honest, my thought was first just for Lynelle, the thought of her being hurt, even upset, really hurt me. This was a new experience for me, these were changing times! I felt I had so much to lose all of a sudden. It had been as though a link in my life had been missing all this time until now which had allowed me to meet this lady, hopefully in the longer term making my life complete! We still had so much to achieve as a fighting force before we could be together on a permanent basis but we at least had hope!

When we began this enterprise, I only had hatred for the enemy and all I wanted was to fight and fight and eventually win. No other thought was in my head. Now if I lost my lady what would all the fighting be worth? Simple nothing! Could I just carry on planning and fighting if, dread the thought, she was no longer in this world.

Thoughts of the rape, murder and burning of communities in the north of England came to my mind and it was a job to think of much else at times but carry on we must!

The leader of this group came straight to Geoffrey and demanded to be shown records of the farms business, he told the others to go and look through the farm buildings, then the fields, then to report back as soon as possible.

They were hoping to catch someone, somewhere, who was up to no good against them. If they couldn't, the main group of men would be along very soon to make a much more detailed check of everything, everywhere. No stone would be left unturned…they hoped!

We, on the other hand, had never been here, it seemed, just as we had very quickly planned. We were lost in the hills and wood lands surrounding the area.

Chapter 36

Norman Search

They made a mess everywhere they went, hurling anything aside that which may have been hiding something. The one in Geoffreys house ripped everything apart he could get his hands on, simple didn't care, no thoughts of winning the hearts and minds of the locals. What a mess!

Geoffrey's wife was in tears at the sight! They were certainly going to make no friends the way they carried on, a real disgrace. They behaved like cheap thugs at best. That was all they were in their homeland probable, so what did we expect?

They Broke Open Doors in the Sheds With No Regard at All

The only good thing about it all was they found nothing conclusive. A few tracks where horses had ridden a lot made them ask who in particular had been going through these areas, those of us who were asked made excuses for farm workers or members of family and they seemed to accept these explanations.

Geoffrey made a point of asking what had happened to the rest of the group that had passed us by, he was simply told that they would be along sometime, it was not our business to know when!

They left as quickly as they had appeared, off to the next house they could find, hopefully nothing to find there either, plenty to miss. Us Saxons were all hidden away in the wolds and woods of the area, out of harm's way, we hoped.

I just hoped our cooking fire smoke would disappear in the bush as they had at other sites we had used, we were all very careful, most of any cooking took place at night normally with guards out in all directions to make sure nobody was near enough to tell of smoking fires. Much training and common sense ruled the day, every day!

Being careful had become second nature, I drummed it into everyone, by not being careful, could mean death to us all!

The papers we had "invented" regarding staff on the farms had worked a treat for us all, even the ones not in our close group, who provided the men for Geoffreys fighting force.

I still had reservations regarding the group of men coming to look through our dealings in the near future. One of the faults with our plan was that a number of the families on the farms could not read or write, would this be a problem?

We hoped not, we hoped the Normans would think at least the fathers of the families would be able to read and write a little. We could do nothing until they came and maybe asked questions, or not?

The owners of the farm next door, in the other direction from the Mordikai's farm, came to see Geoffrey a few days later to tell him the enemy had appeared, causing yet more havoc on their premises, but they appeared to be satisfied with all they found, which thankfully was nothing!

We had done a more convincing job than we thought, it seemed!

There was a scare when a bunch of these men had travelled through the hills behind us and found some of the mess we had made of our old camp. After a panic from us, all they decided was it was too old to be of use to anyone who had caused the trouble they were looking for.

We had disguised it well, it seemed, though if they had looked properly they would surely have found that this was not the case. It was good to have some good luck at times like these!

I found it hard to understand how they had not run into any of our men out in the bush, it turned out later that the scouts had seen the enemy coming and had kept a distance from them at all times, staying out of sight.

That was very good of the men organising themselves so well, a considered plan working.

We had problems with our horses, each group was responsible for their own animals, they had to be tethered near where the small camps were, so if needed they could quickly ride off at any time. Even their horse dung was scattered about each day so could not be traced to a single point.

It did cause some problems but we were up to them, which was good, the men thinking for themselves and getting it right when under pressure. This gave us all confidence in our future planning and fighting together.

These enemy troops were going to be sneaky I felt and would perhaps try and catch us out by turning up when least expected after we thought they had left the area. This indeed turned out to be the case as late one night they stormed the farm next door just as the owners were going to bed for the night, caused a bit of a riot but that was about all, nothing untoward so no problem at all.

Lynelle was even more upset this time, her room was ransacked, no proof of anything untoward was found so a nights rest lost was of little consequence. I enjoyed calming her, her parents thanked me too, so there was a plus in a very upsetting situation. Apart from a bad night with not much sleep and all hating the Normans a little more than before, no harm done.

The panic caused by this onslaught by our enemy was short lived though we made up our minds never to endanger our hosts anywhere, anytime, by living amongst them wherever we might be. That is except in exceptional circumstances.

We started training in small groups out in the hills, not causing much damage to undergrowth so it could not be seen we had been there. We lost some of our camaraderie but that was of little importance compared to everyone's safety and peace of mind. We raided each other's camps just to see how close we could get to each other without the other group knowing.

It became fun and we were learning to outwit each other, we were becoming much sharper, much more reliant on each other, in each little group which in the heat of battle, knowing what your group was going to do, was of the utmost importance. I felt now we were becoming that winning team that we needed to be at all times, that is, if we were going to make the difference I wanted.

This sounds rather as though I am bragging, which is not my intention at all. I was very proud of our progress at this time. I had indeed become very proud of these men, we had become a self-reliant band of hard thinking, hardworking, fighters and I felt we would never give in.

We could make that difference on the battlefield, though I knew we had not fought any running battles as yet, we were certainly going to do just that in the near future, I felt sure and we would learn as we progressed.

Could we get in a position to make a real difference to our nation of Anglo-Saxons, Girvii and Iceni. We began to think of asking the other original tribes of these lands to join our endevour. We talked of little else than setting up groups of fighters up and down the nation and organising fighting on all fronts against these dreadful Frenchie's!

We may be badly wounded, as a nation, but we were not dead yet, and where there is life!

We must learn from Harold's defeat and use our horses in battle as they had proven to be decisive at Hastings. Out with the old ways, onto the new!

Chapter 37

Our Horses had Became an Important Part of Our Team

Our own horses had shown how good they could be, we had used them in many mock battles so they would get used to the commotion, they were real characters as well, they knew when they had done well and responded as such to our voices.

King Harold seems to have become set in his ways of fighting which was a really bad mistake. Adapt and adjust and move forward was the name of the game, I felt sure the result at Hastings might have been different if he had used cavalry as well as men on the ground.

The enemy came back to haunt us several more times in our little valley, but try as they might they could not find evidence of us being there.

When they came near to one of our groups in the hills, we just moved on, always keeping an eye on them, as they encroached on another groups area the other group moved too. This way no patch of woods became used too much so no one could tell if people had been staying there, unless they spent an awful long time looking, which they did not. They had too much of an area to cover with too few men who were quite frankly not up to the job.

Work on the Farm

I worked with Geoffrey and his number two on the farm, it really was an experience working the land, rather than the fen, though I missed that. Tending the animals, there were so many more than we had in and around the fens, and planning the crops was an adventure in itself.

I did not miss being a novice at the cell very much as I had not been doing that very long, though I wondered how everyone was, I did miss the way of life, I suppose. Though, it was hard, it seemed worthwhile.

Time to Move On?

It had become almost fun dodging the enemy but as we felt it much too soon to restart fighting with the local lads, it would bring down the enemy right on our heads. They would probably wipe out the whole community, if they found us as they had done in the north, killing men, women and children and burning their towns and villages. Yes I know, I have mentioned this many times before but it did dominate our thinking so I will keep bringing the dreadful subject to the fore in these notes! We felt it best to move on, south, towards the Refuge of Ely.

That was the place to talk to the real leaders of Anglo-Saxon England, if we could fight with them…what an honour, …..what an experience!

Surely we could make at least a very good fight of it, rather than just meekly giving in as some had suggested we should, as our king and family were gone. It still did not seem possible that had happened. Stories were passed around that he had just escaped the battle and was preparing to re-enter fighting at some time in the future though we believed none of this it was nice to think he just might be able to achieve such a thing.

King Harold.

We had been hoping our future looked very bright with Harold at our head, he had made such a good job of being head of East Angle, he was so popular, especially after the success at Stamford Bridge. Peace and wealth beckoned, we all believed. Sadly, our beliefs were being dashed very quickly!

Moving Out!

Cedric, Richard, Nicholas, Peter, Thomas, Guthrum, Wulfric, Vitt Hal Girvii, Vercingetorix and myself.

So the 'ten' was raised in number to 'twelve' as us leaders had become known, we also promoted the Brightcard brothers, Zack and Xander. They had more than earned their chance at contributing to lead our force.

Bringing on new leaders was essential at all times, as we set to organise our move from here, this was going to be difficult as the enemy had left groups of men along the way they thought they had cleared of Saxon fighters.

All of our groups had to find them and get by without being noticed, we would need to stick to our groups of ten, or twenty, as the case may be and travel very lightly, leaving a lot of our equipment behind, much to the delight of the farmer's battle group, and get used to seeing in the dark as it seemed the best way to move about without being noticed.

This slowed us down terrible, but it was better to be safe than dead! On cloudy nights we would have to set camp with many scouts out with regular changes so all were rested for the next move.

We had become the victims of our own success, if we had just travelled about to find any work for a living and not organised ourselves to fight the enemy we would not have a problem, perhaps.

The Normans would have just carried on taking over our beautiful land and let us be. We would never live like that, cow towing to a bunch of Frenchie's was not our way of life, we needed our self-respect, then we could live as we needed to, work and play hard, but fair to all our people!

It was arranged to move in our teams, quarter of an hour between each one, the track would be in the middle of our two lines of men, moving at a similar pace. Scouts were out each side of us to make sure there was nobody lying in wait to surprise us, all possible problems were covered, I hoped. We were sure the main group of Normans were still moving away from us, following the track as it went north, madly trying to find us just where we were not!

This We Found Quite Amusing

There were a number of settlements to get around, blasted dogs were a pain as they always made a huge amount of noise, especially at night, we did not want to disturb too many people, even if they were Anglo-Saxon, so we went an extra distance away from these places to avoid disturbing animals. This, of course, made our journey take a lot longer so we were not too pleased at this turn of events.

A scout rushed back to our team and said we had better run out of the area we were in as a group of men with dogs were on their way towards us.

We began riding a little crazily away from our area, all in the same direction, we were confused in the dark and did not realise there was a river nearby. It was a large one, though not too deep, we could hear the dogs behind us so we had no choice but to slip in and muddle our way across, we stumbled through and it was damned chilly. We struggled out the other side and rushed for some thick looking cover, dived in and stayed very silent, and cold! Our horses were not too pleased at having to get cold and wet. They snorted for quite a time, we stroked their heads and silenced them.

The dogs were getting very excited by this time, barking crazily, they reached the other side of the river bank, much chattering between the men, though we could not make out what was going on. The men seemed to spread out along the far bank, I thought they must be preparing to come across and challenge us.

The language they used was not clear, did not sound English or French, so I was a little lost as to what to do, if they turned out to be friendly we did not really want them to know what we were about and if they were not we simple did not want them to know we were here at all. Maybe their local dialect made their English sound different, who knows!

There was some discussion between three of the blokes, they obviously did not want to get their feet wet, could hardly blame them for that as it was quite cold, so they called their dogs back and began to leave only for the man to stop near where we had entered the water and call his mates over.

Though we had them covered with our bows we did not want to attack them as it could bring down all sorts of problems on us, so we kept our peace, watched and listened. We still had problems with their language, perhaps it was the local dialect, but it seemed they were going to go back to where they had come from, relief all round, as they pulled the long ropes the dogs were attached to and began sauntering off into the darkness.

There was talk and a lot of pointing in our direction, so some of them wanted to cross the river still to find who it was that was on the other side. Perhaps they did not want a fight anyway so they followed their leader and went on their way.

That could have been a close shave, as they say, we now had to re-cross the water, get back on our track and see if we could get back in time so as to not cause problems regarding us not turning up at the next stopping point with our group.

Problems, problems, whichever way you turned at the moment there was always something. The horses were not a problem at least as we walked them back to the other side. We tried to be very quiet on the return to the track we were using, moving a lot of brush wood as we went, but I did feel we needed to catch up with our time.

Chapter 38

We arrived late in the end and met with the group ahead of us who were waiting, they welcomed us like long lost soldiers. They were worried we had perhaps been caught by a bunch of stray Normans. We still had no idea if those men had been friend or foe.

Even if they were friendly, we did the right thing by not showing ourselves to them as if it had got out that we had been there it could have been revealed to the Normans by accident or under torture. They would have been killed, men, women and children for not telling them. This was the normal way of the enemy warning all to beware of them!

Though I have mentioned this before, the impression was constantly in our minds, we had heard whole areas of northern England had been burnt to the ground after everyone had been slaughtered, dreadful killers these enemy. There was only one way to treat such people, with force, as that was all they understood and respected!

A Good Laugh at our Expense

We experienced quite a lot of laughing at our expense from the next group, as they thought our trip through very cold and muddy water a good joke! They went on their way to the next stopping point, fifteen minutes later we were on our way again, glad to be moving to tell the truth, as we were cold still from the wet. As a rule, we kept pretty still while waiting so as to make as little noise as possible, this did not help to get dry and warm again. More than a little exercise was called for.

We chatted a little as to those we had left behind on the farms, a lot of firm friends had been left, especially of the female variety, we were but young men who had our failings and much to learn. We would all come this way again no matter what, providing we survived the fighting.

Though the future looked very difficult, we could still dream of peaceful, happy lives ahead, normal family life looked fine in the long term, we hoped we would all achieve it, with many children to tell of our deeds of daring.

We had arranged to meet up in the two groups each side of the track when it started to become light, the idea was to find some deeply wooded area, rest and hopefully eat. It sounded good and quite easy but as that time came we could see quite a few lamps on in the darkness, evidence of housing, so we had to keep going as best we could.

All of us were very tired by now, the horses were snorting, tired as well no doubt. They had done well, it had been rough riding, up and down, in and out of ditches.

We had another scare when we heard some voices, quite loud so close by, we picked out a group of perhaps ten men, hunting, for whatever they could get to eat, no doubt. We just hid ourselves in a dried-up ditch which was handy, the horses were getting used to being pulled down to hide, they enjoyed being patted and stroked by us all, they began to expect this treat, they were not stupid! Whoever said otherwise, was wrong. The same as us humans, they could have bad days and moods to go with it but you came to respect that and understand. That understanding was rewarded if given.

Eventually we became clear of all humanity except ourselves and found a well wooded area in which to take the day easily at rest, with time to prepare food, cook at a leisurely pace and sleep some more, ready for the next night's fun!

We quickly got pidgeon from their sleep and rabbit that were running all over the place, good food for all and an awful lot of it around this area we were pleased to note. Both groups camped over the ridge from the track we were following, the distance away from the track was important as it would help disperse the smoke from sight, our scouts were out to make sure nobody approached from anywhere we did not know about.

It was a bright sunny day we noted, it would have made no difference if it had been snowing, as we were so tired we just crashed. Water was a bit of a problem as we could not carry very much, a couple of the lads went in search. They went a little south and found a few small houses with wells from which they helped themselves, there was nobody about, two of the three houses were derelict, besides it would not be missed, even if it was, local families would no doubt help us if they were told we were fighting the enemy. This water would be fine when boiled.

We would never tell anyone we were responsible for the killing of Normans as that would be dangerous for us all in the long run, the less people learned the better. The stories of our deeds would be good for moral, they would usually be exaggerated as they went through the population, they might be fun to hear sometime, as we could perhaps do with a laugh!

Two of the leaders were with me, so we used the opportunity to talk of plans to see if we could set up groups of fighting men up and down the track, north and south, then east and west across the country. Organised resistance throughout the land, there's a thought for us all to ponder. Cedric and I talked about these plans all the time now and we included all to have their say.

No point thinking small when we had such big problems against us, no reason why we could not form a fighting machine of great strength, with correct training and purpose. Anglo-Saxons were a hardy bunch of fighters at one time, if only we could bring back that spirit, with good leadership there was no telling what might be achieved. There was plenty of wooded land and hills up and down the country where we could meet without being noticed and plan the destruction of our enemy.

We decided to rest on that note as our minds were doing overtime!

One of the scouts in the other group came over to talk to us, he had to be really careful as the Normans were still on high alert, moving up and down the track all hours of the day and night. He said all was well with them, which of course was good except that one of the other scouts thought they had been seen and maybe even followed. This was not so good and it worried us all!

We would have to keep very close watch from now on when the light came, and decide what to do then. Otherwise, the night slipped by too quickly, as always, not much I could do about that, so I resigned myself to move on with the rest of my group when the time came, it was quite cloudy now and a cold wind pushed us on our way.

Bearing in mind the possibility that we had been spotted we rode a lot faster, if perhaps it had been a small group of the enemy that had seen us they may have gone back to report or get some reinforcements for the possibility of a fight, we would have to wait and see.

All of us stopped about midnight to let the horses feed and water, ourselves as well. I decided to go across the track to the other group to see if anyone had spotted anything. All seemed well at the moment, I thought I would stay with them for the time being to put my mind at rest as much as possible.

We all moved off, made sure at least one horse was visible on the opposite ridge so we all kept at the same pace, if we were forced into a battle we would have to get together and fight as one as quickly as possible. There were of course times when we could not see across to the other side of the valley, it was simple too dark, we carried on our way and never became parted for very long. Breaks in the cloud gave us glimpses of each other's progress and that was enough. The reason for the two groups was so we could more easily get together when needed, we were not so spread out in a single line.

Friend or Foe!

A scout came in from behind us and said he could hear some movement in the trees behind, so we scattered as soon as we could manage, from the direction we had just come.

Cedric called out to whoever it might be, if indeed it was anyone, asking them what they were doing following us.

There were some people and they claimed to have seen us some time ago. We were not dressed like Normans, they must have seen us when the clouds were clear to let the moonlight through, so they thought they would catch us up and find out who we were and what we were up to. No one trusted anyone these days!

I quickly stepped forward and explained we were taking horses to a farm south of here, they had been bought by the owner for him to use with his staff. Not sure they were buying this though, just to be sure and to get the lowdown on what was going on in this area in general we thought it made sense to have a drink and talk. We sent the hunters out to get food as well so it was not time wasted as such, we could either eat here or take any meat with us.

They turned out to be two middle aged men and their sons, they had just been checking their land and cattle when they saw a few of our horses. What with all the trouble since the Normans had been attacked and the huge search parties they had sent out to find the culprits they felt they needed to know what was going on in their area. A fair comment, I thought, but quickly explained we were merely delivering these horses and we had not seen anybody else on our travels to date.

We simple did not want anyone knowing who we were or what we were really up to, it was for their safety as well as ours. I kept repeating these lines to drill it into my men just how important it was, so we chatted with these men about their farms and families etc.

Chapter 39

Norman Taxation

They moaned about the extra tax they were forced to pay to the enemy, I am sure they guessed that we were not horse traders but we told them nothing of what they wanted to hear, that we were the boys who had struck a blow against the Norman swine and we intended to strike some more. They questioned why we were not using the track, I quickly said we had heard of animals being stolen so it was to keep our charges away from established tracks, thereby, hopefully, avoiding trouble.

I changed the subject and asked what their views were on the chaps who had fought the Normans. They were a little cautious in their replies, which I could understand. What if we were enemy? These men they had found could kill them just for the hell of it!

We talked a bit more about farming, they said they had better carry on with their work, though they would stay here and camp for the rest of the night and feed themselves. They said good bye and wished us the very best in our endeavour and left us to continue on our way.

They may well have guessed what we were up to as some of our fighting gear was on show for them to see. That could not be helped, we could do nothing about that now, just carry on. They had after all just seen a small section of our group we hoped.

Hopefully if they guessed they would not tell anyone.

We were getting careless in letting these men get so close without us realising, though at our next group meeting we would see about putting more scouts out ahead and behind us a little further behind and out front, taking in a wider area, thereby giving us more time in which to prepare for whatever might happen. Maybe a couple each side would be good too!

All of us carried on slowly as before, we could hear many horses on the track, coming and going, one group in particular, was huge. There must have been hundreds of horses and enemy soldiers.

Just hearing them was demoralising, as we got an idea of what we were up against, we could just make them out in the half light. Very organised these men, not a horse out of place in this regiment, very impressive, a show of strength was what it was, to knock us Saxons down a little further, make us smaller. Well, it may have just become more difficult, but it will not stop us, we decided, we had no choice but to fight on!

We formed a group together between a hamlet called Threekingham and Horbling, this place provided some thick forest so was ideal for us, a decent stream for water and plenty of food nearby. Maybe, fish as well as meat, space for decent fires as well that would not be seen, though we would be careful. We must get a lot of course bread baked as well, if time permitted, as, if we became hungry, we could munch away as we travelled along, filling the hole if we did not stop for food mid-day. It generally kept us going, if faced with starvation! We were still growing boys, don't forget, well maybe not boys any more, but still growing and needing plenty of food for energy.

Surprised by the Enemy!

We were just settling ourselves, when we heard noise in the woods behind us, coming in our direction, we quickly spread out and hid in our usual way, pulling down our horses and patting them to comfort them. As the noise became louder, we could make out comment and commands in French, we could not make out the numbers but there were quite a few, They were unsettling all the birds and animals in all directions, as they crashed through the undergrowth.

Suddenly, they were upon us, this could be awful fighting as we were at such close quarters, did not have time to think. Anyway, some of their horses crashed into ours lying down. We had no choice but get up as best we could. I shouted for all to stand and fight, we stood almost as one, startling the French, several of their horses reared and threw their mounts, as those men stood we attacked, several of the enemy were pulled straight off their mounts, they were easily dispatched.

On they came, the French were barking orders to each other, sounded to me like they were in a state of panic, our arrows flew into them, the few that had enough room to let them loose, that is, the rest were left to attack us, they were battle ready troops, so were pretty good. We had the upper hand, again, the element of surprise, so we attacked with all our strength with swords. Crashing through the bush, we all made a lot of noise, the sound was hemmed in by the woods around us and the still of the night.

The noise from our swords hitting each other was pretty deafening in itself, then there were the horses snorting, and quite an amount of humans shouting and grunting, the odd scream from a hurt soldier and bashing our way through the undergrowth made for quite a theatre scene.

Some of our lads on the ground were still firing arrows and dodging horses from behind trees. There were not a great deal of them to begin with thankfully so as we knocked them about their number dwindled quickly. They were getting thin on the ground by now, our constant harassing and dispatching of them was telling, I was very pleased to note. Close combat was difficult but good if you were winning! We were not suffering huge losses, the French were.

Several of the them tried to make a run for it, presumable to warn others or get help, or possible both! I sent two men after them but two more slipped away in the frenzy and I could not send others after them as we were all occupied with our swords!

I saw one of the enemy knock one of my lads off his horse, so I attacked, bashing small trees and bushes out of my way. We stood facing each other for a moment before attacking, what a crash when our swords met!

He was damned strong and going to be difficult to deal with, we passed each other and attacked again, swords flashing and crashing against each other. I took a huge swipe at him, met his sword, and scraped down it. It hit his arm, between wrist and elbow, through his clothes and along his arm, made a bit of a mess. He responded with a great show of strength and determination, tried to unseat me and cause me more damage. He failed but did some damage to my right leg, did not feel a thing in the madness, what a rush! I reacted a bit late, as he came at me, missed my blow but was able to give him such a shove that he fell off his horse as I went by.

Chapter 40

This was interesting, I leapt from my horse and stood a few paces from him.

He launched himself at me and his arm brought a huge blow to despatch me, or so he hoped. I very quickly stepped aside, as I had other ideas and even surprised surprised myself, this was a good move as his sword arm went by me towards the ground, I thrust at his chest, he was wearing mail, but the force I hit him with sent him reeling. He staggered back and tried to get his breath, I launched myself at him again, hitting him square in the chest.

He did not fall back or anything but I could see he was hurt, not only in the way he stood, defiantly, but swaying, he tried to come back strong but was noticeable weaker. I knocked his weapon away from me and went for the killer thrust.

He quickly moved, which surprised me, but I caught him in the neck, unguarded, as usual, and managed to finish him.

What a rush doesn't do justice to the way I felt, my first major one to one sword fight, I had won, hadn't I?

Not too sure, I was in a bit of a daze. There was a cheer, well actually more like a grunt as couple of my lads who had seen the fight recognised the fact that I had won.

Though the French carried on I felt their hearts were no longer in it, we despatched them all with only slight damage to seven of us, sadly we lost four more gallant lads. We looked better all the time, even in these conditions, could we become the force I hoped? Or at least part of it ! Could we train more and more groups of soldiers like ours to fight as well as this? Only time would answer that!

This was not the peaceful night's sleep we were looking for, I felt sure two Frenchmen had escaped so we had better get moving very quickly, we must get out of this area as quickly as possible. We did not want to be traced to this place.

All of us wondered if it had been part of a larger group of enemy, we could not take the risk of being attacked again that night. We needed time to recuperate.

The damage to my leg was showing through now, it bled quite badly, so I had one of the lads bind the wound again, hoping that would establish it in healing mode! It looked worse than it was, I kept telling myself. The sight of one's own wound was quite chilling.

We would have to take some risk and travel on the main track, I thought, to get the distance we needed quickly, so we travelled back the way we had come onto the track leading south.

We all split into our groups, cantering over the land as quickly as we could push our horses.

After a time, total darkness hit us fast so we sent out our scouts to find somewhere suitable to spend the rest of the night, thinking the French would not be able to travel in search of us in the dark. We knew it would take them some time to respond.

We must be careful though, as I thought the men we had just despatched may have been hunting for food, the best time to catch some animals was at night as they fed themselves, maybe to feed a large battle force staying in the area. Maybe they could have been looking for us? I always tried to think of all eventualities and I have to admit it can confuse an issue, at least in my mind! Sometimes, it was useful to talk to Cedric or possible Guthrum or anyone come to that to get the correct view on what to do or indeed where to go.

The scouts soon returned having found a decent spot to spend the night in some kind of peace, we were dead on our feet by now, we rode as hard as we dared push the horses and settled quickly to getting food and water from the area. On a normal day this is what would happen, now, in the dark, we could only dream of eating, we crashed out, virtually where we stood!

First Light

At first light, we woke, still pretty tired and cold come to that, very hungry and angry, worst camp ever! We immediately moved out to get more distance between us and the enemy. We talked of the fight, how quickly the enemy had come upon us, we must be much more careful in the future, check out the area as a whole before deciding to camp somewhere or we would get into more trouble than we could handle.

On reaching those woods, we had recalled our scouts, something we would never do again! This of course would slow us down.

The overriding ambition of us all was to get to the Anglo Saxon base of Ely and see what sort of force had become established there, organise ourselves properly and begin the fightback against our enemy.

Hereward the Wake.

We were sure we could learn from the leaders there, people like Harold's brother Earl Morcar. There was a fighter called Hereward, we heard, who was already termed "The Great Saxon Leader" of our time. Maybe, even the Last Great Saxon Leader, we would do all we could to stop that being the case! A great planner and fighter and very popular, we would add to his strength and fight the good fight! Not that there is much good in fighting but when you have no choice and we had none, put simple, you fight!

That is if we could extract ourselves from our present predicament which might prove difficult.

Again, we had to travel as lightly as possible, so we left quite an amount of clothing etc. We split into our groups and trotted out onto the track, making sure no one was on it before us.

We rounded a corner and could hear some commotion behind us, we all got off the track and hid from view, pulling down our horses as usual. The commotion turned out to be a very angry troop of Normans in pursuit of something and it did not take much of a guess as to what or who they were after!

The ones who had dared to kill many of their men as we had just done. As before, I supposed, they were setting up groups of men and leaving them at points along the way to try and find out where we had gone.

Williams plan, featuring Estienne and Roland.

Williams force established to find our force and kill us! 100/200 enemy in total.

The Norman group sent out by William to destroy us was instructed to kill us off at any cost to Norman lives, he had little regard for the average soldier it seemed. His main concern in forming a battle group was to achieve the result needed at any cost.

He called on Estienne Enguerrand and Roland Vauquelin to form and lead a group to attempt to kill us off. They had both been involved in such sorties before and had accomplished much against several French areas William decided he wanted to take over. Both of these men were no rules fighters, there was no place for chivalry in their lives. They just had space in their minds to kill the enemy, wipe them from the face of the earth!

They in turn called in Guiscard Onfroi and Piers Roul and pulled together 96 other men of dubious quality and set about their task. It would take them some time before finding us and then attacking.

Chapter 41

Immediate thought, stay off the track from now on, it was much too dangerous to continue as we were, at least for the time being. We would not last long at this rate, without another fight at least, we needed rest and plenty of it!

When the track was clear, the leaders came together to talk of where exactly to go from here, all decided to make our way further to the coastline and continue as soon as possible, leaving this track altogether. To be sure of our safety we would send out more scouts as we progressed. This was the way forward, we decided, you could never be too careful and to train more scouts would be a bonus!

We went over some small hills and found a very small track, probable used by shepherds walking their sheep. This could be a problem as our horses would make the path so much larger so we stayed in single file so it did not leave too much evidence of our passing. Anyway, we took it and off we went at quite a pace which was encouraging.

There were many overhanging trees and this slowed us, which was a real problem, still, we progressed quite well, with a few sore heads to add to our day.

My blasted leg was still bleeding, off and on, I kept tightening the dressing around it, hoping that would finally sort it out, it was a pain. I was at least better off than a couple of the lads, I suppose.

I always tried to look on the bright side of life!!

It never failed to assist me in my darkest hour, of which there had been far too many of late, and probable there were many more to come.

The scouts from behind and to our right came in and said horses could be heard, still some way off, but coming our way. No evidence yet that they were enemy but we assumed the worst under the circumstances. Cedric and I decided to carry on, we sent both scouts back just a little way behind and to the right, we would need to know approximately how many Normans there were, and find a clear patch of land in which we could set a trap and dispatch them if we could.

Our horses were getting tired now, another problem, they could last well, about twenty-five miles, on an open track. This was no open track and it was taking their strength.

The scout came in from ahead of us, he was excited, he had found somewhere clear and open just up ahead, to the left of the tiny track. We quickly made for it and I set men and horses in low lying points around this clearing. There was a ditch all around, that made it easy, as we could probable hide in it, readying to attack the enemy. I tried to calm everyone, no easy task even for myself.

We had more time than expected, but soon the approaching horses could be heard, there were exclamations crying out in French so we knew there was trouble ahead, they were excited but sounded like a rabble rather than a trained Norman unit, they could be both, I thought to myself!

I had said to all that they may have a scout out front as we do, so we must prepare to let him come through and wait until the whole unit was with us, or at least as many as could ride into the clearing in the trees. Then six of my men, still in the open, would quickly run their horses from the track across to the far edge of the clearing. Hopefully, leaving them to believe we had all gone that way, the enemy would then follow into the middle of our trap, then presumable all hell would break loose as we fired our arrows into them, then the battle proper would take over. The moment was nearly with us!

This is what we were here for and had trained for all these months past. We must stand together and teach these people that we will not just lie down and give up as a nation. We were going to fight and train and fight some more, we would make them pay for thinking they had us beaten! And for causing so many deaths among our people.

Time for a Battle!

Our first real battle! A long time in planning, in a short time going to happen! How would we fare? No time to even consider, as the lead scout came into the open from the track, he was going so fast he did not look at the clearing properly, he saw our six men at the far end of the clearing and he carried on and took an arrow for his stupidity. His horse continued and went from view. He was supposed to be let go, past the clearing, never mind! All of us must follow orders, I made it clear enough, surely? I would have words later!!

Let's See What Happens Next I Thought!

The noise of the rest of the enemy became deafening, we concentrated our attention on it so much, they bashed their way into the clearing, the first saw my six men, supposedly surprised and running from them, at the far end of the clearing and cried out that all should give chase.

Because they were more or less in single file due to the track being so small they attacked more or less in a line which was very stupid, the first group would die cheaply as a result!

We let them run towards the end of the clearing before opening fire on them, the six of my lads turned to fight. Shock hit the enemy as they fell like flies from their mounts, the horses were reeling and neighing. The noise was awful, men screaming in pain, more horses and men coming to their aid, this was very silly of the enemy! The leader of the French group shouted orders to add to the mayhem, though nobody seemed to be paying attention..

Some Normans stopped their horses and began firing at us at the edge of the clearing. Others rushed in to help some of their men who were in need of attention, they were quickly dispatched, no quarter was given as usual. We knew we would be given none.

Some enemy began running along behind the quite deep ridges, and ditch, where we were hidden, I sent four men to dispatch them. I was very pleased to see that Cedric did the same on the other side of the clearing, he was catching on!

Some stiff sword fighting took place at these points, the crashing of the blades was severe. A lot of blood was spilled, not from my lads I hoped. I knew of course this was not the case but I hoped our losses would be minimal.

I took a moment to look around and saw movement behind the lads opposite, more enemy coming in from a different direction.

I shouted and shouted, eventually, someone noticed, I cried out to all to watch their backs, they did, just about in time to save the day by putting a sword into an onrushing Norman, more followed. Guthrum, Zack and Xander lead the fight up the bank behind as things looked a little better. The fighting continued non stop at a mighty rate, it was intense at the very least.

Chapter 42

Pandemonium ensued, as we were attacked by what turned out to be the rest of the enemy, some of my men rushed out to finish the men on horseback, while myself and the rest of our boys turned to try and wipe out the new attack.

A Norman took a dislike to me and heaved his sword in my direction, I deflected it to my right, quickly bringing my sword back to attempt to hit his chest, he followed his sword to the right, so I missed! Quickly he turned, while raising his sword towards my head. This I simply deflected, followed by a jab to his left arm, the cut went quite deep, though was not where I had aimed, as for a big bloke he was agile, took the cut well and went for my chest.

I managed to leap out of the way, just, he caught my side as I moved. I could feel the blood straight away.

I was somewhat miffed, I don't mind saying, but I was not close to giving in, …ever, so I just stepped back, adjusted my tunic, and fully launched myself at this man with great speed and abandon, or so I thought. He stepped away and mockingly made a gesture with his hand waving as I passed him. He followed as I turned and jumped out of his way as he tried to get me in the back. Very unsporting, that, I thought later. I somehow managed to damage his other arm as he was slow to adjust from missing, not just a little nick this time either, a proper cut as the madness continued. It was to get worse before it got any better

The fighting in the middle was now gone, some horses were still in a dazed state but all Normans were either no longer with us, or were injured and out of the "game". Then when I was thinking we were at the winning end of it yet another group of enemy attacked into the clearing, it was almost too much to bear as all the leaders barked out orders to our men. They responded well and immediately took out many of the enemy, some with bows from around the edge of the killling field, then by sword in the middle, it just went on and on!

My opponent was not pleased with my attempt to rid him of his arm, I gave him no rest, as I attacked again and made a jab to his side pay with a decent cut.

He just seemed to be getting stronger, maybe he was just brassed off at being cut in a fight, as he again hurled himself at me, I noticed blood on his sword as I matched his sword against mine the next time he tried to defeat me, the arm wound was taking effect now. He was tough, no doubt about it, though I was still scoring the most points in this contest.

He seemed a little groggy, standing away from me, as though he was trying to make up his mind what to try next, when suddenly he leapt at me, sword held high, big clash of steel, and whoosh! The sound of an arrow close by our heads, he took it right through the neck and he was gone at my feet, eyes staring into nothing. Dead and gone in a moment. That image stayed with me for an age and it wasn't pleasant, I can asure you! Damn all this fighting and damn the enemy for causing it.

No time to look around to see who had fired the arrow, so I began clashing swords with the next Norman, this was going on all around the clearing. The noise had been awful and something you could not plan for coping with but cope we must. The only good thing was that it was getting less as we began to take control of the fight.

I fought off the man who had come from behind, he turned and ran, I followed across the ditch we were in, up and out the other side, I took my bow from its holder on my back, put in an arrow and fired at the man, he dropped right away and just lay in the dirt. Another gone!

I turned back to the main fighting, there was quite an open view from here, many bodies, clearly some of our brave boys had paid the ultimate price in the last half an hour but you could clearly see we were winning, and winning well.

We must try and let no one escape, as that would bring a whole lot of fury on us much more quickly, we would have little enough time to escape as it was. I had no doubt the enemy would stop at nothing by trying to kill us off as soon as possible.

Our horses were already tired, using some of the Norman horses would be possible but we were attached to our own, we had given them all names and regularly talked to them. I swear, they understood a lot of our comments, they might appear daft at times but as a general rule they were part of us and our fighting force.

We would take some of the enemy horses with us I decided, just to give us an extra option if and when needed. Our stores caravan was getting bigger all the time, so we needed horses to carry that if nothing else. Spare animals were always a good idea, if one was having a bad day we could simply change to another, roping the aggressive animal to the caravan.

We just needed to finish this fight as quickly as possible, so I rushed back to take on some more enemy. I was met by not one but two of them as I re-entered the main fight area, down into the dip at full running speed. I hit one sword, knocked out of the man's hand with ease, as he quickly leaned to regain it I slashed him through the side and into his chest. I still felt pretty dreadful when anyone "went down" as it were. I kept reminding all, it was them or us and I certainly knew which I preferred!

The other bloke was clearly not pleased at losing his mate, he attacked with fury from my left, I took a large leap to get out of the way. This did not look very dignified, but it was enough to give me time and space to try and hit back. I parried his blade, so we broke and sort of leered at each other, wondering what next the other might do. I was a little out of breath, so I did not mind being slow to attack this fellow. He had other ideas, he just flew at me again, straight at me, easy for me to see what was coming.

He had hold of a short spear from somewhere, this was quite new, it gave him a lot more range to do damage to me. Not good, but no time to think or plan, he hurled it at me and in a flash of instinct I got out of the way, more, I fear, by luck than judgement. Really simple to deal with on this occasion at least!

He followed this by another head on attack, he was slower now so I easily brushed his sword away. At this moment, in a second, I pulled out the knife from my tunic and stabbed him in the side. Though I did not think this method of dispatching the enemy was quite right, it had been brought to my attention by the enemy trying to kill me off in this manner so I considered it justified on those grounds. A loud grunt saw him fall to his knees. Another one gone!

I looked around to see if I could see any stragglers running off to perhaps get more soldiers to help them here. Nobody was going anywhere, except maybe to hell!

Very little fighting was happening at all, some of the chain mail was being removed from the dead for use by our boys already, much of it being superior to ours.

I called out to everyone to dispatch the enemy completely from this ground. To wipe them out was the only choice we had of getting enough time to get clear and maybe separate as a group for a time. Soon after I called this out, we could clearly hear a number of horses running away from the clearing, some enemy had managed to survive and get clear. I cried out to at least ten of our men to follow and try and catch the fleeing enemy, we must finish them off I called as they sped after them. Our adventure could end very badly if we could not get them.

The ten returned later with the bad news that the enemy had in fact got away from them. This was the news I feared most!

We would have to discuss everything pretty soon and decide what to do.

We learned sometime later that the four who had escaped, were the leaders appointed by Willaim himself to track us down and kill us all, Estienne Enguerrand, Roland Vauquelin, Guiscard Onfroi and Piers Roul. They were to all intents and purposes a bad batch of Normans. They would have to convince another bunch of rogue soldiers that to track us and kill us off was the only thing to do though some might be right in thinking the last group of 96 soldiers that tried this task found it to be somewhat harder than they were told. They may have a job recruiting!

There would be Normans everywhere in a short space of time, perhaps killing everyone of fighting age to try and get to us, this was exciting but very frightening for every one of us. I hoped our people did not think the price of success was not too high!

We all knew there was no choice if we wanted the return of our country and the freedom it gave us.

Silence Descended

All quiet now, we took the horses we wanted and all else, the spears and shields were particularly well made so we took most of them. Our men discarded some old weapons and clothing that was well worn. We had not come across the spears a great deal, we roped them quickly onto the new horses, made sure they were fed and watered and prepared to leave. Training with these spears would have to be implemented by us all if they were going to be of use.

The dreadful part for us remaining soldiers was to bury the seven men we had lost, we were not going to bury them here as they would perhaps be desecrated by the Normans. We tied a couple of pieces of wood together and used them as beds for them to be pulled by horses some way off and buried there.

Maybe the enemy followed the tracks we left but I don't think under the circumstances they would have wasted a minute of trying to track us down by digging them up for no gain, we did not want our boys buried near the Normans, they would never be at rest. Most of the enemy had been dispatched by arrow from the ditch surrounding the clearing, that was why our losses were so few, I was very glad to note. A large number of these Normans had not been wearing chain mail which was also a major factor in our favour. Cedric suggested later that he thought they may have been hoping to catch up with us and have time to prepare themselves to fight and that we had indeed been lucky again by enticing them into the clearing to fight straight away. Perhaps the leaders thought we would be a walkover, easy to destroy.

It was a very peaceful spot and I often think of it today, my lads at rest after that dreadful, fierce battle. A huge win for those of us remaining, experience was the only way to become better, much better than the enemy, and today we proved we were, we could match them.

All of us now felt we were a good team of men fighting for the survival of our race and that of our country. These were hard times in which to live, one honourable thing to do and we were doing it. We were not the aggressor after all, I kept reminding everyone. We wanted peace and security for our people and we would never get that if we just let the French take over.

Chapter 43

Cedric sent out our scouts as always to find another track, nearer to the coast this time, we felt we needed a larger one as we left too much evidence of our passing on that last small one as they had followed us easily. We moved slowly through some wet lands, seeing the reed beds made us all a little homesick, just those who came from the fens, there were track ways even here so we were not making a huge impression as we went.

The scouts returned with a few ideas regarding other tracks but we decided to stay as we were at present. Still plodding along! It seemed quite slow at this point.

We were very tired by now and the day was ending, our lead scout came in to say there was a good size island up ahead. Cedric noted that we had much to do and not a lot of time to do it in the light. The fishermen prepared to fish, the game catchers went off to see what they could find on dry land, the rest of us to set up camp/latrine and to see if we could get enough wood for fires to cook on and keep warm. It was a little drafty at this spot but we had little choice. We were very hungry men now.

My leg was considerable better at this point, though I thought about loosening off the bandage, I decided to leave well alone in the hope it would heal more quickly. Other damage was coming along quite well, healing fast. We all seemed to have many bruises and cuts to contend with now which I suppose was better than coping with a great many dead as the enemy had to as a result of meeting our force.

There was always the chance the damned Normans could follow with a large force at any time to try and kill us off. We were good in a fight but numbers were still against us, if they came in droves we would not be able to cope. It was more than a little frightening to think of what might happen.

The reed beds were pretty thick around us, so I hoped the smoke from our fires would not be seen, we were lucky in that it was a cloudy night so anyone would have a job seeing it. There may be a storm coming, but at least we could eat good hot food. We needed to restore our strength for the next fight and the march ahead. Winning fights was exhausting, though it was exhilarating!

We were still aiming for the Isle, but it seemed further away each day.

There was quite a lot of noisy talk between us all, though I instructed all to do so quietly. We were all excited as never before, our hand to hand fighting had been good though most of the enemy had been dispatched with arrows, we had never experienced anything like it, fast and very loud and pretty painful as many of us had injuries, myself included. It was probably much better being forced into sword fighting as we had been rather than carefully planning a large full-scale sword fight, too much thinking could easily cloud a battle.

Our medics were busy doing the rounds to help us heal as quickly as possible, washing and binding any wounds.

They were very busy chaps! One came to me regarding my damaged leg and arm repeatedly saying, "I must take it easy to give it a chance of healing, my arm too. Could I not stop leading the group for a time for it to heal?" He asked.

I thought about it and said, "I will swap with Cedric after the next fight, if it had not healed itself."

I felt like a naughty boy being told off at home by my parents! He was probable correct, I should take it easy though that was easier said than done. If the wounds became infected I would be in all sorts of trouble.

I liked to lead from the front, I kept being told by the men that Cedric and I were indispensable, with our knowledge of fighting and spirit that we passed onto everyone else, our cause may be lost if we were indeed lost to this world.

Both of us laughed it off but we were very pleased to hear our group thought so much of us and our abilities in fighting these battles. We still, all of us, had so much to learn.

We talked to the whole group and decided to let others lead at times, as if we were just injured and out of the game, it would cause problems. Every one of our men seemed at peace with this so that was the way forward, we decided. When I stood back, Cedric would lead with another leader, then Cedric would stand back as another took over and so on. This way all the leaders got the experience that was vital to help us all in our quest. We could then pass our experience onto other groups, leading the force was never going to be done by just Cedric and I ever again.

Food was coming in all the time, loads of fish, then three large deer about which we all became excited as it was some time since we had tasted such good meat. To top it all, some boar were made into lovely cooked sides which we took large slices which never seemed to end, a very good way to end our day.

We didn't have the time to think about how many of the enemy we had dispatched, but it was our biggest battle to date and though we had lost some great friends and fighters, we knew in our hearts that they died trying to do the thing that mattered most in the world to them. We would all give the same, not willingly, we would fight to the last breath, but we knew the potential cost in all our minds!

They may have to pay that price, if we could not outrun the response we knew was on its way to greet us over the next few days, if they could find us, that is!

The night passed, wind and rain battled around us but we were so tired, only a few of the men stirred. Before light came up in the heavens the fires were relit and we finished off all food and drink, we would travel as lightly as possible to give us as much speed as we could muster.

Horses were prepared and we were off, on our way towards Boston, through the roughest land we could find. No one of sound mind would come this way or so we hoped the Normans would think, the bush was really dense, if we were followed they would only travel slowly. The thick bramble in some of these woods was dreadful, it slowed us which was not good, we just hoped we could lose the enemy and make it worthwhile coming this way.

We thought we had a decent chance, what really would count against us would be the numbers of the enemy that they could get together quickly to hunt us down, if indeed they could get maybe three hundred or so together we would be over run.

As we had taken a good supply of enemy horses from the battle, we changed them as our horses became too tired to help us by riding as quickly as possible.

It occurred to me that we may be able to recruit replacements to our group from among the lads of families of the town, there was great hatred for all things Norman and our passing close by, if we did, would raise hopes perhaps of the re-emergence of our Saxon fighting force, why not?

Cedric pointed out that we could increase our number by a great deal, perhaps, as I was always talking of becoming a major fighting force, like they had on the Isle already. We would be of more use if we had under our command an ever-larger number of soldiers, fully trained and fighting fit, and for all us leaders to be used to commanding them in battle.

Cedric and I decided we would no longer hide and run, we would perhaps try shouting from the rooftops that we were the boys who were starting a rebellion, possible throughout the land, though we had not yet even got as far as meeting up with the rest of our fighters at Ely.

I wondered by doing this, if we could take some of the pressure off the lads on the Isle, maybe the enemy might send more troops to look for us, that would create more problems. I was feeling more confident as time went by, but this maybe a step too far! On reflection we decided to keep silent on those thoughts, at least for the time being.

All of our men reached the end of this bush filled area and stopped to feed and water the horses and ourselves.

We had actually travelled south too far to go through Boston, in the back of my mind was the thought that we might lose the men following by going slightly back on ourselves from here.

The main track near us was the Grantham to Boston one so we packed our gear and headed off towards Boston, if we were being tracked they would lose us with all the civilians using this one, so we hoped.

We still had our scouts out, front and rear, so if any soldiers were about we would get off track quickly and hide until the danger was gone. Our caravan of supplies and arms were following slowly off the track and out of site. We were pretty well spread out, there were quite a few other people going to and fro, taking goods to market, or whatever.

I heard a couple talking quite loudly about the attacks on Normans, they seemed pretty pleased, but were more than a little troubled by the fear of reprisals. This is something that constantly bothered us, time would tell on that one, I thought. We could not stop what we were doing now if we wanted, we could try and disappear somewhere, maybe in Boston, among friendly types of our own persuasion, good Anglo-Saxons.

That was where we were heading anyway, so we would put the word out when we reached the town, providing we reached it of course. The day was bright and fine and at this moment we were mainly all right, the wounds were healing and the bruises were coming along as they do in the circumstances of our fighting.

One of our scouts at the rear came hurtling to our side, telling us that a bunch of Normans were coming up quite quickly from Grantham, so we had better get off the track and into the low brush. We all proceeded to do so, not leaving much time to spare, for a group of about fifty enemies to come past us. Not sure what they were doing or where they were going, we may just bump into them at little later.

They were in full battle dress, so they were up to no good we thought, fifty was a quite large number as well, if we had to fight them later we would need to be at the top of our game. I still found it difficult to get my head around, I really was in command of a fine force, trained and fighting fit, men of the Anglo-Saxon race! And others of course.

I was proud to lead them, our movement would grow and grow, I hoped, until we could take on, and defeat, the dreaded enemy! To retake the throne of England for our race, that was the aim, though Cedric and I knew it would be a long hard road from here, we had at least begun the fightback!

It was a daunting ambition in itself, we had periods of doubt as the enemy were so strong and experienced but in the main we were getting stronger and stronger in our belief from this time!

At the end of the day, we stopped to catch food and eat, we pulled off the track and settled in the woodland, well off the track, got some nice fires going and cooked to eat. I talked with the other leaders and they agreed that stopping in Boston might be a decent plan, settling with some families if we could find some work, the money would be useful at some point.

We had to buy ingredients for our bread as we travelled on our way and other food we wanted.

Cedric and I went into the nearest settlement, Northorpe, to ask if anyone knew of enemy soldiers in the area.

Some large movements of soldiers had come and gone in the last week, more than usual, but no word of what that movement was about. Some of their men had stopped for ale, taken a shine to some of our favourite drink, had spoken in broken English of searching for something or some group of men, they only tried to communicate when more than a few pints had been sunk so no real help there, they were almost certainly after us. We were ready at any time I liked to think, to take on these men with confidence and that we would prevail!

All of us trudged on our way, feeling better for the break, near Bicker and onto Swineshead, we stayed near the track, I knew we were not far from the destination of Boston, Lincolnshire.

The Outskirts

On the outskirts, we very nearly stumbled onto a block across the track, every cart was being searched, it looked as though the soldiers were taking anything off they fancied, including the women, and they seemed to fancy quite a number of them! These soldiers were a damned disgrace to the human race.

We went off track, into the woods, and made a detour to the nearest point you could go to enter the houses of the town.

Cedric, who had family here went to explain what we were looking for and see if they had an idea who could help. My group of nine went with him and myself. Our leaders group number often changed as we wanted to hear what the rest of the lads were saying, we never wanted a "us and them" situation. We were fighting and learning together, leaders and soldiers of the ranks alike. All of us had the same aim.

There were an awful lot of enemy soldiers here now, almost on every corner it seemed, this was going to be more difficult than we thought.

We stood at his family house and knocked on the door, no response to begin with, a small window opened, quickly, and Cedrics mother appeared. No sooner had it opened than it shut, the door was noisily unbolted and we were ushered in.

Great laughs and smiles and hugs for Cedric, he was obviously very popular. This was good to see, you do see people in a different light when they are with family.

Chapter 44

Everyone had apparently been very concerned for our safety, as it seemed to have become common knowledge that it was our group that was fighting the enemy, word spread fast in these parts, the stories doing the rounds were more than a little exaggerated but it was good to hear everyone seemed to be supporting us no matter what. It did really help us that we had called ourselves the Boston Defenders. Without any thought by us, the people here had adopted us as their own force and were very proud to acknowledge our achievements to date. It was an unwitting masterstroke! I had not thought a name could help so much. We had only called the group that as a bit of a joke.

It made us all feel damned good, as a matter of fact, we were making a real difference, we were indeed showing that Anglo-Saxons could train, organise, take on and dispatch the enemy and live to tell the tale. Most of us that is, our dead left a cloud over us all of the time. It really was a major task coming to terms with our losses.

After we had sat down and been offered an awful lot of food we chatted about what we were looking for, we only had the older members of the family here as we did not want the youngsters to know anything as they might be questioned at some point, we could take no risks.

Cedrics parents talked about getting the word out to those who they thought would be best placed to help in hiding our lads out of the way for quite some time if possible, giving them room to put their heads while lying down would be enough, hopefully in full view of the enemy as that would be best we all felt. Not dossing in a shed as they may be seen and talked about.

Seasoned Fighters Now!

There were around sixty of us at this point and we said we were looking to replace those who had paid the dreadful ultimate price, we may be interested in taking more if we could, it just depended on how people felt about saying goodbye for a time to their young ones.

They may never return, come to that, so this would be a very big decision, and it took some courage to decide one way or another.

We had left most of our men protecting and feeding our horses in the woods near the town.

The youngsters of the area talked of nothing else but putting up at least some kind of fight so we were told we would talk to parents first, then the lads themselves. We were getting a little ahead of ourselves as we had to go and arrange for most of the rest of our force to come into town and be placed wherever we could be put in a safe house. This took some considerable time as we had to get them into town in small numbers at a time so as not to raise alarm among us Saxons or obviously the enemy. Loose talk by our own people in the ale rooms could cost us our lives we knew only too well!

We placed just one of our force with large families, quite well spread out, it worked pretty well from day one which was fantastic for us all. We all helped the families with building work on their houses or gardening or help with their business, no one was idle, we made sure of that. In one way or another we relied on each other, Boston families and soldiers alike.

Often room was made in the loft spaces of houses, well hidden from prying eyes. We just needed room to lay down and close our eyes. Clothes were made so we fitted in everywhere we went. We began to meet in the ale houses, to plan our next move towards the Isle.

The most important thing we did was to look to adding to our number, bringing us back to the original seventy odd men. So many lads were interested in joining us we had to decide who, and how many, lads we needed.

This was difficult, we knew we needed to be as big a force as we could be as the enemy were intent on killing us all, things were going to get more and more difficult as they put more men into the bush to try and find and eliminate us.

New men. Planning a Force of 100+ men

We looked at maybe a hundred men, this would be very different from anything we had known to date and would require an awful lot of thinking about to get right. Our battle plans could be much more adventurous with one hundred soldiers, and of course we could protect each other better in response to enemy attack. We decided to put out feelers among the town to see what kind of response we would get.

We would need to get people from the surrounding area as well, as that many lads leaving would probably cause comment, the Normans had spies amongst us so we must be careful, we knew the enemy would punish those who may have helped us in any way.

You only had to think of what they had done to the poor settlements north of York, burned to the ground, and all Saxons murdered! Men, women and children, all gone! It really was sickening what William had ordered his men to do. I shuddered to think as to what was going on in that man's head! How any human being could think of doing such a thing was beyond me.

We talked to all those youngsters interested, some were simple not strong enough, so I am afraid they were told nicely that they would need to train a lot to get fit enough to join our ranks, those ranks would be open to all who succeeded and they would be allowed to join up at a later date.

The majority were big and strong, so we took them under our wing and left town in the dead of night to camp and train in the woods in small numbers at a time. This proved very satisfactory, we had a set of training methods to be done in a given time, the ones who made the grade couldn't wait to go and fight the enemy, we had to hold them back. Progress was very good!

Huge amounts of arrows were made and stored and wrapped in sacking and put in holes in the ground, ready to take with us when we left, we got hold of many swords and spears, it was a major task and began to take all of our time, though we made a point of not letting anyone down from us helping our hosts point of view. We made sure every household benefitted by us using their houses.

Some of the new boys were not much use with swords in particular, so we gave them extra tuition, all seemed pretty useful with bow and arrow. The swords were really heavy. It was a task to get used to carrying them let alone using them in combat.

Horses were going to be a problem, those who were not much use on horseback were helped all the time, practice made perfect.

Enemy Stables

The enemy had some horses in stables south of the town and if it came to it we could take some of their animals when we made our break for the Isle, we decided, though we were told that they were not very good animals. They would surely be better than nothing. We were bound to add to our collection as we fought the enemy in any case, we confidently thought and hoped.

Quickly, we got our number of extra men. To get the other forty seemed a bit frightening, putting all these chaps together in groups of ten so as to not alert the enemy was hard, getting them together for a battle would be even harder.

The more I thought about it I decided that getting the original group together at the start had seemed hard but we managed that alright, so we would work it out as we went along. No stopping now! I only knew that we were going to be a force to be reckoned with and no mistake!

Chapter 45

There was dense woodland to the north of Boston, so we built a small area in which to train in small numbers. This would have to be small as I did not want the enemy finding this camp, hopefully, until we were gone, if ever, and deciding it was too small to be of use by a large group of soldiers, as that was what we were now considered. It became referred to as "base camp". A group of us, not more than ten, would go and train and fight for a number of days and nights, we really pushed ourselves and stuck to a set programme. Time and again we all went through it.

One of the men counted us over the whole course, it became the thing to do to beat the last group, we just got better and better and as a result more and more confident, though we all knew that combat with the enemy was the only real trial. We knew that many more battles would come soon enough and we would all have to prove ourselves many times over.

Normans Sent to Destroy Us

Estienne Enguerrand and Roland Vauquelin, the leaders of the enemy group set up to kill us all, began to wonder where we had vanished to as our fighting the Normans had ceased, this was as though we had just disappeared altogether, they had not given up trying to find us. They had gone through most of the woods nearby thinking we had gone to ground there and seemed pretty miffed to have not discovered our lair. As our base camp only consisted of a small area, they had missed it, which we thought was funny. We managed to move our horses at night away from their search area though this had been more than a little difficult doing so without getting caught. As our horses had made quite an imprint on the main area we left them, we left about a dozen horses there and had a friend tell them that they stabled their animals there for safe keeping. The enemy accepted this story but took half the horses as they looked good animals. It was worth losing those, as it took the pressure off the rest of us and made the enemy feel as though they had achieved something for their days work.

We thought they had increased the number of spies in Boston as well, just to see if we were living amongst the population. We had all by now got some kind of work so we could justify our living there if we needed to.

We may have to leave in relatively small numbers thereby not raising suspicions as to a whole group leaving together, as they would punish the Bostonians if we indeed lived with these fine people, many would be tortured and, or, put to death!

Even though we never met as a whole group there was a camaraderie we all felt, locals and fighters alike, we knew for the safety of all we would have to make our next move soon. To get on our way to the Camp of Refuge, as The Isle of Ely had become known.

We paid a spy who worked for the Normans to work for us, if the enemy used spies, we considered it only right we turned some to work for us, though I did not like this side of warfare at all, if they used them against us they were fair game to be turned, and received information that they were planning to take Boston apart, house by house, if needed, to try and flush us out as they had decided this was where we had gone to ground.

Some ten days before this was due to begin, we took apart our rooms in lofts where we had been staying so there was no evidence of us being there and began leaving in the dead of night. We were going to stick to our groups of ten, but we raised it to twenty as we would not have enough time to get clear of the town.

Each ten or twenty, or a mixture thereof, had a last meal with our householders, said our thanks, and we were off on our next adventure. Our scouts would hopefully give us enough warning of the enemy approaching for us to be able to pick our ground to defend, rather than them having any advantage.

New Horses Needed

Those who had horses, went south in the direction of the Norman stables, to get new horses for the new men, we did not have any idea how many men protected these stables but we needed to take these buildings so we waited until we were about sixty in number.

We approached and surrounded the place. I called out to the leader of the Normans in the stable. We demanded he come out and let us in to take the animals. He had other ideas as he and his men sent arrows out to try and either kill us or chase us away! They closed the gates so we could not enter.

We were never going away, so a couple of us approached and called out that we only needed the horses, if he let us take them we would not kill him or his men! We would give them safe passage. We had no idea how many men were here so we called out that if he did not come out we would set alight the gates and buildings, force our way in, and fight to the death. It sounded good, however, it seemed to have no effect on the enemy, so we set about burning the wooden gates, at the front and back.

More arrows were aimed at us, this was not a well defended place, they could not stand at the height of the gates and aim, they just sent arrows into the sky in the hope of killing us on the way down, they missed. We had to dodge a number, needless to say! Our shields gave us some protection from above.

Both gates were roaring and crackling by now in the fire as it was taking over so we stood back a little, out of the heat.

They fell, we could see the enemy now, so began to fire, and hit the men inside. The fire began taking the fence towards the buildings now. The men inside ran for cover in their buildings, we pushed our horses to enter the stables, leapt off our horses and began running after the horse handlers.

Using our swords now, we attacked as we met our enemy. It was quite easy, really, they were not soldiers at all, the trouble was they were trying to kill us so we had to take them on! They should have given in when we offered them safe passage, bad judgement on the part of their leader! This man was not going to be available to make more bad decisions!

The men cleared out all of the horses quickly as they were disturbed by the fire. It was time to go and meet the rest of our Saxon force. We left the remaining enemy to lick their wounds, them being horse trainers and not front-line troops, they were not "fair game" to be killed off we decided.

There were more than enough animals for all to have one, with spare to take with us, so we cantered off to find the rest of our force.

Chapter 46

The large Saxon force we assembled at this time was 116 men in total.

102 Saxon, eight Girvii and six Iceni soldiers. A much larger force than we thought we could manage but we simple could not leave these men behind as they were simple so good.

We were now all out on our own, one hundred and two men of the Saxon race, plus Girvii and Iceni ready to do battle though we were not sure where, that would soon come to us as our enemy would not be far behind now we had broken cover.

The whole group began to make our way towards the coastal track alongside the wash. We soon realised there were just too many of us to be altogether, we were putting on too much of a show, more so than before, someone may well tell the Normans of our whereabouts, even inadvertently, and that would never do! The track here was quite open as we needed to get as many miles between us and the enemy as possible, as quickly as possible, we thought it worth the risk staying in view for the time being.

We split into our groups, with a considerable gap between each. We decided to put out double the amount of scouts we had before, just to make sure we were not bothered by the enemy. If we were bothered by them, we would at least be ready for them, not be taken by surprise, or we could hide, whatever was the best plan at the time. This was always a worry, as I knew that at some time in the future we would be ambushed. We needed to be ready to act at a moment's notice!

I still had a job getting my head around the fact that we were one hundred strong, 116 to be exact, the group seemed huge but I was sure that these next battles we had in particular were going to need that many men, if not more, we knew the Normans had to try and kill us all. Maybe we should consider several groups of men, we had enough leaders, after all. Cedric and I were really beginning to think big with a very confident approach, our dreams really were taking shape, in our minds at least ! They had some way to go in reality.

If the enemy realised how many trained soldiers that they were up against they must crush us or die trying, at least that is the way we saw it. In their place that is what we would be compelled to do.

The Saxon Fight Back!

This was the beginning of the fight back, we were by no means finished, and if we were to join the Isle of Ely, we could maybe even start to think of organising groups of fighters up and down the country. We could build a future for us, Saxons, Girvii and Iceni together. Let us rid ourselves of the dreadful Normans and build a new peaceful future for England!

We had crossed the river below Boston and now moved to the area the seventy of us had stayed in earlier near the river estuary to the wash.

We found the spot straight away and moved in, more space was needed so we got that sorted quickly, the fishermen and hunters got busy catching our first meal together and so our adventure began, again!

This all seemed new with so many new "boys". A lot of the new boys joined in catching food so we were not left alone to do the job.

Boston was not a large town at this time, a lot of its food was caught by its youth so these lads knew what they were doing.

Fires were lit speedily as dinner began to turn up pretty fast. We were now 116 fighters in total and we were hungry again! I had to keep reminding myself that I was leading all these fine fighters of whom I was very proud.

Fifty-eight new fighters of the Anglo-Saxon race.

Aart Dwerryhouse
Aldin Elvis
Arlrigh Gebhard
Hollis Elwyn
Hall Forester
Merton Green
Morton Foss
Ramm Hogarth
Ray Jinks
Rowe Kipling
Ward Fabian
Winston Everitt
Wylie Ibbott
Wynchell Marley
Taite Maddison
Tate Farney
Toland Gosse
Tredan Murgatroyd
Elmer Ackerman
Elswyth Anselm
Esmond Abram
Orvin Blakesley
Osric Bloodworth
Osmond Chandler
Daegal Adair
Dell Courtenay
Denton Dabney
Drew Dannel

Berkeley Betli
Brimlad Byron
Kipp Adcock
Nodin Alvey
Norville Aston
Byron Barrington
Bartlett Talmac
Billy Binney
Brad Burney
Carlyle Chancellor
Charlie Cooper
Iggy Dob
Earwyn Thomas
Rand Grimshaw
Kipp Hadwin
Peter Hargrove
Ralph Beothtric
Jack Kendahl
Walter Aelfraed
Algernon Cimberleigh
Kyndra Beorhtric
Milton Cyneburg
Nesbit Cynfrith
Kendra Kenelm
Ogden Cynesige
Pierson Dudda
Watson Wills
Ricker Rumford
Tadleigh Saxton
Tedman Weylin
The fifty eight new men, (Boston Defenders)

Chapter 47

I called the leaders together to decide how we were going to organise our force, we needed more men to lead the others and trainers who had become important as they were of a different mind-set. They led our men through training and had become back up for our leaders in times of action.

We asked them to talk amongst themselves and if they liked to vote as to who should lead them then to let us know.

We said it worked for us and we talked about voting someone else into the post but we felt a change was not needed, we stayed as we were. This may or may not work for them. They continued to talk away through their meal and came up with possible six men…Zack and Xander Brightcard, the only brothers in our force, these two lads came into the original force but they had proved so good that they just had to lead a number of men to see where that leadership took them. I put their names forward from our group, Carlyle Chancellor, Osric Bloodworth, Tredan Murgatroyd and Wynchell Marley were put forward as well.

Sixteen Leaders, including trainers in total! Now we were a real force to be reckoned with. I really thought we could begin to plan for larger fights from now on.

We could begin to make that difference, to hopefully wake our sleeping Anglo Saxons, Girvii, and Iceni to train and plan, and become not as good as the enemy, but better!

I was thinking of meeting, us leaders, every day, and talking about our men, how they were reacting to training, did any have ideas to make our force better. Should we go here, or perhaps there in the country, whatever, to make this force all inclusive, a much better fighting unit! One whole group of fighters, not small units, with one aim, that of taking back our land from the enemy! We could attack enemy units of perhaps twenty men at a time, depending on the size of the enemy force, watch the battle, then send in more to finish the job. A proper fight plan could now be envisaged we all felt. This of course depended on the number of enemy that were thrown at us at any time.

We may not need anything like as many men to run this battle group as time went by, but it was a good way of getting to know everyone and how these chaps spoke for one another. The groups could be led by as little as two or three men, in total, in the long term but that could wait.

This first night went by very quickly and the weather was fine so we had no problems sleeping rough. This could change pretty quickly, as our weather did just that at times.

I woke early the next morning and as Cedric was awake as well we decided to go out and see our scouts, we had left two on the way here and sent two more out front, along the coastal track.

I was afraid the enemy might have thought that a lot of men of fighting age didn't seem to be in the town, they may have joined us perhaps? That may force them to act quickly perhaps, find us and attack, before we had time to organise ourselves as a fighting unit.

However, my concern was unfounded, nobody had even come close to us during the night, so we thanked these lads and returned to the fold!

There was a little too much noise coming from the camp so when we arrived, I said as much and everyone calmed down a notch or two, our security depended upon it, I explained. I also said we must get to know each other but we must do so quietly.

There was a patch of ground we had cleared for training when here last so we made for it, cleared it a little more, and began to go through the paces of our training in groups of twenty, then ten.

We would compete against each other just to see who was best, whoever won would be spared hunting for dinner duties for the next week, this got quite a response so I felt it was the right thing to suggest. There seemed to be quite a bit of comment between each group as to how they were no longer going to have to hunt for food ever again. Some groups were a little over confident and somewhat brash as to their accomplishments in the past hunting wise. As far as I could tell, no single group was better than any other, time would tell on those claims.

The run was set up through some woods behind us, on getting back to "base", we went through our paces with climbing over great logs, of which there were six close to each other. Then we climbed up and down some trees, they had to be climbed and not jumped off as I did not want injuries, then a run through the marshy ground alongside the estuary and back to base, as quickly as possible.

The first two groups went through, very quickly, I thought, then it was our turn. I always tried to make sure my group won, I tried to encourage them as much as I could. There was no holding them back this time, as they left me trailing. I pretty soon caught up, bashing through the undergrowth, around trees at the turning point, I was about in the middle of us all, we had to climb those trees now, out of breath and ready to drop, it was more than a bit heavy going, very fast. We reached the trees, they were laid out in more or less a line, one arm on, then a huge leap over and try and keep your balance and continue running as fast as possible.

I had never known the lads go so fast, they were getting into the spirit of this alright. The trouble was, I didn't know if I could keep up with them. I must train harder I decided, cannot let the side down, I will lead by example on all fronts if at all possible!

My team were important, we must try and show how things should be done! On and off the battle field, we tried to be the best, to set an example.

We were in the marshy part now, what a mess, much slipping and sliding around, we just managed to keep our feet. Legs were now so heavy it was painful to run at full tilt but we encouraged each other to carry on, we left the water and made a sprint to the finish, though it was not much of a sprint it was thankfully the finish!

Having collapsed, amidst much comment and laughter, the next twenty ran off, I only hoped they were much slower than us. To be honest it didn't matter who won, it was good camaraderie for us all. This mattered a great deal and that was my thinking. Some group would set the mark and all the others would try to beat it, that was the point of the exercise!

Two of the groups ended up with more or less the same count as us, we decided that though it didn't really matter that much, we would run the course again.

The two groups were led by Cedric the fen and one of the new groups, Richard Eltisle, who seemed to lead everything very well. Cedric was really up for this, he was very enthusiastic about everything, a really good bloke. His group set off first at a good pace and went through the course quickly. He was tiring towards the end, he had put his all into it.

Richard roared off to much encouragement from the new boys, as you would expect, no sooner had he started then he was up the trees and over the tree trunks, then the water. He didn't seem to slow down at all, the last section saw him sprint to the line, he was damned fit and very fast. A certain Zack Brightcard caught up with Richard, he was really moving through the field, have to keep an eye on him! His brother, Xander, wasn't far behind him. The two of them were always trying to "out do" the other. This normally meant they were first into a battle, or whatever was required of them!

Our turn again, I was not looking forward to this very much, we were off to shouting from our lads, did the running, climbed the trees, leapt over the trunks, the water slowed us it seemed and with a mad rush to the line got very close to Richards count, but not quite.

The new boys had beaten us at one of our own games. Whatever next!! Cedric and I said to each other, having congratulated them heartily. It appeared the group had a programme of fitness training of their own and had been using it for about two years, I felt a little better after I heard that, regardless of that they had done well and competition heated up after that so it was good for us all, I liked to think. Not good for our Norman friends, they would soon discover just how fit and strong we were!

I told everyone off for the noise they had made but we were well off the beaten track so it wasn't too bad. It was something I must get them to do until it was the norm, to speak in a controlled manner at all times, depending on where they were, then they could not be wrong!

We went back to camp much more of a complete unit than we had left it and packed our belongings.

I spoke to all about what our objective was, to join up with the fighters on the Isle of Ely, and hopefully lead a revolt against the enemy across the land. Cedric also mentioned that we were hoping to avoid fighting on our way there, but there was little hope of that as we knew the enemy would be trying to catch up with us as we spoke, we might encounter them at any time so be always prepared was the only way!

116 Soldiers

58 surviving men from the first force, 58 new men from Boston. 116 in total.

I hope I have recorded these numbers correctly, if not, I hope you can appreciate I am recording these numbers from notes some time after events and forgive me for any errors!

A note, just to remind me, from the original time of events, I had to keep telling myself that we were that strong a force now and that we would grow and grow in number. Cedric and I were confident for the first time, these men were great fighters and we had a great future, no doubt about it!

Then we were off in our groups of twenty, or ten as the case may be, one hundred and sixteen fit and ready soldiers, it seemed like a dream to me, that I could be leading such men made me proud and somewhat apprehensive.

There was an awful lot riding on our shoulders. We had much to prove, to ourselves and our race. Maybe we were daft, thinking we could cause an effect across the land, it would not be for want of trying, of that I was sure! Forgive me if I have noted this before, but it was often to the fore of my thinking time.

All the horses we had "acquired" from the enemy were doing quite well, the ones we did not take to, were let loose and chased away a fair distance, or kept as "spares," to use if and when, or used to carry our equipment. It would take the enemy some time to round enough up to try and find us, if they needed more horses.

The River Welland. Our first battle with a complement of 116 men.

We followed a track, small, towards the river Welland and used the very small and not too safe bridge to cross.

On reaching the other side, our back scout came hurtling along the track to inform us of a big troop of enemy horses coming our way. We all got off the track and hid with our horses down, the new ones were not amused to be put in this position and they struggled and made plenty of noise.

Two of our lads and one of the new recruits who were good with the animals tried to calm them, we just had time to take them further into the woods behind us.

The enemy were on us, kicking up clouds of dust, they hurtled by as if chased by a dragon. They must have taken a wrong turning, they were on the wron; track, if they continued the bridge would be no more, it would certainly fail. Th lead horses slowed and stopped, called for all to stop behind them. The two m began shouting at each other, one rode off in disgust, he was heading right us, he came through the tree line and saw a pretty large group of our men, turr and roared something at the top of his voice. He had found the enemy, perh;

Battle Ready or Not!

I cried out to all to stand and fight. Very effective it was too, everyone not on his horse leapt onto it, those lying down encouraged to stand and prepare to charge out of the woods to fight this enemy force, no time to think or plan, just charge and fight!

The enemy were surprised by this huge change in fortune, one minute, passing through a nice silent, wooded area, the next attacked from their left seemingly all along their troop line, this meant an awful lot of Anglo-Saxon soldiers. No time to think about bows and arrows, straight out with the swords, and try to defend their space on the track between the trees.

Our soldiers charged like crazy men. Shouting defiantly, they hit the enemy line with huge force, a number of them ended up on the ground, their horses throwing them. Give them their due, they pulled their swords and ran towards the fight, these were front line troops, and no mistake!

Having said that, we considered we were as well, all along the line, not straight any more, clashing swords, and cries as men were injured. Cedric and I cried out to kill all, we could take no prisoners.

We had a long way to go before we could finish this battle. I did not have time to think, "hopefully" win it, perhaps it was better this way, no choice but to get stuck in and fight to the death, or victory!

I attacked an enemy on horseback first, he wasn't quite ready, I hit into his sword as he raised it, he just managed to hold onto it as we passed each other, I turned quickly, he began his attack, thrashed at me with his sword. I moved my horse, fast, pulling it away from him, his sword cut into the belt that was holding my saddle on, It cut like a piece of cheese and I fell with it to the ground. The ground was quite soft, I remember thinking, that was handy!

I almost bounced on the moss that covered this part of the ground, back onto my feet, I had kept hold of my sword, so I was ready for anything that hurled itself towards me, horse or man.

One enemy came straight at me, even his horse seemed angry, perhaps it did not like its exercise today being disturbed!

Our swords clashed again, as he sped by, he turned his horse and came at me again. I had to leap out of the way of the oncoming animal, in time to try and get the soldier on his back, he aimed his sword right at me with all his strength, I knocked it out of the way and managed to get hold of his arm with my left hand. I pulled him off his animal, that made us equal!

He was not pleased at this turn of events, though he quickly pulled himself together, we ran at each other and clashed again, he tried to stab with his knife in his left hand, I just pushed him away. We met again and I managed to cut into his arm with my sword this time, quite an amount of blood showing right away. He was not impressed but it did not stop him coming at me again, he was not any slower, as I had expected him to be, my sword hit his halfway to the ground, it knocked it clean out of his hand and I finished him with a thrust to the chest!

The next man was on me, right away, we were both standing on the ground, though we were being bothered by the now stray horses getting in the way. They were running all over the place, again, first clash of swords, a lot of energy wasted, as both went towards the ground. We both picked them up and sword fighting continued, clashing, again and again, sapping more and more of our energy.

A man in Norman uniform backed into our fighting area, being attacked by Cedric, my friend had him backing away like crazy, he realised he had nowhere to go, so tried to fight back, Cedric finished him, and I attacked my enemy soldier again. I caught him again, this time in the side as he tried to move out of the way of my sword, he was clearly slowing, more so now as he had something else to contend with. A lot of these enemy were not wearing their armour, they were not expecting to fight here, I suppose, and it could be quite clumsy. That made it easier to damage them!

I "launched" myself at him and struck him through the chest, a killer blow!

This was going on everywhere there was a fight, which in this locality, was everywhere. Another enemy attacked, with much the same result, again and again they died. As I have thought before, such a waste of life, why couldn't we be left alone to get on with our lives in peace in our own country?

It seems wherever man found a decent place to live, someone else had to come along and try to take it from him. It was a hard fact of life, especially in these days!

We were winning well, were much the fitter force, and I could not help but think we will last a lot longer than any enemy as we had so much more strength than any other force, maybe I was being too optimistic in this thought!

I hoped we were stronger and that it gave us an edge over our enemy. Hopefully, the Normans would never realise this was relevant. Perhaps they relied on the fact that they were renowned the world over as "the" fighting force during this period of history. They may be getting lazy in their ways! You just needed to think what had happened to the Roman Empire to see that these forces did not last forever. Maybe, just maybe, we could begin to force the end of these Normans as a fighting force!

The battle was coming to a close, thankfully, body's and horses cramped the area, injured soldiers staggering about, some in a complete daze, all around us. There were a bunch of the enemy towards the centre of the fight, we made our way there, and began to fight again. Everyone was fighting on the ground now, our men from the other end of the fight were making their way towards us.

A number of the enemy tried to run off into the woods, I called for men to follow and finish them off. About eight men followed and caught them before they vanished into the forest.

The rest of us fought and fought these last few enemy, then we were nearly finished. We could not afford to let these men, who were injured, go so we had to finish quite a number who were not quite dead. The only way I could stand doing this, or giving the order for others to do so, was by telling all that the enemy would do the same thing, given the chance, to us! They would also be likely to show off our dead bodies as a warning to others to not follow our actions, letting our bodies rot in view of everyone.

Silence came along, as we surveyed the scene, it was not pretty, though we had no choice but to fight. I told all the men, it was them or us! I had said this many times before. It was, however, a major battle and a major win for us, again, this boosted our confidence no end. They appeared to be a front line group of fighters, we had taken a big scalp from the enemy!

15 Good Men Lost

We had lost fifteen men, and had many injuries to contend with but just look at what we had achieved, I exclaimed to all!

William will not be at all pleased when he gets the news of our fighting, and his losing, again, at the hands of our brave Anglo-Saxon soldiers! We were a force to be reckoned with now, he will have taken note!

We took our fallen heroes to one side and said more than a few words of kindness, understanding and prayer as we buried them to be at peace with one another. More than a few tears flowed down our cheeks, a solemn sobering moment followed! Farewell my friends!

Continuing With Our Journey!

When we had calmed down, I called everyone together, I said how impressed and indeed proud of them all I was, this had been a great test and we had won the day. The troops we had killed off would be expected to arrive somewhere, sometime.

Groups of enemy soldiers would be out looking for clues as to where they were, their bodies would be found and Williams wrath, led by Estienne Enguerrand and Roland Vauquelin, would be on its way to find us, whoever, and wherever, we might be!

That is of course if they could find us. We heard later of the leaders of the group of enemy soldiers sent to destroy us, they were instructed to stop at nothing in their pursuit of us. They were a fearsome bunch we were to discover time and again.

So our plan at this time had to be to get clear of the area and disappear again as it were.

We had an abundance of horses to pick from now, plus new fighting gear if we needed, only the best for my men!

Though it was second hand, I thought and chuckled to myself, it was all appreciated. Some of the gear we had taken earlier was discarded, only the best was kept, we had no need of a great store, it became too much to carry with our caravan of horses.

There were a large number of dense woodlands/forests locally, so we could lose ourselves, make sure we left out a large number of scouts, well hidden, so keeping a very clear view of any enemy troop movements. I planned building a training camp of sorts wherever we stayed to keep us sharp.

The next place of any size was that of Holbeach, we decided to take a smaller track this time to Moulton Seas End, near the edge of the Roman Sea Wall, in the hope of avoiding any further enemy soldiers on the same path, path being the word as it was a very small path indeed. Our scouts went ahead to see if there were any soldiers about, couldn't see any, so we trotted through this tiny settlement in our groups.

There was a startled cry from the lead group, we saw a horse being pushed to the limit, moving like crazy, away from us, just as fast as it could run with a Norman uniform and its user on its back, he had been disturbed by us, saw we were not in uniform and thought he had better get out of here rather quickly, trouble was we needed to stop him as he would tell of our passing this way, so I sent four men after him.

They returned some time later with the bad news, that in fact they had lost him in the woods, couldn't be helped, we would have to learn of the consequences later. I knocked on the house door where he had come from, apparently the daughter had been seeing this Norman fellow for a time, we were not too happy about this but had little option but to carry on.

Fraternising with the enemy was more than just frowned upon by us all. We were just trying to make sure nobody was being held against their will, hopefully he didn't see more than two of our groups, that would be possible forty men, so maybe no problem.

Chapter 48

We turned towards Holbeach Clough, which was on the road to Holbeach itself, just another small settlement, probable farm workers, fishermen etc. Several of the occupants rushed to their front door, it was as if they had never seen so many men on horseback, we found it really funny as we passed by.

On the outskirts of Holbeach, we saw a number of horses, they were being guarded by a couple of Norman soldiers.

We could hear a lot of noise in the village and could see smoke coming from one of the houses, they were causing all sorts of trouble with the locals so we put our heads together and decided we would relieve them of their horses and attack them where they stood.

Four of my lads went to pass the two Normans, instead of going past they turned into the field and began untying their animals, the soldiers started shouting at them and took up their bows and arrows to stop them, they were soon dispatched by our men. We proceeded to the field and while a chap acted as lookout we took all the horses and led them away, quite some distance, and tied them as they had been where they were now out of view.

We then went into the village, there seemed to be two groups, working from each end towards the middle, so we asked the first group what was going on, they ignored us completely, took hold of a man from a house and threw him in the street.

That was too much for us, at least twenty of our men, jumped from their horses, picked the man from the track and placed him back in his house, having pushed the enemy away. This caused a mighty fight between our men and the dreaded Normans, out came some knives and it all turned pretty nasty, very quickly.

Normans at the back of this group drew their bows and arrows, we did likewise and fired before they let off more than a couple of hastily, badly aimed arrows, they missed, ours did not. Swords drawn now, we did battle, we had caught them out, they were not expecting opposition, just a few locals to bully was what they wanted and so died as they stood.

The group at the other end of the village heard the noise we had made and came scrambling down the main street to help their mates. Much too late they realised, they were in trouble as they saw their colleagues were dead. They loosed arrows at us, two of my lads took them in the arm but as we were on horseback, we had the advantage and attacked, they split up, our group took the nearest and wiped them out without a thought, as they tried to harm our horses and then us. We watched as our other group took on the rest of the enemy.

Nobody was hurt, as we struck them down, one by one, one horse was hit and suffered a broken leg, so we had to put him down which was a shame, he would be missed. We had plenty more to pick from, awful thing to think really, they were animals but they were a very important part of our team now, most had great personalities and we were fond of them. It was Peter Ganning's horse that was lost and he was very upset! For a laugh he had named it Guthrum 2, after one of his friends and fellow leaders.

That was the end of our second engagement with our contingent of one hundred and sixteen men. Minus the poor men we had lost in the last battle. I could not bring myself to think of their deaths yet, I had not found the mechanism to cope. I was still trying to get my head around the fact that we were that many soldiers now, let alone admit we had lost those men.

Good Men Lost

101 was our number now, having lost fifteen brave Saxons in that first battle. Considering the number of enemy we had killed it was a little too easy I had to admit, we had knocked that Norman group of soldiers to pieces and though I hated losing any of our men we had done really well compared to enemy losses. Twenty of the lads who were involved in the sword fighting had small injuries to treat, but most important no more deaths to report.

The need to clear Holbeach of all evidence was apparent, so we talked to many of the people who came out of their houses to kindly greet us, there were some hollows and dips in a field nearby so we arranged to help bury the Normans who had fallen, and cover them with some earth, then small trees to disguise the earth, plus our horse, he was a job to move!

Rowan and Whitney were busy cleaning and binding wounds for quite a time, a lot of groans were to be heard coming from my men as the wounds were touched when cleaning. These men brightened up as soon as they were bound, though some would not be ready for action again for some time.

Against my better judgement, we stayed afterwards to eat with these people, it seemed they did not see friendly faces often, they began cooking a deer outside not long after the fighting, they had a lot of cold meat and smoked fish which we could have as well.

This could take some time! We had to stop and eat at some point, so why not here with food prepared for us by somebody else for a change? If the enemy were following they may catch us at some point anyway, why not here was what Cedric and I thought, their force may not be very large yet so we would have no real problem fighting it. Our first really confident thoughts, it really was a "sea change" in our approach. We felt very strong and confident from this point, not too confident I hasten to add as that may be dangerous. We had not met the enemy in huge numbers yet, I wished to delay that for as long as possible!

The food was quickly eaten and some ale drank, we waited and talked of the present state of affairs regarding the takeover, they were impressed with the way we had fought the enemy and wished us well for the future. We did not tell them we were responsible for all the other attacks they may have heard of, the less people knew the better we decided, for them as well as ourselves, as always. I kept instructing all our force that we were really just passing through the area and to tell people we were going to Kings Lynn, known as Bishops Lynn at this time, if anyone asked, nothing more or less.

It was a nice area and at one point we were going to stay the night here, we considered we had really spent enough time in this particular place so on reflection, we changed our minds as the trouble that may come their way as a result of our fighting, made us go and collect some of the better looking horses, and leave the rest to go wild, or, again, maybe get used by the Saxons, that would be poetic justice of sorts and so we moved on with many a hearty clap on the back as thanks for helping them out of their predicament with the enemy.

We kept to the small tracks out of Holbeach and headed for Fleet, just a couple of houses, and then onto Gedney Broadgate, small again. We then followed the track to Sutton St James, even on this small track our scout at the rear came forward to tell us of soldiers on the way, we were a bit battle weary by now, so decided if it was a small group we would hide and let them pass us by.

This didn't quite go to plan as one of the eight men spotted one of us and called his men to stop and investigate, bad idea for this group of Normans as before they could do much except approach the man they could see, they were shot to death by our arrows. I was getting more concerned that this was too easy, we may have to pay for this good luck sometime in the future, again time alone would tell on that thought, so I stopped worrying as there was no point!

So we continued on our merry way towards the Isle, we reached Tydd St Giles, before finding somewhere to camp in the surrounding woods. Our usual rush for enough food was just getting underway, we were settled and about to light our fires when our back scout spotted a number of men on horses passing a nearby clearing, we were getting more than a little fed up by this time. We laid low and the men passed by into woods in the distance, relief all round. Though there were only six of them, it would have been more hassle than we wanted at this time. They were not in uniform so they were probable friendly, if we had stopped them they may have inadvertently told someone of our whereabouts so to stay unseen was the best plan of action.

Food appeared in the shape of wild boar and deer, this was much appreciated, leaving a lot to spare for the morning. The low bush here kept out the pretty savage wind so we slept well.

Morning appeared, much too soon for my liking! as we ate leftovers and cleared any mess we had made, didn't want anyone passing on that a large force of men had been through this area, though the camp was well off the beaten track and if someone looked carefully enough you simple could not hide the fact that so many horses and men had been this way, we did our best to hide what we could.

We left as usual in our groups of ten or twenty, leaving a gap between each group and made pretty good time. Floods and small rivers were an ever increasing problem, but we managed alright and approached the town of Wisbeach, it would be interesting to see how many of the enemy there were here, it being a quite large town.

On the outskirts there was a block across the track and the soldiers were searching all wagons and anyone carrying goods, or in fact anyone who had a bundle for bedding on the back of his horse or anyone they didn't like the look of, lots of people were getting angry at the hold up this caused, the ones who made the most noise were either beaten or insulted. It paid to keep silent!

Port of Wisbeach

The whole of our group went into the woods to the right hand side of the post. A small group of us entered town via a small bridge, apart from the fact that there were Normans almost everywhere, especially in the centre, all seemed at peace.

We spread out on a street and entered some ale houses, thirsty work this horse riding! We really just wanted to find out what, if anything, was going on regarding the enemy. To find out if anyone knew anything.

The soldiers were apparently looking for the force that was attacking their men. Everybody was excited that we were, as Anglo Saxons, fighting back at last, all the talk was of our exploits, which we thought was great. Obviously we had agreed nobody would tell who we were, if anyone asked we were just looking for work in the area, we were in a small group so nobody was interested in us.

Beatings

Some of the locals had been beaten, but not too badly, though they might not agree regarding the severity of the beating as they must have been in pain, in the search for information regarding our whereabouts, nobody knew anything so they could not tell anyone. As always, we were sorry for causing any problems but had to look at the bigger picture. Most of the moaning concerned the blocks across the tracks in and out of town, sometimes it caused food shortages.

There were a very rowdy bunch of soldiers outside one of the ale houses, a fight began between them and some of the locals, it really caused a stir. One of our men stupidly became involved and mayhem ensued, crashing chairs and tables across the street, one of the lads knocked the leader of the soldiers down and began kicking him, everybody piled in, what a mess!

We were out for a simple pint of ale and some information if possible and were now involved in a mass punch up, again. After much shouting, kicking and punching, the enemy who could still stand, ran off, leaving their injured pals behind, we just ignored them and continued with our ale and chatting. Nobody bothered us as we stood.

I pointed out, yet again, to the men that we should always make a point of avoiding bringing attention to any of our group by getting involved in a brawl, though I had a broad smile across my face at the time, apart from the fact we may become injured, therefore no use as a fighter as a result, we did not want added attention from anyone to our men.

It was getting towards the end of the day now, so we began getting the men together to leave town so as not to draw attention to ourselves. We made our way out and began leaving to where we had hidden our equipment and horses. We had left the rest of our men with them to look after them, feed, water and a graze which they had more than earned, this area was surrounded by woods, they had let the horses graze for a time, then taken them under the cover of the trees, which made it a useful point to stop for a time.

We then headed off into the local densely packed forest, with a good bit of low bushes, trees and grass at the edge in which we could pass the night with ease. We found a good place between Wisbeach and March to the left of the track we used towards Elm, and settled down for the night. The horses were a little unsettled but they became at peace in the end.

It took an age to get everyone together, when spread out we covered a huge area, I contacted the leaders of each group to make sure all was well, and sent out our scouts to make sure no enemy approached.

Unknown to us at this time, the enemy group charged with destroying us had not been far behind. Goodness knows how they managed to keep track of us. We thought we had been so careful, evidently we had much more to learn. Somehow word had been passed when our small group had been in Wisbeach that we could be part of the fighters that were causing them so much trouble, so someone had followed us on leaving town. That fight had cost us dear, bringing attention on us!

Chapter 49

In the night, I was woken by one of the scouts, he had heard some voices not far from where he was hiding. I quickly woke and got another of the leaders to come with us, this particular scout had never let us down so I was more than a little worried.

We crept over to the left of where he was hidden and crawled into the low bushes. Sure enough you could make out distinct voices and they were definitely not speaking English, so we were in deep trouble again it seemed, it was just a matter of how much, how many soldiers were there and what arms they had. And, of course, were they aware we were here and was their purpose to attack and attempt to kill us all! There could be no other reason for them being here.

We quickly retraced our steps, crawling, as we went through our ranks we shook everyone to wake them and get them ready for battle, explaining where they would be coming from and that we had no idea of just how many enemy there were.

We had heard horses whinnying, our shield walls would have to be impregnable. With any luck they would not be able to use horses, too dark at the moment, though there was some light in the sky, there was much low bush and trees. We prepared our bowmen to fire on command from myself. The moon kept coming and going with the clouds so we were constantly trying to make out shapes of soldiers coming our way. The trees did not help a lot either, they shut out the moonlight at times.

We had time to sort out our battle lines, but only just, as there was definite movement up ahead.

They were in range easily, so I shouted fire! With a great schoosh, the first arrows were off, they made a lot of noise in the silence of the night, I was surprised at that. We could not be sure how far they were away but the arrows hit home as the cries of the Normans, as they took arrows into their bodies, was remarkable, though not good to hear. Damn this war, the Normans had much to answer for! An awful lot of trees took arrows as well.

I called on our bowmen to fire at will and hoped they would continue to hit home, the cries and the cussing became more and more evident that we were still getting them. They simple did not expect us to be ready for them, luck was again with us, good soldiering as well I had to admit. I should add good scouting was with us!

The Normans who were left standing, were ordered to attack us again, they did not seem very keen on the idea, but attack they did. We formed our shield wall and held it no matter what they did to try and dislodge our men, we had some men at the rear who began hurling spears into them, this was very effective, from our point of view.

The remains of that first attack began falling back to their lines, they were followed by our arrows, harassing them as they went. Another line of soldiers came forth to try and break our wall, only to be rebuffed again. Perhaps the leader of this enemy force was out of alternatives, he was certainly losing a lot of men for no gain.

Our whole line straightened up and seemed to stand firmer, impressive and very determined our men had to be, if we had any chance of survival. I couldn't really refer to them as boys any more, they were well trained, very fit, and very strong men ready to do battle, ready to take on the best of the best. As the clouds moved we got a pretty good view of where and how we stood.

These Normans were no slouches, they hurled their men at our wall. Not one member of our team let us down, as they crashed into it. In doing this the enemy could not get close enough to use their swords against us, our men behind the shield line threw spear after spear into them, through slight gaps in the wall they cut into the enemy who came close, making them constantly wary.

The battlefield was getting congested now, injured and dead all over the place, some animals and men shared the mess.

Then the enemy sent in more men and a whole lot more arrows flew towards us, we held up our shields and mostly they brushed harmlessly away or became embedded in the shields. A couple of our men who were hurling spears into them were hit by their arrows.

Our shields consisted of a line of men and shields to front the enemy crouched down, then a line as another group stood behind and held their shields overhead to form a double wall, ahead and above.

The new onslaught of soldiers was more of a problem though they hurled themselves against our wall again and did not stop.

We were now all in our defensive wall, apart from a few who were still throwing spears, I shouted to the men to stand firm but if a chance arose to stab the enemy between the shields then go for it. This confused the French to begin with and we caught more than a few to put them out of the fight.

We began moving forward, slowly to begin with, the horses had gone back to their lines to regroup, so we went further and further, hitting more enemy as we went. Blasted bodies of Frenchmen all over the field of battle, they were in the way of our movement forward! Though they were dead, and out of the game, they still caused us problems!

One of the leaders noticed movement at the end of our line, it appeared Normans were going to try and come around the side and rear of our main line, this was tricky as we did not want to shorten it. I called for thirty men to move to cover the side from attack, thirty more from my end of the line to do likewise. It proved a very wise move, lucky our man, Xander Brightcard, had noticed the movement in the first place, the two brothers did not ever miss much, him and

Zack were making a name for themselves, good, strong, thoughtful and disciplined soldiers.

We then saw more horses going round the side of our line of defence, perhaps to attack the sides or rear or indeed both sides of our force. We could not allow that, it could be the end!

I turned twenty of my men to face backwards from each end, we had a few minutes to adjust and they were upon us again.

So, we had enemy with swords and spears on the ground plus men on horseback with the same, we also were being attacked at the rear and sides. Our soldiers in the middle were still throwing spears at the enemy, though there were not many left now, spears or men. As we moved forwards we collected some already thrown before, which was helpful! With replenished stock they threw some more along with their arrows.

The enemy at the front seemed to be losing strength, we had dispatched most of them which was excellent in the near darkness.

Perhaps these enemy had heard of our exploits and thought they may catch us unaware at night and find us an easy target while at rest, they had perhaps better think again!

Suddenly, a horn sounded and first the horses returned to their lines followed by the men on foot, they looked a rabble now, dispirited and weary from a night of hard work, losing!

A lot of shouting came from the direction of the enemy, we just sorted out our lines and cleared the dead from our path. I had no doubt they would attack again as there seemed to be many more soldiers waiting to fight, this was more than a little alarming!

Chapter 50

In the Midst of Battle!

Now they came again, at least three lines brandishing their swords and shouting. They had no new ideas so they floundered against our wall, quite a few died by our spears and arrows on the way and again by our swords that flashed out of our shield wall, killing or maiming, the rest returned into the night.

This was a dreadful scene, though we couldn't actually see a great deal of it but it was going to have to be fought up and down the country if we were going to rid our land of these dreadful enemy soldiers.

All were tiring now, we were obviously winning as well so we just kept on with the fighting, though it was getting harder as time went on. The three lines of enemy had been dispatched, just the odd soldier wandering around in a world of his own. The last roll of the dice appeared to be yet more horses coming along to join the fight so we prepared our defences to not yield an inch. Our line stood strong but it was taking one hell of a battering, we were all of us fighting for our lives, and were by now even more exhausted. I had no doubt that we would have been finished if we were only the original sixty odd fighting men in our force, they would have killed us all by now I felt sure.

Somebody or something was prompting me and my decisions I was beginning to think or had I just been lucky! One of Cedrics men was fond of telling everyone I was being guided from above! That certainly was an interesting view as I confided with Cedric and he smiled. I lot of our men gained confidence through these comments through the ranks so it was no bad thing. Anything that gave us an edge over the enemy had to be good.

The line of men attacking was becoming less and less, still a lot of noise coming from them, crying out, mostly in despair now as they made no real progress.

A bugler sounded for retreat to the Normans and they were quick to take up the call, they severed all links with the fighting and pulled away, back to their lines, accompanied by quite an amount of cheers from us, with plenty of arrows following them as well.

To give them no quarter, I called for my bowmen to begin sending in more arrows and they were very effective at this range. They soon realised they were too close, as many more men fell, and moved further away, we could just make them out from a noise point of view. It sounded as though there were not many left now.

The tiredness began setting in now, dead and injured everywhere, not a pretty sound or sight. We would have to get more used to this, though it did not seem to get easier with time. The noise of the battle had been dreadful though we did not think about this until afterwards. In the still of the night and the silence after this fighting the atmosphere was strange. The only noise was of soldiers moaning because of their injuries.

What a waste of life! And time, come to that. We should all be busy earning our keep, possible raising families etc.

My Lady!

I could be spending time with Lynelle, hopefully understanding the amount of the day I seemed to be spending thinking of her. Was she the love of my life? I certainly hoped so! She certainly was an important reason to continue fighting, the immediate future of my life was, fighting, and hoping she was well, then more planning and more fighting and yes, more hoping she was well! it was quite a combination, I can tell you!

Hoping we could be together, when peace was the order of the day. She had a grace about her that was charming, a laughter that was lovely, and a smile that was always with me. She warmed my heart when all about me was cold and death.

I could imagine no life without her! Was I being a little silly to think of such things at a time like this? Odd how one's mind worked? A sort of self-preservation, to think of something completely different at a time of great stress.

Move Out

I called to all to quickly get our equipment together and take any spoils we wanted from the dead, we had fared very well for the amount of enemy we had dispatched.

We had lost twenty men in total, the most we had lost in all our fighting. We were down to eighty one soldiers now in total, we would have to get the number up to at least 116 again as we had become used to using that number in battles.

I sent men out to collect as many arrows, lances etc. as we could find. I was thinking of another large increase in the number of men, possible, in the not too distant future.

It was much easier than I had expected to fight with the increase in our numbers we had made from Boston.

Maybe I could send Cedric out as leader of an entirely new group, there's a thought! Two groups of the Boston Defenders, maybe 200 strong each, we would surely begin to make a mark against the damned enemy then. Cedric came to where I was and asked if I was all right. I explained what I was thinking and he thought much the same but he also felt I was protecting myself from thinking of our dead by thinking of more battles and many more soldiers. He was probable right, he knew me too well!

That did not take away the fact that it was the way forward!

New Leaders

Two more leaders of men were coming to the fore, Zack and Xander Brightcard, from Cedrics group of fighters, or one of the others, as I must admit to becoming confused as we were so many now! They began by training longer than anybody else, and then they became great in the fight, beating all before them. They then began suggesting plans to trap and settle battles before even Cedric had suggested what to do, he often said they made his job so easy he need not be there most of the time. I believe I mentioned this before but they continued to stand out from the rest, so I felt it worth mentioning again! the reference again being in these notes so I have repeated them here.

They were put forward to lead the next group available. Good to see new blood making a way for themselves, we would make sure they were rewarded as an example to all.

Losing men from my force was an awful thing, Cedric and I had problems dealing with this as it was a dreadful waste of good men, men who would be needed for the future of our country once we were rid of the Normans. Though this was all a long way off it seemed at the moment, it was an important thought.

The long term future of our kingdom was of the utmost importance. As we did not have a kingdom at the moment we had some way to go before it became relevant.

I felt for them all and their families as we moved off in the direction of Ely.

We left Elm and travelled back into the deeper water towards March. It soon became really heavy going as we slowed almost to a standstill by the depth of the water and the bog. Eventually, one of the scouts came in and told us he had made out the dry land on which March was on having crossed the river Nene. There was a track section of land out of the water and he told us it was the remains of the Roman causeway that travelled from Stanground, near Peterborough, to near Denver, close to Downham Market this was some sixty feet across. In its day it must have been a great help to all who lived or just travelled through the area. Nothing defeated the Romans in those days, or I should say, their slaves!

For all their faults, and the Romans had many, they brought much progress and enterprise to their empire. We lined up on this causeway and managed to get a little dryer, which was a relief for a moment or two, only to plunge back into the deep water again.

Stonea Island

Our next dry land would be the Island that was Stonea, providing we could find it through the tall, thick reed beds. There was evidence of a very old settlement there of earlier humans and Roman remains of their headquarters for the entire waterways area, the remains of their buildings were apparent. It was a very good area to camp for the night. As always we were tired as it was such heavy going through the water and bog.

We made dry land at last so we prepared fires and began our ritual of obtaining food from the area, ducks and fish were in abundance, needless to say they were not so abundant when we left!

We were still nursing wounds from the last battle so a number were spared any duties and were left sitting by the fires, some cutting wood for the fires if they could.

I felt a real sense of history for our land, when on a site such as this and Cedric joined me in this view, a really special place set in the silence of our waterways. We just wished the Normans had not ruined our present existence here!

After we had all cooked and eaten well, we sat and talked of our ambition for this country and just how bad things looked for the near future and how we hoped to change the outlook for the country as a whole. As leaders we all walked amongst our men and encouraged them to tell us how they felt and what they thought we could achieve. Not many of them disagreed with our plans, some thought they were over ambitious, pointing out the strength of the enemy.

We would have to work on changing their view I said to the group of leaders and all agreed. I encouraged all to come up with ideas to improve our training, where we could pick places to organise fights in the future and where we could perhaps get more men to fight with us. We must look forward to constructing training bases up and down the country with new groups of fighters, we were all getting excited at this prospect. To us the future was plain to see. A lot of recruiting, training, organising and fighting. The evening and sleep took us with the darkness after we settled. Survived another hard day!

Langwood Hill

We left Stonea and travelled towards Langwood Hill, the ground was very boggy and inundated with water here, the reed beds were solid and a job to get through but I felt we needed to get a little lost, away from it all for at least a few hours.

Travelling through this section of the waterways was very slow going as it was so thickly embedded with reeds, it took some time to all arrive on the dry ground of the hill. We may have to fight more to get entry onto the Isle so a bit of an unwind was called for. Some time to regain our strength was imperative.

We Had Some Food Left Over so That Was Quickly Consumed

More was quite quickly caught and we settled down with some good warm fires and began to unwind, the cold wind was really bad, and the rain had started again. Extra spare jackets were distributed to all. Cloudy and pretty miserable was the order of this day now.

We were all subdued, conversation was not easy, but as we rested and had our food we began to settle and begin talking about the fighting.

That had been pretty ferocious as battles go, and we did not want too many of them, heavy hand to hand fighting. Though we had won, we had all lost friends who we would really miss, this was not good as we had become a community on the move and we were hurting.

The more we talked about it we realised that this was what we had to look forward to on the Isle, sending raiding parties out to the enemy and defending our island against William and his men.

Surely this was not the way forwards!

All of us must take the fight to the enemy, it was simple no use just sitting back and trying to keep William at bay. That was no future, it was failure and we wanted none of that!

We did not know what Herewards forces consisted of on the Isle but from what little we had heard they sounded very strong, he and his men were defending well but at some cost. No matter what, we would find out soon enough,

We got some good rest as we were all tired out. We all prepared to move on after food, we were refreshed again and ready for the next challenge, we hoped.

Our scouts had reported movement of the enemy to the edge of the wild and deep waterway, so we might end up with another fight on our hands. We hoped we had dealt with his main force yesterday, so it may be little more than a skirmish. All of us would have to wait and see.

Our scouts were at the front, sides and rear these days. We relied on them as our eyes and ears and they did not let us down, at least they had not done so to date! Following the battle we made sure they were out a lot further around us, giving us more time to prepare ourselves in possible defense.

These men were always sent out in twos now, their work was so important, it guided us in all we did, we had not lost one in battle yet but if we did we had to make sure at least one of them would get word back to us.

The Normans may have lost us, or just marked where we had entered the waterway/fen, and were waiting for us to exit somewhere. They may have a large force waiting for us so we had better be prepared for that eventuality, I warned everyone there could be trouble around the next clump of reeds so to be prepared to fight again at a moment's notice.

Wardy Hill

There was a hill, Wardy, in front of us and a couple of us decided to go and see if we could see anything from the top. It was more of a slope than a hill, but in these flat lands they gave us an advantage over the bogs and reed beds. This hill was a real job to get to as there was a wide and deep flow of water between us and it which we had to get over. Having accomplished this we scrambled to the highest point, very wet and cold even when travelling on horseback.

We could see from the hill that the Isle was ahead of us. It still seemed an awful long way across the massive reed beds that were so thick and tall, plus the water and bogs. It was almost like another world. As our horses entered the water we became so low compared to the huge reed beds around us we could see nothing but reeds, it was more than a little disconcerting. We called out to all the force to join us on Wardy Isle/Hill and spent the rest of the day at rest as we were in need!

We hoped we could be a major part of this other world on the fabled Isle in the near future.

We had nearly reached our destination at long last. Would we ever get there?

How many men would we lose trying? These were difficult questions and they were endlessly on our minds! All of us leading our men were concerned with trying to avoid any more fights before entering what had become our Isle. We knew that William and his men would throw every soldier he could muster at stopping our entry. Our future was looking more and more difficult the more we looked at it!

Our point of entry was on the other side of the island, so we would have to skirt around the opposite end, and hopefully not be seen, the enemy must know we were trying to join up with Hereward and he would do almost anything to stop that happening.

If we did get through, he would have a whole lot more trouble on his hands. An extra force for him to contend with, this would alter his whole army movements, it would stop him taking over the whole country. We would give him no peace in "his" new kingdom, of that I was sure!

The scout we had sent on to tell Hereward we were on our way must, we hoped, have reached him and he would hopefully send out a few of his men to guide us through the bogs and waterways to get us onto dry land, keeping our losses to a minimum.

Our force was together again and we told and showed them how close we were, plus the enemy that might be between us and our Saxons and Britons. We would have to go around to our left through the fen reeds to avoid detection and make our way to the other side, around the Littleport end of the Isle, hopefully without seeing anyone. There was little hope of getting through anywhere in this area, enemy eyes seemed to be everywhere! Even if they were not it was good to imagine they were for the sake of safety for us all.

There was a small track which we followed, on Wardy Hill, it led towards the island on which Chatteris stood. It was a quite large settlement, on ground just above the fen. We rode trying to make no noise as we went for fear of disturbing anyone or anything, a flock of birds going up would cause a problem, it may well give away our position, we had no doubt the enemy knew we were about this area by now, they may even be bringing up reinforcements at this moment to stop us in our tracks. We turned to our right towards Manea just before the huge waterway we had ridden/swam across.

We could see a place slightly out of the water with just a couple of houses on it, over the top of the reeds, but the fen was deep and boggy, as it seemed to be everywhere here, so we continued on our rather slow way. This was very frustrating as the crow flies we did not have that far to go. The water level was very high at this time. Very little land at all. All of us were very wet and bedraggled now as it was raining heavily, the cold wind made things worse. The reed beds were like a forest, especially from water level, they towered over us all.

From here we discovered we could not get directly where we needed to reach the Isle which was a real bind, the combination of reeds, bog and water were just too thick. We could plainly see why William had not been able to take these islands under his control.

Manea

Our only hope was to go towards the island of Manea, where for whatever reason the reed beds were not so thick and would hopefully enable us to go around the far end of the Isle near where Littleport was, it would be on our left, or so we thought. It was much further away from where we thought it was so it took an age to find. Though we were on horseback we were low in the water so our view of the area was, as always, really bad. Just water and banks of reeds were our view as usual. We had to cross the huge waterway again to reach Manea which on reflection was a waste of time; we had in fact become somewhat lost.

I have talked about how difficult it was to travel through these waterways between islands and this proved it, anyone could lose their way here! If we had travelled closer to the Isle of Ely we could have avoided crossing the main waterway again. The reed beds here were impenetrable, set in the deep bog, so we could never have got through to the refuge. This added considerable to our time.

Plus the fact that it was damned cold and wet, so we were not pleased at making such a mistake. A lesson learned, we simple must use our scouting network to find the best way to reach a destination before we attempt to get there. These conditions were, of course, a one off in particular to this point in this area. The area around Ely was as good as cut off, almost like another world, as I have already mentioned.

We even thought we had perhaps gone the wrong way at one point. We thought we had lost Manea altogether. All of us had to take a chance the movement in the reeds we created by our passing would not be seen so we spread out to find out where we were. We all just about kept in touch with each other, only just.

All of us had several hours of being lost, wet, confused, worried and very cold. This was not a good combination!

A number of our men to our left cried out in anger as we could hear a commotion from them. It turned out the enemy had stationed soldiers on Manea to try and find out where we were. Arrows could be heard slewing through the air, cries could also be heard, possible from our men being hit, I quickly called all to come to where we were.

Would These Enemy Never Give Us a Break?

I asked all to spread out around the island, I sent a scout to view the place as to how many enemies were in position.

There could not be many as it was only a small island, surely! Apparently there was quite an enemy camp established but the numbers difficult to tell accurately.

The scout returned and it appeared there was not much cover on the island so the enemy could not hide very well. If they chose to stay and fight we could surely dispatch them with arrows relatively easily.

The reed beds went right up to the bank of the island that was Manea so we approached with as much stealth as we could muster. We could clearly see some enemy soldiers so we began firing into them, as some fell those left dropped back to the tree line and took cover.

When our men from the other side began firing into the enemy, they found they had dug a ditch near the trees and they settled into the cover provided. They would therefore be a job to finish off.

I did not want to get involved in yet another drawn out sword fight but it looked like the only way we were going to clear this place. I said to Cedric we did not want to think the enemy could get this close again and threaten the Isle, to which he readily agreed! We would see to it that a number of our men would be placed here to tell us of any enemy approaching in future, on a permanent basis, then we would be forwarned!

I sent out another of our men to tell the men on the other side of the island to look out for a single arrow shot in the air as a signal to attack, a time after that we would launch an attack from our side as well, so hitting them from both sides.

After a time we sent up the signal, we could hear and see some arrows being sent up as the other men attacked.

All of us could hear the skirmish unfolding as the enemy were surprised. Our arrows that we continually sent onto the island from our side to act as distraction had worked well.

We moved forward as a whole unit, well most of it, out of the wet and onto the bank of Manea, spreading out all along the front of it. Some arrows came our way but they were now in hand to hand fighting with our fellow invaders from the other side. The horses shook off the water and we attacked. They were glad to be out of the water as well as us, as it was damned cold!

Most of the enemy were fighting the other side of the island, some turned to be mown down by our force. As a skirmish it did not take a great deal to finish so we quite soon finished it, without loss of life on our side.

Just a few more injuries were all we were left to contend with!

There was quite a defence trench dug here, which could be used by us another time we noted. This trench work was utilised by us when we sent our men to defend it. We made it a lot bigger and deeper and it became a practice we used in quite a number of battles. It was not only good defence but it also kept out the quite dreadful wind and snow that was thrown at us at times.

I said to Xander, who was by my side at the time, that we should station a group of Saxons here for our defence which he agreed. We could see the land mass that was the Isle of Ely easily from here, it did not seem far off as the crow flies but it was going to prove to be a job actually setting foot there. A huge amount of tall thick reed beds we could not see through at water level made moving around anywhere almost impossible! When you were low in the water on horseback these beds might as well have been huge trees as you could easily become lost as if in an impenetrable forest. Guesswork was the order of the day!

So we quickly set off again, back into the water, bog, mud, river and reeds.

Now there was no chance of being able to see any land or Littleport itself as the reed beds blanked everything out. We trudged slowly through the bog here, some places were blocked, reeds, bog and water and then some more!

As we scrambled through the reed beds, we heard some horses approaching, they were travelling quite fast. As fast as the water would let their horses move, that is with little care as to who might be about, which I thought was very careless.

If it was the enemy, they would soon die and if it was anything to do with us they would be reprimanded on the spot for being stupid, not thinking, and putting a lot of our lives at risk if they brought the enemy down upon us.

I signalled all to be silent and to stop moving, this took some time, we had just a few moments to wait and see if they were friend or foe!

Book Two

Chapter 51

Entering the Isle at last?........Possible!

We prepared to at least halt whoever it was and find out what was going on. The pressure on us all mounted as the moments ticked by, the sweat on my brow became profuse as the noise of their animals made increasing noise coming through the reed beds, we sat low on our horses and prepared our bows! Just who was coming towards us?

It turned out to be two horses with riders, just who were they? that was the question on all our minds, then with great relief I recognised one more or less straight away as our lead scout. We all heaved a sigh of relief, didn't fancy yet another fight if we could avoid it! the other turned out to be one of Hereward's men. So no more fighting for the moment, at least!

Edric Dickenson.

They had come to lead us onto the Isle. Though Herewards man had great knowledge of the area, they had not been able to locate us and they had been looking for us for some time. The fenland was truly a wilderness, we were 94 strong now and we could not be found even by Herewards men. There was no doubt in my mind that he would have eventually found us but with Williams's build-up of forces trying to kill us off time was of the essence! We needed safety on the Isle and time to unwind.

They had found us more by luck than judgement and it was the best news we had heard in a long, long time, that hopefully we would in fact reach the safety offered by the Isle, was it true that at last the Isle was to greet us as prospective inhabitants?

The chap with our scout was named Edric Dickenson, one of Hereward's men. Most of us leapt off our horses to meet him, crashing about in the water, no thought regarding our security at that moment. He did likewise, much cheering and talking went on, though we were supposed to be silent. It was so good to meet someone from the fabled Isle. He had been fighting from the start and had fought at Hastings with Hereward. I called for silence from everyone as we listened to the him talk and it was interesting, to say the least!

He said talk about us had reached them long ago, if half of what was said was true they were overjoyed to have us join them. It would encourage others to do so he hoped.

Edric confirmed we were the wrong side of the Isle to gain entry easily, though entry was difficult at any time, this was its attraction. If we had gone the

Cambridge side of the Isle there were too many enemy soldiers, we would have problems with major fighting to get through.

More of the Normans had turned up in the last week, probable to try and stop us getting through. They had been placed relatively close all around the Isle, out of the water obviously. We may have to enter little by little, a few horses at a time.

If we went around the outside of the Isle, to the right of where we faced, around the Littleport end, and back towards Ely, the hidden entry through the bogs and reed beds and rivers/floods was there, if we were careful we could gain entry without loss. This sounded much too optimistic! We all knew we had no choice but to give it a go. The future of the Anglo-Saxon Kingdom depended on us and we felt that pressure as never before!

Anyway, we set off on the final leg of our journey, one leg we had hoped we would not have to make, right around the Isle to the other side. Not far now though! Hopefully.

All of us were very silent as we pushed our way through yet more flooded land, quite deep in some places, it was really deceptive. If enemy soldiers were in fact looking for us, as it seemed, then they would be listening and seeing if they could make out regular movement in the reed beds. This was impossible to stop, we had a lot of horses with us. It was decided to go further away from the Isle to make it easier. This was a pain as we just wanted to get onto the Isle, not away from it. We would take a wide circle around the far end thereby keeping our losses at a minimum, at least that was the great hope!

Chatteris

We became close to the island that ran between Chatteris to March, this was near the landing stage for boats from Earith and we could hear a commotion, so approached with care, there was another guard post here checking what was in trailers and on horseback packs. This track petered out some way the other side of Chatteris back into the waterway and you had to travel by boat or maybe horse again to get to March, after landing near Doddington.

Some people were objecting to having their property thrown about in a careless fashion by the soldiers, the Normans were having none of it, put up with it or get beaten and arrested, or worse. This was the order given out.

Our people did not get a great deal of choice so they tried to keep their tempers and carry on with their day as best they could. The Normans confiscated whatever they wanted, hard luck on anyone ! We left our pack horses and most of our men in the huge reed beds well out of sight.

Cedric and I looked down the line of carts moving towards Chatteris and caught sight of some people struggling to carry off various things, they were trying to go through the fen, round the enemy guarded gate and back to their carts further down the road. This was somewhat doomed to failure as there were so many enemy soldiers milling around the area in general.

The thought was of going to stop them, or help them in some way, but, alas, we were a little too slow, and some of the soldiers beat us to it. They charged down upon these poor people and started to beat them senseless, we were all itching to get onto the track and knock the hell out of these enemy. The trouble was it would bring every enemy in the area down upon us, so we stood by and did nothing. This was really not our style and it hurt a great deal, nobody was killed at least.

Somehow we had to get around these soldiers without being seen. This needed some thought, as the track was straight, we could not simply go round a corner and be unseen. We had to have a plan and it would have to work!

We decided to send twenty men towards Chatteris, through the reed beds so unseen by the enemy, to have them go across the track in full view of the enemy, make sure they saw them, and goad them into following, we sent the fastest horses in the hope nobody would get caught.

We planned to meet up at a point further along the track, nearer to where we should turn around in the direction back into the water towards Littleport and head towards our point of entry. That was the plan, though it was some way off.

Our twenty men went off through the reed beds and about a mile along the track they showed themselves, made sure the enemy saw them as they travelled across the track and quickly disappeared amongst the woods and reeds on the other side.

The effect it had on the Normans was incredible, they looked in true amazement that these men should show themselves in broad daylight, obviously they were enemy and up to no good so they left what they were doing and raced after them. They could only have guessed who these men might be but maybe they had been reminded there was a large reward waiting for capturing any enemy, who knows, they sped along as if chased by the devil. Our men were certainly not Norman soldiers in uniform so they were enemy!

Quickly they disappeared into the reed beds and we leapt into action, pushing our horses to get us over the track and hidden by the woods and reed beds again.

There were just eight of the enemy past us on the track now, they followed us immediately, we knew they would chase us so we just waited by the first reed beds to give us some cover, and shot arrows into them without any trouble from them, we took their horses with us by rope, we may need them in the near future or they would be useful on the Isle, who knew at that point?

The bodies we pushed into some low lying bushes to hide them, their compatriots would no doubt discover them some time.

We were able to make good time to the point where we were to meet our men who had gone further up the track to entice the enemy to follow them into the bush. We didn't have much time to wait for their arrival.

But wait, something had gone wrong with our little plan, as they were being chased by an awful lot more enemy than when they went into the reeds.

We very quickly turned to meet them, sending in several volleys of arrows. This dented their stride and at least twenty men hit the ground. They didn't actually stop, they came at us at quite a pace still, swords brandished to kill us if they could, quickly we sent in a lot of spears at great speed which slowed and confused them.

They did not cope at all well now, they were in disarray, so we charged them with swords at the ready, they were pretty much finished when low and behold, another batch of the enemy appeared. Just what was going on! Our plan hadn't considered there maybe many more enemy in the area but we simple hadn't time to check before doing something, anyway we were where we were!! To try and deal with the situation was the only way forward.

They Tried to Split Us Up into Smaller Groups

Where did all these enemy keep coming from, I asked myself, with the thought that they could pick us off as they wished any time with so many soldiers at their beck and call, surely?

We would not be split, I cried out to all. They had a damned cheek trying, I thought, as I encouraged all to fight to the finish, arrows, spears and clashing blades, what a noise, what a fight, absolute exhausting madness!

So much for being silent, we were tired out but had become used to big fights now, and we were not going to lose as we were so close to our destination. Our determination began to show through.

Fight, Fight and more fight was the order given out, a really big bloke came hurtling towards me, no time to think. I attacked and we met with a mighty clash and grunt from him, we passed and turned to clash again. He managed to knock away my sword but as it passed him on his horse, it cut into his left leg and part of his saddle, he had to adjust the way he sat or he would have fallen off.

My horse reared, which took me nearer to him more quickly than he had anticipated and I was able to strike his back, this nearly un-seated him again, he was more than a little miffed and shouted in anger.

I was told to not lose my cool in battle, as you do not get a second chance in this game, concentrate and dispatch your enemy. He fell off his horse and I ran him through with my sword, to shout at that point in a fight is to admit defeat to your foe. I needed little encouragement to defeat this one.

We were all clashing and smashing our way through this batch of enemy, what a difference experience and confidence makes.

Also, our numbers counted as never before, it helped us no end, though there were still many enemy to try and deal with yet.

We had to be quick as we needed to get away from this fight and on our way, the enemy would certainly know where we were now, they had lost yet another batch of soldiers. They were paying dearly for trying to get us and we wanted to make sure we kept them paying.

Some of the lads to my right looked as if they were in trouble, six against two, so I pushed my horse and joined them, just to even up the numbers a little, took two away from them straight away by running one through and clashing blades with the other. This one was about my size but he could move very quickly, he just pulled his horse out of the way of my sword as I thrust it at him and came back brilliantly with a jab, just managed to move my arm in time, but it was too close for my liking, better take this one more seriously!

I pulled my horse several paces away from the fight to give myself a second and a bit of room, I think he may have though I was removing myself from this fight so he confidently launched himself at me but I easily brushed his blade away and proceeded to cut his arm as we passed. He was in pain and annoyed now so I felt I had the upper hand. I was proved wrong as he brandished his sword at me and hurled his horse at me with such speed that he caught me out, he hit my sword with such power that he knocked it out of my hand, perhaps it was my turn to cry out, but I didn't.

I used my left hand to immediately pull out my dagger and as he followed through with his sword action, I neatly pushed it into his throat, killing him quickly. Again I note these killings with more than a degree of horror now as I sit here recording these details, some from memory but most from these notes.

I still have dreadful nights when I am reminded of all this violent, dreadful killing. To kill or be killed was the order of things at this time, it was not good however you looked at it! I would far rather be in my sleepy fen area getting on with my life!

I cried out to all to not let any enemy get away as I didn't want any telling them what had happened here, or which direction we had taken from this place.

Chapter 52

Hand to Hand Fighting Continues

More hand to hand fighting ensued, it was bloody, but we were on the winning side, so became stronger and stronger, until we had wiped out this assault.

No time to do anything but move on, quickly, so although we were exhausted from the fighting adrenaline kept us going as we were really trying to move fast now, cantering along in the water to try and get to a place where we could get onto the island, ………..still some way away. Maybe to even find some peace at last, that would be good. A nights rest without feeling constantly on edge, what bliss that would be! not having to spend some part of each night guarding our camp would be bliss!

We were only cantering, as we were aware our horses had done several days' work today and the water was quite deep and boggy, so it was hard going for them and it was certainly faster than walking, plus it kept us out of the wet. Our plan was to head towards the Isle from here, the Doddington end of the March island. We had no idea what lay between us and the Isle, we were disorientated by our surroundings and we gave no thought to who saw us at the moment as to a certain extent we were beginning to think we could beat anybody, though if numbers were against us we knew we would be overrun, that was a fault we were going to put right on joining with our fellow fighters.

Though I had to admit we were still way off where I thought we should be from a fighting perspective, we needed to train even more than we were at present. Training and fighting real battles was the way forward Cedric and I felt sure. You never stop learning was a favourite mantra of my fathers and I held to that each and every day.

As we won fights, our strength and confidence rose no end. We ended that day settled on an island which was very secluded and secure, all exhausted!

We swam, or rather our horses did, over some very deep sections of fenland. Some parts were open river, huge amounts of water travelled through here on its way to the North sea.

The fens, as a whole, were the sink, for no less than thirteen counties rainwater, I think most of it was flowing through this section at this moment. It flowed fast, wide, deep and very boggy! The only good thing about it was that it provided the security we needed from the enemy and it would give us time to train and organise ourselves to take back our land.

For us all to get through was an achievement in itself. I was very glad we had our guide to assure us we could get to the other side. This waterway we faced right now was daunting as it appeared so vast, deep and fast flowing water. It was not a good combination when you no alternative but to cross it somehow! The first of us set off across then, we were in the open so we hoped there was nobody watching though it was so very wild I couldn't think anybody could possible be here, as was the case. The speed and depth of the water was deceptive and it unnerved the horses as well as ourselves, this was difficult as we calmly tried to encourage the animals. Edric had gone ahead to show it could be done and it helped a great deal as our progress was slow for some time. Eventually my group reached the other side as well thankfully and we called others to follow.

After what seemed as age we were all over on the far bank with our pack horses, all very wet and a little uncertain we moved off again following Edric cautiously. How deep was the next bog we might come across? Clearly we had no idea!in the backs of our minds were the comments we had heard of horses and indeed boats disappearing altogether, never to be seen again, though logic dictated this could never actually be the case, who really knew! We were riding into the unknown most of us having never been in this area before.

I was glad to get back into the thick rooted reed beds on the far side of the waterway. We all felt considerable safer once out of the main flow once again.

Edric assured us that was the worst section between us and the safety of the Isle and we were very pleased to hear this was the case..

Littleport

We travelled around Littleport, away from the island as you could just not get close and made our way towards Brandon where the track we were going to use to get back towards Ely, all of us had settled back into our groups of twenty, there was no track to follow, just gaps in the reeds where horses had been through, as we were in water all the way now, some really deep, some not so. Back to our beloved fens, for the forty of us that came from here, or where does this damned water end for the new men, it depended on how you looked at it.

I kept thinking, we were still 116 in total number, alas we were not. We would have to increase our numbers back to our full complement as soon as possible. Again, I was thinking of another group of perhaps 200 for Cedric to command, I had talked of this to him, he thought it was a little too soon, didn't feel confident as yet.

I thought to myself, chuck him in at the deep end, I knew he would do well.

Maybe, we could get a batch of Herewards men to train up to our standard, that may well work. Two groups of "Boston Defenders", each 200 strong, then maybe some more to add to that! We could become a whole army, "The Isle of Ely Army". Cedric and I did not lack ambition! This was felt to be more of an appropriate name too. Even maybe "The Great Saxon Isle of Ely Army".

That had a Certain Ring to it

The river was in full flow, a mighty water to those who had not seen it before, we had to cross a river to get to where we wanted. We struggled on through the water as best our horses could, very slowly encouraging them as we went. Some of the men slid off into the water, holding the bridles of their mounts, less weight for the animals, helping them over the worst parts. Deep, sometimes, swirling water was not what these animals were used to so it was difficult to deal with, for them and us!

Eventually, we all crossed and were very glad to have done so. We pulled ourselves together and set off on the next leg of what had seemingly become a never ending battle of one sort or another. It would hopefully end with us all gaining land on the Isle, dry at last!

Possible Entry onto the Isle, at Long Last!

Apparently, according to Edric, once we found the track which led from Brandon towards Ely, travelling became a little easier, the track then died out in the water, or appeared to at least, therefore it ceased being a track, surely? I had my doubts about this! We were assured that it was the very tried and tested way of gaining entry, not only that but it was the only way, so choice was out of the question! All we could do at the end of the day, was follow, so we agreed to do just that.

We continued on our way towards Brandon which we began to feel was in the wrong direction, we knew it was but we were assured by Edric that it was the best way to find the track, the fastest way was the best way to get to our refuge, unseen by others. I agreed with him but it still rankled that we were going away from Ely! We found an island and settled as our horses were exhausted. Edric told me not to worry and we would soon be in the right place to turn and go for home as it were.

We settled for a time and began drying out which made us all feel better, some warmth returned to our cold and wet bodies, pushing the reeds away from the horses to help them through the reed beds had made a lot of our hands bleed which added to our discomfort.

After a time, Edric called me over to him to explain that the track was not more than a few hundred yards away to our right, which I was very pleased about. It certainly was not a track I had ever thought could be described as such but you could make out a few horse marks in the bog, he assured me things would get better as we progressed! I hoped he was right, though we still had our doubts, I can assure you.

From this point which we reached there was deep water, provided we were careful, in not more than two horses at a time we could gain entry to the Isle. We were a long way from safety still but we were on our way at last! Our spirits began to rise as we became engulfed in yet more reed beds, it was indeed a forest.

It would take a long time, but it could be done, guards would have to be set at several points to protect us, in case the Normans found out what we were up to, they would be looking now, all over the area as they must have found their dead and be even more annoyed, if that were possible!

There were thick reed beds a plenty in this area so we sent men in groups to stay in complete silence in them, or on small islands, the horses did not like staying in water but it was the price to pay, if they became unsettled then men looked after them, by stroking their heads and talking to them.

They seemed to know what was expected of them at all times, these wonderful animals. They had become pets, friends and battle ready work horses all in one. Provided they were set somewhere to feed and drink at the end of the day they were incredible animals, an asset to any force.

The guards were set in place in groups of four, with plenty of extra arrows, clean water and food. Then we would begin sending men onto the Isle as it would be a slow process I had no doubt. It may be a long stay for the guards! Cedric and I, and the other leaders, arranged to go between them at times to make sure all was well, to add to their number if and when needed.

I thought it would be good for moral as I did not want them to think they were being left out too long alone. They were all very good fighters, with bows swords and axes, I pointed this out to them, I am sure they felt better as a result, being the best of the best is no bad title and with us backing them up we were beginning to feel confident as the day progressed.

One of the problems we faced was the amount of mud/bog we stirred up, as more and more horses rode through the area it would be relatively easy to trace for the enemy.

In the worst sections, we decided to cut a lot of reeds, tie them, and lay them in the fen, ride our horses over them, thus not stirring up the mud too badly. We simple had to try something and this worked pretty well. The one problem it was causing was that it took a lot of time, time we really did not have. The enemy would be getting closer every moment. Edric encouraged us in our endeavour, whilst lending a hand as best he could.

We were having to cut the reed from a long way off so as not to give our position of entry to the Normans, bring it back on foot, if that were possible, so as to not cause the mud movement that horses caused, tie it in bundles, put it in place, then walk a horse to tread it in. It was very frustrating time wise but it did seem to work and our confidence became stronger as we got on with the task.

We all felt we had no choice, this was an awful lot of extra work for my men, who were already tired out, we all of us settled into a routine and we became much quicker at it, working together, almost as one, it was really good. We were so consumed in our work that we were slow to realise the sound of arrows being unleashed not too far away.

The lads were busy again, ambushing a number of the enemy no doubt, the noise didn't last for long, I was glad to note. A bit of splashing noise was quite clear as the lad's probable removed the dead from the scene, then they would have to lead away their horses to remove all evidence.

We were just about ready after such a long time it seemed, to lead on our first men and horses onto the island. It was a great moment for us all, particularly myself as it had been my idea to begin with.

We said goodbye to our first two lucky lads. Off they went, to our Saxon refuge, no rushing so the minimum amount of stirring in the water, then they were gone and it was the turn of the next guys, on and on, they went, following very close to each other so the horses knocked the cut reeds into the fen.

It was time for us to check and make sure all our guards were all right, the ones that were sent towards Cambridge were not troubled. The ones who were protecting the way we had come were not so lucky. The furthest one out had dispatched twenty of the enemy as they had come in search of us, they were silly appearing in small groups as surely they knew they had little chance of fighting us and winning. This was our home turf, after all.

We hoped they would not learn the error of their ways!

As always it may be that the enemy were being offered money for information leading to our deaths or capture, so a few finding us may be rewarded rather than a lot of soldiers, or maybe finding our route onto the isle, that may explain it, we were never going to know anyway.

Yet another fight!!

The scout/guard we had sent out towards Cambridge rushed up to us in a state of panic and exclaimed that he was sure a number of enemy soldiers were on the way, so we had better get as many men over to the Isle as possible, and prepare to fight, yet again!

This was very disappointing, as we were doing really well, number wise. On reflection, we should have counted the men as they left, I actually had no idea how many had gone onto the Isle, we were all too excited was my excuse. Bad leadership on my part, made a note to not do that again!

I sent six men to go and give us an idea of how many were coming, four of the lads with me kept helping more and more get over and I and ten other men went to see what was going on regarding the fighting towards the Littleport/Feltwell area.

There was a lot of sword play, you could hear the clashing, and groaning from the victims, quite a number of bodies were lying all over the area, I did not recognise any so I hoped none of our men were down.

The fighting was taking place in a pretty narrow place, so it was difficult for us to lend a hand, however we did just that as we had to do something to take the pressure off our men. We took out a few enemy with arrows, they took a look at us and began to cease the fight and move back to their lines, which were through several thick batches of reeds and across a stretch of water.

We quickly followed and were amazed to see just how many Normans there were waiting to fight. They could only come in small numbers as there was no space for people to move about, let alone fight, a good place for us to set the trap we had, by design, of course,.... well possible! As being truthful it was more luck than judgement.

Chapter 53

Enemy Feltwell force.
We went back into the wilderness of the reed beds and began firing arrows into the enemy, you simple could not miss, they were so tightly packed. Many cries could be heard, they began to thin out, back towards Feltwell, we kept firing our arrows, they began to fire back now, though they could not see us, we moved back into the fen to avoid problems, where too many arrows came our way we protected ourselves by using our shields as best we could, inevitable some of our men were injured.

Our fingers and arms were getting sore now as a result of constant firing, we felt we had to keep going as the further we sent them back towards Feltwell the more time we had to get security on the Isle.

We could hear "battle" noise coming from behind us, our lads must be taking some stick from the Normans that had come from the Cambridge direction. What to do, we could not be in two places at once, the trouble was, we must do something.

I decided to take fifteen men with me, and for the time being leave these brave lads to take on the huge force facing us here. To be honest the enemy had no idea how many of our forces were here, they just faced an almost constant onslaught from our arrows, I hoped they could keep it up while we were gone.

The fifteen of us, Cuthbert Damian, Morris Kynaston, Jo Jo Jepson, and Martin Marmaduke and of course myself, plus Alrigh Gebherd, Hall Forester, Wylie Ibbott, Osric Bloodworth, Eleyth, Daegal Adair, Berkeley Betli, Norville Aston, Byron Barrington and Carlyle Chancellor moved as fast as we could through the fen towards the fighting we could hear.

We got past where our point of entry to the Isle was, past quite a few thick reed beds. There was a small open space and it was packed with fighting men, splashing and dying, fighting and crying out in pain. It was not a pretty sight!

This did not look too good for us at this moment as we were outnumbered, I took my bow in hand, slid in an arrow and fired it into a Norman, the other lads did likewise. Fifteen enemies less to worry about, we did this time and again, until some of them stopped fighting and took the time to see where the arrows were coming from. The enemy split in two, as if cut down the middle, and made to close the gap between us and them and take us on with swords. They were quite slow in the water, this enabled us to knock down a lot more of them as they came towards us, through the reed beds.

The ones who got to us were looking very dishevelled, soaking wet, some covered in blood, what a state! `

We took out our swords and parried their attempts to kill us, I took out my little knife and dispatched the first one, then another, then another. This was quite a skirmish; more enemy were coming out of the fen to take us on., some on horseback, some not.

Cuthbert was going extremely well by my side, cutting and thrusting as he went through the Normans. Jo Jo was behind us, firing arrows into the enemy as they appeared from the reed beds. I could not see Martin for the moment as he was a little behind us. The other half of the group of enemy came upon us at this stage of the fight, another major clash as they came at us side on, we were not properly prepared for this as it took us somewhat by surprise. They were a damned tough bunch of warriors but we battled and met them head on. What a fight these men gave us but with a little time we began to overwhelm them.

I could see two of our men down in the water, they were not getting up in a hurry, they had left this world for another I was very sad to see. I hope they took some enemy with them though I suspected they would be going to hell, but then I thought from their point of view they probable thought we were doing likewise, funny old world? …….I know, too much thinking, again!

All the remaining men were now involved in close combat, sword to sword, the whole clearing was full of desperate, very wet fighting men and horses.

Again, the noise was extraordinary, hard to imagine, hard to think of afterwards, in the peace of these fens. Blood and bodies all around. More and more men lunged into the fight area, two were in front of me, one stuck out his sword as if daring me to attack, I needed no second invitation. I knocked his sword down, as I did so I kept the speed of my sword going and hit out at the man by his side.

I damaged his right arm, he quickly lunged at me and very nearly got my left arm, just managed to move in time, I was on quite shallow ground here so I kicked out at the first man, sending him sprawling in the cold water, I thought if that doesn't wake him up, nothing will!

With the forward motion I had, I skilfully, I thought, pushed my sword into the other soldier, killing him. By this time the other fellow had got up, he was not at all pleased with the way things were going, so he attacked me again, I parried his sword behind me and struck him in the chest with my dagger.

Time to move onto the next enemy, I should have noted, no time to move on, as he was trying to get me right away, moving skilfully through the very muddy water, he went for my chest. I turned sideways to move away from the sword and managed to punch him in the jaw with my glove and sword arm, he was so close now it was frightening!

This was no mean feat, especially for me, as I simple don't do things like that, a spur of the moment type of thing, nevertheless it threw him completely as he fell over. Suddenly mud and water where everywhere, mixed with the entrails of battle, none of which were pretty I might add!

Another man attacked me to my right, he thought he had time to finish me, tried to strike me through the side. I jumped back, threw my sword out to move his and stabbed him with my dagger. It was very useful today, I noted in the back of my mind.

Another one down. Still they kept coming. Was this particular brand of madness never going to end? Though it was a lot slower than earlier I thought, perhaps wishful thinking on my part?

Some more of our men appeared from one of the other posts, this was useful as the Normans saw this and seemed to pull back for a moment or two. We used that moment to good effect by attacking with greater ferocity, pushing forward the advantage, more and more, knocking them back further into the fen.

Could we actually win the day? My goodness I was tired, my clothes were soaked and really heavy, it felt as though I was being dragged into the fen bog!

Could we pull this off? The new men who had joined us rode towards them, pushing them away.

They began to pull away then, looking like a defeated rabble right now, not a fighting force any more. Suddenly it seemed there were a lot more of us than them as the remainder of the enemy turned to run. Not that they could run but you know what I mean, I hope. That was a huge relief to us all, we were on our last legs, energy wise, couldn't keep up with that pace for very much longer!

Things quickly settled, we sent the injured men off to get treatment and arranged to carry those off who couldn't walk. We lost some brave souls that day. They had all fought so well and now I couldn't tell them how proud I was, they were fine men and would have helped rebuild our nation, what a dreadful loss!

On the other hand, of course, we had a major victory on our hands and though we were tired out our whole army would benefit from this fight, I would add that that sounds rather filppent and that is far from what I am trying to convey to you, the reader, I hope you understand?

Fighting was still brisk at the other fight site, we prepared ourselves as best we could, took a breather, and went back to battle. Was this madness never going to end?

Cuthbert was still excited about knocking out so many of the enemy, Morris was nursing an injury and insisting he should go on with the fight, no matter what, Jo Jo was moaning about a strike he had taken on his leg and Martin just wanted to wipe out the whole Norman race, rather like every man in this fight! More of our men joined the fight now, we certainly needed the boost they gave us.

Chapter 54

The other lads with us kept reasonable silent, I calmed everyone down, told them all to keep silent, listen for the enemy who could be anywhere, and prepare to enter the next battle with no distraction, no other thought but that of wiping out the enemy. Some of our badly injured were taken by the men who were still riding onto the Isle.

We rounded the last batch of reeds. What a sight, it looked rather like we were taking on the whole world, mind you, we have seen that before and still won the day, somehow!

We began sending in arrow after arrow after arrow, well you get the drift! The enemy fell like nine pins; it was almost funny, though none of these actions were in the least that way!! Funny and fighting simple do not go together.

We were more accurate than the enemy, simple because of our experience to date it seemed.

They should group before going into battle, organise themselves, then try and take us out!

We did not mind if they were led by foolish men, though it did seem very strange, it had lost them a great many soldiers, would they ever catch on?

They caught on to this particular fight quite quickly but only after we had felled a whole batch of them, the main force moved further away and their bowmen moved into range, protected by other soldiers who held shields, they fired at us and took down more of our men, things were getting bad right now! What to do was the question?

Though we took yet more losses, this was not going as well as I had hoped to say the least!! There was no choice but to carry on with the fight, I called out to one of the lads to get some more men from the main group, he rode off very quickly indeed under the circumstances, which were by no means easy and it seemed in no time we had another forty five men with us and that made all the difference as they began to knock down the remaining enemy soldiers, we sent men out to our left and right to go through the reeds unseen and attack them while we constantly fired into the bowmen.

When in place we fired and began moving forwards, the men each side did likewise and we started to crush them together, some realised what was going on as we heard horses running away towards Feltwell through the reed beds, the remaining ones drew their swords and readied to do battle. Spears were being thrown by both sides and I regret to some effect as some of our men were laid low! Theirs also so it was not all bad.

More than I had expected had escaped but it did mean we had less enemy to deal with, though it was far from easy as we began to take control, as arrows,spears, axes and whatever else came to hand was used to diminish these enemy. This constant bombardment took effect and eventually victory again was ours, though our losses were bad I am very sad to have to admit! Luckily the men going onto the Isle had stopped riding through the fenland as they heard the noise of battle become so loud and made up the forty five men who joined our fight.

The brothers, Zack and Xander Brightcard, had been at the front of this fight, I was beginning to wonder where they got their strength from, they never seemed to slow down! They would soon be great leaders of men, no matter what they did with their lives, providing of course they survived the fighting. The way things looked the entire Norman army would not survive their fighting against them! to be honest all the men did really well, especially the leaders. I suppose I note them as they were our only brothers and that thought stuck in my mind as it was brave of their parents to let them both join us in our endevour.

We were feeling the strain now as the pressure mounted on us to finish and get on with the task of entering the Isle, then peace returned to this particular area and we slumped where we stood for some time, when our strength returned, we began looking around for the next attack. Perhaps they were lulling us into a false sense of security, just by thinking we had won the day for a time, then reappearing to try and wipe us out.

Nothing else happened I was very pleased to report so we rose and very loudly cheered each other. What a fight and what a victory!

Many more good men lost, many injured, though we must have killed off at least eighty enemy. Our Strength was now down to the lowest number yet, this was dreadful. We all knew there was no choice but it was very hard to take, so many dead or injured. We were losing men at other points as well. It was always the price we had to pay, we all had to look to the long term. The long term gain, freedom on our Isle, then all of England!

We must now round everybody up that was still outside the Camp and get admittance as soon as possible, it was time we rested, I am sure the enemy would agree!

Slowly, we were in no rush now, as we were worn out by our efforts, we were elated to be here at last, but were weighed down by our losses.

We made our way back to where the track was for getting onto the Isle, we called it a track but it was far from that, we led our horses through the water between small islands. They were not at all used to really deep water, so we had to talk gently to them and try to assure them there was no danger to them, eventually we won them over and they sort of swam over the worst bits being coaxed by us. We had a group of lads that went out onto the fen to clear anything that had been used to get anyone onto the Isle, to leave as little trace of our passing as possible. Mainly the reed mats we had secured in the bog which could in fact be used any time in the future to aid access or entry to our refuge!

Chapter 55

The camp of Refuge at Long Last

Eventually, we were all on the Isle, I couldn't settle until we were, I felt responsible for this whole situation, though it was the damned Normans who really were.

Ely Monastery was vast, no other word for it. Its hospitium and dependencies would start to become more than a little crowded all too soon, as more and more soldiers sought refuge. A lot of priests began to appear, plus families who could not ever see themselves living under enemy rule.

These would have to stop coming here and arrange to go and live where they could be protected as much as possible by our forces in local communities, as we simple could not have space for a huge number of "normal" families on the Isle.

As we expanded our forces we would look after these people, we felt sure. In times of danger they would be shielded by our soldiers. A lot of small islands in the fen were fenced and used, an ever expanding ring of settlements surrounded the Isle on land where we could hopefully protect them when needed.

The Great Hall of the Lord Abbot was filled to the brim with Anglo-Saxon and Girvii nobles, chiefs of great fame and church heads. They all knew they would be maimed or killed if they showed their faces to their foul Norman enemies.

They would all be shouting "Misericordia", oh, mercy on us!, and would be shown none, this enemy had none to give! To kill and control those remaining was their ambition.

Some families were ferried by carricks, skerries any flat bottomed boats to these small islands for them to live on. They would put up with much to be safe. Their diet was fish, fish and more fish, they could of course trade fish for other foods on the Isle. This was, of course, better than being killed, which was the alternative for some!

Those of us who had come onto the Isle earlier had been taken to some buildings where they could get the dirt of battle off them, this they had done and felt much better for it.

They wanted to know what had held us up for so long, when we told them they found it hard to believe. They could hear quite a lot of noise, yelling and clashing of steel against steel, could even see some of the arrows going up into the air and down into the enemy. What they couldn't understand was why had we not called them back to fight with them, they felt sure that would have been the best thing to do.

I explained that I didn't want everyone to get killed, or damaged, I had a responsibility to all. Plus the fact that it would have taken ages to get enough out to make a difference. Everyone agreed in the end. I still had my doubts to be honest, would less of our men have perished? We would never know so let's just get on with fighting and winning this war!

We felt like new men once we had cleaned and rested, I still had trouble with the idea that we were in fact on the Isle at last. We all stood outside, talking about the last fighting, the new boys were exultant in their joy at surviving and killing so many Normans.

We had teamed up well, there was no doubt about that. Things were looking up for the future of the Saxon race, we needed to go and talk with Hereward and the rest of the leaders of the Camp and see if we could organise some kind of national resistance to evict the dreadful Normans from our land.

A Great day

It would be difficult to put our horses into a pen, we tied them with rope to a certain area where our men looked after them, they would want for nothing. This place seemed like a garden of Eden, it was perfect, everything was grown food wise, and cattle were penned in everywhere, all sorts and sizes, fruit trees were all around, fruit bushes too.

Chapter 56

Earl Morcar

Earl Morcar, King Harold's brother, appeared, introduced himself and asking if we, the leaders, would like to meet Hereward and the other leaders.

We jumped at the chance and suggested a time after lunch which was agreed. A time after lunch sounded awfully grand to us as we were used to grabbing food where we fell pretty much exhausted. This was very civilised and would take some getting used to!

He suggested we go and survey the Isle, it was approximately ten miles long by five miles wide, as it depended how much rain had fallen, it dictated how much flood there was. It was a lot larger than we had assumed, the islands we were used to were ones that could just about cope with forty men, to begin with, sleeping, the area we needed to stay together at camp was now huge! But still not on the scale of the Isle.

Kick the Normans Out!

Everyone was of one idea, keeping the Normans out, off the Isle, then challenging them in their back yard and then beating them. Nobody talked of kicking him out of Cambridgeshire alone, we wanted him out of England. We must put our ideas to the leaders and see what they thought.

Some of the land was quite low, near the water towards Littleport, we were told it got a little wet in the winter months, but nobody really bothered about it, they just moved any cattle when they needed to.

We were greeted with great enthusiasm wherever we went, everybody here had been hearing of our "heroic deeds" as the Boston Defenders. They were thrilled when they heard we were trying to get to the Isle, they claimed to have heard some of the fighting, they may well have done as we had fought near here out in the fenland floods.

We were quite embarrassed to be honest, but it cheered us up no end, one of our tasks was to show we could take on and beat the enemy, we all could! The enemy were by no means supermen.

They were good well drilled soldiers but that was all. They were not some kind of super race as some would have us believe and they were beatable as we had shown.

We made our way back to the main buildings where we were to meet the leaders, we were somewhat apprehensive as we didn't know what to expect.

The Meeting Hall

Two guards at the doors let us in, greeted us with big smiles and claps on the back. Eleven of us were at this first meeting, we said we would relay relevant information on our return to our men.

A large room greeted us with a big table and room for about fifty, I would think. As soon as we entered talking stopped dead and we were met with a group of about thirty men looking straight at us, which we found a little disconcerting at first.

That soon changed to very loud cheering and the biggest smiles I have ever seen. They all rose from the table, moved over to where we stood, and began shaking our hands and shouting well done, time and again.

Eventually they became silent, Hereward came forward and introduced himself, he was surprisingly small, but very well built and had the look of a chief, dignified and strong.

I introduced us and Hereward did the same, he said stories had been reaching him from almost the beginning of our fighting, a lot of people travel through the fens, buying and selling at various times of the year and the Camp used spies, as we used scouts, to keep an eye on what was going on, so they were well placed to note what was going on and where it was happening.

From 40 lads to 116 trained soldiers/full complement at this time though we were somewhat short of that right now!.

To think we had started off with just forty lads, we were now nearly one hundred and sixteen strong, this had been reduced to 80 fit soldiers, trained and ready to fight. Plus the ones we had just lost in the fenland battle just now, I really didn't want to know the total as yet, though I knew full well I would have to come to terms with those losses sooner rather than later, it was still very hard doing so.

We had come a long way in a short space of time, we were not lads anymore, we were definitely a force of fighting Saxon men. We would ask the men on the Isle if we could take charge of more men to take us back to our original number, plus Cedrics possible new force of 100 more soldiers!

Asked to explain ourselves we told of how we had begun, myself from the cell at Spalding being a novice, and training by ourselves in the fens away from everyone, and how we progressed along the coast, then back inland and of the group we had trained and of our ideas for setting up armed resistance throughout the land.

Boston Defenders

Hereward was truly bowled over by our stories and most of all our ambition. They genuinely seemed impressed with us taking on the enemy as we had.

Most Saxons seemed to be scared of fighting, they were so pleased to have had some of the pressure taken off their shoulders by this "other" force, known as the "Boston Defenders", yes, even our name had carried this far, we were amazed as we only considered it a joke name really. Strange how these things stuck.

We were served a rather large meal, beautifully cooked, what a difference to our usual food and company! We could just about get used to this!

The rest of the force was given the same type of meal as well which was a good thing, as I was feeling guilty. If my force went hungry, I did too, was my mantra and I stuck to it!

Talk continued of our proposal regarding setting forces up and down the country, training them, and showing how to take on the Normans. We would make the enemy take notice, no matter what! Cedric stated that our plan was to coordinate attacks up and down the nation on the same day, this would astound and confuse the enemy. This was what we had been discussing for a long time now and it was set as our plan.

We could perhaps divide the country, let them use part of it, perhaps not, when we got them on the run we must destroy them, lots to plan, lots to think about, lots to get right.

The great King Alfred.

King Alfred had taken back part of the country from the Danes, Wessex, when he first defeated them, he then went on to take back the whole country following more fighting, uniting it.

Why could we not do likewise? I boldly stated! We had a once in a life time opportunity to right an awful lot of wrongs I bravely claimed!

I was very unsure as to the response I would get but I need not have worried as Hereward said he now had much more to think about now, he shared the dream but was it just a dream? Could we turn my words into reality?

All of us then returned to barracks, having consumed a little too much ale, we were pleased to see the force had eaten and drank well too, some were asleep. We were all really tired so we chatted for a few minutes and decided to join the rest, asleep in moments.

Up bright and early in the morning to go and watch the Ely "boys" do their "stuff" on the training pitch, they had a large area of things to climb over, to carry, to sword fight, to ride horses around, to race each other on and off the horses, they had targets for arrow shooting, lances, spears, axe throwing and even tree climbing as we had on our own training pitchs.

We decided once we knew the course, we were going to race against an equal number of the Ely boys. We took our places and ran off, two at a time, over the course. For my part I ran with a chap called Byram Eccleston, he was about my size and seemed to be a good bloke, all smiles at the start, hopefully we would end this race with the same, for all of us that is, one big happy group of very fit fighters, with one aim!

Byram took off at a brisk pace, the fighting had taken more out of me than I realised. The Boston Boys were suffering, to begin with at least.

One arm on the huge logs, then leap over four logs, each one more difficult than the last, then to pick up some quite large logs and run with them to a set point, next, we picked up a sword each and had to fight off one of the Ely lads for a few minutes, this was all getting a bit much, we then leapt onto a horse and ran the length of the course and back, then we raced each other on foot, he was still a little ahead of me to begin with, I all but caught up as we ran to the target shooting, we loosed off twenty arrows, each into targets which were compared later.

Pretty exhausted, we took to using the lances on horseback, these were about six feet long, judged later, then half a dozen spears were to be used at a dummy. We were both clearly exhausted as we took to the tree climbing, we were still nearly level but would not know how we got on as we had to wait for the judge's decision.

This went on for what seemed an age, we were both tired out, many more of the men had to go yet, so we were not going to know anything until later. It was quite fun watching everyone, all were really trying and laughing at each other so it was good to get to know one another this way. Overall we seemed to be fitter than they were, so it was a wakeup call for them.

They had not been riding horses, walking through thick muddied fens, running, and fighting everyday as we had, and it showed. The course was new to us but I thought we had possible won, we had set the standard and we would use this as a mark to improve on. We would continue to train and practice our fighting more often than Herewards men as it gave us an edge over our enemy, it also showed them all that they needed to be better than they were! It was a rude awakening and there was no doubt about that much comment was seen to be going on between Hereward and his leaders.

Chapter 57

Push them Back to France!

We didn't want to just stay safe on the Isle, we wanted to get at more Norman soldiers, chase them all back to France!

That afternoon I saw a couple of the men from the meeting with Hereward last night, greeted them and asked when do you plan to go out in search of the enemy. They replied that plans were being made to chase away the enemy at the door, we wanted much more than to just chase them from the door, of course, but that was a start. Hereward would want to discuss it with us shortly which sounded good.

Hereward to be Knighted

For Hereward to be accepted by all his soldiers he had to become a Knight. He was put forward for this honour by Abbot brand, his uncle, from Peterborough Abbey. He had returned from Flanders on 23rd of December, 1069, and had pledged to find the men who had killed his father, and kill them! The revolt in the fens had begun in May 1070. He arrived in Ely on the 24th April. 1071.

He travelled to Peterbouough with a large group of his men and was knighted around this time.

This happened a long time ago it seemed to Hereward, so much had happened in so short a time.

The day dragged to a close and we were called to eat, the same as before, sixteen of us now in the building, the rest in their quarters, really good food again, we thought we might begin to feel like human beings again soon if we continued to be treated in this manner, not merely dogs of war.

The meal came to a close and Hereward said he wanted to test the men's steel, to actually get a feel as to how good our force was.

He, and his men, wanted to pick an area locally that was held by a Norman force and attack it but for him to hold back and basically watch us fight. He had heard many tales of our capabilities but needed to know how far we would go, how we would attack and not hold back. I could see that he did not want to put his forces future in the hands of others, that was sensible, but he had watched us in training, still, if that was what the man wanted!

The Soham Fight

We decided to have a look at the Soham force of Normans, so we set off towards the settlement the next morning, at first light, to go and take a look, see if we could muster a plan of attack that might be agreeable to all, except the Normans, of course!

Just us five and five of Hereward's men let ourselves off the Isle, and followed the track towards Stuntney, we took this way as it was closer than the Brandon exit area, as usual this track was under a great deal of water, so really it was not a track, it was the bottom of the fen! But, of course, it was our best track to this part of England!

From the hill we could see parts of the Norman camp quite easily, between areas of trees, we were not at all sure what they were doing here, but they were settled at camp.

We estimated that there were about one hundred soldiers, they would put up quite a fight I had no doubt. If we managed to catch them unawares we might be able to cause them a lot of trouble, I hoped.

As we looked very carefully, scouts were about, so they were expecting trouble, we would need to be very careful. I didn't want to risk losing many men, some would no doubt be lost but I had to show Hereward's men that we meant business, to start as we mean to go on was the order of the day. If we could impress him then I believed we could impress upon him our plan of taking back our country, this was our goal and we needed to establish other fighting groups now! and to move these plans forwards, sooner rather than later!

We made the short trip back to the safety of the Isle and sat and planned what we would do. With the advice of Chris Calvin, one of Hereward's men, as to where ditches, rivers, were. We hatched what we thought was a decent plan of attack. Chris, and his team, worked closely with all the attacks carried out so his input was of great use.

We carried out more training in the afternoon and settled down to a quiet evening, all the leaders talked of where they were going to be stationed to begin with, and where they were going to attack first, which section of the camp they were hopefully going to destroy to start with and so on.

Our scouts had the first job of putting their scouts out of action. Then with the rest of our force in groups of twenty, I needed them in place ready to attack at the same time. It was difficult to get them in place in time as they would have to go quite a long way out, away from the camp to not be seen, and then come in to be near enough to fight at the same time as the rest of us.

Battle of Soham

Eventually, all prepared and ready, which indeed took some considerable time as expected, at the set time we took on the enemy for the first time from the Isle.

We were just short of one hundred and thirty men, Hereward had made our number back to what it had been with some good fighters, we were flattered when a huge amount of his men offered to join our group. We attacked from five places, around this camp.

The enemy were thankfully not ready for battle so we had the very important element of surprise in our favour.

The men with me were shooting arrows in all directions after we had entered camp, with Norman soldiers running here and there, they were well trained and some were soon on horseback and trying to organise a counter attack. We quickly cut them off and I shouted for men to loose off their horses and make it more difficult for them. This done, we continued to wipe out as we went, swords, axes and spears cutting away at the enemy.

I could see other groups making progress so things were ticking along nicely, not a very professional way of looking at it, I thought, but here we were doing what we had trained for all this time. I must have been too busy thinking and not fighting, heard a horse hurtling itself at me, snorting, somebody crying out loud to watch out, I pulled my horse to the right and the big beast just missed me with the sound of a sword swishing through the air.

Bloody hell! Was my immediate reaction, I aimed my horse towards my present enemy and tried to catch him. He was off after someone else so I decided to follow, something made him turn back. He saw me and came straight back, collision inevitable! I swung my horse to the left at the last moment, to give my right arm freedom to try and clobber this bloke.

His sword was raised, damn it looked big, I tried to catch him in the side as he passed, he saw it coming and nearly knocked my sword out of my hand, this was not good! We turned to face each other and attacked again, hope these Normans were not all like this one, this time he didn't have his sword up. Just as I was about to raise mine I saw he had hold of some kind of short lance in his other hand, he clipped his sword up out of the way, and proceeded to attack me.

I had not faced one of these before and was more than a little surprised. I just managed to pull my horse away in time to not be skewered. He seemed to go off the idea of using this form of warfare, he ditched it, and had another go at me with his sword, he missed and I was able to take a batch of his chain mail off, plus a lump of flesh off his arm with my effort, this must have hit home as the resulting blood flow proved. This did seem to take some of the wind from his sails, but he was more annoyed than dying so more work for me to do yet!

He aimed at me again and came at me at some speed, held his sword high, for a bit too long this time, and I struck him in the ribs, pretty deeply.

This time he fell off his horse, still the bugger managed to stand, and defy me, he stood still with sword and challenged me. I leapt from my horse and confronted him. It was as though the whole world had stopped for a few moments. We just looked at one another, I leapt towards him and went for the kill, he still surprised me, lent away from my thrust, so my sword missed, and tried to slice me open with his sword.

I managed to jump clear, in a most unprofessional manor, almost fell, turned and caught him in the back. I retrieved my sword and damn it the man turned and tried to slice me in two yet again. This time I managed to put him down with a clear thrust to the chest, he groaned and went down.

Thank goodness for that! I was nearly at a loss at what to do against him.

The battle was hotting up in a few places around the camp, my men had seen off this section and were heading, mostly together, towards the middle, where the greatest concentration seemed to be, probably where the senior officers had placed themselves for maximum protection from any attack, the brunt of any fighting would be taken by the chaps on the outside, pretty cowardly I thought to myself. No time to dwell on any thoughts, just attack, hopefully finish off these swine, and scuttle off back to our haven on the Isle.

I could see the first of my group meeting the enemy in the middle, swords slashing confidently, from right to left, knocking tired looking Normans into the next life. Soon we were all there, some off their horses taking the fight to the enemy. We were fit and fast and clinical in our destruction of the foe.

Some arrows, well aimed, from our men, finished off this little batch of enemy and we moved onto the next challenge. Several of the groups were looking up to move onto somewhere, I signalled to all to join with us and finish off this bunch as soon as we could.

This was much easier than I could have imagined, maybe it was just that we had surprised them. Maybe it was because we were good, their scouts were definitely not up to the job, we had already made them pay the ultimate price.

I began worrying about our losses, I had made out several men injured, some on the ground. I made myself stop as I had told everyone to think of nothing else but winning in any battle, concentrate on winning, help anyone of us Saxons who you could if they needed it. Win first, think about all else afterwards.

I pulled myself together, severely told myself off, and got back to the job in hand. I aimed my horse at a couple of the enemy and attacked with great ferocity, well, I thought so at least. They were not too pleased, as they appeared to be trying to run away from the fight. I struck one with a spear I had recovered, and hit the other with my sword, did not finish him by any means, as we drew level I struck him again and he fell from his mount to the ground where he was run through by one of our men on the ground. Job done!

Chapter 58

I turned to view what was going on and was pretty delighted to see most of the enemy had been mopped up, things were going very well, I hoped Hereward's men agreed. Some of our men were already selecting any swords they liked the look of, jackets too. The enemy had not had time to put on most of their chain mail so we helped ourselves from their stores.

I called for all to make sure and finish the fight before doing anything else, I did not really want any Norman left alive to tell the tale, much more of a worry for William the Bastard to have this force wiped out, totally!

We also had to convince Hereward and his men we were up to the job!

Clearing the enemy after battle is an awful process, in this case it had to be done. We had to show Hereward we were up to the mark, no lose ends! Warfare is a pretty vile exercise at the best of times, however we had a job to do and we had to do it, therefore no option.

The Battle Was Coming to a Close, Mopping up Began

I thought it was over when clearly it was not. At least ten more horses charged towards us in the middle of this ground. Not at all sure where they had sprung from. Swords at the ready, Cedric and I and six other men met them. With shouts of encouragement from our men we clashed, the man in the middle came straight for me. He brought his sword up and smashed it into mine. He really had some power in his arms, made my arm shudder I can tell you! We turned our respective horses and flew at each other again, another mighty clash. We turned again, trotted towards each other, sword fight on horseback was not easy, then again when is it?

I managed to turn his sword away to give me a moment to thrust at his chest, I hit him quite hard, it knocked his mail really hard, knocked him back in his saddle. He was not pleased and he very aggressively tried to hit me back with his sword. I had moved fast past him in a moment and turned my animal. He turned and we hit each other again. This time my sword carried to the end of his and hit him along the arm, more pain for my enemy!

He leapt off his horse and challenged me to do likewise. I did so and yet again we clashed, much more firmly as we were on the ground. We must have hit each other at least eight times when we stopped for a breath of air. This bugger was tough! I leapt at him quickly and caught him early, before he was quite ready, cut his arm again.

He was not just tough but angry as well now as he came at me fast and hard. He nearly knocked my sword out of my hand as he hit me but I managed to recover, though painfully, and finish him with a cut through the chest, as his mail had come lose. That was a hard fought fight. No time to recover as another soldier attacked me. I did not have the strength for a long drawn out fight. I managed to dispatch this one with ease thankfully. This particular fight was over and all the ten enemy were gone. Some time later I watched as the rest of the battle was coming to a close.

I took my first look up to where Herewards men were, the group seemed larger than when we arrived, but thought no more of it.

We then set about rounding up any of our men who were injured and able to ride, then the poor chaps who could not ride, we hung them over the saddles of horses and led them off as quickly as we dared, so causing them as little pain as possible. We took our dead, with respect and dignity, and placed them at the side of the battlefield, some dreadful moments spent justifying their loss of life. It was a gift, this life, and they died as a result of doing what was the most important thing in this world to them, ridding the land of the foul Normans, they were fine Anglo Saxons indeed and would not be forgotten ! We had all of us played our part in this fighting and had shown Hereward and his men that we were determined fighters that would not slack until the job was finished!

Back on the Hill

On our return we were greeted with wild applause and hearty shouts of "well done" as we approached the hill. There were indeed many more soldiers than when we arrived, Hereward had asked his men to come a little after battle began, as we might experience some difficulty. They might have had to come into the battle to help or save us, thankfully they were not needed.

All his men were pleased to see how well we had coped and were glad to have a lot more fully trained, and above all, experienced men to call on at any time.

I tried to not let those who we had lost bother me too much, they would not have wanted that, we all of us understood we were living in difficult times and that may be the price we paid for having at least tried to bring about the change we needed, back to Anglo Saxon rule.

Back on the Isle

We calmly trotted home to the Isle which was not at all far, pleased with a good day's work.

As soon as we entered, we took our injured to the place where they treated "damaged" soldiers.

They had a number of beds in a separate unit where they were brought back to health, if possible, it really was very organised and it helped the soldiers in general if they knew they would be helped to get better quicker, not just left to rot, become infected and die, as would happen in the "old days".

Hereward's men had left us to report back to the man himself, he had left us earlier as he had a meeting with some of his leaders. He came out and congratulated us all, even shaking the hands of the injured, if possible.

I thanked him for sending the other troops out to help us if needed, he passed that off as nothing, and said he found it hard to believe we had wiped out the entire group of enemy. William would not be at all amused.

It was clear Hereward was delighted with his new fighting force!

Norman Army Mainly Based at Cambridge

He said he had had word that William was massing troops at Cambridge, probable with a view to try and take our Isle and finally finish the threat of the Saxon forces, something he would find even more difficult now we were there, increasing Herewards fighting power, and indeed confidence, by so much.

Time to clean ourselves of battle and prepare for some ale, followed by a hearty meal. We had earned it, without doubt, a fine days' work. We were proud of our achievement that day, and no mistake. There was much singing that evening by a pretty large bunch of Saxons, with the odd Briton amongst them.

Chapter 59

A rather fanciful illustration of Cambridge Castle drawn in Elizbethan times, By this date only the Norman mound and Gatehouse remained intact.

King Tonberts Girvii

We had eight Britons among our ranks who had become fine fighters and good friends to us all, they had learned to live alongside us after our early battles from when we arrived on the island that was Britain. It was a fine place to fight over, growing crops on the low lying land was comparatively easy and grazing cattle was easy too. A small population made it an ideal takeover target when we seized control.

It was good to have the six Iceni with us as well, it showed we could work together despite our past disagreements and work for the same end. Together we represented the population of England against the foreign invader. We were thinking of trying to bring other of the original tribes of these lands to fight alongside us as we were aware most had trained a fighting force on standby, ready if needed, why not persuade them as to the justice of our cause, surely it made sense!

Upto Date Plan of the Enemy Encampments

Hereward said a plan was drawn of the whole area and of the Norman troop movements which were amazingly kept up to date.

The estimated numbers were recorded and brought back for him and his senior staff to look at, he sent out scouting parties with the raiding parties to get more information when he was not clear as to what was going on. They tried to cause as much havoc as possible on these excursions, as it gave the enemy no peace.

His scouts were left out to carry on with their work, as always. This was very advanced thinking we all thought, though it was mostly common sense, putting it all together and constantly keeping it up to date was a major task. It gave us a clear advantage over the enemy.

Having a group of dedicated men whose task it was to keep this as up to date as possible was a master stroke. They sometimes went out for long periods and often concern was raised but they had always reappeared to date.

They did have to hide for quite some time at times, they became encircled by the enemy who had no idea they were there. There was no reason to think they were exaggerating. Sometime they stayed with friends. For food at times they took from the Normans and waited until they moved off before returning with all the details they were looking for. They certainly were a very useful and clever bunch of men. A huge asset to any armed force.

All details of the enemy were set onto plans before any fighting commenced.

At meetings, us leaders and Hereward's would often stand in amazement looking at the detail they put together. I did not believe to begin with that so much detail was up to date.

It always had been to date, I was told, so had better get used to it, all our lives depended on these plans being correct before fighting began.

As the Norman troops moved around in their groups, so the plans were altered. When they became a bit cluttered they were put to one side and a new plan was produced. These plans were stored in a special room, locked and bolted, well away from prying eyes! They were also never talked about outside an inner circle of leaders and the scouts were sworn to secrecy.

Tomorrows World.

We had never heard of anything so organised, let alone seen it. It was like a tomorrows world, only it was today, right in front of us!

Hereward said we needed to keep the enemy on their toes, pushing them away when they came too close. We also needed to attack, in large numbers, his stronghold at Cambridge I exclaimed. We would sack his confidence, teach him we were afraid of no one.

He had been unable to attack on a large enough scale to date but now felt confident, with our group helping, that he could take the fight to the enemy, and without doubt cause him major problems, if not wiping out at least parts of his forces.

This would weaken his resolve and delay any action against the Isle. It would give us time to organise ourselves on a national scale. The more we could delay the eventual fighting of the main battles for control of the Isle the better prepared we would be to fight him off.

If we could organise our forces up and down the country we may even be able to sneak off the Isle if and when needed, fighting as we went, all of us together, or in separate groups, come to that, for specific purposes.

This was the challenge laid before us I said to all and no one in particular as I made sure everybody in the room heard!

So we began to put our heads together to hatch a plan of bringing these ideas to life, we knew of a large number of the enemy that were now based at Cottenham, around the dock, this was not far away at all, so we sent out our scouts to look at the area as a whole. Just how many concentrations of troops were there? Were they well defended, did they have cavalry, and if so how many, we needed to know as much as possible. Where there any floods about? What condition were the tracks in?

Could we be delayed by any such problems? We needed to know how long it would take a large force, that we were proposing to send, to get from the Isle, maybe to Cambridge or even beyond there.

Taking the Fight to the Enemy

This was both eye opening and interesting, we were proposing to take the fight to the enemy for the first time in what seemed a long time, on an unprecedented scale.

If William thought we were a beaten race, we would make him think again! We were now a force to contend with! As a force we would get stronger and stronger I felt sure.

Earl Edwin

News reached us that Earl Edwin had sent a scout to us to let us know that he and a group of loyal men would be approaching from the Newmarket area, they were coming to fight with the Saxon might Hereward offered and hoped they would be welcomed.

They had fought at Hastings, and had been harassed as they travelled up from the south coast. They would be a great asset! Battle weary they maybe, experience could not be bought, and it was vital to our cause! Plus the extra numbers would be great.

This brought a huge cheer from Hereward's men and he immediately set out to send a group to fend off any enemy that might be about and guide them onto the Isle, probable have to be at night as we didn't want any spies to see and tell William.

We took a plan and tried to make out the best way to achieve this, we had to avoid tracks where possible, travel through woodland where possible and make sure there were no large waterways between them and us to slow them down. This was quite difficult and it took some time but we did get a sensible plan, if there were no unforeseen problems they would be alright.

If we could add substantially to our numbers of trained soldiers we could take this fight to the enemy sooner rather than later, it would also be very good for moral, the Earl had several hundred men under arms, coming up from the far end of Suffolk, he was coming with the usual array of arms. He must surely be moving in small numbers, as we had done, or the enemy would be on his tail. Maybe they were! We simple had no idea.

Space was going to be a problem, the island could only take so many. We would deal with it somehow. If needed, we would set up a camp outside the Isle.

Tonbert knew of areas you could quite easily hide hundreds of men on islands or even patches of land throughout the fens.

We sent out several scouts with his to meet Earl Edwin, our men were to go over the plan we proposed, and one was to return at once if agreed. The others were to return at intervals to let us know how they were getting on and where they had reached at that time. We would send men out to escort them in.

As we did not really have room on the Isle for yet more soldiers, we asked the leaders of groups if they knew anywhere we could possibly hide this force, close by.

It was difficult as a lot of places came to mind and were discarded. Tonbert, of the Girvii, came up with a wooded area he knew very well, near Downham Market, which was not too far away. It was our side of the village, near the river Ouse.

The Earl and His Men Join Us

The Earl grouped his men near Soham, some way away from the battle area where we had just fought, approximately two hundred strong they were for the run to the Isle.

He did not know it at this time but he had been shadowed by a number of Norman soldiers who had sent for reinforcements to fight him and stop him joining our force against William.

As he grouped his men, the Norman soldiers caught up with the shadowing enemy and the leader decided to challenge the Saxons right away before they could link up with our men on the Isle.

The Normans caught Edwin by surprise with a full on attack. Arrows flew into his men, quickly his leading men took control and turned to fight to the death!

Arrows were returned en masse and swords drawn to fight man to man. They clashed at high speed, no holding back, both groups being anxious to win quickly and get to security with their respective groups of soldiers.

Edwin and his four leaders and men attacked from the front, hitting the main groups of enemy, a huge clash of iron occurred, both groups of men meant business, tough, strong and experienced as they all were.

Edwin took the first man easily and prepared for the second. This Norman was good with his horse, he turned it at the last moment, as he did so he threw a short spear at the earl, it thudded into his shield with great force, made his arm shudder but that was all. The earl aimed his horse after the enemy and as he caught him he slashed at him with his sword, catching his side. The angry enemy was hurt and it showed, he turned and tried to catch our man. Their swords met again, he was hurt but tough and clash after clash they met with great ferocity.

Neither was giving an inch so to speak as they hit each other again, the earl came in quickly and caught the Norman who was not ready. He struck him in the side this time and blood showed quickly but the enemy was having none of it. He seemed to not accept defeat of any sort as he tried to claim the earls head with a wild thrust. The earl ducked out of the way and thrust him through the chest, another Norman to fight no more.

The fighting continued over a large area, the earl cussed to himself that he had been foolish to bring in his scouts a little earlier as he prepared to meet with Herewards men from the Isle, clearly not a good move!

No time to dwell on that, he thought to himself, must continue winning this battle and nothing else. Another lesson learned!

In the still of this early morning the noise of battle was alarming as they were somewhat hemmed in by the surrounding trees, though they were on open land now.

He pulled back a little with his leaders, up a gentle slope, to get a glance of how the battle was progressing.

It looked quite good at present, his men on the left were making inroads well, the ones to the right not so. He spoke with his leaders to take some men from the middle and reinforce the right hand group.

This they did and the difference was incredible to see, easily overrunning the enemy. It was good to be able to see what was going on, he thought to himself with a degree of confidence from this point onwards. He re-joined the fighting with renewed energy at the front section closest to where he sat on his animal, pushing his horse back into the fray.

There was no doubt that his force was tired with all the battles and travel, just laying your head in yet another camp at the end of a hard day was exhausting, no peace really at night as you had no idea when the enemy might appear to take you on again.

Fighting continued, though a little slower as the earls group appeared to be winning, the pace of the fight being dictated by the Saxon force.

A batch of the enemy tried to make a run for it, to escape the inevitable destruction that was on the horizon. He took a number of his men in pursuit, rode round to the left of the fighting and followed. Their horses seemed slower so he caught up quickly and immediately got to them side on as they fled. He took out the lead man and went for the next closest, he tried to turn quickly and basically run, ….cowards! Thought the earl, though he did not blame them. They were on the receiving end of some very sharp fighting from the Saxons. He liked to think they had no chance and recognised this fact.

They were despatched with ease and he and his men went back to the main fight which was nearing its conclusion. They finished the few soldiers left and joined his whole group.

That was a very unexpected battle he exclaimed to all! A sharp lesson to us all he claimed, we should never have let these enemy get as close as they had, we simple must keep a much better watch on any area we camped in at all times. That was a lesson to us all he repeated!!

They agreed and continued on their way to meet Herewards men without much comment. They had become so used to battles that it was second nature. As always they were sad to have lost some more good men, it was the price to pay, they all understood.

These were hard times, we had forgotten what peace was like, though we had not stopped hoping it might be around the next corner, that was some hope, as we knew full well what a determined army we were up against. We all must keep believing or else there was no point continuing with the fighting.

His lead scout came in to say there were a group of soldiers coming their way, he thought it was Herewards men coming to escort them to the Isle. They had to be careful they were not enemy, especially as they had already made one bad mistake that day! Another would be unforgivable.

It was indeed our men and they quickly arranged to follow them to safety. They reached the Brandon area, guided by our men, and could clearly see the Isle ahead of them, it was exciting for them all, they had thought and talked of getting here so often, after so much fighting along the way it was hard to imagine, here at last!

They had a real job going round to the point of entry and filing slowly and frustratingly, two at a time, onto our Isle, but it was well worth the effort to be greeted by all with such enthusiasm. Edwin thought we may have a future after all! it took an age for them all to reach the refuge!

Hereward and the leaders themselves were here to greet this historic moment. Another great step forward in the salvation of the Saxon race. We were indeed getting stronger by the moment.

Once they were on the Isle we sent men out to clear an area for them to camp, partly prepared, we sent them to await further instruction and finish the camp as they wanted it. They set up a training area, based on ours. We would soon find them plenty of fighting to do.

That night it was decided to send them out to near Downham Market in the woodland nearby, as room was now in such short supply, guard camps were set up all around their area so they were secure for the time being.

The Earl wanted to stay with his men but we felt he could contribute more by joining with the other leaders in planning our fighting, so he left several senior members to run their camp.

Chapter 60

William the Conqueror Plotting to Fight Back

In the meantime, William had heard of losing all of his men in the group that had camped between Stuntney and Soham, and he was not pleased to say the least!

I would have liked to have listened to the conversation between him and his generals at their headquarters in Cambridge. He was not one to suffer fools gladly, these men had been fools to not guard themselves properly, to let us attack as we did was plain bad soldiering, and they paid a mighty price!

He ordered a large party of his best men to exact retribution, somehow, he must get a plan that will work to get onto the Isle and get this Hereward fellow and put down his rebellion once and for all.

He got together the best minds available and set them to work.

To make matters worse a couple of soldiers came to the Cambridge castle informing him of the fight with Edwin and that most of his force had been able to join up with Hereweard on the Isle, this, he considered a disaster!

Plans were drawn up and discarded, if not by William himself, then by his generals. Every time he sent scouts to look to see how the land was, if it was capable of letting the weight of a large force over it to get to the Isle, they returned and said there was no way even a small force could travel through that depth of water unnoticed. If their horses arrived in twos, they would just be slaughtered, fodder for arrows!

These men went right around the Isle by boat, most didn't return, said to had been killed by Hereward's men, who seemed to be everywhere, living amongst the locals as they did. The ones who returned only got back by the skin of their teeth, having been followed and then chased by the local men. There seemed no way through. Contrary to Norman opinion the men of the waterways were proving neither slow in the head nor weak in the arm. A little rough in their manner perhaps, that was all.

Williams's admiration of their behaviour was becoming apparent, much to his generals concern.

William decided he ought to go and see for himself the problems that existed. He knew he would have to be careful as Hereward's men would possibly find out his plan soon enough and try and arrest him, a painful death would be the least of his worries!

He got some of his best men to surround him as he went, he was disguised very well. He didn't recognise himself, made everyone who knew what was going on laugh. This was too important to not go, he had to see for himself. He simple had to devise a plan and somehow make it work. He was, after all, William The Conqueror! And he thought he could not be beaten.

Cottenham

The group set off early one morning on the track to Cottenham, this had a dock where boats would take goods to the Isle in peacetime and for fishing from for food, though some boats were there they were plainly not in use for that purpose, just a few were there for fishing for the locals, the view across the water was really something to behold at the time. He was devising a plan to build some kind of causeway to the Isle so he could get his troops there in a quantity large enough to defeat the Anglo-Saxons. Where to site it was the question in his mind?

It was clear that any wood for bridges and stone etc. would need to come via Cottenham as it was the nearest point to the Isle and it was a decent size dock, he would have to build larger boats if and when needed.

The locals were coming out of their houses and commenting on who were these soldiers and what were they doing, wondering around as they were was very unusual.

They were not in uniform but these days any man of fighting age was classed a soldier by the local population. This must have unsettled William and his men, he must have realised Hereward's spies would be interested straight away, they could be watching at this very moment, counting the number of soldiers there were and were they armed and what was under their cloaks etc. trying to guess what the purpose of their being there was.

They would get back to Hereward right away and see what could be done quickly, it wouldn't matter if they worked out who he was, though the likelihood of that was non existent, obviously they were Norman and they must be stopped and sent packing at the very least. Every Norman was enemy!

They stayed at the dock for a little more than an hour and took the track to Rampton, a small settlement between here and Willingham, all flooded on their right all the way to the Isle, a great expanse of water, quite forbidding! Mostly hidden behind great banks of reed beds, these, in turn, stood on huge bogs in which he could lose his entire army. He began to see that it was indeed a huge problem. Exactly what were they going to do about this? To get a large enough force there to do battle was a huge problem, there simple must be a way!

There were some small boats on the water, mostly fishing, but it crossed his mind that they could easily be soldiers of the Saxon nation that he was trying to squash. They could be on their way to tell Hereward of this comparatively small bunch of men, possible Norman, and arranging to have them attacked and killed off!

It was a little unsettling to say the least, there was no time to lose! The Saxons had just won a huge fight against his men, they would love to get some more William had no doubt.

They reached Willingham quite easily, got to the near side of it to see how far the Isle was away from there. They rode along Irlam Drove, a section of which became Belsars Hill, named after a Norman general as the staging post for the defendable position for the construction of the causeway, to the highest point they could find and could clearly see the land rising in the distance, where Aldreth stood, defiantly, rising from the forest of reed beds and waterways. At this time it was the only remaining section of land, and water, he had not conquered in England. The rustling of the wind in these reeds was unsettling to William as he was not used to it. He would tame this land and its people!

He could see the land rising out of the fen on the other side, which was not far away. This looked interesting, he thought, they might be able to build a great causeway and bridge over the main river that he knew flowed through these reed beds, from here and get onto the "Camp of Refuge" as it had become known and clear it of the blasted Saxons, once and for all! As he thought about it, he could clearly see this causeway, massively impressive, a statement of his intention to take these vast wilderness lands under his control, with a huge bridge as a monument to himself. "My" Norman fenlands he thought! A wilderness today, a structured Norman controlled area of the future, paying him taxes!

There was quite a noise coming up behind them, quite a number of men with cutters and choppers in their hands, they appeared to mean business. This is trouble, he thought and said so to his men !

They were apparently demanding to know what this group of men wanted, what were they doing in their village. Two of Williams men spoke fairly good English and they tried to explain they meant no harm to anyone, they were just looking at the fen area in general.

The men began shouting and getting very excited, rocks began to be thrown at the Normans, hitting some and their horses. Several reared, sending their mounts flying. William took charge and shouted for all horses to charge the local men and scatter them, to kill them if they objected, this they did with great delight, sending all in all directions.

His group left the area very quickly, towards Earith, he was glad to have lost none of his men.

Chapter 61

The Norman men skirted the fen, water each side now, they felt isolated and it was strange. They entered Earith via a not very good bridge, which took some time.

The Normans sat and ate their food and set up a camp and fire. The men settled in for the night with half the men as guards, they knew word travelled fast in these parts and they would not be welcome. William wanted to test the Saxons as much as anything, he thought they might be disturbed in the dead of night.

As indeed they were, half way through the night a scout woke all, with the disturbing news that a quite large band of what appeared just locals, no soldiers as far as he could tell, were coming their way and the purpose was not to toast some bread by the fire!

William and his men had time to prepare themselves, he sent out the two who spoke English, to see what they wanted. There was much shouting and some noise of fighting, one of his men reappeared, the other it seems, was dead, so not good news.

William and his men took to their horses and charged the Saxons who were still coming towards the camp.

The Saxons threw whatever they had in their hands, several of the soldiers were caught unawares, as they took hits to their bodies, fell to the ground and were attacked. The skirmish went on for a few minutes more, Williams men and horses chased the locals and they dispersed carrying their injured with them.

William knew now what he was up against, not just those on the Isle, but the whole population around was not scared to take up arms, of any sort, it did not matter if it was a knife or a scythe, or just a stone, they would still cut and hurt the Normans. They were a hardy lot these fen men, even those who were not trained in the arts of war. Perhaps they were encouraged by the stories doing the rounds of the Boston Defenders and of Hereward's resistance on the Isle.

No matter, thought William, we had better get back to our stronghold at Cambridge and see if we can use what we have learned these two days to our advantage. A plan was already in his mind on how to tackle the Isle and Hereward.

He made his way back towards Cottenham, before he got as far as Willingham, he realised there were men on horseback following them nearby, away from the track to not disturb anyone, but obviously keeping pace with him and his men. Thoughts of a trap entered his mind, there was a thick spinney before the village, he had noticed on the way through, he thought at the time what a good place to ambush someone.

Now he considered the likelihood of his men being the target. He quickly told his men to watch out for any movement ahead. He was a little short of the spinney as one of his men said he thought he saw a stirring in the trees, William could see nothing at first, but as he kept looking he too made out movement of the trees where there should be no movement on this still evening.

William told everyone of his men to spread out across the track and the clear space each side of it, then he called to attack.

This was not the wisest decision he had made as soon as he obviously made his move a fierce and constant flow of arrows shot in their direction. This caused many of his men to take arrows, plus, sadly horses, the ones that carried on the attack reared and threw their riders off.

Some Saxons showed themselves, stood in front of the spinney and fired even more arrows into the dreaded Normans. The Normans began to fire back, they hit a few Saxons, most of them leapt back into the spinney and hid behind groups of trees, out of harm's way.

The Normans who were on foot now, attacked with swords. The locals tried to put up a fight but they were not very good. One or two were pretty good and made the enemy stop their advance, the others retreated through the spinney.

They had a stash of short lances, spears, at set places in the wood, they retrieved them and began to attack again, causing many more deaths or maiming the enemy as they went. I am sure the enemy had never known peasants to fight like this without a recognised leader of experience.

This was truly amazing of the Anglo-Saxons, as they had not trained very much, they knew this was helping Hereward's cause an awful lot and they were prepared for any consequences, so were their families.

The hatred of their new masters knew no bounds. They were never going to let anyone tell them what to do again. This was the beginning of payback time!

The Normans were now all walking or running if they could through the trees trying to catch the Saxons. These brave men had tied their horses on the other side of the spinney, as they got there they leapt on their nags and sped off towards the village. Williams men tried to bring them down with their arrows, to be honest they didn't have many fit men left, many were dead or injured.

This trip was a disaster from Williams point of view, though he had gained some ideas, it would sap moral at a very important time.

He would put this idea of a causeway and bridge to his generals on his return. Maybe someone else had come up with a better idea he thought, with little confidence.

As he and his men staggered through the village, he let it be known that he and a mighty group of his men would seek retribution for the men he had lost. This fight was by no means over.

The locals had not felt this good for many a year, so for the time being they celebrated! The plan they had discussed was for the men to get onto the Isle and continue the fight against William. They may be able to get to their homes now and again to help the farming community from starving.

They knew when William returned all the men would be massacred anyway so they would have to leave if they wished to stay alive! They had shown what they could do and were mighty pleased, they were concerned for their families but it was time to make a stand!

Chapter 62

Sulking William!
He returned to Cambridge, everyone was stunned at how many and who had been lost, some of his better men had perished, these men had fought by his side for years, what a waste evedryone was saying behind his back. He was having a job trying to make out just how successful the trip was from a planning point of view, he tried to look cheerful and confident, but did not convince many.

If we knew how close William had been, we would have spared no one in trying to kill him, it would have saved a great many lives in the long run. The story came out some months later, we were astonished at how close they had been. We only found out about it later when he returned to his camp as Hereward had a spy in the enemy's lair, plus the fight became known well locally as a victory for the locals!

Williams Obsession
He held a meeting with his senior staff and talked of building a causeway across the fen and river to Aldreth, one that could carry horses as well as men.

He was very determined to make this work as there was no option, so began to set a huge group of his men whose job it was to construct this causeway. They would need masses of stone, chalk, trees and all sorts of anything to make this work, a massive construction job, probably the biggest he had ever undertaken. Stone could be brought up the river Cam and along the Car Dyke from other parts of Britain, clunch could be brought from Reach. In his mind he could see this coming together, it could really work! 'How deep is the waterway?' was the only real question and how much deep bog was there to soak up the foundation he would need to secure the causeway.

He would have to wait and see. He was not the kind of person who liked to wait for anything in this world so he was not happy!

He didn't think for one moment that it would not work, Williams mind was made up and that was all there was to it.

The Planners!
As plans were put forward, they all wondered just how much stone, clunch, wood etc. they would need to support a big strong bridge and causeway over the deep river and fen.

There was not much stone in the area, let alone Cambridgeshire, so wood would have to be the main ingredient, it was the easiest to move, though this would be a problem to fix in place, he was confident any problem could be overcome, he had not lost a major fight yet and he was not about to start!

William was bringing nearly all his troops together to fight the battle that was looming against us. The enemy were getting stronger and stronger it seemed and more confident, he thought to himself, proof could be seen as they killed off the whole battle group near Soham, he couldn't remember when he had lost so many men in one battle and to have them all killed off was a nightmare. The Saxons were becoming a very efficient army and he was beginning not respect them.

He had tried to hush it up so his troops did not hear of it but these things will get out no matter what, there was no way the Saxons could be kept silent about such an event, they made sure the enemy soldiers soon knew what had happened. Our people were laughing at William and he would not have it. He would make them all pay, soldiers and civilians alike!

He had some more strong boats built to carry the materials for the causeway from Willingham to Aldreth and commandeered all that were there for the purpose, strengthening many so they could do the job required.

Belsars Hill.

Things began moving quite quickly, a protected base was built to defend it against attacks, named Belsars Hill, and from there the foundation was begun to be put in place for the causeway. It surely sounded simple enough.

A huge amount of manpower was needed just to get it off the ground, but over time it begun to take shape, a large circular, protected base, from which to deposit the materials and push them out over the fen.

It actually began to take shape; no one came up with a better idea so they carried on regardless. Not only did they use Cottenham Dock, they built another near Somersham, boats were bringing materials from that area as well, this improved the rate at which the project progressed. We began to have a grudging respect for William, it surely was a huge undertaking.

Hereward viewed this with some alarm, especially to begin with, we knew that William had bitten off more than he could chew, so to speak, the fen/bog was very deep in places and at the bottom, who knew what lay there or in fact just how deep it was, it seemed to go deeper forever, no matter what you pushed into it!

It would surely take a massive amount of foundation, he was using mainly trees and brush and earth and chalk in sacks, not the best material for this purpose. Who knew how much material would be needed to secure this causeway, to make it strong enough for William's army to travel safely over it? Nobody.

The amount he would need to be successful would be huge and when asked I said he simple would not be able to get enough to do the job. If it all looked like it may work, plans were discussed regarding setting it alight! All that wood burning would make a fine spectacle, a statement from us to William and we all of us looked forward to seeing it!

After we had decided it would not work, providing we could set it on fire, we calmed down and had a team watching progress.

They were a long way off and it was interesting to watch them at work, the leaders were pushing the actual work force very hard, they were not testing the depth of bog they had to go through, they were just pushing and trying to sink the wood and earth and hoping it would be enough to make a strong enough foundation to take the weight of his force going over it.

They pushed out more and more bales of earth and wood, then they tried to put weight on it, it just sank into the depths, when pressure from the next load was put on top of it, that sank out of sight as well.

It really was funny, all that effort for nothing or at least very little, we thought.

We had several men working with the Normans, they had quite a number of Saxons supposed to be helping them, as slaves I hasten to add, they were doing what they could to slow down progress. Our spies told us there was no real plan even now that anyone knew about, they were instructed to just get on with the job.

More and more wood kept coming, so they moved it out to the furthest point and sank it, more often than not watched it sink out of sight and then get cursed at by the Normans.

Eventually, after huge amounts of effort and time, several months had gone by, they reached the main flow of the river Ouse, this was where the water was fastest and deepest. This could be fun we decided!

Chapter 63

Planning the Bridge Over the Ouse and Fen

They sent out boats with long poles to try and get the depth, they dropped large stones tied to rope to be more accurate. It had a huge amount of water going through it on a daily basis, so this alone was difficult. We were told they were planning a bridge, where would the wood come from we wondered. Any decent sized wood was quite a distance away. It would take a huge amount of work to get it here, build it, and float it out through the fen. Then they would have to fix it in position. Clearly, it was up to us to stop this happening. It was time to plan our next move.

We could infiltrate the work crew and see if we could set it on fire, we knew the Normans guarded it night and day, as it was an open target for us otherwise.

It was decided that Hereward would lead a group of men and take the place of some of the Saxon work force building the bridge for maybe a day or so.

Thankfully, he picked myself and four others, Ned Beake, Kimball Brassington, Neville Bentley, and Odel Acka, the last two being scouts as well as good soldiers, set off one night from the other side of the Isle by boat, out towards Stuntney, and made our way over towards the track to Cambridge. I had friends at Denny Abbey and as we were so close and may need their help in the near future we thought we would stop and see how things were with them, I was not at all sure what sort of reception I would receive.

I need not have worried as I was welcomed with open arms, as were my "friends", we needed to stick together like never before, they claimed.

They had heard all sorts of stories regarding myself, I had to try and explain which were somewhat exaggerated and which were not, an almost impossible job as they wanted to believe the most colourful ones. To be honest, even the battles we had fought in sounded really good now, we had won quite a few and I was very proud of the men I fought with.

Hereward and I had discussed leaving the Isle by our normal route, or via Stuntney or maybe going across the fen from near Aldreth and over from there to the mainland near the bridge.

It made perfect sense to go via Aldreth, I thought, Hereward said we ought to go by our normal route as he wanted to get the low down on just how good the work of the scouts was. We needed to know how accurate were the plans we had, we were going to have to rely on their efforts so much.

They were convincing, when talking in our planning room, were they that good in fact! I said it would be a good idea to take at least one scout with us.

Though I still had my doubts regarding going all that way in enemy held land, when all we needed to do was travel by boat from Aldreth and land near Willingham.

There was of course much to be learned by going overland regarding any enemy forces being prepared, where their scouts might be etc. I went along with what Hereward said in the end, looking back, it was not really my decision. If we had been caught, goodness knows what would have happened! Our force would be without their leader.

The men I was with, I introduced with different names as they might have heard of them and that may have caused problems, it was good to catch up with the Abbot and all who were not having an easy time themselves.

They insisted we ate with them and were sad to have to say goodbye, they hoped we would meet again soon in happier times. Those happier times were a lifetime away, I feared.

Cottenham

We then rowed over from Denny Abbey to Cottenham, the dock there was filled with piles of wood, sacks full of soil and ropes in and around the boats ready to move it all to Willingham, it was hard to imagine the amount of man hours this was taking. By this time a great deal of the wood etc. was taken direct to Belsars Hill as a track had been constructed to make the work faster.

William didn't lack ambition, this was a very impressive effort, he was not going to be stopped easily.

Our boat was hidden at an agreed spot with Saxon friends, we borrowed some horses to finish our trip to Willingham. These were left at some more friends and we travelled on by foot.

Six of the men who worked on a daily basis for the Normans trying to build the causeway changed their places with us as arranged and we joined the large bunch of workers who were working by taking trees from the circular protected area out across the causeway that was being constructed to get to Aldreth.

There were places we could see straight away that could be put on fire, where they had left piles of wood that would be easy to set alight, the type of timber that would burn ferociously with no difficultly this time of the year.

We worked pretty hard that day and got cussed at by the Normans for being lazy. They might have said a lot more had they realised just who they were talking to, Hereward and some of his best men, and myself of course, not sure where I fitted in yet! Though Herewards men listened to what I had to say and for the most part went along with it, I still had a job considering myself a leader with this fine group of men.

While talking amongst the other Saxons working here, they told us they had heard of a huge bridge being built off site somewhere near here. It must surely be being built as the bridge for the causeway over the river.

We decided the time to burn it all would be when they had struggled to put it in place. Burn the whole thing if we could, it would set them back months, a grand plan. We made notes of the best places to put fires, though we could come and look at it again before putting the plan into action, or at least try to.

It would be interesting to find out where the bridge was being built. It must be near the water somewhere as the only way of getting it to the river would be to float it into place, that didn't matter too much as we didn't intend to burn it where it was being built.

There was not a lot more to be gained by risking staying longer this time so we decided to head off back to the Isle in the morning. We enjoyed a fine meal and evening with our friends and listened with amusement to the way our lads were slowing down construction as much as they could.

They cut part through ropes and sent loads of wood off across the fen, or better still down river, when they had nearly got it into position, they had a job catching it then and bringing it back if they were told to.

Often they used horses to pull great logs, the horses would be spurred to leap into the water, taking the wood with them, then they would be brought back, silly, but very time consuming and a pain for the Normans. Normally they caught on and someone took a beating.

At the end of that day, we returned to our friends nearby, spoke nothing of what we were proposing, we said our goodbyes in the morning and left on horses. We were approaching what is now Rampton when we noticed a disturbance in the first few houses, we slowed to try and see what was happening.

It appeared that some Normans were causing trouble with the locals, it was getting nasty, we said to each other that we ought to pass by as it might risk what we were doing here.

Could we stand by and let these awful enemy maybe kill some of our people, I doubted it, we slowly made our way up to the houses, Hereward asked them what they were doing.

This just made them even more angry, they stopped what they were doing and attacked us, there were six of them to begin with, we drew our swords and began knocking them about, into the next world, if we could, as fast as we could.

I hadn't realised just how good these five men were with their swords, they just cut these enemy to pieces. One was heading for me and I was conscious of the fact that I was not perhaps as good as my new colleagues, the chap fairly threw himself at me, I defended myself badly, but was able to strike back as his sword went down, I luckily caught his arm quite well, not for him I might add, this left him a little disorientated and gave me time to finish him with a thrust through his chest.

We all had time to smile at one another in a congratulatory manner before we were knocked out of any thought of victory by the fact that there were at least ten horses riding right at us, more of the enemy we had not seen. We should have checked all of the area before attacking, it was not exactly large. A little late to tell ourselves off !

There was nowhere to run so we quickly lined up to meet the attack, in a moment I suggested we took the soldiers horses so we could fight the attackers. We met in the middle of the street, a pretty loud clash ensued, thankfully they were not as fast as us, we knocked several to the ground and slashed them with our swords, several of their horses reared, not used to battle, so we hit their riders. We had passed through the enemy so turned to face them again, charged, and all hell seemed to break loose as more and more horses joined the fight. Apparently the men of the parish thought they ought to join in the fun, much slashing and bashing over a few minutes and the enemy were all down, done for!

Peace returned, thankfully, two of our six were in a bit of trouble with cuts, and six of the village men were damaged as well.

We simple could leave no one to tell what had occurred here so we finished the enemy off. We had no choice as the parish would be wiped out if left to the Normans. The clean-up took longer than we thought it would, even though we moved at a fast pace, they agreed to take the horses far away and let them loose.

We shook hands with our new friends and quickly left the area, making sure they would clear the area of all evidence of what had just occurred. It was great to see us Saxons getting the confidence to fight back at last, we were making the difference. We just hoped we could carry it on, now we had the fightback started!

We quickly rode back to Cottenham. These enemy camps were huge, a great many soldiers were here, and seemed well protected by guards, we made notes in our heads as to where they stood, if they stayed in the same places or moved on a regular basis. These things we may need to know when we came back to at least try and burn the causeway. We would try and damage the dock here as well as that would slow any damage repair attempted by William and his men.

Back to Denny

We rowed back to Denny Abbey having got back to our boats, all was not well here, as we approached we saw about fifty horses tied in the grounds, so we slowed until we got quite close, tied our boat, and approached silently to find out what was happening.

There was a lot of clattering noise coming from one of the barns, several novices came running out of the main door. They were being chased by blasted Normans, nobody was left in peace any more it seemed, they were caught and knocked to the ground by these swine. The soldiers hit them, time after time, they only stopped when some of the senior staff came out shouting angrily for them to do so.

Takeover!

It seemed the Abbot was being replaced by a Norman, this was not going down well at all with the rest of the staff, no doubt he was French and spoke no English, Latin would be no problem, it's just to be extra awkward we had no doubt services would be conducted in French, so it was an awful wrench for everyone and some were not shy in telling the Norman he was not wanted.

The trouble with this very brave attitude with the enemy was likely to kill everyone here and perhaps torch the whole place. Common sense prevailed but only when the Abbot appeared to calm everyone.

This was what was going on in every area of the country, it was appalling to view at first hand, we knew we could not do anything at this time, the enemy took the Abbot away, goodness knows what his future held but whatever it was it was not going to be good. Quick and easy death, or long drawn out and painful death were not very good options!

We sadly made our way back to our boats and began the long way home to the Isle, there were nowhere near enough of us to make a difference anyway, we simple could not risk all we had planned to save Denny.

Even if we had the enemy would send out more soldiers to fight until they won, though we wanted to, we were desperate to get our plans together with the rest of the leaders and decide what to do and when to do it. We must strike back as soon as possible with a very heavy hand and maybe, just maybe, start to slow Williams progress over our land.

Spinney Abbey

We decided to make our way to Spinney Abbey and see if that lovely place of peace and quiet had escaped the Norman onslaught.

All approached slowly and could see nothing untoward, we sat in the boat and just watched to see if daily life had been changed, if any new men had been placed at the building.

We could hear chanting from the church, it was beautiful as it drifted across the water towards us, in English and Latin too, which is what we wanted to hear.

We moved our boat to the higher ground and walked over to the entrance. We were warmly greeted by all and took the Abbot to one side to tell him the disturbing news regarding Denny Abbey.

We were surprised he took it so lightly, he knew what was coming, he didn't expect it so soon, that was all. We invited everyone to come and join us on the Isle, close Spinney altogether and bring all they could carry with them that they needed.

The Abbot said he planned to do that anyway, to at least invite all who wanted to stay free to come with him. That turned out to be all here, so our party became somewhat larger all of a sudden.

They had three rowing boats, we began stacking books etc. into them.

A lot of items from the church were carefully packed so they would not get damaged, I tried to rush everyone as the enemy could appear at any moment and that would not be fun at all!

Eventually, we set off toward the Isle, they looked somewhat apprehensive as this was a leap into the unknown for them, though we tried to reassure them all that it would be exciting, never dull, like some of their life to the present had been. We had many people on the Isle who would need their services/help at times, so they would not be idle.

The boats made a little line in the water which created a lot of clanking of the oars!

Chapter 64

As we pulled away, we saw a number of horses coming through the shallows towards the Abbey, we had only just made our escape in time, but were very thankful we had done just that.

A couple of the men on horses saw us escaping and cried out to their fellow Normans to chase us, enough distance had been gained between us and them to be able to escape to deeper water where they could not follow, not easily anyway, this did not however stop them firing arrows at us.

We were able to jeer at them for letting us get away, much to their evident disgust.

We made our way to Barway, another small community on a dry piece of land before Stuntney, where we had some dried meats the men from Spinney had brought with them. The people here were friendly and brought us hot drinks to go with our meat.

They asked many questions, as to why the religious men were with us, we told them what had happened at Denny and Spinney. They were saddened by the news and wondered if they might get attacked, we tried to set their minds at rest by saying that often places like theirs were left alone as there was not much to gain by fighting over such a small piece of land.

We also added that they were welcome to come to the Isle, we would protect them to the best of our ability.

Back to our boats, heading for Stuntney, we were getting close to home and safety now, we were quite excited at the prospect of home and a good sleep. It had been quite a long trip with very little rest.

It was beginning to get dark when we left Stuntney for the very wet trip to the Isle, we had to navigate through the dips, bogs, and river before we got to dry land on the other side, as always.

Though we did not look forward to this part of our journey, we knew it was the only thing that kept the Norman army out of our refuge. If they ever got here in numbers, we would be in a lot of trouble.

The overall plan from my point of view was to have parts of our army up and down the country, training more and more groups, to prepare to take our country back, it was not to stay on the Isle and hide from reality.

After much groaning regarding cold water and mud we all stood on dry land and shook hands with each other. We had gained a lot of knowledge that would give us confidence when we came to bringing our next battle into being.

It really was an eye opener just to see the lengths William was going to try and get us out of the Isle. No matter what it was going to take him a long time, cost a lot of money and ultimately cost a lot in Norman lives, plus cause us a lot of pain no doubt.

We made our way to the main buildings, showed the Spinny brethren where to wash and clean their cloths and introduced them to the clergy already here, then went to get all of us leaders together to discuss our ideas regarding destroying Williams causeway and bridge.

Chapter 65

Hereward first thought a large group of soldiers would be best to make as big a dent as possible in Williams forces, to just smash our way through the enemy as we met them, I thought we would suffer huge losses and that would dent our confidence to such an extent that we may not carry the Saxon population with us afterwards.

Hereward reconsidered. I thought maybe I had gone too far against his idea, I then added that maybe a distraction battle might help to take some enemy soldiers away from Cottenham and Willingham to add to the force at Cambridge, if we were to send a large force to Cambridge, might that work?

I was surprised at the opposition to this and listened to other men saying it would be easier for a small band of men to get onto the causeway, set it alight and make a quick escape.

Hereward considered my proposal, his eyes lit up, he shouted "great idea, let's think about this!"

Arguments went to and fro, for and against, one good argument I put forward was to send a group of our fighters to Cambridge as a decoy, then a small band to the causeway to hopefully have some of the forces there moved to support Cambridge, thereby making it easier for the men at the Willingham/Belsars Hill causeway.

Another decoy group could be sent to St Ives, in the Huntingdon area, for the same purpose. With Earl Edwins force we could do so much more now.

We would make the Normans fear us, and leave. We would show them who ran England!

This idea was the one we stuck with in the end and everybody wanted in on the fighting.

At the end of the day a big meal followed and then some rest. Details would be worked out in the morning.

Most of us did not get much rest that night as our minds would not settle, it was exciting to think we were even considering going to fight an enemy group near or maybe even in the town of Cambridge.

We did not know how many men would be used, or indeed whose group would be going, would it be best to send a number of men from each group, or just one whole group?

The enemy had not even constructed the bridge yet, let alone put it in place, so there was quite a wait before the time would be right for this attack. We were just excited to be getting into a position where we could even think of inflicting real damage on the enemy.

There was little doubt the Normans would increase their force at Willingham camp as the work became nearer completion to protect it from our forces, so the more of Williams men we could get to rush to help their fellow Normans at Cambridge, as a distraction, the better.

A big fight against as many enemy soldiers as possible in the city itself, hopefully drawing men from Willingham, then a dash with a small group to light the bridge and causeway, possible the following day, allowing for the Willingham force to leave, seemed a great idea, it all sounded quite simple really, though we knew it would be far from that, actually bringing it to fruition proved to be a major task!

Then of course there was the other group to go to the St Ives and Huntingdon areas. These men would probable go the day before the thirty left to set the fire on the bridge. They would, hopefully, make more enemy go from the Willingham area to protect their own men from our other distraction force.

We made our number to 116 easily, it was an odd number but it worked for the time being, so many men wanted to join our unit, it was great! For the time being we stuck to 116 men as it worked well, the men were worried if we changed the number greatly we might lose the good luck that seemed to follow us about during fighting, though I considered that a little daft at best!

I had told all the leaders of my plan to add maybe 100 men to our number, so it would not be too much of a surprise if this happened. They were told to let their men know.

All the groups of fighting men were training more and more, everyone wanted to be involved, though no one knew the details outside the leaders, they all knew something was afoot soon.

Our spies at Willingham kept us in touch with progress, we even had some lads at the site where the bridge was being constructed.

Any of the existing Saxon workforce would have helped, but we felt men we had specially trained to get all the information needed was a better idea, so we were well placed to put into operation whatever we wanted whenever we wanted. We were ready.

Normans Attempting to Get Onto the Isle via Littleport

I suppose we had become a little lazy with our confidence on the Isle, being un-reachable by our enemy, so it was of great surprise to hear that they had landed at the far edge of the island. We had no idea how many boats or men were involved but we knew this had to be crushed right away, could you imagine the boost this could give the enemy? Part of our Isle held by the enemy, this could not be! They might establish a base there as a springboard to take the whole Isle. Surely not many invaders had managed to get onto the far end of our island!

Hereward was enraged that they had not been spotted in time.

Rather than go off in an un-disciplined manner, he got together about one hundred men from different groups, myself included, he always talked of using different troops as he wanted to get to know how they fought and how to command them and so we set off to sort out this problem as soon as possible.

We raced quite quickly along the track from Ely to Littleport, as we approached we could make out plenty of noise relating to a battle in progress. At least our men here had not waited for other soldiers to turn up, they had taken on the fight by themselves.

The French were at the towns approaches, our men were firing volleys of arrows at them, this had slowed them down or they could have taken it. It would have been much more difficult to fight house to house than in the open. So we rode straight into action.

There must have been approximately one hundred enemies here, it was really bad that they could have got here without being seen approaching, we must put more men defending this place right away, and make sure they do their job! Any more must be repulsed before they could even attempt to land, ever! The enemy must have spent an awful long time getting to the end of Littleport as it was cut off by massive banks of reeds and deep water, they must have travelled via the Downham Market area, then through the water to avoid detection of any sort. In future we would have a considerable force based in this area at all times.

Chapter 66

Littleport

Back to the matter in hand, Hereward said we should attack in line as they were watching the flight of arrows from our men near the houses, as a result they were distracted so we got quite close before they realised we were there.

We met them sideways on, our men stopped firing as soon as they realised we were attacking, clashing swords made a huge noise, as usual. Much shouting from the French to fall back and hold their line, though it seemed not many soldiers were listening. A full force of men on horseback now going at some speed with swords drawn, shouting attack! Attack! Tended to have the desired effect on a force on foot, the effect was to run away as fast as possible!

As our horses met the somewhat bedraggled line, we threw our swords into the mix, shouts, screams and death mingled with some unrepeatable cries from the French, as one would expect I suppose.

The whole line scattered under the weight of the horses, we reached what was the other side of the line or at least where it should have been, and turned the horses, attacking again, thrashing swords against the enemy.

We Had the Advantage and We Used It to Great Effect

Some men had stayed with the boats and they were frantically trying to get at least some of their soldiers on board and then to get away. I shouted for at least ten men to go and stop anyone leaving, no time to check which men. I saw a few of my original fifty men quickly leave, plus a few I did not know at present and hoped they would sort out the situation quickly.

I turned to see Hereward bashing the living daylights out of a couple of Normans over to one side, I suddenly saw some movement.

About six Normans had decided to get the man on his rather outstanding coloured horse, they were aiming their bows right at him, I shouted to Hereward at the top of my voice to beware, the group were suddenly bashed apart by one of our lads on horseback, one was hit by a sword and would take no further part in this fight.

The others quickly stood and fired their deadly arrows, as they had done so quickly they were not very accurate, Hereward by this time lay down on his mount to one side of his horse opposite to the Normans, so he was hidden from the arrows of death! One actualy flew into and struck into his saddle, which was much too close!

I decided it was time for me to enter this particular fight again, so I urged my horse forward. It was not far so the men began to alter their attack from Hereward to me, this could turn nasty, I suddenly thought, no time to re consider!

I ducked under the first arrows and was soon putting one enemy out of this fight, Hereward came crashing through and knocked another to his death. We glanced at each other, Hereward nodded to me, as we both surged forward to finish the job. Both of us got several more of the enemy, defending ourselves as we went, thrashing our swords to left and then right, moving fast.

Other battles were occurring all around us, we were fighting quite a number of the best armed and trained soldiers who were up for this fight. No need for Hereward or myself to talk, that could wait until after the fighting, it was by no mean easy.

Several of our men were down we could see, a great many more French were in trouble which was good, a number were still attempting to escape, we had that area sealed off and we would continue with our policy of wiping out the opposition, no one to tell William and his leaders! That would make him reluctant to send more soldiers this way, hopefully.

A few fights were on going where the number of our men versus the Normans was on the side of our visitors, we rounded up our men who were not otherwise occupied and pulled them back into the fight to even up the numbers.

This proved decisive, as we hacked our way towards victory, though none of this was easy, we were beginning to lay waste to these invaders. We were very angry they had come so close and we took it out on these soldiers.

Hereward was again setting the standard from the front so I thought I had better re-join him. It was scary stuff, leading from the front, swords clashing, horses grunting, men shouting. I saw a lance/spear hurled at Hereward and cried out for him to move. Luckily he did, it missed him by inches, too damned close!

We all just kept moving forward, even if someone fell, exhausting and killing these hated enemies. How dare they invade our Isle! We would have none of this! We would have the last word and we were going to win this war, this battle first, then the war. Make no mistake.

We came to the end of the Norman line and turned to see much devastation of the enemy, much better for us. Hereward and I shouted, at the same moment, to all to stand in line and move towards clearing all enemy soldiers.

They were trying to decide what to do, one or two small groups of a somewhat bewildered enemy. We trotted towards them, they organised themselves as best they could and attacked us. Silly really, they knew we could show them no mercy and we didn't!

When the job was done, we all went back to silence, it could be a little eerie this place. Their boats were nearby hidden in the reed beds at the edge of our Island. We may have to consider cutting all the reed beds close to the Isle, so we could easily see what was coming and going. This would be a lot of work but we would be much safer so it was without doubt worth doing.

We isolated the parts, a few weeks later on land and in the water, that needed cutting away and then set it alight, very successful it was too!

All of us were more than a little exhausted after this fight, we took care of our injured and left the scene, back to Ely itself.

The soldiers left here were instructed that they must keep an eye on the reed beds at all times, no excuses! We would be sending more men to make sure nobody came this way again. We also said a well done for taking on the enemy by themselves, and sending a couple of guys to warn us of their situation.

Hereward and Myself

No time for words but looking back this was a huge moment for me, so important for Hereward and I working, planning and fighting together. I felt I belonged with this force and that we had much to do. I knew I could help Hereward and his men, he knew it also.

I hoped they didn't lack the ambition I had for our enterprise, that of taking back our land by force. I would press to impose my thoughts and plans, I would not stop either until all saw the logic of those ideas.

Cedric and I knew this would take a long time to plan and even more to bring to fruition, I hoped my powers of persuasion were going to win the day, and eventually the war, for us all, certainly not just ourselves.

News of the battle travelled fast, as we approached the main buildings, people began cheering us, this was new to me. I obviously liked winning, I could most assuredly get much more used to being cheered as well, though I must admit to being embarrassed.

Hereward said he was mighty pleased to hear my shout regarding the spear, thanked me, and said he looked forward to working with me, on the battle lines or with planning. We must talk more as time went by. Great news for me, just what I needed to hear. Imagine, for a moment, what it was like to receive such complements from the greatest man of the moment, Hereward the Wake!

Chapter 67

After much excited talk we cleaned ourselves and went for our meal, much more talk, plus the obligatory ale, or maybe two!

Hereward shouted for me to join the main table, I said I felt I had a duty to stay with my group of men, he cried, nonsense! And even asked my men if they minded that I join his table if only for this meal.

They all thanked me for fighting well and especially for making sure Hereward did not get sliced in two by the spear. So I joined Hereward and his leaders.

Hereward told them of our shouting out commands at the same moment in the fighting, I was somewhat embarrassed by this I must admit, not used to taking complements, I did not know how to respond.

The atmosphere was fantastic that evening. Our mission had properly begun. All of Herewards men treated me as though I was a kind of long lost friend, I was treated with great respect, when I spoke, they listened and it felt great!

Planning the Battles

The next morning, planning proper began for our "excursion" to Cambridge and Saint Ives/Huntingdon to fight and distract Williams soldiers so we could send our party to burn as much of the causeway as possible, when the bridge was in place, that is. We found it was under construction some way up river so it could presumable be floated into place, that made perfect sense, it was by no means finished yet so we had a bit of time to make sure we got the plan of attack right. We assumed it was being built off site as they could protect it better than if it was put together slowly on site as it would be much too easy for us to attack and very difficult to build over the river in sections.

We needed to know how many soldiers were around Cambridge, how many in total could William call on in an emergency, so we sent out our scouts to get this information as quickly as possible. We already had much of it, we just needed to make sure it was as up to date as possible.

William moved his men around as a matter of common practice, so that it was a job to keep tabs on, our scouts would probably have to stay out until we sent out our force towards Cambridge.

They were sent out in twos, not singles as we once did, so one would stay at all times, the other would report back to us any major changes. Some would stay out in the bush, others would be staying at friends around the area.

They would have to be very careful they were not caught and tortured, William might well be expecting an attack on his beloved causeway as if he was in our position he would do the same, our scouts had no knowledge of what we planned so they could not help him anyway.

We sent them out, twenty men, to find out who, and how many enemy were where. Some left with horses, some on foot, the foot ones were not going far so they did not need them, horses could be seen too easily at times and if not needed were not used.

Chapter 68

We did not hear from anyone for quite some time, I began to think they may have been caught, then a couple of them returned with the bad news of new groups of soldiers coming from where they did not know. Clearly William thought something might be afoot with us, though maybe he was just bringing these men in to protect his causeway, we might just have to wait and see, though clearly this was going to be more difficult than we had thought to begin with.

We were going to have to use more men than we anticipated. It all seemed so easy when we first talked about this fighting, William's forces seemed intent on trying to stop us in our tracks!

The 500. Earl Morcars Group
Plans for the Fight at Cambridge

We began selecting men to go with the earl for the distraction force to go to Cambridge, this was to help get them to know each other and fight as a unit. Hereward put some names together and so did I, a couple of his leaders did likewise.

This really took an age as we were desperately trying to get this right first time. We all felt it was important to get the best people to do the right job first time.

Looking back, we could have chopped and changed as we went along so it was not that important, we just felt it was at the time. In retrospect we were being too picky, all our men fought well, and they all wanted in on this fight.

Trying to integrate all these different soldiers from different places who had different military backgrounds was quite a job.

Eventually we had a list of five hundred men, the largest amount I had ever dealt with, looking at it the ones I had picked were not necessarily the biggest and strongest, many of them were good thinkers under pressure, men who got it right first time, no matter what, especially in the heat of battle and that would be what counted. We had so many people on and near the Isle now food was having to be brought onto it. Things would have to change in the long run as to how we managed our population on our Isle.

The level of fitness was not good with some men so we devised a program to get all up to about the same level, some grumbled about it not being important, couldn't be bothered. They were either dropped from the group or helped through the program. After a time, these men felt so much better in themselves, I am sure that it made them better fighters, more confident, that they agreed it was good.

This was an important fight to win, I have always believed being as fit as possible at all times was a good thing, being fit and able to march and fight long drawn out battles can only be an advantage over your enemy.

Lazy Human Beings Simply Do Not Achieve Anything!

Even Hereward was surprised at how the groups improved with fitness, he initially thought it was a bit of a silly idea, almost a waste of time. I was glad to prove him wrong, as we pushed our force harder and harder, after our experience of all the fighting we had achieved, we knew it made sense.

The up to date plans of the area were getting filled out now, we had all the groups of enemy soldiers noted, there seemed to be no particular pattern to cover it, we could not see why William had put a group here or there, most were near tracks, to move them at short notice. It was clear his intention was to take the Isle as soon as possible, if at all possible. We would have to try and place more spies at Cambridge in particular and try and find out the timetable, though we knew there was only a small chance we would get the information we needed, it was worth a try!maybe some free ale could be given to some soldiers in our ale houses in the search for information.

We would then disrupt these groups of the enemy each and every day as much as we could as often as we could to drag down their confidence and ability to fight. We determined to not sit and let them dictate the time and place of battle.

I was not going to let our spies stay with Saxons for longer than was necessary so we moved them around a lot as we knew William tortured people nearly to death, treated enemy's dreadfully, cutting off hands, legs, blinding people etc. if they had helped his enemy. The stories going around in relation to him wiping out whole communities in the north of England and burning their houses to the ground were dreadful. He simple did not give a damn for his fellow human beings on this planet, if you were against his thoughts.

Most of our spies were living rough now, it was becoming more of a job to stay undetected, enemy troops all over the place!

Earl Morcar Confirmed as Leader of the 200

We had to decide who was going to lead the fighting force to Cambridge, and who was going to lead the group to set the causeway alight, the earl Morcar was told of the privilege. It was clear that this group ought to have to be much larger than we had planned as the enemy defending it was much larger than it had been when we first talked about it.

We kept to the 500 in the end as we needed to be able to move fast if needed and felt more men might just cause more problems, movement wise, this was also our first mission and we wanted to learn before we put out maybe 800 men at a time to fight. It was so exciting to be thinking in such numbers! The future looked good for our dreams and ambition! as they amounted to the same thing in reality.

All the leaders stepped forward, most wanting to lead the fight at Cambridge, to fight the enemy at their strongest, was something nobody could resist, it seemed.

Before the Fighting

We arranged all the soldiers going in the earls group, there looked many more than 500 men, it was just to get an idea, and it was a good one, of the force going, they all claimed their usual horses and that more than doubled the size of the group.

It was very exciting looking at them all, just thinking of our project, made it all encompassing, it had taken over our lives, we all felt we were born for this fight and what happened after would be a fantastic success or a disaster, though I much preferred the former to the latter!

The day was approaching when we would be set loose for the biggest fight of all in this fenland of ours, quite a few drinking sessions, I mean parties, were happening each night, everyone was letting off steam, I swear you could cut the air at times, it was so thick. There was a joy as we were about to do what we had trained, and talked about, for so long for, at long last.

It was decided we had to halt the drinking three days before we left, when we did they all knew we had those three days to properly sober up and perhaps do some more training, then the day was upon us.

Chapter 69

The 500 prepare to leave. Cambridge in our sights at last, Morcar to lead!

The Earl Morcar was appointed first in command of the Cambridge group, he had a great deal of experience, gained not only from Hastings but many battles before that, especially the ones at Stamford Bridge against the Vikings. I was asked if I would like to be his second, and to be frank I was amazed at the complement, but I wanted to be involved in the destruction of the causeway if possible.

Hereward had already said he would command this group, I enjoyed "working" alongside him, and could learn much as well, plus I hope I don't flatter myself in saying we got on very well, our ideas in battle seemed to be similar, though the objective was to win, how you got there, from a command point of view, was helped no end by knowing your fellow leader was on the same wavelength.

The Earl appointed Kendryek Albert as his second in command, this was quite a surprise, though he had fought with him a few times, we didn't know what they had both been through, he did prove to be excellent on the field of battle. He was a silent fellow, except in battle, and that was what we needed above all else at this time.

The earl and Kendryek fought planned battles against each other, they began pressing us to let them go and fight one of the enemy groups outside the Isle, just to prove to each other that they were ready.

Eventually, we submitted, though we would take a number of our men with us to help out if needed, we could not risk losing men at any time, let alone now, that would be a devastating blow from which it would take some time to recover.

We looked at our plans as to where a similar number of men were grouped. Near Newmarket seemed about the best test nearby, numbers were similar and there was quite a distance between the next enemy group, so they would have a job calling in other soldiers quickly.

This was put to the next meeting of leaders and was agreed.

The Earl waited for a pretty wild stormy night, it became quite dark early, and the soldiers began leading their horses off the Isle. After the 500 left, so men cleared any markings we had made to disguise our passing, this group had become invaluable "cleaners", the earl led his men on a route through the trees so no one would detect his force.

We were about five hundred and thirty men in all so it was quite difficult staying in touch, good practice for another time, I thought? We seemed slow but it was not far to go, we made it well before sun rise as planned. We ate and drank that which we had brought with us and made ready. Some didn't eat before fight.

We wished them well and stayed back within several rows of trees for cover, not too far away so we could get involved if needed. I thought we may be needed to "tip" the balance if the fight looked like going the wrong way.

The camp had sentries so from a safe distance the earl sent his men to deal with them, we could not make out how it was going but saw the men return so presumed that went well. He sent out four groups of twenty-five at points around the camp and was quickly ready for the attack, which he signalled. He held back the rest to attack a little later.

The silence turned to mega noise, horse noises, arrows slewing through the air, swords crashing against swords and shields, fires being disturbed, it all looked an awful mess from where we were, enemy horses cut lose in terror, small huts on fire, an awful lot of enemy soldiers plainly dead, a lot dying from injuries and a lot more to die, a truly dreadful situation really but I remind those who might be reading this sometime in the future that we were not the aggressor in these dealings, that was down to the invader of our land.

We thought jokingly we might as well pack up and go home at this point, the earls men had broken into smaller groups and they were systematically knocking out the enemy as they went through their camp. They were ferocious in the way they sought a quick conclusion to the end of this fight.

There was one group of the enemy towards the middle, the earl noticed in the mayhem, pulled a number of his men to him and attacked. This was a desperate attempt by the enemy leaders to fight and survive, he drove his group from the front and smashed into it with speed and strength, knocking out three or four men as he went for the leader, he smashed his sword into the man on the grounds sword, almost knocking it out of his hands.

He quickly turned and went back for him, he turned too quickly and his horse bucked and threw him off. He only just had time to stand as the enemy leader moved quickly to kill him.

He managed to brush off the first strike and hit the other fellow in the head as he went close by. He was angry now, sword at the ready, he closed on the enemy.

Now was his chance to show who was boss of this fight, he thrust at him, I thought a little weakly, and the enemy brushed his effort away, this could be going wrong at any moment. He very quickly turned and caught out the other man, cutting his arm, quite badly. One final attempt by him to rescue the fight with all the strength he tried to catch out our earl, who saw what was coming and thrust his sword through the man's chest, fight ended!

He signalled for his other men to join the fighting which they very quickly did to great effect; they had lined up on the other side of the tree line, just past the ditch, and immediately put many enemies to the sword.

Some more fighting continued but as the men left saw their leaders fall they clearly lost heart, they more or less died where they stood.

This was perhaps a slight exaggeration as one group of brave fellows gathered to make a stand, the earl quickly gathered men around him as he saw these enemy and led a charge, a huge roar went up from him and these men.

All the other fighting seemed to stop, momentarily, and watch the earl almost flatten the opposition with huge destruction. The Saxons turned back to their particular fights with renewed energy! A true leader was earl Morcar! an example to all.

When all the action had stopped, we rode down to talk with as many men as we could, we thought it good to talk to men of all ranks as well as the earl, they had, after all, all fought for this victory, it was good for moral to include all the men involved.

Fighting Was Always a Team Effort

Now was the time to quickly lose ourselves in the woods on our way home, we were not sure if any enemy had managed to escape, if so, he would soon get word to their leaders. He would be sure to get soldiers here to fight us, though he must know we would not remain long after the battle.

We broke up into smaller groups and kept a careful eye on any tracks we could see, nothing much happened until we got quite close to our crossing point onto the Isle.

We could see smoke billowing up into the sky, someone had set light to the reeds.

Just what was going on? We could not tell from where we were but this could be a nightmare for us all!

We were far enough away to leap from our horses, leave them with a good guard, and make haste to the site of the fires. They were some way from our entry point we were glad to see, but clearly a number of boats were spreading this fire possible with the hope of catching our men, perhaps on our return.

Had a spy in our midst let the enemy know a large force had left the Isle? How could they otherwise know we had left? A lot of questions to ask! Maybe they had just chosen a good time for them to light the screen that hid us! We had no idea but all we did know was that something would have to be done and quickly!

Chapter 70

This smelt of one of us, perhaps, being bribed to tell what we planned to do, a traitor in our midst, the lowest of all lows in human terms, could this possible be! One of our own people stabbing us in the back....surely not?

We would go over this later. Now was the time to try and deal with this situation against the enemy who seemed intent on trying to perhaps burn us out.

The leaders were all with me, we were well hidden, behind groups of reed beds and the odd tree on a small outcrop of land, we could see the enemy on their boats casting pieces of wood on fire onto the reeds and helping the flames jump from one batch to another.

This was not good at all, we had to act quickly as this area hid one of our underwater tracks onto the Isle and as this burnt area got ever larger it would be more and more difficult to keep it hidden.

Luckily we had caught the enemy at the start of this burning and if we could put it out quickly, we would not lose much cover.

What to do? There didn't seem to be many men on the boats, possible fifty we thought, the nearest dry land was quite a distance away so even if we dealt with these men it would take some time for more soldiers, if there were any nearby, to come to their aid.

We could see movement on the Isle, so our men knew what was going on. It seemed that no Norman had yet got onto the Isle so they had not found our track, which was good.

I sent Thomas Eltisle back to our men to get the best men to loose accurate arrows at the enemy from this distance, I knew of eight who could consistently do just that. We had to act fast, so I sent out four of our party who were good shots with their arrows, they got to a point I said and aimed at and shot several of the enemy.

Panic went on in the boats, they had not seen where the arrows were loosed from so were looking in all directions. Another batch of arrows fell on them, several more knocked out of the game, amidst shouts of pain and indignation!

They were more or less trapped in the smouldering reed beds so we kept firing to try and finish them off as quickly as possible.

When the new men arrived, we sent them out to points so that the area these Normans were using was encircled, took quite a time as we were all in pretty deep water, I also sent out some of the men who were very good at hand to hand fighting, I doubted the arrow men would get them all.

There was not much wind, so the fire was slow taking effect.

Stilts

I thought that we should have had our stilts at the ready, they were great to use to fight, some of the men were simple superb at using them, a real skill, a great way to travel quickly through water. Having said that you had to be careful of staying near reed beds as it could become very deep, very quickly and, as you can imagine, they were not much use in deep water! Nor were my soldiers.

Anyway, we didn't have them on this occasion so we would attack as we were. All men at the ready, I fired arrows and was pleased to see someone go down, all the other shooters let fly again, many Normans hit the water.

Panic ensued, oars and boats moving in confusion as they had no idea where we were, some went straight towards our chaps with the bows, they were quickly dealt with, others headed for areas not covered very well.

I cursed myself for not sending out more men, however, we were easily dealing with these people. There were not enough men to do this job and leave out scouts to tell if someone was coming, they had not been clever!

One boat made it to the reed root clump which gave them the chance to stand in the water and not sink into the bog and the men jumped out of it, there were six of them, pretty angry as they had been enjoying themselves.

Two of our men fired into the reeds but to no avail. They rushed as best they could to get to where the enemy had gone, one prepared to fire another shot, before he could let it lose, he took an arrow in his side and crashed into the water. Two of our men rushed out to get him, the other man could see where the shot had come from, he aimed and fired into the reeds, there was a cry followed by a loud splash, got that one! I thought to myself!

Two more men left to join the one chasing, they went into reeds, lots of sword clashing and a bit of groaning, we hoped some more had left the fight. All other enemy were dealt with so we waited.

You could hear more arrows being let lose, men crashing through the water as fast as they could travel.

After about ten minutes our men returned and confirmed that the other four were now dead so we set about dealing with the fire, this was relatively easy, as it had not yet grabbed hold on a large enough scale, though trying to clear this mess was not going to be easy. We may even have to find ourselves another way to get onto the Isle, this was not our usual point of entry. It was a sort of back door entry, we knew of it but it was difficult to cross even for those who knew it quite well, not far from the Cambridge end of the Isle.

If they did find the entry point we would have to build some sort of trap on land so nobody could use it any more. I hasten to add that this track we used was not really a track, it went up and down in the water, those who used it had got to know just where the deep parts were, and the shallows, not that there were many of them.

As usual, we cleared the bodies, well away from here, we heaped them onto boats, no easy task as their clothes were all soaking with water, and left them hidden in one of the wilder parts of the fen.

The boats we could use ourselves, we left them in the fen where we left our boats normally, though someone pointed out that if we had a spy in our midst we may have to move them again, not a good thought, having to change everything just because of a possible low life!

In a long line we clambered onto our beloved Isle once more to be greeted by the many people who had gathered at this place of entry, they were trying to find out about the fire on the fen. They said they had seen us fighting, what were we going to do about the now clear area that was our disguised entry point.

It wasn't that large an area when you considered the whole area of fenland but it did take in a section which we would rather not have drawn attention too.

All I could say was we would be meeting later to decide that, talk was easy, there was really little we could do about it, just hope it grew back quickly!

The other leaders greeted us well and asked how we had got on. It had been a very good exercise for all involved, marred only by the destruction of the reeds.

We all talked of possible traitors in the camp, there were an awful lot of people here now, perhaps we ought to start an Isle force to keep order, maybe we could track this person down that way. Interview anyone who seemed to be spending more money than they were paid, there must be a way of finding him, or her, come to that, that is, if they existed.

An awful lot of the families of our men were living in their communities were they came from, that would make the job even harder, we could make inquiries at least, though. As the odd fight was breaking out, not helped by ale, we could maybe keep an eye on that problem too. Order was of great importance, especially in time of war.

Chapter 71

Order Guard, Keeping Order!

So we selected a leader for this group, a Girvii named Oswin, he seemed up for the job, he was to get six men to begin with and we explained what was required of them. He teamed up with Eadgifu, Aescwine, Seax, Suningfu, Edjar, Ecgfrith, obviously it was a Girvii team, we felt they would do a difficult job well under very difficult circumstances.

If they did not, we would appoint someone else! He was to look at faults in stories from earning and spending and anything else that caught his eye. We would monitor them on a monthly basis and see what information they could gather.

We asked everyone to keep an eye open for any odd behaviour from anyone. Many people had been reported to the leaders for odd behaviour since it became clear there may be a traitor in our midst, maybe there wasn't, never the less, it was important to check it out.

Better to be careful than plain stupid! I felt the Saxons would more easily talk to someone who was not one of us, so to speak, hopefully feel compelled to do so. We would wait and see.

They were to start work right away as there was no time to lose!
Earl Morcar.

The earl asked me how the fight had looked from our vantage point, I was amazed he asked that of me, I had obviously got myself a reputation amongst the leaders already which was very good. I said it began as a bit of a mess, this was to be expected, but soon it became clear that he knew what he was doing, each group fighting towards the centre, knocking out the enemy as they went, trying to knock out every soldier in their way, when he rounded it off by destroying the enemy leaders, bit like cutting off a monsters head, the rest died too.

He clapped my shoulder and laughed, liking the way I explained his battle plan.

Viewing the Plans

The leaders took a look at the plans altogether to get an up to date idea of how many Normans there were between us and Cambridge. There were a huge number we estimated, he surely couldn't have many more in the country. It seemed that many! We talked about how our force could go around and just fight in Cambridge, but then we would have to meet some other enemy force on our return journey. We thought and considered just what were we to do?

Hereward and the earl were talking quietly about maybe sending out another distraction force to take more enemy soldiers, more to confuse them, away from the Willingham force near the causeway. We had idly talked before of such a thing but now I joined in that it sounded as though it was getting even more complicated but it could just work.

All the leaders were up for this it turned out, so we began to think of how many men would be needed to form a huge distraction and indeed where to send them, which enemy group was going to get the benefit of being slaughtered by us? Or at the very least attacked.

We could manage men, equipment and horses at a pinch, this was going to need a lot more thinking about!

The Huntingdon/St Ives area looked like a good bet, if we had some fighting with the enemy groups on the way there, William may get the message and send more of his men from Willingham to help those areas.

With all this going on we could slip along, the thirty of us, after the Huntingdon/ St Ives fighting had cleared our way to Willingham by their force moving out to attack our men at the nearby towns and then for us to destroy the causeway with fire. This may sound complicated but it was not, I assure you.

This made more sense all the more we thought about it, a sound plan. We knew of course that even sound plans could go wrong, so I, for one, was a little wary.

Sending out so many men would leave the Isle not terrible well defended but we knew William would have so much on his hands coming to terms with our fighting forces that it was unlikely he would have time to consider doing anything as adventurous as attacking our base in the hope it would be undefended. In fact we left a motley crew who dug trenches along the edge of the Isle from which it was relatively easy to defend.

We got all the latest plans of all the enemy camps together, they didn't change a huge amount, but it was important that we saw the most up to date possible. This gave us all a confidence which at the time we needed, above all else, as these fights were a very big deal for us and our country as a whole.

Chapter 72

Training Force to Attack the Enemy in Huge Numbers! 730 Men to Battle!

Our woodsmen were said to be working twenty-four hours a day making arrows in the main, some bows and a lot of strings for them.

We selected who were going out with Morcar, 500 men, to Cambridge, then one group of 100 men, Earl Edwin and Vitt Hal Biotmonap, leader of the girvii would lead this group who were going to St Ives/Huntingdon, after giving it some thought we decided to add another 100 group as we had the men, the more pain and confusion we could inflict on these enemy the better and who were going with us, the 30 men, which seemed a tiny number considering our task but that I suppose was its beauty, its size, as we ride about unnoticed, that at least was the hope!

All was coming together for our greatest adventure yet, just hoped it was going to work. We were very confident that it would, most of the time, at least, we were a good seasoned, experienced and very fit bunch of very determined soldiers. Us Anglo Saxons were not to be written off just yet!

It appeared the enemy had not done much regarding the soldiers who had burned the fen reeds trying to find our point of entry to the Isle, he must surely have been told of the men who had not returned, with or without the boats they had used.

Perhaps William had too much going on in his mind, what must he be planning, I pondered. We had soldiers camping on the Isle out near where the fire had been set and our landing point to keep an eye on anything that was going on amongst the reed beds. Some boats of enemy soldiers had come near on one occasion, our men shot many arrows into the boats and the men who were left alive soon rowed out of range so they didn't get to see much of the burned area.

They had lost a good fifty men, plus, and they simple didn't seem bothered. It was a nice job for our soldiers, keeping an eye on the area, as they cooked their food, played games, tried to keep out of sight from the water and fished, a hard life being a soldier! We changed to new men every week, a little holiday for these men!

The Cambridge Battle led by Earl Morcar and the 500 soldiers.

This group was the largest planned attack we had ever sent out for the specific task of knocking out as many enemies as possible, we were expecting great things of Earl Morcar and his men. If they could have any enemy troops moved from Cottenham and Willingham to help defend Cambridge that would be good, it would help both of the other groups, that was part of the plan!

Later, we hoped more enemy would be moved to help out their forces being attacked at St Ives/Huntingdon.

Using a Roman Idea! An aside.

Talking of plans, the Abbot of Spinney Abbey, had told of the Notitia. He had told Hereward some time ago.

It was a civil and military survey of the Roman Empire, he only saw the survey for England, compiled at the beginning of the fifth-century, obviously up dated, it gave names and forces at each Roman station and it gave the distance between each. It was him that originally noted this fact, this was originally where the idea came from to help our forces do much the same thing regarding enemy soldier numbers? And to keep these plans up to date! This was not the way the Romans had used their plans, we adapted the idea to suit us. It was a huge advantage before going into battle, knowing more or less exactly how many soldiers were stationed where. We knew which camp to hit and which to avoid if we could.

The 500 leave to fight at Cam-Bridge. Earl Morcar and his men.

Five hundred men and horses with their packs took some time to get off the Isle, they began to leave as it became dark, this should give them time to get away from this area before anyone knew they had left. We knew spies were dotted around us, we often fed them lies to confound them, we would do our best to give our men any advantage we could.

The earl led from the front, as usual, after bidding all farewell, he was wished every success by everyone on the Isle. Everyone was in good spirits, looking towards a future hopefully without Normans, going off the Isle to take the fight to them instead of just hiding from them, here on the Isle, at the Camp of Refuge.

He set off towards Brandon, in batches of twenty, keeping noise to a minimum, once clear of the Great Fen they rode south, there was much water and fenland between here and where they needed to be but it proved no problem to get over. Like the earl said a problem was just something to overcome, regardless!

Then they aimed for the Chippenham area, his men liked this as it was out of the blasted water! They often joked about growing fins and scales, and how it would make life so much easier for them.

They turned right before Chippenham and took the track towards Burwell, then past the Reach road, they avoided being seen by anybody in these settlements, where they could, as word would soon travel. Every time someone was seen by a scout he would tell the Earl and they would try and get into cover in time to avoid being seen, it seemed to work so they carried on. This did become useless after a time as they simple could not move out of the way for small numbers of local men and women. They were just careful when enemy soldiers were noticed. Doubtless word would get out but probable by the time their work would be done!

The force still hoped the scouts had done their jobs and the plans they helped draw were correct, time alone could soon tell on that one. He did not like trusting anyone, ever, but realised he had to on this occasion, if a lot of troop movements had taken place since this was drawn up, it would be useless, let's be optimistic, he thought.

They were seen by a small group of troops near Burwell, they attacked our men much too soon, they had no idea our force was five hundred strong. The first group simple stood their ground, swords ready, and engaged them, basically, brushing their swords away. By this time, another twenty had caught up with them, they used bows and arrows to knock out a few. Swords were drawn and they all clashed. This group of enemy seemed young with not much experience, they were not going to have the chance of more experience as they were killed off! The Normans would have given us no quarter, so we gave none either! You could say we returned the compliment, these were hard times indeed!

The bodies were pulled into the brush and the horse's hind quarters were slapped to get them out of the area though they seemed more intent on feeding. They led them away through a batch of trees, so they were out of sight.

His force didn't want to wait around so they set off, passing between Reach and Swaffham Prior, nice and silent here, one of the scouts came in, very excited, to let us know there was a camp nearby at Swaffham Prior. They had checked the plan, it was only stated as a small camp, it had obviously been increased very recently. More troops brought in to fight the men on the Isle, seemed a good place to begin battling the enemy.

The Earl took a couple of his leaders to where the scout pointed and saw a pretty large encampment, not being very well protected by guards, they moved around under cover of trees and made a note of all guards. The gaps between them were much too large for them to help one another if attacked, or to keep an eye open for each other.

They checked to see if a number of groups could attack almost at once by going in on tracks rather than struggling through bushes and ditches, in small numbers, thereby raising the alarm. Speed was important, keeping the element of surprise.

There were three good entry points that would work, our men could storm the area quite well causing no end of damage to this camp. A couple of other places were going to be used for smaller numbers of men to gather before they attacked, so the force would be everywhere, all around this camp causing as much mayhem as possible. They must remember to let a few get away, at least to the next camp, so William would inevitably get to know as soon as possible, hoping he would draw in support troops from other units from villages towards Ely making the defence of those places harder, so us thirty men had a better chance of achieving the goals we were after for advantage to all three attacking forces. Let me explain better, the main 700 men would go in hard and fast causing mayhem, forcing William to send word out to the Willingham camp to send men from there to help the towns attacked, by which time our 700 would have left their fighting and would hopefully be on their way home so the 30 of us could do our work, having a much smaller enemy camp to deal with! hopefully you have got the idea?

Swaffam Bulbeck

The earl said they must strike hard and fast to cause as much mayhem as possible so the men who were let "escape" thought perhaps the force was bigger than it really was, they must get the attention of the enemy, this was the only way he knew how it could be achieved.

He had done it once before and he liked to think that it worked! Time would soon tell if that were true or not.

He silently returned with his men. He told of the plan, all nodded in agreement, it was decided to walk their horses around to the points of entry. After an agreed time, provided they were not seen, they would attack at the agreed moment after they had split up, having sent up an arrow to announce they were ready.

The horses were led around camp and they were all ready to destroy the place, or at least try!

At more or less the agreed moment, they fired arrows into the air from each group, before they hit the ground, they were off into a daylight fight against the dreaded Normans. They aimed more and more arrows at anyone that moved in the camp, men were shouting and cursing, more and more as the arrows flew, it was rather like catching chickens in a pen. What a racket, a melee of men, horses and fighting, in other words, a normal battle, hard to describe on paper!

All our men had worked hard, training day and night, for this moment, so with great relish they smashed their way into the Norman compound, some cut the enemies horses loose and chased them away, some bashed into small huts that had been erected to keep off the rain, and slashed with their swords at their foe as they struggled to get into fighting mode, most not having time to pull their swords, to cause mayhem was the order of the day and they were all doing their best to achieve that.

Our earl led from the front, as usual, horses to his left and right to support him. Go for the main hut, get the leader of this troop and his underlings. You could be sure that once they were gone, things would get easier, some would lose some of their confidence.

A number of the enemy had managed to get on their horses, they were going to assist their leaders, they could obviously see what the earl was trying to do, in a split second the earl and four of his best men turned to attack these enemy.

The earl and two men struck first at these men with full force and ferocity they knocked them aside, the other two were with them now. They knocked the enemy senseless and carried on their way to get the leaders again, as if nothing had been in their way, it was so hard and fast!

Horses and men running everywhere, it really was mayhem, no other word for it.

The men in the middle had no horses so in the spirit of honour the five Saxons leapt from their mounts to take these men on in equal combat.

The head man gave a sheepish grin in acknowledgement of the Saxons actions and attacked our earl as he stood, the other four were already engaged, battle to live or die!

Swords drawn on the attack, a mighty clash ensued as the swords met, he swore it could be heard above the sound of the rest of the fighting, swords went to one side, they battled for position to be ready for the next thrust.

The Earl caught his footing on something and stumbled, he quickly pulled himself back, just in time to move very quickly to one side, put out his sword to deflect the momentum of his enemy and kick him in the side. Not very manly but it did the job of moving him out of range for a moment while he adjusted himself for a huge attack on the fellow. Clash, clash, clash the swords went at each other, the earl saw in a second a gap in his defence and attacked, the sword went through him like a knife to a piece of cheese, fight finished. Move on.

Another two men attacked, luckily one of his own men took one, the one left came at him like a mad horse, grunting, flapping, and snorting, no control. The earl stood his ground and knocked the man's sword away quickly, he let him pass, as he would have been knocked over if he had stayed where he was. This moment seemed to control the enemy as he turned he had a different expression on his face, he became calm, much calmer!

No time for either man to think much as the battles around were getting closer all the time, they launched at each other, an almost overwhelming crash as the swords came together, quickly they were brought up again, and crashed again, this time the enemy caught the earls left arm as the sword was knocked away. Not a really bad wound, hurt his feelings more than his arm!

Earl Morcar

The earls cool got a bit hot now, he wanted this man down. Enraged, his sword arm moved so quickly he amazed himself, knocked the sword of his enemy away and thrust his sword into the man's chest. Somehow he didn't go straight down, he pulled out his small knife and tried to get the earl with it. Our man was savvy to that and just pushed the man down, he knew he would not be getting up with a large hole through his chest, needless to say he didn't!

For a moment, the earl stood with his four accomplices and took a quick view of how the battle was unfolding, mayhem was going on! Winning on all fronts was the feeling.

They tried to pick out their own horses, little hope of finding them at this moment, they thought they would try their luck with just any animal, grabbing them as they ran past. Even this was difficult, men, bodies and horses running everywhere, all five on horses now, not their own, charging towards the next largest group they could quickly make out fighting with all their might!

The four soldiers tried to make the earl take at least a bit of a back seat, he of course would have none of it. They attacked full on, his usual way of battle, didn't know any other !

Right into the thick of it, knocking swords away and running the enemy through, that's the way to win battles.

Having helped out that group of his men, he looked about again, and saw that the enemy were nearly all accounted for. Time to make sure some got away so they could take word to William.

He saw a few men over at the far side of where he was standing, decided they would do, pushed his horse to get there and made sure nobody had eyes on them to kill them. He only had to glance at his men coming over to make them understand and to leave them alone.

They seemed to dither at the edge of the field, not understanding why they were being spared, the earl urged his horse forward and growled at them, whilst waving his sword. They didn't need to think any more as they just disappeared very quickly, three very lucky soldiers!

He chuckled, as he wondered what stories they would tell William, hopefully just what he wanted, and William would act as he wanted in bringing in more soldiers to deal with these mighty Saxons, thereby making things easier for us to burn the bridge near Willingham. It may help the force going to Huntingdon as well.

Everyone who had jumped off their horses to fight was searching for their particular mount, funny how attached they had all become to these animals, they all had great characters and were friends who didn't normally answer back!

Mind you, get one in a bad mood and you would soon be chucked onto the ground. One had to understand them and treat them with respect. That respect was returned unconditionally.

All was silent now, the fight well and truly over, time to head for Cambridge itself, so they made their way past the little settlement called Bottisham. Some time ago there was a quite large grouping of the enemy here, no soldiers now. Just a few houses here, so no trouble.

There was a substantial track here which led into the town, to their left the track led to Newmarket, the scouts had said there was nobody about and as there was no point trying to stay hidden on this particular trip they took it, as noisily as they liked, riding to their right along the said track.

This Made Quite a Change from Normal

Quite a number of scouts had been deployed ahead of them to try and find rough numbers of enemy and the total number of camps. So far the plans they had been given by Hereward had been more or less correct, trouble was, things changed quickly, especially in war.

The earl and his leaders had decided to hit fast and run to the next fight and carry on like that, if they could at least.

If they were met with a huge force they would have to run as quickly as possible and get back to the fens. They knew that we would all be watching out for any returning heroes and wouldn't hesitate to join in any kind of fight to help them to safety. Save them to fight another day, if needed.

On the outskirts, at this end of town, on the Cambridge to Newmarket road there was a small unit of soldiers, there to check who was coming and going, they thought. They would begin with these men and be led by our scouts to where the smaller units were and see where that took them all!

The earl and the four men who seemed to have formed their own army, within the group, and fifty men approached the check point from behind bushes, there was no need of horses for this fight as they were really sentries, without horse.

They got level with them and waited for a time when no civilian was waiting, then they pushed aside the brush and fell open the enemy, slaughter followed.

Chapter 73

When the bodies were cleared they went further along this track, into town, just to the right of this track, near the Abbey, there was, they were told, a nice well set up camp.

It was so well set up it must be for someone important they thought, their blood was up, so they thought it would do them no harm to slaughter someone important, that must surely get Williams attention. It was surrounded by a large number of the enemy, all the better! Or were they becoming a little rash? Time would tell on that question.

Enemy soldiers.

Some men who had been spared at the first fight rode straight to the castle and demanded to see William, once they were in his rooms they told him of how they had been attacked by a vast force and killed off apart from the six that stood before him. They assumed the worst for Cambridge and that it was about to be attacked, they urged him to prepare his forces as best he could for the coming onslaught!

William quickly considered his position, he didn't doubt he could beat back this force, even if it was as large as he was told but maybe it would be good to have back up at the very least, if all went wrong, he would at least be prepared, so he sent out a group of men to call in some of his force at the camp near Willingham as he knew they had little to do at the best of times! 150 soldiers might tip any imbalance in his favour, so once instructed they set off to call in these men.

Once that was done he sent out orders for all at the camp nearby to get ready for action.

Abbey

They got to the Abbey buildings, off Newmarket Road, and prepared to attack, a couple of guards saw them coming and ran, very professional! our men thought. No real plan was needed, everyone knew it was us or them, so they were in trouble. Our men took the trouble to line up, not really needed, and attacked. Not a great deal of opposition, they just swept all before them. The soldiers were just guards it seemed.

They approached the main building and a man of stature stood before them, in flowing robes, he appeared to look down at them, which was really quite annoying, so several men fired arrows into him. Simple to deal with.

He looked most surprised at this event, couldn't believe what had just happened, how dare these peasants do this to me, his expression seemed to be saying. The rest of the soldiers were taken care of, time to move onto the next target.

A little further along the track there was open ground, again on the right. A large number of soldiers were here also, on The Common, we were told by the scout, who had done a remarkable job. When the earl praised him for his work, he brushed it aside and stated that there were plenty of people ready to tell anyone just where any concentration of the enemy was at any given time, he was right of course, the earl was right as well in praising his men.

As the common came into view, they could see what the scout meant, row open row of covered ground for the occupying enemy soldiers. The leaders were all surprised the force here was not ready to fight, our men had made as much noise as possible just a small distance back along the track, it was almost insulting!

Being a wise old fighter the earl began to get a little suspicious as he reckoned up the amount of soldiers in view to the amount of covered area. Something not right here, he thought!

He took his men back under cover, though most had stayed back as he did not think he had been spotted yet, and talked with his fellow leaders.

This could easily be a trap, he said to them, he quickly stated that he thought there was a large area for horses, two thirds of which appeared empty, the same could be said for the amount of camp space that was not occupied by soldiers.

They approached this camp with stealth, silently does it, the earl instructed, the scout explained that the river Cam was on one side of the camp, away from the track, those who ran would at the very least get very wet, if they escaped the arrows and all else! their escape would be slowed by the water and our men could pick them off probable before they managed it.

They decided to send out scouts, quickly, to find out if this was correct, as they must surely know our men were in the area by now. Time was not on our side at the moment. Our men skirted the area and came back pretty fast.

The earl was right, there were a large number of enemy on horseback waiting in side streets to be given the signal to attack as we entered the common!

The leaders of this enemy unit must think they could outwit our earl and slaughter our men. They were trying to lure our force into the open common and then attack from the many streets where they were at present hidden. It was in fact a good idea and of that there was no doubt!

Our men had time to roughly estimate the number, they were here to do this job, unsettle as many enemies as possible, so that is what they were going to do.

There were several hundred of them waiting at different points to attack our men, they knew where the groups were, this was a great advantage, they would send our men in groups to come up behind these enemy and surprise them where they sat on their horses. The earl thought they could do this, they knew it was a risk, they may be spotted but they had to do something and no other ideas were put forward.

So, each newly split group went their way to battle, quite silently, they pulled back from where they were, and came up a distance behind each group of the Normans. The horses made a lot of noise between the houses, in the tiny streets, the enemy seemed so intent on waiting for us to appear at the front of them that they didn't consider us coming up the rear. Their scouts were clearly not up to the job, again! But perhaps they did not have the time to organise themselves properly, lets give them the benefit of the doubt!

The allotted time came and one man fired an arrow into the air from each group, to tell the others they were ready. Our men waited until they had seen all the arrows go up, then unleashed a huge amount of them into the French.

They were startled to say the least, as men fell off their mounts left, right and centre, the usual melee of horses, running mad as our men attacked the enemy. It was so close quartered due to the tiny streets, it was pretty mad to say the least!

Some of the enemy went forward to give them more space as the streets became wider heading towards the common, our leading men drove forward to stop them getting the chance of any advantage that might be taken.

Chapter 74

They were bashed and broken pretty quickly, surprise had been essential and the fighting was ferocious. The earl was really enjoying himself, in his element, one might say, charging and shouting at the top of his voice, fighting while giving out commands came quite naturally to him. He made sure his men had to keep an ear open for his words of wisdom, most of them knew what to do and when to do it anyway.

From all four points around the common, some enemy were entering the common area itself, being chased by some of our men. Chased to their doom, so our men planned and hoped!

He could see a problem occurring as the enemy soldiers who were left on the ground jumped onto their horses and began joining the fight. He had kept a hundred men back for any eventuality, now was the time for them to be used, he signalled for them to attack as a group and they did so to great effect, taking out the nearest few to where they were stationed.

They turned to their left, a quite large number were here and giving our men some trouble, coming up behind at great speed they spread them in all directions, giving our original group a breather, who then attacked afresh!

Good so far, thought the earl, all his men now in the centre, taking the enemy down left and right as they went. There was a stern defence coming together to one side of the middle. Possible their last stand?

They had knocked a number of our men down, so not too good a day. They began sending arrows into more of our men, this was not good at all, several of his key men looked over at him, nodded and began urging their horses at them, others sent arrows back, they began to make them fall. They could still win this fight and win it well.

Our swordsmen reached theirs with the usual first clash of iron, very loud, and very hard sounding, very painful as well if you were on the wrong end of it.

The Saxons were being drawn into this particular fight as never before, battle madness would be a good description.

The Normans were soon overwhelmed, not just here but all around. Some of the locals came out of their houses to cheer the earl and his victorious men. Though it was a great victory they had lost many men and they would have to live with that knowledge, as always there was no option but to carry on!!

From here, they were heading for the road called Castle Hill, out of town, via the protected area around the castle itself, they knew quite large number of enemy were supposed to be there, they would probably be waiting for our force as well. Quite an amount of time had passed by since the start of this fighting. Peace had returned for a time at least!

They went towards the river and sent out the usual scouts towards the Cam bridge, quickly they returned, and were given the news that there were so many enemies there it would be suicidal to try and fight them at this time. Many thousands they were told in no uncertain terms.

The extra soldiers from Willingham could not have arrived yet but the earl had no knowledge of what William had ordered. He just wondered and hoped that was the case.

He thought William might have ordered in groups of soldiers from outside town, as he had hoped, to relieve pressure on the other groups of Saxons going about their business, in St Ives, and Huntingdon, at this time the force had not reached St Ives yet but he hoped they would cause this effect.

Maybe he had just moved in troops for no particular reason? As a plan it had worked, now was the time to head for home, as quickly as possible, maybe a few more fights on the way?

The order was given to head for home, they would head for the bridge over the river near Stourbridge Common, though it was a little makshift, nobody hung around, they knew they were about to be attacked and would probably lose as the advantage in numbers was so great with the enemy.

The group quickly made their way towards Stourbridge, over the river Cam and out of town, via Chesterton.

They settled into an easy rhythm on leaving the town behind, the chatter was quite pleasant, though everyone was very excited about that last fight, you would never know they had just been fighting for their lives, they were very laid back about it all!

They had not got away with the fighting just yet as the lead scout came in to tell the track to the Isle had been blocked and there was a number of enemy soldiers waiting for them to appear.

This did not sound too good so the earl went with the scout and the four leaders to get an idea of how they could be passed with as little trouble as possible.

Clearly these men had been placed at this point in a rather hurried manner as some old rotting trunks of wood had been placed across the track in a rather hap hazard way, our men could not pass without slowing down considerable thereby putting themselves in danger from the Normans who were in ditches on either side of the track, quite a number of men they decided, difficult to guess at number wise as they were mainly along the ditches to the right of the track, some were on the left.

They returned to their men trying to think how best to get around these soldiers, this would slow them down, maybe even giving the Cambridge troops enough time to catch up with them, if they were now following.

This could really be a "grave" situation, Tredan thought, not his, he trusted, grave that is, his mind always looked on the amusing side of things, he explained to Hereward that was how he coped with stressful situations, that's what probable made him a good leader, Hereward decided he did not get stressed with too much thinking. He simply got around problems by thinking "outside the box", unlike most people who just became more than a little lost when it counted. Hopefully they could quickly get over this and progress to our camp.

Though there were many ditches in the way of getting them around the blockade, they thought they may be able to send some men a long way out to one side and have them attack the enemy from behind and at the same time attack from the front. This could cause a number of problems for them, as they seemed to be concentrating their attention on the track towards Cambridge, a lot depended on just how many troops they had, and of course how battle ready they were.

Speed was of the essence so they decided to send out seventy-five men to the right of where they were, the lead scout said there were less ditches to consider that way, an important consideration!

They followed tree lines and ditches to be under cover, when they thought they were out of view to cross open ground, they did so, and managed to get past the enemy without being seen.

Again when they thought they were past being seen they doubled back and spread out so they could cause as much confusion as possible with the attack.

No need for them to let the earl know when they attacked, by sending up an arrow, he would clearly hear any noise, or indeed see the horses and his men in action.

Chapter 75

Attack at the Barrier on the Ely Road

When the 75 men were ready, they attacked, many arrows to begin with flew through the air, a lot of noise from the defenders as they realised these men had passed them by without their knowledge, many of them turned to focus their attention towards the 75 Saxons.

This, of course, was the idea, they were left open to our main force, attacking from the front. Our men did not spread out to begin with, the ditches were quite deep and quite a problem. So they simple crashed through and over the barriers that were in the way and without firing many arrows went straight into action with their swords. Quite a number of enemy had climbed the ditches and were on the track trying to dislodge the earls force from their horses.

Not sure if it could be described as mayhem or madness, probable a bit of each, that happened, it was difficult as well as the enemy fairly poured from the ditches.

However many were there? Thought the earl. Impossible to tell at the moment, again they were fighting for their lives, they had after all trained very hard for this and it was off the back of a number of victories already on this trip so they were making good progress, they were in high spirits due to the events earlier in the day, it was damned hard fighting though!

Group after group of enemy assailed the walls of the ditches, and from the trees nearby where they were hiding, only to be stopped in their tracks by our brave men, the arrows they were sending in from a little way off to one side were knocking too many of our men out of the fight, injured or dead. Something had to be done and quickly!

Twenty of our lads decided it was time they were killed off. Off they went at good speed, jumping over the main sections of ditch, but slowing as they encouraged their horses to get up the last section. Our bow men sent a stream of arrows now to keep them out of action for the time it took our men to reach them. When they did they just ran amok with their swords and wiped them out. It was a hard battle to win, the fighting intense but eventually, they won the day, though they lost many good men, things were beginning to look quite bad, the losses had become that heavy compared to previous actions!

No time to waste, they turned their horses and charged back into battle. The earl was thinking of pulling out and getting a move on towards the Isle, then another batch of enemy came at them from the other side of the track to the one they had been concentrating on. *Yet more!* He thought, *when was this going to end?*

Their leaders had obviously been told to hold our men up for as long as possible, if, that is, any came this way, these men were coming in waves, they didn't seem to care how many men they lost, their job was just to slow our men down.

Call to Run for the Isle!

Regardless of anything else, the earl thought, we must run, and to do so right now! He called to his leaders to turn from any fight and run for the safety of the Isle.

Almost as one, they turned and made off, it was by no means a defeat, they had nearly cleared out all the Normans, it was just taking far too long to finish them off, before they lost view of the battle site they saw a very large number of enemy soldiers appearing, probable the men from Cambridge.

Without doubt, the earl Morcar had saved many of his men's lives as a result of moving when he did, he may have been caught himself which would have been even more of a disaster for us all!

The enemy force from Cambridge.

The enemy had been instructed by their leaders to chase the enemy force that had just destroyed their soldiers at the Common and to destroy them!

Part of this group had just come into the castle area from the Willingham camp as they had been instructed to add to the number of soldiers in the town at present so they could chase and catch up with the enemy responsible for the fighting. They joined the group told to go into the town via Castle Hill, it was a mighty impressive group and it moved with speed as time was of the essence!

As they came to the site of the battle they were horrified to see their dead laying strewn about, scouts were sent out and about to try and find out where our force had gone, many demanded answers from the locals who were wandering about and of course they told them anything but the truth which exasperated them even more.

They believed they would have tried to return to the Isle, they guessed correctlybut they had really spent too much time waiting for the scouts to come back with definite answers, so as they left town and made their way towards where the fighting was taking place they realised they were somewhat late, especially as they came close and saw the mess of more fighting, mainly of their dead and injured soldiers who encouraged them to ride like crazy and catch up with our force who had by now gone from view. They knew well their was little chance of catching our men but they gave chase as best they could only to lose more men as they approached the massive reed beds, where Morcar had left men to halt their progress as our force had ridden to safety on our Isle. Home again after a great days work!

Chapter 76

End of "The 500" Fighting

Back to safety and friends on the Isle at last!

The horses were slowing a little now, they had had a very tiring and exciting couple of days, so they dare not push them too much as they approached the water they had to cross to get home.

They had to go a long way around it to get back in the way they had left. It seemed so long ago!

They met with no other problems on the way round and found the point where they cut through the water and began re-entry. This was almost too easy! Their scouts had checked that no enemy were about before they entered the area so they knew it was clear.

As they got near the Isle, they could hear a lot of noise, it turned out that it was directed at them, cheering and shouting, masses of men, women and children.

Homecoming greeted by the leaders who were left to defend the Isle if needed

It turned out that a lot of our scouts and spies had kept more or less a record of how they were getting on with their fighting and had returned when the fighting was ongoing on the common.

News was passed along until it reached Ely which was amazing, so many Saxons, and indeed Girvii, were rising to the challenge of these enemy taking over our land, they were afraid no more, they were risking all to help the fight. Without the support of the "friendly" families of England we would not win against this dreadful enemy!

128 Good Men Lost!

The really bad part was to admit that the earl had lost 128 of his men, seventy injured, who would at least live to fight another day, many of these gallant fighters had kept fighting non-stop, though they were injured. We were all saddened by this, though it was part of a huge plan which had worked out very well, his group had killed off a great many more of the blasted enemy, several hundred, plus injured, some of whom would pass away, no doubt.

30 men go for the Causeway.

Before the day was out we let ourselves off the Isle, the idea being we could get into positon to attack the causeway from first light the following day, hoping some of the enemy troops might possible have answered a call to help out at Cambridge and maybe the Huntingdon/St Ives area, however it was just a hope at that point, we would travel in hope rather than despair at least!

Our plan was to leave a couple of men with our horses while we carried out our task having placed then under cover in woods near Irlam Drove, Willingham, where the enemy had constructed a barrier from where the causeway was being pushed out across the waterway/bogs.

The two men were told to let the animals loose if we failed to return, taking three with them to make their way back to safety, one extra for spare if needed, as if found they would surely be chased, possible to their doom!

We were all silent as we progressed as there was so very much at stake, just twenty eight of us now had this huge responsibility on our shoulders, we had to get this job done and if possible in one go as if we failed William would place so many soldiers to protect it we would probable never get another chance!

We had talked for so long about this fighting and burning, now is was almost before us it seemed so big a task, could we actually do it?

We avoided every group of enemy we could find as it was relatively easy as we were so small a group, we did not make much noise and we could hide easily so we progressed quickly. Near the site we camped and ate our food in silence.

During the evening we heard horses going along a track away from the camp so we hoped maybe at least some were leaving, this turned out to be the case as our scouts informed us later, maybe our plan had worked after all, who knew at that time, we certainly didn't!

We left the two men with the horses and very carefully made our way towards the barrier surrounding the start of the causeway in the darkness before dawn the next day. Our plan was to clear the guards and set long fused fires as we went along the causeway, hopefully giving us time to return and get off the causeway, avoiding the enemy by possible returning to land via the water, who knows!

According to our plan of the area there were quite a large number of soldiers in a camp close by the defensive barrier, which was made of timber, so we would have to be careful we didn't disturb their guards or we would be in severe trouble even before we had set anything alight, so we went very carefully, I can tell you! silence was the order given.

There were not many guards to begin with so we split into two groups and attacked as silently as possible, dealing with them with knives, it was an impressive place to see even in the half light, William didn't do things by half, when he had his mind set on a task what he planned was normally achieved, whatever the cost!

When we had cleared the soldiers we began to set the fuses for the fires around the barrier and then as we crept out along the causeway itself, our escape would be a problem as we knew soldiers from the nearby camp would soon be alerted, possible cutting off our way back to the Isle, we had our task set before us and we would complete that, no matter what, and try and deal with whatever followed. If they had in fact taken our bait and sent many soldiers away to fight our other groups then at least we would have less of a problem than might have otherwise been the case! There was no point thinking about anything else than our present task so we didn't, or at least we tried not to!

We had only gone a short distance when two of the men at the front whispered that there were soldiers placed actually on the causeway, this was a problem we had not thought about, the question was how many were there and could we silently deal with them?

We left men setting the fires and cautiously moved towards the soldiers, several of who were just chatting to each other, just before we reached them they saw us and leapt to their feet trying to take us on, they didn't have time to defend themselves as we dispatched them with ease, cleared the problem easily but the trouble was they had disturbed some more soldiers further out along the causeway, all we could do was run like mad men at them and try and silence them before they had woken the men at their camp, could we do it? No time to consider what if! Just get on with dealing with the situation we were faced with and it was scary stuff in those moments, I assure you!

We hit them as hard as we could but they were ready with their swords so the noise as we clashed rose over the water, surely the guards at camp would hear?

In the darkness we could hear the sound of running coming towards us so we prepared ourselves for more fighting. The approaching sounds were coming from further out across the waterway so there must be even more soldiers in front of us, how many was going to be the problem, plus how good at fighting were they.

Eight soldiers took us on so there was not a great deal of room and it was almost impossible to see them properly but somehow we had to deal with this dreadful situation, clashing sword noise was now dominating our space, surely the camp would be roused and we would have a mighty attack to try and deal with, how could we fare with so few men by our sides? I may have commented this before but again this could end badly!

Somehow we knocked these men aside, Hereward called out to light the fuses to all the fires and for all the men to join us to make a stand against these enemy.

In no time the fires took effect and our men ran the causeway where we grouped to fight whatever came our way. Thankfully we had brought a great many arrows with us, all had special back packs with fuses with some oil to light the fires with so at the very least we would take many enemy with us, if this was to be the end!

There was no time to think so we took on the enemy as they appeared before us, as the moon came clear of the clouds for a few moments we could see there were not many soldiers and we were encouraged by this as we knocked them down or back as the case maybe.

This was followed by immediate silence, just where we were that is as there was plenty of noise coming from the land side of the causeway now, some soldiers were trying to come along the causeway now but the fires were taking hold pretty well now, as some did get through we sent arrows into them before they came too close, any boats along the land were being launched by soldiers angry to take us on, it would be some time before they reached us, so what to do?

Quickly we all set about setting the fuses, no other choice really, we would have to worry about living through this ordeal at a later time, though that might only be a few minutes away! When we reached the bridge it got some special attention, it soon glowed with fire, looking back towards the land there was already a great line of fire as it spread towards us.

We decided we would defend the fires as much as we could in the small amount of time we had left, at least we would achieve a success regarding destroying the causeway, even if it meant our destruction!

We gritted our teeth and considered this might just be the end, I mentioned to Hereward, we have at least given our cause the best we could offer, lets go out on a high, my friend! Lets just see what we can do, was the answer given as there was not much else to say, given the situation.

It really seemed we had no way of escape, our destiny was set before us, maybe just a painful end, we could at least give as best a showing as we could. The enemy were approaching, a few along the causeway, leaping over fires and holes as the causeway burned but quite a number in boats coming closer by the minute!

It was mesmurising watching the great fires take hold of the causeway.

These were dire moments, of that there was no doubt! Our backs were against the wall, though, of course there was no actual wall! But you know what I mean.

As the fires increased the enemy began firing arrows in our direction from the causeway and we moved back towards the bridge.

These fires were in either direction especially now in the dark of night, though dawn was breaking through. Could this be our very last day! It was a sobering thought!

Then out of nowhere it seemed a cry went up!

Relief was at hand, hopefully, as suddenly there was a cry from a couple of our men, they had seen four boats in the reeds by the causeway, unseen through the reed beds where they had been placed and the darkness but now parts of them were in view.

It appeared our good luck had held, maybe someone from above really was looking after us, though I personally doubted that was the case, and an escape might just be on the cards, could it be possible, one minute staring at a painful death, then a possible escape route! Was it going to be happen in truth, that was the question! Could we escape the clutches of these enemy?

Possible our good luck, often talked about, had come our way again as

without a word we rushed through the water and bog as best we could, as we clambered on board Hereward told the strongest men to take the poles and push like crazy though they knew full well that our very lives were at stake so they needed little encouragement.

We all jumped off the causeway and made our way towards the boats which all had poles with them to push them to wherever you wanted them to go, though we knew it would be damned hard work getting through the reed beds we had no choice if we wanted to stay alive, by this time we had lost six of our number which was pretty awful though we had put to rest a much larger number of enemy.

We did have a good head start at the time so we had a chance of living to see another day!

The biggest lads we had with us took up the challenge of punting and they didn't let us down as they pushed and pushed the pole into the bog where they met the reed roots to give us the power to move forwards, at times quite fast but then slow as we couldn't break through the mass of reeds.

We could hear the enemy urging their men onwards to try and catch us but thankfully at the time they were some way distant, when we thought they were perhaps in range we fired more arrows over the reeds to where we thought they were much to their consternation as we heard cries as they took injury, this encouraged us no end.

At last we met the main river which was more or less open water, quickly we pushed our boats over and disappeared again into the reeds on the far side, hopefully not far now to the safety of Aldreth and our Isle now, though we knew it would take a lot of effort to actually get there.

The new day was underway now, perhaps a new world for us?.......... Perhaps not just yet! As my mind raced with the prospect that we may be well on our way out of this dreadful situation.

I cried for silence as I heard noise to the right of where we were.

We could hear boats being rowed or pushed through the water, how could this be as surely the whole area was covered in massive reed beds?

There must be a clear path cut through the reed beds nearby we had no knowledge of which they must have made with the intention of finishing their causeway, perhaps they had better think again! the noise these boats made began to get closer by the moment so I called for all to ready their bows to fire into the enemy who were almost upon us!

Two boats crashed through the reeds to where we all sat, arrows were let loose, then the boats met, swords and knives drawn as we leapt into the others boats to try and settle this fight as soon as possible.

As you can imagine it was pretty mad as the boats swayed too and fro as we fought, clearly they were not designed for fighting as there was little space but after a time we beat them down, we did after all, have numbers on our side right now, so that at least was good. It was a question of slash, bash and push overboard. Yet another fight for survival.

Ending this attack.

After what seemed an age calm returned as we were clear of any enemy, hopefully for good relating to this particular fight anyway!

We pulled our injured back on board, the whole situation seemed unreal, many bodies in the water, boats, water, reeds beds all around and enough smoke to cover the whole world it seemed at the time, the crackling of the wood from the causeway and bridge as they burned added to the unreal situation.

We were all of us exultant at long last burning the great causeway, it had dominated our thinking for such a long time, as we had watched it approach our island security during its construction, now it looked as though it was gone, relief all round! Would these enemy give up the construction or would they try some other way of getting onto the Isle, that was the question, again, only time would give us the answer! It would have been a close run fight if there had been more enemy attacking at that time.

We lost some good men that day and we talked of making sure there were no open sections of reed beds anywhere we did not know about in future, so we could not be caught out in such a manner ever again.

We began again to make our way towards the land at Aldreth though it was slow going as the reed beds became thicker as we tried to push our way through towards the dry land.

The enemy had given up hope of catching us by this time thankfully and as we approached the land we heard some of our folk talking, making comment about the burning causeway and the dreadful smoke that enveloped the area.

It was then we crashed through the reeds into open water to appear before them.

We shouted a greeting to all as nobody was expecting us, they were quite shocked to meet Hereward face to face as he leapt out of the boat he was in. carefully we carried our injured from the boats and placed them on the level ground, glad to be there and out of the water.

A good days work, that so few men could achieve so much was quite frankly amazing!

Success indeed as we looked back across the waterland towards the origin of the smoke and fire that engulfed the area where once Williams grand causeway and bridge had stood, now it was a shambles and little else! He would not be amused, to say the least!

We answered the questions fired at us by the men of Aldreth and then began our return to Ely itself.

This was the end of the story of the 30, for the present at least! Sadly 30 did not return but we achieved the mighty task that was set before us, it was to become a victory that would go down in folk law over the centuries as it surely deserved! A tribute to the planning and brave determination of some great people who had set about fighting back against the invadors who were determined on taking our land and freedom very much without our consent. Most of us who survived had injuries to cope with but the experience made us stronger in our belief that we would win the day against this enemy.

We sat that night and considered our overall position, we had a training base at Brunn, Bourne, plus earl Edwins two hundred men set in the forest near Downham Market. I was very pleased at how we were progressing. I, for one, settled down to sleep much more soundly these days, if I woke, I did much thinking and planning for the future, as I truly believed we had one, at last. This thinking included my lady Lynelle, obviously, more often than I would like to admit! I hoped all was well with her and her community. Thinking of her was my release from the tension of our everyday life and she gave me great solace in my darkest hours, it really was a wonder to me that someone could actually mean so much, I was so pleased I had found her, my only worry was that she might find someone else so I began to wonder if I could find an excuse to go that way in the not too distant future, how that might work out I had no idea for the present!

There was so much else to plan and think about, the weight of the nation was ever on my shoulders.

Chapter 77

Trip to St Ives and Huntingdon, the 200 group of men to leave.

Vitt Hal Biomonap and Richard Hokyton led this group.

They climbed out onto dry land at the usual point where the track came onto land on the track that led to Brandon, rode their horses towards Isleham, the two hundred were on their way to fight any group of enemy soldiers that came their way, or if the group looked too large, avoiding it! to make as much noise and mess as they could as they went to try and coax as many of the enemy away from Willingham as possible, they took the track to the Swaffams, then headed to Waterbeach where there was a crossing over the river.

It took them some time to all cross but they made it all right in the end, there was a small skirmish as there were about fifteen guards who had to be dealt with, they thought of letting them go so they could tell William of their passing but this was too early in their action, we would let the enemy know when it was to our liking! Burwell was next on their plan where the dock was very busy loading boats with wood for the causeway construction, they thought it funny as they were on the way to help destroy it! Was so much enterprise going to be wasted? One could not fail to admire Williams ambition. Such was life at this time!

They avoided this area as it was protected by too many of the enemy. They took a wide berth to the dry side of the settlement, made their way towards Longstanton where they took their leave of the old track, the hundreds job was to now cause as much trouble as they possible could, picking as many fights as they thought they could win, letting a number get away so William could hopefully send some of his troops from Willingham to help out around St Ives and Huntingdon which is where they were heading! This was to cause the maximum amount of noise as could be caused as it was important that the enemy thought all hell was breaking lose, clearly with just two hundred men it was not, they just had to try and make out it was. Totally different than normal. No cautiously moving forwards so as to not alert the enemy.

They did a great job as it turned out, saved a great many lives at the site of the causeway later the next morning, by the enemy taking soldiers away from here to try and defend the Cambridge camps as they progressed slowly, urging their horses on as they safely rode across this huge waterway on their fine horses.

Chapter 78

They had left the Isle a little after the 500 had done so and had made their way to St Ives as they knew a large number of soldiers were there, protecting the main track to Cambridge.

Guards were all over the place it seemed, their scout returned to say there was an encampment near Fenny Drayton, the leader of the group went with him to see and judge what was the best approach to tackle these men and to make sure there were not too many to take on.

They had taken over a field, cleared of all trees, quite an open battle ground, he pondered how to deal with these soldiers. He thought he would send in four groups of twenty-five from different corners of the site, the rest a little later to stagger the attack, hopefully they might panic, thinking they were surrounded, catching them unawares and give his men a bit of an advantage. This was the way of many of our battles, if they worked, why change the method of attack!

Here we go again! He thought, an arrow was fired by each group to let us know they were in place.

They fired in a huge amount of arrows from each group, and then attacked as fast as they could on their horses.

They had wiped out their scouts to begin with, they had no back up, two together would have made a great deal more sense, that was certainly not Vitt Hals problem!

They rode into the first men, about twenty in number, and more or less mowed them down, good start, he thought, they were in a somewhat bedraggled line now, but tried to keep pace with each other.

Some of this batch of enemy fought well, some didn't, he didn't get a chance of looking to see how the rest of his men were faring as all our men were busy, very busy indeed. Just keep fighting all before us, he cried, trying to egg his men on. They needed no encouragement as they hurried to try and finish this quickly.

Towards the middle there was a large covered area, probable the leaders covered area, keeping out of any rain.

They were all cutting with their swords, first left, then to their right, pushing their horses as they went forwards.

It Was Heady Stuff and They Quickly Made Progress

At this point, he caught a glimpse across the field, a lot of horses milling around, swords flashing, cries of pain and anger, he hoped just from the enemy, but knew that was not the case.

They would be very lucky if they got away with just a few good men lost and injured but this is what they had come to do and do it to the best of their ability they would, regardless of the losses they might incur! The overall project was what concerned him, above all else!

Some of our men from the group next to his came alongside them, they had knocked out their enemy where he had sent them, and joined his group.

They rallied and charged towards the leaders group. Some enemy loosed some arrows in their direction, they merely laid low on their horses and continued on their way, a couple used their shields for protection.

Some men came out of their hide with full battle dress on, the enemy leaders, no less!

Suddenly, his horse was hit, been his friend a long time, he crashed to the ground, four of his men jumped off their horses to protect him, as soon as he had gathered his breath he cried out to his men to fight towards the centre, to take down the leaders!

Vitt Hal fought his way to meet the Norman with the most colourful armour on, hopefully their main man. Good lord! He was huge!

He must have been at least six foot seven tall and broad as a bear. He recalled feeling like calling out to his men for support, perhaps it was a bad idea going for the leaders! A little late now.

Vitt Hal saw he was running towards him, maybe if he turned around and went for someone smaller perhaps, much too late for that, the fellow seemed to grin, came straight for him. No time to think, so attack, as usual. He slashed his great sword at him, damned great thing it was. He leapt to one side and before he knew it the monster was about to hit him again, he was fast as well as all the other attributes, simple not fair! was the thought that came to mind. Under the circumstances that was quite a silly thought.

He ran a few paces back to give himself some room and stood with sword at the ready, the Norman jumped over to our man, I think the ground moved! Our man went straight for the monster's chest, making sure his sword was not coming his way. This seemed to unsettle him, though it just rather gently hit him and went off the side of his body, the chain mail gave him good protection at the time. He did manage to cut his arm quite well as the blood was soon there.

This monster was not happy, he yelled something in French, sounded rather good actually, he seemed to lose control and in a fit of rage leapt at our man, knocking him off his feet.

Vitt Hal said he saw stars but managed to pull himself together quickly enough to avoid a sword running him through, he rolled over and stood in one move and was ready to parry "Monsters" next blow. This Norman knew no fear, perhaps that could be his downfall, he got out his small knife, thrust his sword at the fellow and stabbed him in the side as they passed each other.

Monsters fury knew no bounds, he almost exploded with rage and hurled himself at Vitt Hal, he was not careful so our man stabbed him again, in the other side this time.

He was beginning to weaken now, one of our men shouted, he staggered before he attacked again, he was still a major force to be reckoned with so Vitt Hal had to be careful.

He growled at him before he raised his sword against him again, never seen anyone so cross in his life, stated Vitt Hal, bursting with hatred he tried to knock our man out of the fight. He quickly moved out of the way of the sword and struck him through the neck, job done! Toughest man Vitt Hal had ever fought, hoped he would never, ever, meet his like again!

Back to battle normal, no more monsters in sight, thank goodness, just normal, your average well trained and fit Normans, that was enough!

Three of the fellows from the group were busy, looked all right, coping well, one was being attacked by two men, Vitt Hal ran over to give him a hand, knocked the sword right from one guys hand and he finished him off. The other one called out to a few of his friends, so he faced four soldiers instead of just the one, he had not had time to calm down yet from killing the monster, worry about being tired later. One man lashed out to try and put him down, much too fast to fall for that, he simply knocked the sword away and pushed him over, very undignified! Richard joined him and took another out of the fight.

Two of the others came for him, one was finished with a sword to his right side, the other reached Simeon Elison, one of the best swordsmen in the group, tried to knock his sword away, failed, and took the consequences, sword to the chest. They were now one against one, much fairer he thought, though after the monster he thought he could probably take on the entire Norman army and win.

Daydream over he said to himself, both these fellows put up quite a fight but they had dispatched them with no real problems. Simeon was busy again.

He looked around, the fight was dying, as were many enemy soldiers, some fights were still going pretty strong but they were without doubt finishing them off.

He pulled over a couple of his men and explained they were to let at least six enemy get away, they were to tell William what had happened, how their force had been smashed, in the hope that he might send in more soldiers from Willingham, some to help the Cambridge force and some towards Huntingdon.

He found out later it had worked a treat, several hundred enemies had been sent from Willingham alone to trap and kill the force at St Ives/Huntingdon, more went to Cambridge to try and attack Morcars 200. We did split the enemy forces, thereby making them less effective as a whole. Our fighting forces battles overlapped, thereby making William weaken his forces at a time when we needed just that.

This fight was done, not a single Norman left standing, time to quickly move onto their next battle. It came all too quickly in the shape of a large force on the track between Huntingdon and Cambridge.

Our scout came back very quickly from the front to tell them of this battle group, he also mentioned they were moving some injured with them, so they had already been fighting.

This could work to our advantage was his first thought, they might not be very alert, so let's go and see what damage we could do.

They were silent as they approached the track, from behind cover they saw about eighty men in a long line, he thought that if we were fast we could break up into a couple of groups and attack them.

He sent half his force back along the track, Simeon leading, they sent up an arrow to let him know they were ready.

Both attacked as one, again mayhem! Horses all over the place, men thrown from their mounts, arrows flying everywhere to begin with, then sword fights, everywhere.

Dead men, dead horses scattered all over the field of battle.

The Norman leader got a few of his men together and attacked the Saxons, he saw what was going on and without saying anything to his men, they attacked their enemy, no one was giving in so this was quite a clash. They were very determined, more so than the last lot they had crushed, long sword fights were happening, up and down the track. These enemy soldiers were quite experienced, but then so were ours!

The enemy group and our leader group met, a huge amount of noise arose from all, it seemed, Vitt Hal took on the leader, bit of a bad habit this had become, the main fight, perhaps!

The Norman knocked his sword arm, damaged it a bit, so he pulled away for a moment, a little blood, but no real problem. Vitt Hal turned and attacked, the enemy was a little slow to turn, so he was more than ready for the him, his sword went to knock his enemies away and out of his hand, our man was much too strong for the Norman, and knocked his to one side.

He turned again, quickly, thrust out his sword and knocked and cut his arm. Enemy blood again! He over compensated for the damage and fell from his mount, our man, rather stupidly followed him to the ground and challenged him straight away. The Norman was not a happy man now, Vitt Hal held his sword in front of himself and the enemy hurled himself at our leader, he tried again to knock his sword out of his hand, it didn't work the first time, didn't work this time! He stood his ground and went straight for the others chest, it hit him hard and knocked him a little silly for a time. This gave him time to work an attack of his own, he thrust at his chest, caught him over his right lung, quite a lot of damage caused. Would he come back, he certainly would, yet another angry man to deal with!

He wasn't standing well now, he waited a moment or two, Tredan stepped forward and thrust his sword into his chest. Another Norman down.

Vitt Hal pondered, we simple must finish this fight as soon as possible and move on, he glanced around him and saw there was quite a lot of work to do yet!

The rest of his group seemed to be doing quite well bashing the rest of the leader group, if they could finish them off it should work well as the Normans seemed to falter when their leaders perished, at least that was what he had been advised.

So let's take another one out, he decided, a quick glance told him that two more were giving one of his men a hard time, back to work, he thought, as he crashed their particular party. Smashed one away to the ground, our other man finished the other with a thrust. Vitt Hal half turned and smiled at Simeon, he returned with a salute to Vitt Hals sword.

Noise to his right, as the chap he had knocked over got up again, he was rather angry, never the way to fight, he tried to run him through, as he came close our man easily brushed his sword away, as he went with the sword he lashed out with his left hand and tried to stab our chap, he must have retrieved this when on the ground. Not fair he thought! Only to remember when fighting the "monster" man a little earlier he had had to resort to such a tactic!

When needs must! He knew he was near to losing that fight at that particular time, it was the only way to end that fight at the time.

This fellow might have appeared tired to begin with but he was damned fast now, with both knife and sword he furiously hurled himself at both men. Vitt Hal had never seen anything like it, the devil incarnate, or what?

He knocked Vitt Hals sword a little out of the way, giving him room to attack his fellow Saxon, who parried his sword, again he tried to knife him with his other hand, cheeky enemy.

He turned, very quickly, and thrust again towards Simeons chest, he quickly knocked the small knife out of his left hand and thrust towards his chest, he fell away from his sword, still more fight in this man. He thought, what was he taking? Better get some for himself, quickly, for us all, perhaps!

They both decided they had to finish this, and get on with this whole fight, so they just stood together, side by side and let him decide how he was going to die, he seemed to register this, and rather stupidly attacked head on. Two swords against one sword and a small knife, even if he was another "monster" he should have thought better, could be was tired and not thinking clearly, anyway his accomplice knocked his sword enough to give him space to go for the kill, he died an honourable death. It could have been much worse, perhaps!

All the groups did really well, they fought as separate groups, took on whole sections of the enemy and killed them off, very, very effectively, Vitt Hal made note in his mind, he would talk to them all later, to encourage all was to lead.

Chapter 79

His new second in command, Simeon Elison, and Vitt Hal looked back at their group to see they were nearly all accounted for, they went back looking around to see where else they were needed.

They were both pleasantly surprised to realise most of the enemy were in fact dealt with, horses running this way and that made it all a lot more of a mess, so they could not see clearly before, it was apparent now, a lot of injured enemy, out of action.

They would not "deal" with them as they thought, quite rightly, it would demoralise Williams forces to see these poor fellows in such a state, with the main force dead or dying later.

Time to break away, deal with anyone still able to put up any resistance, and go and find some more. Apparently, there were plenty to go around!

Simeon was very good at seeing any part of any battle where he and Vitt Hal could make an instant difference to winning more quickly.

These men had been fighting hard for a long spell now, they needed to get lost if they could and recuperate, to mend damaged parts as needed, as quickly as possible.

They left the scene and found a thick wooded area near a place called Houghton. There was a river nearby so they could refresh themselves and perhaps get some food, they all needed it by now, the end of the day was approaching. They were on such a high, such success against our foe, all was going so well. They wondered how all the other men were getting on with their particular fighting.

They hoped they would all live to find out, sadly many did not return.

Back to basics, they had to get any animals/birds and fish they could and set fires that could be disguised by breaking the smoke in these woods, they were very thick, especially towards the water so they were lucky, they covered their tracks as best they could, and after food, plus a lot of almost silent chatter between our soldiers sent out their scouts to guard for the night, it was not cold by any means so they basically crashed quite close to each other. The scouts were on a two hours on and two hours off duty, so they could all be as fresh as they could be in the morning.

The 100 Continuing!

Morning, as usual, came all too soon, they were all very stiff from yesterday's endeavour, everyone knew what was expected of them so they got on with it. They were to get food and repairing anything that needed it, body parts included, or at least try.

The scouts all came to meet the leaders and talk of the night's events. Nothing had happened in the dark, some troop movement had begun as the light appeared. Nothing spectacular yet, they knew of course, William would know whereabouts they were so they would have to be careful, he would be somewhat mad at having yet more of his troops slaughtered and would try and guess our groups next move, he might find it odd, them not killing all his men and would attempt to guess what was going on!

They Just Hoped He Got It Wrong, Whatever He Acted On

The fishing and wildfowling were good here so they ate well and were about to leave when one of the newly sent out scouts rushed back with news that a huge military unit was going by on the track they had left to get here, utter silence descended on them all. They could but await events.

All moved to prepare a defensive wall, a little way in from the water, very silently! This was just in case they guessed where they were, if in fact the soldiers were searching for them, maybe the enemy force might not be looking for them at all. All things considered, they probable were trying to find where they were, or were these men preparing to fight for the Isle, to finally try and take it away from us Saxons?

Tredan took two of his men to have a very careful look at these soldiers, it certainly was a very large number of men and they were travelling in earnest. It was difficult to tell the number as they were only two abreast at this point and some had gone by. They marched with speed and discipline that was impressive! Some were on horseback; most were marching on the track. Suddenly they heard some very loud horse noises, coming from where our men were camped, they froze on the spot. Surely some of these troops would hear this, luckily, it seemed they could only hear the marching of their feet. How they never heard was very strange, perhaps our men were indeed blessed, it had been suggested a number of times, perhaps our cause was!

Our men kept well hidden in the bushes and waited until they had passed, nothing to gain by staying so they made their way back to the water.

After reporting what they had seen, they packed up again and made their way back to the track, carefully making sure no troops were about in either direction, they carried on towards Huntingdon.

They heard quite a lot of noise some way ahead, the scout returned to tell them of a great many enemies just ahead, he was very excited, so they stopped again and hid in the trees and bushes nearby.

He followed the scout and saw the largest concentration of troops he had ever seen stretching over fields and through woods beyond, a pretty dreadful sight for us all.

No time to hang around! Quickly, they returned to the very small group under his command and told what he had seen.

They all thought Hereward and his group would have done their work by now and decided to get back to the Isle, or Camp of Refuge, as it seemed to have been given that name, it did have a certain ring to it?

Chapter 80

Return Journey

They had kicked up a huge stink in military terms, there was nothing to be gained by them getting slaughtered now, if they got away, they would live to fight another day.

This journey began easily enough, made good time, they were all in good spirits. So far, a job well done, and no mistake!

The group avoided tracks they arrived on but sent out a scout to see what had happened to the debris of their fight on the main Huntingdon to Cambridge track.

It remained a quite dreadful scene of destruction and death, a very sad sign of the time.

The number of men he had massed so fast the other side of Houghton was extraordinary.

They wondered just what Williams plan was to try and find our group of Saxons. He had placed them too far past us which was good for us, in his place they thought he would send troops out in all directions to find evidence of their passing. He definitely had enough men to do just that.

Enough thinking of him, they must stay off tracks now, if they could, and return as though they had never been here. Tredan decided to try and avoid the river crossing anywhere near here as they would probably be manned by troops.

This proved to be so as their scouts checked the nearest one to find at least twenty soldiers there, this would mean slow movement but at least they would not be found easily, hopefully at least!

They made their way back around St Ives, plenty of cover in the shape of many trees and bushes.

Suddenly to their right came the noise of men on horseback, men shouting in earnest, and in French, which made matters worse! They could hear commotion ahead, to their right and to the rear.

The Normans seemed to know they were in this wood, how they knew would perhaps become apparent later, Tredan called the heads of each group of twenty-five together, it was decided to ride as silently as possible out of the woods the other side, away from the enemy. To try and not ride in a state of panic, aas that would raise too much noise and no clear pathway through these woods would mean many unhorsed men rather quickly with sore heads, they could not afford to lose men before any impending battle. They could not afford to lose men at any time as a matter of course, the odds stacked against them were only too obvious in this area.

On reaching the far side, there was some cleared land, they made great haste to the far side and quickly disappeared into more woodland.

The Normans were not that far behind Tredan and his group, out into the open, not as many as they had feared but enough to cause major problems. A lot depended on how much battle experience they had and indeed if they guessed which way they had gone.

They sent out some soldiers, presumable scouts, to get an idea of where he and his men had gone. They would soon catch on so our leader called for all to follow him, …….rather fast.

He had no idea where he was going, but staying was not an option he wished to consider, a couple of pathways existed here so they all took them.

If a battle was going to take place, they hoped they could find a place where they had the upper hand to begin with.

They travelled through this wood fast, the French were in full cry now, you could clearly hear them getting excited about chasing our men to their doom. Our men had other ideas regarding the outcome of this particular fight, only time would tell!

There was a smaller clearing at the end of this wood, our men quickly decided to use the gap to lure the enemy into the open and finish as many as possible. They covered the space fast and turned, hiding in the trees opposite, bows at the ready.

The first enemy burst into view, our men would leave it to the last minute to open fire, to let as many as possible of these French men in the open, to hit as many as possible first time, before they realised they had easily fallen into the oldest trap in the fighting world. They should have been much more careful in their pursuit.

Arrows flew at a mighty rate, very impressive, as they cast the French aside all too easily. As usual, rider less horses all over the field of battle. Dead and dying enemy everywhere.

There was a command from the enemy, obviously to withdraw, the ones who were in a fit state to do so did just that. Calm again, at least from our men.

A couple of the enemy had got through the clearing and had sword fights against several of our men, they looked accomplished and battle ready which could prove our forces undoing yet. An eerie silence flowed across the field of battle after the sword fights.

Our men had just one problem, they were running a little short of arrows, they may have to do some sword to sword fighting. This was really not the time to make some more!

They still had no real idea of how many soldiers were left against our men, quite a few they thought. It occurred to Tredan, what if the enemy had sent some men back to the Norman lines and reported where our Saxons were.

Think of that later, they had enough on their hands now. Deal with one thing at a time!

Out came a rush of arrows from the cover of the trees opposite, hitting several of our men, they returned to the same effect. Our force moved back into the woodland so they could not reach them, some of the men began picking arrows from the ground or where they had stuck in trees, waste not, want not, was the expression springing to mind.

The enemy stopped firing and began walking on horseback around the clearing, it was easy to hear.

Our men steadily walked back further yet into the woodland, it was thick so they walked their horses, giving them a rest for a time as well which was no bad thing.

As they approached the end of the wood, they stopped as they could hear horses. The Normans surely could not have got behind us yet thought Vitt Hal?

They hadn't, it was another group of the blasted enemy, this fight was by no means over. What to do now was the question on all their minds.

Ralph of Spalding turned to see perhaps fifty men on horseback, ready to attack our line. They could hear the soldiers behind so they were more than a little trapped!

Vitt Hal thought they were about eighty men now, they had lost some great friends and soldiers, and they were damned if they were going to lose any more, without taking out a huge amount of the enemy, at the very least!

The odds were not good but at the same time they were not awful, if they kept their discipline, and fought like merry hell they could emerge victorious yet, they must believe they can win!

He quickly spoke to all his leaders to encourage the soldiers under them to make a massive effort against this dreaded enemy, make them understand they could simple not march into our county, or indeed country, and take it from us. No matter what the odds we could win!

Again, they fired arrows into the unsuspecting enemy, they stupidly stood their ground, many died doing so, would they ever learn? Led by stupid leaders!

After losing at least thirty men, they ran to our right and left and disappeared into the cover of the trees.

Vitt Hal and his men broke cover at this time and rode over the clearing into yet more woods and kept going. They did not hear from the enemy for some time.

They came across a small settlement, which went by the name of Woodhurst, an appropriate name he thought considering where it was, in the middle of woods!

It was a very pleasant place, hidden on all sides, small cottages were all there was to it, quite a few individuals were walking around, some asked who we were and what we were doing. The leaders just said they were trying to elude the Normans on our tail, any place to hide out for a time?

These people were startled at the thought of the enemy nearby, understandable, they supposed. Vitt Hal asked how far it was to the water of the great fen, maybe they could hide on an island for a time, or maybe some islands, who knows? Could they manage to get lost in the vast reed beds and waterways? Could they get away from these chasing fiends or not. If and when would they have to fight them?

They had to a certain extent slowed much too long at this Woodhurst, they could hear the enemy approaching, quite fast. A couple of the locals told them it was not far at all to get to the sanctuary of the waterways so they had better move fast!

They followed the track through the parish and found themselves on the bank of the West River. It was a mighty piece of water, this time of the year and as they did not want to leave tracks of their passing on the river bank, they made for a bridge. It was possible guards would be there but it was more than a little off the beaten track at Somersham, which was a tiny community, and they were quite right, no guards!

The river was flooded but the bridge was visible, they didn't hesitate, stumbled their horses into the flood and crossed to the far side. They quickly concealed themselves in the wood and turned to see what the enemy would do, they needed to know how many there were before deciding whether they should try and wipe them out, thereby giving their main force no idea about our group from any survivors.

Chapter 81

The Enemy

They stopped before the bridge, and chatted in an excited manner. There were quite a number of them, but not too many to scare our men into believing they could not defeat them, relatively easily.

They came over the bridge and flood water and stopped quite near us, peering into the woods.

One of our horses began to make a noise, strangely it reared onto its back legs and charged.

None of them were ready for this but without giving an order all Vitt Hals men charged forward, crashing through the undergrowth which they were hiding behind.

A huge sword fight ensued, many of the enemy were thrown off their mounts by the speed and ferocity with which our men attacked. This was a mad battle, swords flying everywhere. The first time they had fought before taking out a lot of the enemy by arrow.

As had become usual Vitt Hal attacked their leader, their horses brushed each other and the swords came together with a mighty crash, just knocked each other and passed, no time to turn as another enemy attacked him. He had time to adjust and prepare his sword arm to take on this next fellow, he was much stronger with his thrust and nearly knocked our chap's sword out of his hold, our chap turned well and came back before the enemy was really prepared, he knocked his sword away and managed to hit him in the chest, clearly knocking the wind out of him.

Vitt Hal very quickly turned and dispatched this enemy. In the meantime, the enemy leader was back on the scene and was not too chuffed to see his mate destroyed.

He let out a somewhat mad cry and attacked without thinking, never a good idea! He tried with all his force, and no brains, to finish our leader, to no avail.

Though, he survived for a time, he was lucky, both men turned to face one another and tried to force an end to this fight. Their horses leapt into action, met, and the swords clashed again. Our man thought the enemy looked somewhat tired, as he lifted his sword arm for the next encounter.

Both horses were being hustled by others, they still went for each other, the Normans horse came at an odd angle which put him at a disadvantage, this time our man did some real damage to his arm, he let out a cry and became even more unsteady on his mount, he didn't stop for a moment, which one had to admire, turned and attacked, yet again.

He must be running on adrenaline alone, thought Vitt Hal, was he never going to give in? He noticed a glint from his other hand and realised he was going to try and stab him with his other hand as they passed. A split second to think this one! He knocked his sword arm away and managed to thrust his sword through his stomach, the man's other arm still came through with his small knife but it came to nothing as he slid off his horse, leader gone! It still pains me writing of all this dreadful killing as I sit at my secure desk now in a time of peace but at the time we simple had no option, as always it was kill of be killed!

Continued Fighting

Still too much fighting everywhere, perhaps he had bitten off more than he could chew, Vitt Hal said to Simeon. Two of his best fighters came alongside, without a word they all attacked the biggest batch of enemy they could see, to lead from the front was the only way he knew and he was going to do his best, no matter what!

These men had become like brothers, fought alongside each other no end of times, and always helped each other and always won, they gave confidence to all under their command.

They crashed into a group of about twelve men, killing two straight away, they had knocked a hole in this group, kept going for a few paces, turned and attacked again, they were now a little disconcerted and did not have proper control over their horses, so two more were dispatched as our men did their duty. A lot of hand to hand fighting was happening now as everyone seemed to be desperate to get the fight over with.

The four Saxons cut and thrust at anything that moved causing chaos amongst the enemy, their horses were rearing and snorting, two fell.

Six remaining! This was damned hard work they thought, couldn't stop now. All four together in a line now, just go for it and hope they came out the other side the winners.

They met the six, knocking a horse over, one gone! Our Leader smashed a sword out of an enemies hands and pierced him roughly through the heart, two gone! Vitt Hals, second, Simeon, went to the right and met his enemy with such strength it knocked his sword clean into the air, he finished him with ease, four gone!

They turned, two left to get, they charged at speed, the one on the left went down easily, the other, had other ideas, he pulled to one side, just had room, and went for Vitt Hal. He came at a funny angle, with sword and knife visible, at the last moment he straightened up and thrust his sword, knocked Vitt Hals weapon downwards, he was able to save it and himself but as he passed the enemy he thrust out the small knife with his left hand. The man had tried to prepare for this but he had hit his sword arm with such force that he was in the wrong position to fight the coming attack. It caught him towards the back of his side, didn't feel a thing to begin with, just some blood. He quickly turned again, he knew he must settle this fight now or it would get worse. This time our man came very fast and caught out the enemy, he simple was not ready, as he raised his sword he thrust him through the chest.

Fighting like this was going on everywhere, it was spectacular, and very loud And of course dreadful, as per norm!

The main body of enemy was now looking sad, blood and bodies all over, some seeping into the water making it look much worse than it was. All their leaders seemed to be gone now, there was just a rough fight for possible survival from them, the leftovers, as it were!

They could let no man survive this time, it would take William some time to find out what had happened to these brave enemy, it should give them time to get back to the Isle, that was the idea, at least. Let's see what happens, Vitt Hal, said to Simeon? Simeon said that two of his men, in particular, Zack and Xanda Brightcard had fought so well, he was considering making them deputies in command, this was almost unheard of, Vitt Hal thought for just a moment, and said Simeon should do just that, if he felt these chaps were up to it. It was decided! Zack and Xanda would no doubt be delighted that their work had been recognised.

Several quite large fights were still going on, no need to intervene as we were on top in all of them. Winning was becoming a way of life to this group, Vitt Hal thought, though they must never take anything for granted!

Simeon said they couldn't just stand around so they attacked the largest group of enemy still standing. They hit them hard and finished quickly, he encouraged all our men to help to finish this fight everywhere any enemy was left standing, if he wasn't standing, but was alive, to quickly dispatch him.

Eventually, all was silent in the area, he quickly called everyone together, congratulated his men, and said the next stop was to be the Isle as things would get very nasty around here, pretty fast.

Oh, and by the way, Zack and Xander Brightcard had been promoted due to their outstanding contribution on this trip! Promotion was up for grabs to all who excelled!

Some nursing nasty injuries, himself included, they settled into a trot, trying to not think of their pain, whatever it might be. Simeon was full of the joys of spring, though it wasn't spring at all but you know what I mean! at the result of the last fight, and the fact we were nearing the Isle.

Chapter 82

Car Dyke

The old Roman Built Car Dyke was the barrier to the flooded fenland, at this time. Presumable it had been created to take goods and troops to the north. It was not deep water in these parts so he knew he could quite easily lose the Normans in the huge reed beds, he may even be able to break them up as a force and attack them in smaller groups. He didn't come from these parts, some of his men did and they knew how and where to fight in these conditions.

They easily crossed the dyke and entered what he would describe later as a new world. The whole place seemed to slow down, calm down, the effect was truly amazing. The horses slowed, due to the water, bog and reed beds, some places it was deeper, some not so they were careful.

They travelled some miles and found several pieces of dry land where they stopped and ate the supplies they had left.

Everyone had lightened up, the sun was high in the sky, even the breeze was cheerfully making joyful noises swishing the reeds from left to right!

The leaders sat together and munched away in a jovial manner. They all wondered if the Normans maybe on their tail, and if so would dare risk getting lost attempting to find and destroy their group here, it was so peaceful that fighting seemed as though it could never happen, it was a world away, and no mistake!

It was at the back of Vitt Hals mind that maybe a soldier had escaped from that last fight and got back to Williams men. He would have plenty of soldiers at his disposal to try and find our Saxons and erase them from this earth, or at least die trying!

He sent out his scouts to make sure he could not get stuck in some deep water, tales abounded of men and horses disappearing altogether in boggy ground, whether they were true or not, nobody seemed to know, it was best to take precautions, no matter what!

No real plans existed of these lands, he knew of Carrs Dyke, or Car Dyke, spelt depending on where you came from, and that was about it. He was not sure that the fen area had ever been mapped properly. The end of the day was on its way, he decided to go a little further into the wild fenland, just in case the enemy approached at night, best to be sure they were all as safe as possible. Plus the scouts, always sent out in pairs now, had been out and returned with the news that there was in fact a large section of land out of the water not too far away, in what they thought was the right direction to get them nearer the Isle, safety and home!

Food was for once, all about, fish, eels, ducks, geese, seagulls etc. Now they had long ago brought in many other coarse bread making machines that were left in the fires to cook and gruel was a staple, providing a supply of grouts, crushed grain of sorts and oatmeal could easily be obtained, they always carried a store with them. There was a lot of brush that could be used for fires and he threw caution to the wind and lit many. Food, warmth and relaxation were a wonderful tonic to all. He had fed his scouts before sending them out quite a long way onto dry land. Wounds were cleaned as best they could be, though a few were quite bad.

He totally trusted these scouts for their skills at remaining unseen when it mattered and returning with any news that was important in time to act on it, a great part of his team, he always said. In fact we all did!

The night passed well, no problems at all, which made a change, always being under pressure took its toll when faced with as much fighting as they had had to experience of late.

Vitt Hal was told by these men that he was about to cross a waterway. It was quite deep and wide and probable quite fast flowing at this time of the year, though it should not be too much of a problem, the horses had crossed a lot of the waters of late. It split from the river Ouse below Earith.

There seemed to be nobody following, no Normans at present, though they did not give up easily, they had knocked out the last group, hopefully. Often following a success like that they came back at you even stronger. They had plenty of soldiers nearby too, maybe they had not discovered them lost or dead yet, then of course they had to find his Saxon force, no easy task in this wilderness of water and reeds! They all felt comfortable, enclosed and safe in their own little world, for the time being at least.

The men moved off and soon came upon the expanse of water that was presumable the waterway, it was flooded back some distance, there were patches of bank which marked the edge of the river proper where bushes were growing. They had some distance to go to get over the river, let alone the extra water from the floods. The area was all waterway but the level was high due to extra rainfall.

They walked the horses through the shallow floods and grouped at the river itself, could not see the bottom it was indeed deep! So this may be a bit tricky for some of the horses, let alone the men.

A couple of the leaders set off with about twenty men, all riding their horses, it did not seem as deep as they thought at first. As they reached the middle the bottom seemed to almost disappear, the horses struggled to swim, all the men dismounted, held their bridles and sort of floated by their sides. It was a struggle but they reached the other side and waited for the rest to follow. The third group got into a complete mess, several of the men lost their horses completely and others had to go and get them and their riders out, very wet and very slow progress! This worried both Vitt Hal and Simeon.

Attacked, Yet again!

As they turned to move away from the river flood, arrows came hurtling from the heavens. It caught them all out, they thought they had left the enemy behind some time ago, they had called in their scouts to get over the river, the Normans must have been waiting for a break to get close undetected, they did not miss a trick!

They must have been following quite close for some time, to totally evade our scouts was a real talent, more training required! Tredan, of course, had called them in a little too soon! He will not make that mistake again, he thought to himself.

Two Saxons went down, never to rise, they quickened their pace by a huge margin, running for what little cover presented itself on some nearby land.

When settled a little they looked back to see if they could make out where the arrows were coming from, a pretty large group of reeds were now ejecting arrows aplenty it seemed. They could not make out anything else, so they set about sending arrows back into the enemy.

Some cries followed, as they hit home, they did not have much of a stock left now, so they began looking for the next point where even a little cover existed. There was a high point, some distance away, with trees on it. They decided to make a run for it, they had no idea what depth the water was but they had to do something!

With arrows coming in a little less frequently, most of the men made a dash for it, our leader and some of the other soldiers stayed behind in the hope that they would get an idea of just how many men were following us, and maybe slow them down a little. They also began collecting as many arrows as they could find that had been aimed at them from the enemy.

Splashing noise filled our ears as the horses entered the water, no problems to begin with, about three quarters of the way there the first horses crashed into deep water, they began swimming as their riders urged them on. This slowed progress to almost a halt, as the rest of the horses lined up to get across this barrier.

It wasn't all that wide at this point, the leader urged the soldiers who had stayed back to keep their eyes open, he expected the Normans to break cover soon. The Saxons completed their way across and continued towards the other island.

It wasn't long at all before the enemy began showing themselves, just a few to begin with, then more. Tredan urged no one to fire until he gave the word. He thought there were probable no more than fifty men against him and was surprised to see them keep coming, possible seventy to one hundred men.

It was going to be hard to fight these men in these conditions, they would have to devise some kind of plan to finish these enemy off. Hopefully they could win the day.

Chapter 83

As they turned to move away from the river flood, arrows came hurtling from the heavens! It caught them all out as they thought they had left the enemy behind some time ago, they had called in their scouts to get over the river, the Normans must have been waiting for a break to get close undected, they did not miss a trick and it showed! They must have been following quite close for some time, shadowing them, to totally evade our scouts was a real talent, more training for our scouts! As they could ill afford to make that mistake again, thys might not survive.

Two of our men went down, never to rise as they quickened their pace by as much as they could under the conditions, running for what little cover presented itself on some nearby land.

When they had settled a little they looked back to see if they could make out where the arrows were coming from, apretty large group of reeds were now ejecting arrows a plenty it seemed. They could not make out anything else, so they contented themselves by sending arrows back into those reed beds, returning the complement as it were!

Some cries followed as at least some hit home but it became obvious our force was getting low on the arrow front so they had a problem. The decision was taken that to find the next point where even a little cover existed, there was as a high point with some trees on it some way distant so they made a run for it as they had to do something.

Vitt Hal and some of the men remained to slow down their advance, even a little would help as some kind of defense could possible be organised on the new island.

Splasing noise filled their ears as their horses entered the water again, no problem to begin with, about three quarters of the way there the first horses crashed into deep water, they had to swim as their riders urged them on. This slowed progress almost to a halt as the rest of the horses lined up to get across the barrier. It wasn't all that wide at this point as the leaders urged their soldiers who had stayed back to keep their eyes open, he expected the Normans to break cover soon. Our force completed their way across and continued the other island.

It wasn't long before the enemy began showing themselves, just a few to bewgin with, then more.

Vitt Hal urged no one to fire until he gav e the word, he thought there were probable no more than fifty enemy that faced them and was surprised them keep coming! How ever many were there? It was going to be hard to fight these men in y.these conditions and they would have to devise some knid of plan to finish them off. Hopefully they could still win the day!

He gave the order to fire and joined in, they must make every arrow count now, they were too easy to finish off as they were in the open, they scattered in all directions when it was obvious we still had men on this particular piece of land. They could not see our men as they were hidden, so they had no idea how many we were.

The rest of our group had left most of their arrows with us so we could knock out as many as we could before racing off to catch up with them. Some were getting close to our island now, but as they approached our men finished them off.

The enemy must have got some idea that they were here still in numbers and they attacked in fury.

They had held them up well, now was the time to move on, they turned and left the cover given by the trees and leapt into the water out of view of the enemy.

The enemy were encouraged on hearing our men leave, they stormed the island, the Normans were welcome to it, Vitt Hal decided.

They reached the deep part of the fen and sort of swam over, Vitt Hal, looked back across the fen, the enemy were safe in the trees now, it had been costly for them in lost soldiers,

His force had lost more men than he wished to think about at present but there was no doubt he had done very well with the task set before him.

Their force was largely intact, they had done what they had set out to do, as a group, they only hoped the other groups had at least done as well as themselves. Vitt Hal expected both Earl Morcar and Hereward to have set a fine example for all other Saxons to follow.

They joined their men, in a pretty good hiding place now, this island looked quite a lot larger than the last so it would serve them better. The Saxon men decided they would stand and finish this fight now, no matter what happened. They needed to protect any entry onto the Isle, they had to find one themselves to begin with, as they were the wrong side of it to get in by normal entry.

They tied their horses to trees and made their way to the water's edge, stepping back into cover, the leaders asked for anyone willing to go out each side of this island to protect each flank. Ten men came forward, they sent five out each way to cover these points, the rest settled back into covered ground to remain unseen by the approaching enemy. He would change these men after about half an hour as the cold water got to you.

The odd splash could be heard from the reeds in all directions facing the island, so they knew they were on their way. All went quite for some time; the tension became almost unbearable.

An arrow was shot up into the air, from our boys, this was the signal, many more followed. The noise in the water became louder as the men were trying to get around us, no one appeared at the front, Vit Hal and Simeon had thought some at least would appear at the front. All the action was happening at the sides and he had not placed enough men there to deal with this.

Our men were crying out for help, so twenty more rushed out into the water each side, the noise was of swords clashing now, not arrows being fired as they had few left, so they were meeting face to face. The enemy had thought this out, Vitt Hal had underestimated them perhaps.

The leaders still had no real idea how many enemy were left, it seemed a lot more than they had hoped. Arrows began to be fired at them from the front again, they hid after one man caught one in his shoulder, very painfully from the scream that came from him, this seemed to encourage the enemy and they began to show themselves.

Again, they let them get into open water before firing, an awful lot had been hiding, where they had all come from he had no idea. Maybe another group had heard the fighting and joined in or maybe a soldier had got help from the camp, though this seemed daft as he surely could not have got new troops here already?

The noise from each side was getting less, then suddenly it became more, much more noise, much more fighting! This was difficult to understand for all the men on the island. What was going on, just where were these men coming from. He sent out more men to find out, if they could, what was happening.

The men disappeared into the reed beds, yet more fighting could be heard.

There were now a large number of dead and dying men at the front of the island, were there any more soldiers coming through, or had they at last stemmed the flow? That was the question.

Chapter 84

No more arrows came through or over the reed beds, they thought they might be winning, even the sounds of fighting on either side had become more or less silent.

The men they had sent to their left came in, very wet and bedraggled, but glad to tell us no more enemy seemed to be coming through the water. The men to their right were still clashing swords so the leaders decided it was time to show they could lend a hand.

Off they went in pursuit of more Normans! They pretty soon came face to face with these fierce fighting men, swords thrust at them from a couple of directions.

They clashed with these men, they were damned strong, and spread out as best they could, in a wet and very muddy line they attempted to attack, difficult to do when you are fighting in water, but they did their best.

Tredan was in the middle, he had his sword almost knocked out of his arm, he rallied and lashed out at the Norman attacking him, knocking his sword to one side, the other fellow tried to stick him with his small knife, again he thought, very unfair! They both tried to turn quickly, the mud had other ideas, their feet stuck quickly and they both almost fell over. This could turn into a comedy, well almost, he quickly thought, hopefully not a tragedy.

They faced each other, the Norman threw his little dagger at Vitt Hal, who just managed to knock it away in time, only just in time, a reflex action. They jumped through the water at each other, feeling rather silly, not as dignified as running on dry land, or on horseback. Swords clashed again, Vitt Hal knocked his sword away and managed to cut him in the side, he let out a great groan as he slipped into the water. Job done, perhaps not, as the guy jumped up out of the water and again thrust his sword at our man. Vitt Hal thought, don't these people know when they should give up?

Plenty of blood in the water now so surely he must realise he was in trouble, best for him to try and get away and get well to fight another day…surely!

His sword was up and about to hit Vitt Hal so he almost reluctantly parried it away and finished him off with a thrust through the chest, job well and truly done!

The fight was coming to an end, at long last, every one of our men had been fighting like Vitt Hal to wipe out this group once and for all!

Then, of a sudden, silence everywhere! Except for the wind rustling through the fen. This wind noise was very settling on the soul, he noted. They all made their way back to the middle of the island, more bodies lay strewn in the water here, but that was all, just bodies. Not his problem anymore. The usual riderless horses stumbled about in a state of shock, no one to command them anymore. Our brave and hard fighting Saxons had not escaped death, we had lost a number of men, many more than our leader had expected. This was grim to see!

How these enemy had crept up on us in such numbers was worrying and more than a little confusing? Maybe their luck had just run out, they had had some good luck along the way, maybe this was pay back! Vitt Hal did not believe in all that kind of thing, you trained, fought hard and you won, hopefully! Pay back? What a load of old tosh, he thought. But still,...... maybe?

Of the twelve men he had lost, he buried on the island, they were all pretty exhausted so they said their goodbyes and settled down for the night at the far end of the island, they caught food and cooked it, ate well and settled down. After a time excited talk of the battle came from the group, they were all very happy to have at last dealt with that batch of enemy. Probably more to follow!

As always scouts were placed on any small islands nearby, tiredness took over, not a great deal of talk now, it was night and time to rest. They were lucky to be alive still and they all knew that!

The winds rose that night and by first light rain was almost bashing them all, the island included, into some kind of submission. Though they had lost friends yesterday they were in good spirits, they had finally rid themselves of the blasted enemy, at least for some time, maybe they could actually get onto our Isle this day? Away from being continually chased, that would be a change for the better. To rest among friends again was a great ambition!

They set off in the direction of Ely but soon found themselves in an area that was more deep bog than they had experienced before, this slowed them down considerable, some parts they let the horses drag them through the really deep water, they were that bad.

A scout had returned and said there was a huge glow over the reed beds, as they progressed Tredan realised it must be fire. And what a fire it soon turned out to be, obviously Herewards men had set the huge causeway on fire. At long last, could it finally be gone as the main threat we all faced? It seemed the sky was alight as they became nearer, the smoke was being blown all over the area. It was spectacular, no other word for it! It had been many years since Vitt Hal had felt this good, what a huge positive leap forward for us Saxons he cried out to Simeon.

All the force was delighted, they clapped each other on the back and shouted for joy.

Eventually, they were all across the deep section. The water was damned cold! Dry land appeared at last in front of them and much cheered they landed between Aldreth and Haddenham. Everyone cheered at this happy place, relief all around.

Chapter 85

Return to the Isle with much celebration. End of the 100 raid.

They supposed, they ought to report as soon as they got here, everyone was feeling exhausted, nonstop fighting had taken it out of all of these men. They knew they were very lucky to have got back in such numbers.

Their clothes had dried a little now but when fires were lit they cleaned their tunics and dried them. That evening and night much chatter was to be heard until really late, they were now very excited about their return to their Isle and their loved ones. A couple of the people who lived here rode off to tell all Vitt Hal had returned and would be with them by first light.

Return to Camp

They had no water to wade through, so they made good time on horseback, a scout was sent forward to tell of their return. When they got near a great many folk were waiting on the outskirts of town, much cheering and laughter. They were offered many drinks as they progressed, many were taken very quickly, and very quickly their contents were emptied! Civilisation again! At long last. They may have been on a short trip but so much had happened in so short a time!

They all dismounted and walked their horses to their respective stables, Vitt Hal and Simeon called them together and said how proud they were to lead such a fine body of men. This unit would never be forgotten, they said, while they had breath in their bodies,they would make sure details of their strength, bravery, commitment and skill would be written down for people to refer to in future as an example, this was how Saxons and Girvii should be remembered.

They emotionally thanked them again, had a tears in his eyes, quickly brushed it aside, ' don't do tears', they thought to themselves, they are just tired, as they were led away to an even greater reception in the meeting hall, from the council of leaders.

The men eventuallyreturned to their families, to be greeted even more, stories were demanded from all, people also listened outside their huts, this was all good for moral, a good victory for us all.

Vitt Hal, Simeon and their men had done a fine job fighting the enemy.

After a feast and some ale, everyone crowded around the leaders who told them of their battles, some sounded farfetched to begin with but as they progressed through the fighting they realised that the stories from the Isle scouts/spies that had come into camp matched what they were being told now.

We were to become bolder and bolder from this time. Bad times ahead for William the Conqueror!

Perhaps we were not quite so conquered after all!

"The 30"

The 30 of us followed on quite some time later that day, so as to give time for the 100 to make enough trouble for a lot of enemy soldiers to leave Willingham camp to help protect Cambridge from our force of 200 which was led by Earl Morcar, plus the St Ives and Huntingdon areas to give more freedom from the enemy soldiers so burning the causeway would be easier as it would be less protected! The plan was to get close to the Irlam Drove site and stay under cover, then attack in the darkness the next morning.

Thirty Men and the Causeway

All of us followed the 100 at quite a distance so we would not get involved in any fighting, we were still very silent as there was so much at stake. We were only thirty men in total and we had a huge responsibility to get this job done, to destroy the causeway completely or to at least try! We hoped some enemy troops had been moved from the Willingham area to help their forces at Cambridge and the Huntingdon, St Neots areas against Morcars attack etc. we travelled in hope rather than despair for the moment. The lads had talked themselves silly about what they were going to do. It was a little more difficult actually doing it and here we were about to go into action, could we achieve this major task?

Most of us carried packs of fuses and some oils to set alight the timber of the causeway, as well as many arrows with which to attack the enemy if and when they did likewise. We would leave two men to guard our animals in hiding in woods close by, so hopefuly so we could make our escape after the deed was done! When hidden close by the causeway we camped in hiding and ate the food we had brough with us, tried to get some reat for the very difficult day ahead.

During that evening we heard horses going along the nearby track, we hoped it was soldiers being called to the two battles we had started in the nearby towns.

The plan was on reaching the causeway, to creep onto it, kill off the guards, make our way to the end and plant our fused fires there and at set points back to dry land. It sounded like a fine plan. Escaping may be a problem but we would have to deal with whatever came our way as and when. We were as silent as we could be possible be.

Though it had been dry of late, the timber should burn well so as the fires took hold we may be able to make our escape, otherwise we would not live long, I feared. We were confident and strong fighters and the element of surprise had been on our side so often, why should it change now? Somehaw this work had to be done, if it cost us our lives we were prepared to make that sacrifice!

We approached Willingham with stealth, there were a group of soldiers before the settlement according to our plan. It was correct and they were easy to pass, so we continued through the street in darkness.

There was a quite large camp of Normans just before the circled area, built to protect the entrance to the causeway, so we had to be very careful. It was easy to see a lot of enemy men had quickly left to go and fight the two battle groups, good to see our little plan had worked, we had a lot less enemy than otherwise would have been here, we felt sure.

Hereward took one group of fourteen men and I the other, two were left to look after the animals, complete with our arms and things with which to start the fires. Both groups wished each other well and set off to go around each side of this camp. Both Hereward and I thought we may never see each other again so it was not an easy parting, though we did our best to keep our nerve.

There were just a couple of sentries each side, or so we had been told. This was not the case as there were at least ten! Somehow we had to deal with these enemy without causing too much noise, as that would inevitable bring the enemy camp down on us, as it was close. Silently we crept to the edge of the wooden heap of wood that formed the defensive circle that formed the start of the defensive wall to the causeway. They could see each other just over the top and made out the guards moving around, everyone crawled onto the top around the edge and leapt onto the guards who were instantly immobilsed and out of the action,....... so far, so good! There was no noise from the guards at the nearby camp.

We were slower than we had anticipated and didn't want to run out of darkness so we egged on our men to move faster if possible.

We heard a bit of rustling up ahead and all froze. The man at the front crept along to find out what could be making this noise, some soldiers were actually camped on the Causeway, he thought there were no more than four, we couldn't go around them, there was only one thing to do with the enemy but this time we had to make no noise as it would carry across the water. Six of us went forward, we dispatched three but the forth woke, I grabbed a leg and pulled him down as my second jumped and put a hand over his mouth to keep him quite. He was then finished.

How many more groups would we find, we had no idea, I only knew time was not on our side and we must get moving if we wanted time to try and get clear after it was on fire. To a certain extent we threw caution to the wind and quickened our pace.

We began setting the fires as we rushed along, The fires themselves were doing well, the wind was just right, just enough to encourage the flames to greater height.

Two other groups of four, we almost bumped into, the second group heard the noise we had made and called for all to wake. Something was wrong, or some such words in French, we fired into these men and knocked them out, over the side they went. The trouble was the fight was now on! Could we hold these men at bay and set alight the causeway enough for the flames to take over and do our work! Suddenly there was a lot of noise coming from the camp nearby, it appeared their guards had indeed raised the alarm, their task set before them, to gat to us at all costs and at least try and put out the fires!

We tried to hold the enemy up, so they could not get near the flames to put them out, they were in the main, still some way from the fires.

We reached the end and straight away began setting more fires, the great bridge was something to behold, it seemed a shame to destroy it, but destroy it we must! If we possible could. Looking back towards the land side it was all alight, the flames eating at the entire construction, it was spectacular to say the least!

A Stroke of Luck

There followed some sombre moments as we realised there would be no escape for for us, we had not given a great deal of thought as to getting away, the primary objective was the destruction of the causeway and it looked as though we may have achieved that as smoke and flames surrounded most of the area, the rest was in darkness.

The fires were now taking hold properly, much crackling in the flames, our men moved towards us as it was getting too hot elsewhere. We were all firing arrows now, we had a longer range than the enemy bows, and this was forcing them to begin to move back a little, at least. Quite a few had been hit, I was pleased to note, quite a few not moving and many more injured, I quickly noted.

The Normans who were on land, could be seen running along the bank of land each side of the causeway, carrying lamps, to where I supposed, they had their boats, they would not give up on trying to kill us yet it seemed.

The end was facing us all it appeared as the enemy would destroy all who had dared to destroy Williams ambition of taking the Isle. It really looked fantastic right now, as though the world was at an end, well…almost.

Then it began to dawn on us that we were about to meet our end! The full force of our situation hit us as the enemy could be heard getting closer by the minute, Hereward called out to all to put on a brave face and fight bravely to the death!

As dawn fully broke through there suddenly was a cry from one of our men at the rear of where we stood, he cried "look boats!" As one, we turned, not believing what the man had said.

Sure enough you could clearly see four boats, partly hidden by reeds and darkness previously, now in the clear light. I can tell you we didn't wait around as we leapt into the water and clambered onto them. There were four poles waiting for us to use so the strongest of our force grabbed them and began pushing for dear life towards the river we would have to cross, plus the mass of reeds we would have to get through on our way towards Aldreth.

We punted with a pole and used oars as fast as we could to give us a chance of making a getaway, we had a little head start which we used to our advantage, the trouble was they were much more used to these particular boats than we were so they began to gain on us.

Our best arrow men, Hereward and myself included, began firing at will at any of the enemy we could see. We hit home a lot, forcing them to slow, we only had limited arrows so we tried to make everyone reach its target, even more than usual, we did not aim just to make the enemy slow down as we sometimes did.

As our firing slowed, they got closer, we had kept some back so we selected who looked like a leader and shot him dead if we could. As a result they seemed to lose some of their fight.

We had got over the main river and were more into the fen now on the other side towards Aldreth.

Chapter 86

A new world perhaps!
We were moving quite well by this time as the new day was beginning. Perhaps, a new world for us? or so we hoped. So much of our lives lately had been dominated by our plans to get this job done, to rid ourselves of this threat from the Normans.

Though we knew the enemy would not simply give up their pursuit of us, we felt much of the pressure leave us, we were nearly home, the Camp of Refuge was nearby, we hoped! Could we get through?

Our boats had slowed, as the reed beds became thicker, we were making a lot of noise on the water. I cried out for silence as I heard noise off to our right.

All rowing stopped immediately, silence did not ensue! Rowing noise was not too far from our boats and it was getting louder, the enemy must have found a way through the reeds, there must be a clear path they had followed we knew nothing of.

Two boats came at us at a fair rate of knots, straight through what looked like a huge clump of reeds, it caught us all out!

Quickly, we used our arrows to inflict as much damage as we could, the boats met, men began jumping from boat to boat, the fighting at close quarters was mad, swords and knives drawn to dramatic effect. Luckily we had numbers on our side for the first time and we were able to use it to good effect.

A lot of our men were down, we were still fighting like mad men but clearly winning, no space for any skill. Slash, bash, and push overboard was the order but we no time to give it.

After what seemed an age, calm returned as we wiped out the last of the enemy. Never would I feel secure again after a battle, until I had confirmed it myself!

We pulled back on board our men who were still alive, and finished off the last few enemies. This whole situation seemed unreal. A number of boats, a lot of bodies in the water, smoke billowing above us from the fires we had started.

Some of the reed beds burned as well adding to the chaos. What a feeling though, to have destroyed the causeway at long last, flames and smoke shooting up into the sky and having won this last desperate fight with the enemy, they never seemed to know when they were beaten. We all respected and admired that of them.

There was, we were told later, a section of the fen that had been burned, or cut, by the enemy so they could get boats through if needed. Our spies had not been good enough it seemed, perhaps we had not told them to report anything out of the ordinary, we would instruct them differently from now on!

Many of our men who did not return would agree, we lost some good soldiers, clearly they deserved better.

We collected the other boats and tied them to ours, we might have a use for them some time. Maybe they would just be used by our men camped at Aldreth for fishing and wild fowling, keep them in fresh food at least.

We settled, hoping to god that the days, and nights, events were over, and began rowing to the dry land at Aldreth, both Hereward and myself were now rowers! Not very good ones I have to admit but we could get by with the task.

Aldreth at last!

We could hear men on the land at the settlement but could not see through the dense reed beds as yet. Their voices spurred us on, as we managed to push our way into a bit of open water.

We all shouted together, nobody was expecting us, but I think they could be sure we were English/Saxon, even Girvii or Iceni, and not Norman/French.

Hereward, leapt out of our boat, followed by myself, pulled it onto dry land, as did the others.

We all stood as a group, injured as well, those who could, that is! And answered as best we could the questions fired at us.

The main question asked of us was, how did we set the Causeway alight!!

They could not believe our story to begin with, it did sound a tall tale, even to us who took part.

The result was quite outstanding, though I say it myself! We lost some great fighting men, as always, it seems, but at last real progress was being achieved.

These events would shake William and his forces to the core, they seemed to believe we were a lost cause, we were far from that and we would show him more and more as time went on! We were restoring our peoples pride in our race, our confidence roared forever upwards from this time, we could almost see our kingdom being reformed, though we knew the tasks ahead of us were still immense!

Chapter 87

The two Horsemen Left at Willingham, Had their Story to tell! Rowan and Tait

The two men, who had been left to care for the horses at Willingham had been told to leave and make their way home as best they could, if they could, if we did not return. The horses were to be let free, given to some of our people if possible. They would have to be hidden well as they would be accused by the Normans of helping us if they were found, and that could only lead to one thing, certain torture death!

They had seen the huge fire of the causeway so they were in a good mood for some time. They waited for the return of the victorious men. This did not happen, they left more time in the hope that they may have been delayed, still no word!

Eventually, they gave up, thought they must have been overpowered by the Normans, and thoughts were needed to get them back to the Isle, so that is what they did. They knew that with all the confusion caused by our attacks the Normans would be looking for any number of Saxon men of fighting age in this area so they needed to be extra careful.

They would doubtless kill anyone on sight.

They kept three horses back for themselves, one spare, and left the others with some Saxons who lived nearby who were overjoyed!

Rowan and Tait then set off for Rampton for their trek back home, they knew they would have to be careful now as the enemy would be everywhere, trying to catch some of the Saxons responsible for the fighting.

Rampton itself was a bit knocked about from their earlier encounter, just to make sure there were no enemy about they circled the parish, did not see anyone. They then aimed towards Landbeach, in the hope of getting a flat bottomed boat to get across the fen and river Cam.

They got to Landbeach quickly and began looking for a suitable boat, one that you could tie a few horses to and lead them through the water. Third time lucky, they found one they were looking for, a decent size flat bottomed boat, with a pole to push it along the waters.

As fast as they could, they tied the animals to it, grabbed the pole and pushed themselves towards the river Cam. It was quite difficult trying to push it through the reed beds, it was easier trying to find an open space of water and stay on it for as long as possible.

Suddenly, they heard noise, splashing, over the water nearby, they quickly made for cover, cries of excitement in French as they saw their enemy, Saxons, fleeing the site.

Rowan and Tait reached cover, they both got their bow and arrow and began hitting the enemy as they approached over the clearing in the fen, the enemy tried to send arrows back but they were moving unevenly and could not get accuracy. As our men were very good, and fast, they were scoring well, so well in fact that they pulled up and went behind the reed cover.

Tate untied their horses, pulled them in, leapt on their backs and rode off with Rowan at his side.

They met the river, could see the small island on which Horningsea, a small hamlet was built, so made for it. Tait had a relative living there, so having carefully crossed the river Cam they made for their house. He knocked at the door and nothing happened, they about to leave when the door was flung open, his uncle and aunt, beaming with smiles at how pleased they were to see him, invited them in to talk.

They did say they could not stay long as they said they were busy travelling to Royston to do some farm work. They clearly understood and gave them a drink, chattering non-stop, mainly about the Normans taking over, where would it end? They did say no enemy had been on the island yet but our men did not want to be the ones who were responsible for changing that. So, with big hugs, they were off again.

They reached dry land quickly and began making their way towards the Swaffams, no enemy could be seen trying to find them so all seemed well! But for how long? Being just two strong lads was a great help in staying out of sight! Them not being a whole troop., so they thought they had a good chance of getting back to the Isle.

They went around the Swaffams, only just missing some Normans on horseback, and went towards Newmarket to reach Devils Dyke about mid-way between Reach and the New Market, hopefully missing any troop movements along the way. Hopefully they had not been seen.

They led their animals into the dip of the dyke, as they approached the top of the mound, they stopped to make sure nobody was about. It was clear, thankfully, so they mounted and sped off towards Burwell. They travelled across the shallow fen to Wicken, nobody seemed to be about at all, it was ghostly and silent, so they carried on, With Soham Mere on their right and the fen coming towards where they were. Everything at peace with the world here, the fighting with the Normans seemed a lifetime away, reeds softly swaying in the breeze giving off their familiar sound.

As they approached the end of dry land, they could make out the island of Barway, it was low in the water and the reeds disguised it, very difficult to make out, if you did not know it was there you could easily miss it. Just as soon as they could make it out they urged their horses to leap into the unknown water. This turned out to be surprisingly deep, as you progressed the reed beds became thicker and the horses became more confident, it was quite easy going. Six little houses here, owned by fishermen with nice compact boats. A couple of men returned their cries of hello. They were over the land and back in the water towards Stuntney, very quickly. This part was very deep in patches so the horses were urged to take things slowly.

As they approached, this island they could make out movement so they slowed their animals to a stop. Arrows began flying towards them, too damned close for comfort.

They quickly moved to where they could not be seen, dismounted, and walked in the fen to try and see how many men they thought might be here and against them. It was more than they could hope to cope with so they thought they would try their luck at getting through to the isle direct from where they were.

All sorts of stories did the rounds about how men and horses and boats had disappeared over the years on this part of the fens, so they were a little worried. They did not consider they had much choice, so after a few minutes they set off, taking a wide berth, away from Stuntney Island.

It was deep to begin with and difficult for the animals, moving between the batches of reeds, they were a lot deeper and stronger so they settled into a sort of stride. They were not happy though as they came up against the main river Cam/Ouse. A lot of rain had fallen so there was an awful lot of river to cross. There seemed to be strong undercurrents as they could see the water swirling.

They were too busy looking at the water to notice two boats of enemy coming from the left, the Cambridge direction. They turned their horses and disappeared behind some reed beds, hoping they may not have seen them. Some hope!

Arrows began to arrive, they jumped off their horses and began to lead them away from where the arrows were landing, leaving them safe. They tied them and carried their bows and arrows to a spot some way away, and began firing back at the boats, they could tell quite well where they were. They hit their targets well as cries of pain and exclamations of hatred, they supposed, came from the boats, they did not know a great deal of the French language, they were certainly not cries of greeting anyway.

One of the boats came through, a reed bed not far from our boys, they knocked off a few of these men before they jumped ship and hid in the reeds, mud and water! This could be fun, or not, as they could hear the French trying to encircle them, close in for the kill etc.

Our men quickly moved before they were able to close the circle so they were not going to win just yet!

A few shouts in French, as they began moving to the centre where our men were thought to be, our men began shooting arrows into any enemy they could make out. Shouts in French abounded! Agony and hatred were again the topics. Several died where they stood, the others tried to rush away in panic, not being used to the water they were too slow. Had our men not collected arrows as they travelled along the way, the only problem would have been a lack of things with which to shoot the enemy! It was a waterway of killing!

A couple managed to reach the other boat, clamber aboard, then it quickly turned and went away from where it had come as fast as possible.

Our men were free to try and cross the main river now, somehow it did not seem such a problem, they led their horse through the water. The shallow parts they walked but the deeper parts were a different story as they had to aim them in the direction they wanted them to go and hope they would take it. After some time they managed to cross the deep river section. All three horses were snorting and quite angry at being made to get wet and cold, they were clearly not amused! Both the lads thought this was very funny as they tried to stroke them into good moods for the final leg of this trek.

Some shallow sections followed over which the lads rode two of the animals all the time gentle talking to them as they progressed. The other horse carried lances and bows and some rather wet bedding.

Eventually, they made land on the Isle and scrambled up the bank to safety and home at last!

They were utterly astonished to find Hereward and the majority of our men had returned after setting fire to the causeway. The tales they told each other would last a lifetime!

Chapter 88

New Blood Among the Ranks

One of the best things that happened as a result of our fighting was a huge increase in the number of men wanting to join us. We trained these men really hard, the ones who did not make the standard were told they would be kept note of and contacted in the future if and when needed. They were asked to keep as fit as possible so hopefully they could become useful at a moment's notice.

Some of these men came from far away, it was a risk to travel, Williams men were told to stop anyone they came across, if they could not convince them that they were moving around for work, or family, they were arrested or even killed on the spot, that made them very careful, and useful to us straight away. Some actually were taken, and escaped, even better prepared for us. Their hatred of the enemy knew no bounds.

Space was in short supply now on our wonderful Isle, it didn't seem possible when my group had arrived, it didn't seem that long ago but if our plans were going to mean anything then we must get more and more troops trained in groups up and down the country and take the fight to the enemy.

The fact was that we must make the Normans not just wish they had not taken us on, we must send them packing back to where they came from, France, and make them stay there. To think that just a small section of France was trying to take over all of England was crazy, to say the least!

We were much encouraged by our recent successful fighting at Willingham, Slepe, now known as Saint Ives, Huntingdon and Cambridge. We were not frightened of anyone, we knew we could fight and win! We also realised it might well become harder before it became easier. That was in the future and right now things looked great for the Saxon fight back!

There were huge forests, where we could accomplish much regarding troop camps to train our men, and of course the fens, where they would not be confident of fighting, an awful lot of our men would be quite at home here.

I told Hereward of the men we had trained on our way to the Isle and he was much encouraged, hoping that they had carried on the training and maybe even taken out some enemy to boot!

Maybe Geoffrey had begun to set up other groups around his area, that would be fantastic!

We must send out some men to make contact and see what they were doing, Hereward and I both thought.

I was warming to this Hereward and I believed he could lead us in our quest right across the country, everyone wanted to follow him, he inspired so many people, most of all, myself!

Earl Morcar believed the same, not a word was uttered against him, at times he gave Hereward advice, but that was all.

He was so important to our cause that I wondered if he would ever be allowed on a battlefront again, if we lost him, we would all surely be lost.

I did mention this to him some time later. He merely scoffed at me and said 'nonsense, there were plenty of men to lead after he was long gone,' He even suggested I might like the post, this I laughed off, folly to even make the suggestion I said, thinking I would never be up to the job.

We got along so well, we thought the same battle wise and had the same ambition, I was amazed, truly amazed, by the man.

Chapter 89

Site of Hereward's Castle at Bourn, the buildings now long gone!

Up and Down the Country

A lot of local groups were being trained with bow and arrow and sword play, on a part time basis, already. This was in the local towns and settlements so we had back up at a moment's notice if needed. Obviously the training was taking place in secret in the woods near these places well away from enemy eyes. They tried to make sure no enemy were getting into these camps. They all knew they had spies almost everywhere, they traced families background where they could, to see if they were spending more than they were earning as by selling information to the enemy. They knew the Normans tried bribery where all else failed, which was more than a little low in my opinion, to stoop like this was awful! They didn't care how they won, just as long as they won.

Brunn/Now Known as Bourn. First Training Camp

Hereward suggested a forest near his estate at Bourn, for another camp to be established which he knew very well, it was very thickly wooded, and full with game to eat, so food would be no problem.

It was decided that a party of twenty men would go and see if it could work. My hand was first up and it was decided, I could pick my men and prepare to leave in a few days. Hereward had stopped opposing my wish to go and begin the camp at Brunn.

These men would probable all come from my original group of forty as these were people I knew and would trust with my life, though to be honest I would gladly trust all on the Isle with my life. Maybe I was wrong, what with spies about, time would tell on that one.

The Group of Twenty, for the Training Camp

I decided to take two Girvii as well, Vitt Hal Girvii Biomonap, and Bikassim Girvii Sunningfu, their help and advice had become more and more important to me over the time we had spent planning and fighting, I also felt the Girvii had more than a right to be represented in this force to upset the mighty Normans. I had it brought to my notice many times how all the men under my command listened to these two Girvii, men who in the past would not have even looked in their direction now stood, asked and listened and above all took note of these fine fighting men of the Britons.

Cedric Wenoth was my constant companion, as a true friend and indeed fighter so he was next chosen, Guthrum was a must also, with his sword and arrow, he could not be beaten, Winchell Millhouse was a master hut maker, and expert at making bow and arrow etc. Woodrow Huxtable was always on hand when you needed something, anything it seemed! Roe Leofwine was always available to make anything with wood, huts or arrows. Ware Jerrigan was a master butcher and a fighter to boot!

Rowan Meginhard was our doctor, Mathew Upton Cynesige was a great fighter in general, Warinus Bassingbourn was cook amongst other things, Acton Dickman, arrow man and food getter! Aiken Eads, great with a bow, plus food gatherer, Hugh Fishman, bow man and fire setter! Manton Espenson, bow and food. Ripley Kersey, bow man, Montgomery Haggard, bow and sword and Aart Dwerryhouse, Acton Dickman great all-rounders! Two other young men were recommended to me, Zack and Xanda Brightcard. Both were being talked about in the most complementary manner for soldiers, strong, with bright minds, and without doubt future leaders of the Saxon cause.

I have to include myself in this enterprise as I shouted louder than anyone to get this training other groups outside the Isle under way. Plus the fact that I had already set up a training camp with Geoffrey, north of Brunn.

It was the future, as we had lit a great fuse that, hopefully, would burn until we had driven these dreadful men from our lands!

The "22" Camp. First of Many

We prepared ourselves and set off, taking with us as much as we could muster, on our first trip away from the Isle. It was very exciting as this was our first attempt at setting up another main force to rid this Kingdom of the dreaded Normans.

This base should be far enough away from the Isle and well enough hidden from them to do the job we required.

Chapter 90

The Enemy Amongst Us

We trudged through the water on our exit from the Isle, having said our goodbyes to all those in the know of what we were trying to do. Not many actually knew as we were now being informed by some people off the Isle that spies were now amongst us, actually on the Isle! Just what was the world coming to?

We simple and suddenly, did not know who to trust. In a way, it was a complement from our enemy, we knew we must be getting to them. Having said that, it was going to be a constant worry from now on. The "Boston Defenders" were never going to let me down, I would swear that to the end of my days! As the force had grown it was not possible to be as close a group as I wanted. Just one of the major problems of growing a fighting force!

We exited via Stuntney to Isleham, then Fordham, skirting Burwell and the Swaffham's, Prior and Bulbeck. We had skirted the troops at Burwell, it was a little more difficult at Bottisham, they had more guards. Our scouts at front and rear were well tested in the forms of Matthew Upton Cynesige and Edgar Kenulph so our progress was quite fast.

They were both given time to look around Cambridge, as we had fought there recently we were afraid William would have made his camps much stronger, better defended and guarded, this was indeed the case.

We sent out the scouts to the other side of Cambridge, having secured ourselves good cover, and waited. This was very difficult for us all, we were so eager to get the training place organised, we had no choice but to sit and not be seen.

The scouts came back with the news I expected, there were not many soldiers to be seen south of Cambridge. They had found some little routes via Little and Great Wilbraham which were clear of all except locals, hopefully.

The group, in batches of three, travelled through Fulbourn, close to Cherry Hinton and onto Grantchester, here we settled for food along the banks of the river Cam/Granta. This was beautiful, sitting on the meadows and they all felt cheered as we packed up and went on our way.

Quite a large part of this area lay in ruins, many years ago it had been a city and it was destroyed by the Danes, never to be replaced it seemed. The next settlement was tiny, went by the name of Coton. It soon passed us by.

The next place was Madingley, where a large estate existed, large house, taken over by the enemy, of course. What had we come to expect!

Edgar put us across fields, behind trees to pass unnoticed, to Dry Drayton, more fields to Knapwell, then Elsworth to Hilton. It was slow going, through the woods, we tried to keep hidden behind trees and bushes at all times. This was difficult, as there was nobody about, except farm workers, it could be slow going, we had put out two more scouts to make double sure no soldiers were going to surprise us.

Our path took us near Godmanchester, then around Brampton away from tracks again as the scouts said there were quite a lot of enemy movement nearby and we did not want any soldier seeing us and bringing a mass of enemy down on us! Barham was next to pass, then Buckworth followed by Hamerton.

This seemed an awful distance to travel but to be using Hereward's friends and contacts in a secure forest away from everything was a good plan. William would surely never imagine we would be moving a training camp so far away!

Steeple and Great Gidding were next on the track, across to Luddington in the Brook, what a lovely name, and place come to that! Well-kept cottages as well.

These tracks seemed to go on forever, small settlements everywhere, as we next met Hemington, Lutton and Caldecote. Quite a few cleared fields were here, being used to grow corn for bread and grass for winter feeding for cattle probable.

We passed through Folksworth, some clearance done in this area, but not continued with, as trees were taking over again.

We stopped here for the night, an awful lot of deer could be seen and heard, we thought we rather fancied their meat for our meal. They proved quite skittish, difficult to kill, and very energetic, they ran so fast and zig zagged as they went. We did bag one in the end, along with rabbits, but I think we used up too much energy in the process so it wasn't the best idea, still, it did taste really good from our open fires.

The evening was turning into night when Edgar came into camp with a couple of local Girvii and a Saxon, he had met them in the trees and set about talking about the enemy in the area.

Chapter 91

Peterborough had a large Norman camp, they were led by a very nasty Norman, Frauque was his name, he seemed particularly fond of accusing people of being spies and torturing them, sometimes to death!

He had several squads doing the rounds of the area, this was how he got virtual slaves to do work for him and the Normans in general, building castles, churches or fortifications in general, walls, etc.

He often worked these people to death which seemed counterproductive, teach them to do a job, kill them, and have to find someone else to teach. He sounded a really nasty man to us all.

We asked what the defences in the town were like, where did he live etc. how many men guarded him. Would it be worth at least getting near him during the day with the thought of killing him off! The more these chaps talked the more we thought of a plan to rid this world of him, hoping his replacement could not be as bad!

We were in no immediate rush, so a change of plan began to form in our minds, and I thought we would go wherever he stayed and take a quick look and see if anything could be done about ridding this world of him.

On the one hand killing him off sounded good all around, the problem would be if we lost anyone, we needed all the men we had and more!

If we could get in fast, do the job required, and get out fast, we stood a good chance. He may think of himself as being so strong, untouchable, that he did not protect himself well enough. Sometimes being the "tough guy", if only in his head, could very well be his undoing.

We Slept on it!

The following morning, we decided we must at least go and get as close as we could and see what we could do with this dreadful enemy. We went into Peterborough via Haddon and were told the track to the main camp was along a certain way.

Two of the Girvii said they would take us there which they quickly did, the camp was pretty large, the building in the centre was where he stayed most of the time.

We were told he left it only to stretch his legs, this might just give us the chance we needed, I had brought my best bowman, Wulfric the Black, who we were sure could get the range and hopefully finish him. The trouble was we would probable only get one chance at this.

I thought, with a bit of luck, we could all get arrows into this compound where he walked, we could all aim in an awful lot of them at one time to cause maximum chaos, this sounded as though it could really work! At the very least it was worth a look, maybe even an attempt on his life! could we achieve it was the question?

We were guided to the area in the town by these locals we had met and were told of the regular times he showed which I thought at the time could be a mistake being made by him making him a regular and relatively easy target.

We had to wait some time and walk around the camp wall to the nearest point to where he walked, there were several gaps in the wall, this was more than a little strange. We were told there had been several attacks on the wall recently as he was so hated, so we just waited in the hope of an appearance, maybe he had changed his timing? Who knows!

Eventually, a couple of men dressed grandly appeared out of the main doors, we got excited and prepared ready to fire, only to be told they were not the main man, though one of the Girvii said they were awful men as well. So, we waited some more, trying to walk in a casual manner up and down the inside walkway of the wall, so as to not look too conspicuous. We left our horses in a yard nearby as there were plenty of people who were willing to help the cause!

Then our time came, the awful man appeared, Wulfric, first to aim, then we quickly followed suit.

We fired virtually together, just a second to see how good we were.

To say, we hit the jackpot, would be an understatement, the Normans just fell like leaves, lots of soldiers quickly gathered round so we fired into them as well. We had never seen anything like it, we had killed a large number of the enemy changing the place, hopefully for the better, plenty more were injured. This must be some kind of divine intervention, to be so accurate at this distance with no practice was unheard of, by us anyway! I had never hit such a target at this distance in my life before, and believe me I had tried!

Without a second thought, we turned and ran, thought could come later as we disappeared into the lanes of houses, the Girvii showed us the quickest way to exit the town and believe me when I say we left very quickly taking their advice.

I have never seen a couple of men so happy as the two we left standing on the outskirts. We knew the reprisals would be severe, whatever they were, they would be worth it. We only had time to take note of these very happy guys! We vowed to come this way again, sometime. There might be some interesting stories doing the rounds about the strangers who had appeared out of nowhere, killed our enemies, and disappeared as soon as they had come! Or some such wild tales!!

Chapter 92

Bourn, Brunn

Back to our trip to Bourn, we left through Longthorpe, and followed the track to Marholm, then Ufford.

Nobody was following us at this point, so we thought we would have a look at Barnack, the stone was used for buildings all over the area so we considered it worth a look. Most of us had heard of Barnack stone. The quarry was understandable impressive, there was a camp set to the side where the men who worked at the face lived, a lot of thought had gone into this development, there seemed to be a huge amount of stone left to cut and use.

We quickly carried onto Tallington having had to cross the East Glen river which got us rather wet, it being a lot deeper than we thought, the mud stuck to our cloths. We led our horses through the water which was clearly a mistake, the mud was difficult to remove, we did have other clothes so it was not a total disaster. We needed to be clean and look decent as we had to meet Herewards second in command, from his farming days, as soon as possible.

We were not far off now and speeded up as we could be being followed by the Normans we had no doubt, as a result of our fighting at Peterborough. Hereward had told us, if it came to it, we could easily lose ourselves in the forest near his family's estate, now controlled by some Normans!

We made our way across more fields, crossed the water at Greatford, it had quite a large bridge and that was about it! The forest began to show itself from here on, some parts had been cleared, but it was getting thicker and thicker. We felt, after a struggle, we were reaching our goal at last.

The track to our left was the way to enter the treeline, so we took it. It became a different world all of a sudden, one of quiet peace. The hustle of the outside world went away to be replaced by woodland noise, mainly birds singing, almost constantly. No reed beds, fen or bog.

It took some time to acclimatise to this, it was to become our new world and fill our lives with a great peace we had never known. The deer and foxes and badgers and bats and nightingales and wild boar came more into their own at night time, it was like two different worlds that missed each other.

Our way into this paradise was clear, we made it slowly, we didn't think we were being followed, we hoped at least that this was the case, so time no longer mattered, it seemed that way anyway.

Some of the old trees looked as though they had been growing for hundreds of years, they were huge and knurled and majestic all in one. There was space around them as not much grew near, it was as though they were the kings of this jungle and they were given space to do as they pleased.

We all sat under the canopy of one and ate what food we had left, didn't say much as we were in awe, just listening to our new noises and looking at our new surroundings was all encompassing.

After food and a deserved rest, I stood and suggested we look for somewhere to camp, a little further into this new land. It was no good going off in twos and threes as we would probable get lost, so we continued in line.

It was heavy going as we had to make a way through, making a pathway, to where, we did not know. That was the exciting thing, I think! Cutting our way to a new future.

Eventually, we came across a large clearing where we decided to stop for the night, the hunters went out to get dinner, in pairs so they did not get lost, hoping it would not take long, the rest decided where they were going to spend the night. It was not at all cold with no cloud, so, no covers would be needed to keep the rain off, not that much could get through the canopy overhead provided by the trees.

We just needed fires to cook by and that did not take long! The odd forest here and there, timber a plenty!

The hunters didn't take long, either, several deer and boar were enough to get us busy preparing food to cook, good fresh meat. After food, before we settled down, I sent out scouts, not too far out in four directions around us, the lads asked why I bothered with this as nobody was about.

I explained that they were all my responsibility and I would protect them each with my own life and I expected them to do likewise. Plus, we did not know if any Normans were following from Peterborough, they would be very angry, we killed a number of their leaders don't forget? Not so long ago either. The scouts would change at around three hours, so we could all be up bright and early!

The dark seemed to pull the camp closer, it was a very pleasant way to spend the night. The dawn chorus was so loud it woke us all early. It was very special, that first morning stayed with me for an awful long time. As usual food and wood were gathered to begin the day, feast all around. And damned good food! A lot of excited chatter amongst us all regarding our new surroundings.

All of us talked of going further into the forest and trying to find a large open space where we could perhaps set up a training area for the first group of troops that we were going to train. We cleared away most of the evidence of our being there as a matter of course and moved off, further into the unknown.

We stumbled onto a stream, essential near a camp, the area was not too overgrown and we decided to follow it into the forest, the trees were definitely thinner, it looked promising, they were a different type, most of them. I thought the soil composition must be different. The only problem with it was that there was a small track along the stream, it might have been caused by men or deer or something else. We found no individual prints in the ground so we could not tell.

Our travel continued slowly forward, as I heard a cry from behind. We pulled up sharply as our rear scouts came in to alarmingly tell us there was a group of perhaps as many as thirty enemy following our trail, obviously from our Peterborough fight, trying to find us. There was only one thing they wanted and that would be us dead!

We had time to call in our other scouts and prepare for the encounter that was inevitable. One group of six men were left at the rear end of where we decided to defend, three each side of the small track we had made. These would wait until all enemy had passed and then would attack the last eight. Five each side of the track would attempt to take out roughly fifteen of them and the remaining four would hopefully finish off the rest. We spread out and did not have long to wait!

The French were chattering quite loudly as they came into hearing distance, I was in the middle group so when the allotted moment came we attacked with swords quickly knocking enemy out of the fight, out of this world actually as we could take no prisoners. We had caught them by surprise as they were concentrating on following our tracks, a bad idea on their part.

There was no room to fight, trying to turn horses was just about impossible, so we thrust swords and knives as best we could. Many of the enemy were now knocked off their mounts so we leapt from ours and shoved the horses away.

We fairly leapt at each other, swords clashing, dealing with these men who had come to do us no good!

It was really exhausting, trying to mind the bushes and trees in our way and dodge the enemy, this really was a rare combination of effort and you had to get it exactly right to stay alive to be able to fight off the next cut from the enemies sword.

There was no time to shout orders or advice, just get stuck into this fight. Cedric fell to the ground near me so I jumped to his aid, thrust my sword into the side of his opponent and knocked the next fiend into the next world, he would bother nobody anymore! My friend was not badly hurt I was glad to note as he returned to the fight, a little blood showing from his left arm.

The six lads from the beginning of our fight line joined us, clearly they had dispatched their enemy. They began hitting the French in our group, which took some of the strain off us as we took control.

They were quite a hardy bunch of fighters, these enemy, but we began to take over this small fight.

I hoped there were no other groups of these men following us as we did not want to be easily followed, we did not want to be followed at all come to that!

It was of the utmost importance to set up these training camps out of view of anyone, Saxon and Norman alike, for the sake of safety.

After a pretty huge effort, we dispatched the last of the enemy and took their animals with us. Another days work done, we had fought well and received only a few injuries I was glad to note!

A problem occurred to me! If these men were followed, the enemy might be able to find the track we had made and surmise we were in the forest still. This would never do as we needed to keep out of sight of everyone.

Cedric suggested we should take the bodies completely out of the forest and lay them perhaps near the main track to Bourn. It was decided to do this so we lay the bodies over their horses and led them to the edge of the forest. We stopped to make sure the way was clear and rode across open land to the track. We had to rush across the last piece of open land as we could hear horses on the track and we managed to hide behind trees and low bushes until the track was clear. We began placing the bodies around the open land as though there had been a fight. We left a few of the horses here just to make it more believable and quickly made our way back to the cover of the forest.

First camp here! We settled on the right hand side of the track and began to make camp, cutting trees and tying them together with bark, sides and walls up were very quickly just away from the stream in the trees, out of view! Room for just twenty two men took no time at all, I sent out Matthew Cynesige and Warinus Bassingbourn and Cedric and Guthrum just to see what or who was in the area, Matthew and Warinus were group scouts anyway. Cedric and Guthrum were really interested to see just how far the forest went, they knew what to look for and to take care of themselves and not be seen if needed so it would be interesting to know details of what they found. Cedric and Guthrum would probably have to mark trees as they went on their little trip through the forest, as they would be bound to get a little lost which would not be good.

Acton Dickman and Aiken Eads went off to search for food, Aart Dwerryhouse, of Eel catching fame, went off to see what could be caught for food from the stream. I thought there may be plenty of trout, duck was a firm favourite of mine, there may be some about, possible not in all the trees. Good clear chalk streams were well known for trout, we would wait and see! Zack and Xander Brightcard claimed to be fishermen, so they set about catching some. We may soon see just how good they were!

There was plenty of wood, fallen and dead, so we didn't have to waste time cutting wet wood that was full of sap, it burnt straight away. This was the easiest camp ever to set up to date at least. None of us could quite get used to the beauty of the forest, the wind rustling through the trees, the animals and birds contributing their individual sounds to a very rich tapestry. We did, however, miss the sunshine that graced our skyline at this time. We had to make do with the odd flash of light as the wind took away the trees cover.

We settled and began chatting and feeding our fires, waiting for the men to return with any food. This didn't take long, fifty more minutes and we had slices of deer, boar and some nice fresh trout ready, cooking and smelling really good. One unfortunate duck had been collected and it was set aside just for me, I was rather embarrassed to discover. The flavour was pretty special though, the open wood fire added to it! A great way to end the day we all thought as we talked about the future.

Trout first, then a wait for sections of the meat to be ready, it took a time but was well worth the wait!

Chapter 93

During the night, my thoughts turned to Lynelle, this often happened, as if I did not have enough to think about! They were important thoughts that I cherished, though, gave me a great pleasure I had not known before. I hoped she was well, I imagined only good thoughts, thoughts of a future together, in peacetime, perhaps with our own family. The only future I could imagine now was fighting, and hopefully winning many battles. We had an awful long way to go before peace arrived. One could but dream and hope at this time!

The morning came, all too soon, we ate the rest of the meat, disguised the camp with more bushes so it could not be seen from the track by the stream, and continued on our way into the wilderness of this forest. We were in a wonderland and it was a joy to be here, so different from our waterways and reed beds back home. These British Isles were only small but there was so much variety in the land it made it special.

In some places, the wood bowed over towards the water and we were unable to stay on horseback, so we dismounted and led them through these patches. There was never too large an area to be a major problem, it did slow us down and I was getting annoyed that we had found nowhere yet to base our camp.

Hereward had told us of several places that existed this end of the forest, we could find neither to date!

Cedric and I decided to split up into two groups, where the lower bushes were not very thick as we could stay in touch with each other relatively easily. This way we covered more ground than by staying in the one group, we hoped anyway.

We still had scouts out to make sure we were not getting lost, the one at the head of the other group rushed in with the news that he had found a large open area, he thought it just what we were looking for!

We all got together and followed and sure enough it was a very good place to hide and train, with a lot of bush growth around the edges where we could hide our huts from anyone taking a glance to find if anyone was here.

Building the Training Base

We talked and talked about how we should set up the huts, exactly where we should put them.

It was decided to put two lines of huts behind bushes on the far side of this clearing, we should be together for safety's sake, scout camps were placed all around us, well hidden. The scouts would be changed regularly, at some time we would all take responsibility for guarding, no one would be let off that duty.

Work got under way with the cutting of trees and building huts, we would set up fire areas near the huts to cook and keep warm when needed and to dry clothes out of the eye line of anyone snooping around the area, it all looked almost too easy. As we intended staying here for some time, the latrine area was dug some way away, well hidden.

The buildings were finished quite soon, we would build more as we received more men for training, there was plenty of area left well hidden from the far side of camp that could be used. Having one side of camp hidden meant we would only have to properly guard one side. We were such a small group and couldn't have as many guards as I would have liked, maybe we should increase our numbers as time went along? I had no doubt we would get a set number of men needed to train and guard these camps up and down the country as we progressed!

We were a huge distance into the woodland now, well away from human contact of any sort, surely no enemy would travel through this patch of our land that seemed devoid of humanity. Hopefully no enemy would be able to follow their comrades into the woodland to where we had fought.

We thought the one problem may come from a group hunting, possible with dogs. What we would do in those circumstances we couldn't say as we simple didn't know. We would have to devise some kind of plan! Maybe build fences, areas where you could lead a dog chasing you with the far end shut off, run into it and trap the animal by closing the door you entered by, perhaps more thought was needed!

The lads began to set up the course for training, the open ground wasn't really large enough for what we wanted, but it would have to do!

Close combat in the open was going to have to be replaced by close combat among the trees, on and off horse, all would get the general idea anyhow!

We set up racing marks to test each group between certain points, we had targets for testing who was the best, or most improved as time went by, we raced horses through courses we set up. It was all go and we were ready to take in our first batch of men for our new army against the invader!

Hereward had told us to contact certain people from Bourn, they knew a great many men who were straining at the leash to get to fight the invaders, we needed them now! To get them trained, fighting fit, ready to begin to take back our land! A long and very hard struggle was on the horizon. We were all up for this, no matter what! The caution of the past was long gone and it was time to begin planning to attack in numbers up and down the country.

Chapter 94

From Camp to Bourn

Cedric and I left camp to ride to Bourn, to find these friends of Herewards and organise them to get at least forty men to begin with as our first trained soldiers outside the Isle in this area. We knew we may not be able to handle that many men in one go but the others could watch and learn and who knows, even contribute ideas to our training course. These men would need to be not doing an awful lot, work wise, or they may be missed and the enemy would become suspicious, we would all need to be thoughtful and careful. They would have to return home to help out with the work load some days.

Early the next morning, we were off to find Bourn for the first of many times. We travelled through the woods, hoping, more than knowing, if we were going in the right direction. We found the stream and followed it easily.

Eventually we reached the edge of the woods, sat and ate some of our food by the crystal clear stream. It ran quite fast, made quite a noise as it went on its way. We chatted about how different things were here and about how excited we were to be at this point at last in our lives, we both had so much fight in our souls it was hard to explain.

We were so eager to get many more trained men, so we could begin fighting to get our land back. In our minds we were thinking of establishing maybe as many as fifty training bases around the country. This really was a grand plan, we could at times bring these groups together when needed, or not as the case maybe. It all depended on how the enemy reacted. Who knows where these plans might lead? We certainly didn't as it was largely talk but we at least had ambition!

Cedric said we needed to get a move on, so we went on our way again. Crossing fields with not much care, it was difficult to think that war was around the corner. We met the main track again and followed it behind trees so now we were not in view to anyone from the track. We carefully looked back along the track and could see the bodies had been discovered, quite a number of local residents were milling around. It would not be long before the enemy appeared no doubt! What they would make of their dead comrades we had no idea, they would certainly not be too pleased!

Just before Bourn itself there was a track to our left, Hereward had said that at this point we must take it as it was the track to his family's house. Though we knew it would be housing some damned Normans now, we also knew his right hand man for the estate should be there, or at least around the back of the estate house. We were to find him and set up our camp with men to train from here initially.

Cedric followed me to the back of this house, I knocked and the response was immediate. I stood looking at a man's face and he at me. After what seemed an age, we had to be careful here as he could be a Norman spy, he could be just anybody come to that.

I introduced myself as Eldwyn Aaron, he said he was Dudley Dannel and asked what he could do for us, I mumbled something silly like, what do you produce at this farm that we could buy as we were traders and were interested in organising a network of farms that we could buy from and sell to where we came from. Sounded pretty daft really, but on the spur of the moment it was all I could come up with. We should have sorted out what we were going to say before we had come to this moment.

The chap looked a little confused, said this was not the normal approach but to come in and talk with him.

We followed him into the kitchen area and sat down at a table, he offered us a drink, gratefully we accepted and sort of sat there looking at each other.

Cedric began talking about crops and cattle, another chap came into the room, he was introduced as under manager of the estate, went by the name of Norville Aston, he at least had a good Saxon name, though that meant nothing as a plant would also be given a Saxon name! Clearly Cedric and I were not used to this situation, very new to us! It seemed we had much to learn as we were not confident and it showed.

How was this meeting going to progress, I couldn't blurt out that we were Saxon fighters, Hereward had sent us, can you get us a batch of fighters to train, to take on the enemy. What if he was the enemy!

I ventured to ask if there was any Saxon opposition actually fighting in or around Bourn, they immediately became silent, and said they were dangerous words to utter in this vicinity, I said I was sorry but if I was going to trade here I would need to know as I did in other areas.

He seemed very unsettled, but he said he understood my question. The trouble from his point of view was that we could be spies trying to catch him out.

He said he had not heard of any fighting but everybody was unsettled and very unhappy at the foreign takeover, where was it all going to end? We all agreed.

They left us in the kitchen to get information regarding their crops. I said to Cedric how the heck do we proceed with this problem; how do we find out if he is the Saxon Hereward talked of. Cedric said that Hereward had had a fight with this Dudley Dannel when he was younger and had left him scarred on his fighting arm, on the back of his right hand there should be a scar, there should be more scarring on his arm. They had practiced sword fighting from a young age and Hereward had become more than a little excited and didn't stop when he should have.

On his return, we tried to look for the evidence of wounds, it was not hard to see he did in fact have what was now a very small scar on his hand. I was not totally convinced this could have been caused by a sword, it looked too small.

I made a great effort to take off my coat and signalled Cedric to do the same, saying we were not used to the heat. Both of the men we were with took off their coats and it was obvious to anyone that this man had been hit with a sword.

I really couldn't stand not revealing that we worked with Hereward, that he sent his regards, and would he help us in our quest! A few strange moments passed.

Big smiles all around, Norville gave us both a hug, and said why did we mess around with all the twaddle regarding business, or did we just like to waste time!

Talking of wasting time, I said let's get down to why we were here and how many men could he get together as soon as possible so we could start another front against our enemy from here.

He asked where we had set up camp, I roughly told him, he suggested another clearing much further into the forest, but was sure it would do for the time being, as long as we were careful, with noise and damage to that area. We must also be careful to not make too much of a track coming to and from the camp.

He sent off his number two to talk to the leaders of the resistance, it wasn't a resistance yet, but we hoped it would be soon. They had apparently been taking part in mock fights in the woods, so things were moving in the right direction! It was a start at least. Sword practice was also being organised, about fifty men were involved in this but we would only take men who would not be missed from the family farm or whatever they did. So they settled on thirty good men, fit and good to fight!

No point hanging around, possible being caught, so Dudley Dannel arranged that he would deliver these men to us, probable in small batches so as to not raise attention among the enemy.

We thanked them for their hospitality and were about to leave when there was a very loud crack at the front of the house, it frankly made us all jump.

We knew this was not good, Cedric and I put our backs to the wall behind the very substantial door, Dudley just said to be calm, he would go and see what the problem may be.

Another bang at the door, Norville rushed to open it, the bolt was no sooner pulled than the door was smashed into and Turstin Fitzron appeared, followed by Eustace Ralph, two of the enemy who were apparently living in Hereward's house, demanding why they were not doing the jobs that they were instructed to do at this time!

Dudley struggled to his feet and made a pretty limp excuse as to why they were still here, one of the Normans apparently belted him across the face and he fell to the floor. The enemy cussed him no end in very bad English. Dudley said it would not happen again and he would get right to work this very moment!

Cedric and I grabbed our swords to launch ourselves at these thugs, only to be stopped by the manager. We were shielded by the door and side wall of his office so they could not see us. Though, we were sure we could have defeated these enemy, we realised we could have made a mess of our plans so we stood down, much against our will.

This Was Hard for Both of Us!

The two enemy left and crashed the door shut, Dudley came to us and told us to leave in a few minutes, he told us of a better way to go where we could not be seen, so we thanked him. There were tears in his eyes as he gave us both another hug, said he was never so pleased to see anyone as us in his life, maybe our country had a future after all. He had often thought it had none! Hereward was alive and well and preparing to fight the good fight, they were so pleased to have tiding of him. Not that there was that much good in fighting, but when you had no choice! It surely was the only way.

This was all good for us now, we had to make our way back to the camp and spread the great news!

We left the house, went through the wooded area to our left, and made for the track to get back to what was now our base, that sounded really good, our base! We had our very first training camp, with the first batch of soldiers as good as on the way! We had begun the fightback, we all felt and it was a release in itself!

The scale of our plans, perhaps fifty more groups and camps like this, up and down the nation hit home from this point.

Could we possible, actually achieve this I said to Cedric and Xander who stood close by? Both assured that this was indeed the beginning and we would win this war, no doubt! I think they were a little over enthusiastic with their claim but merely agreed.

Chapter 95

Meanwhile

Back on the Isle, trouble was mounting, the enemy had decided there was no further point in staying around Cambridge, they left quite a lot of soldiers to defend it if needed, and decided to move to another point, quite a long way off. Hereward had no idea where they proposed to go so he arranged for some of his men to follow them and see what transpired.

They had to stay a long way away from the enemy as William had taken to having groups of scouts rather than just one to cover a certain area.

No major difficulty there though, as so many men on horseback could not hide if they tried.

They followed the group via the parish of Cherry Hinton, where they had arranged for a small camp to be set up, another station was set up at Fulbourn, nearby, this was to guard a track leading out of Cambridge. His lead group was cheered by these men as he passed, they followed much the same path as we had made to Teversham, the other way around of course, crossed the river near a settlement and their camp at Bottisham. A number of his men came out to add encouragement to the moving troops.

William took his men alongside Swaffam Bulbeck and Swaffam Prior and stopped for a time at Burwell. He met and talked with some of his men at the causeway where he had a camp alongside the dock/causeway.

He asked where the shallowest point, in the vast waterway, was, at least to begin with, to a track to try and get onto the Isle and break this deadlock that was taking all his time and energy to try and beat.

He was told that it was a long way off from here and would take his army quite some time to get into place for an attempt, but they had looked up and down the waterways, the best place to at least try was to go nearly all the way out to a place called Brandon, via Mildenhall, and travel across towards the Isle from there. A number of the men at Burwell had spent a long time attempting to find the shallowest route possible to reach dry land at the Isle, they would find a likely place, go as far as they could, through shallow and deep water, over islands and the river, huge deep bogs and reed beds, only to date run out of daylight, and have to return, or as some had, to disappear.

Nobody knew if they had been swallowed by the bog, or perhaps been killed by the men on the Isle. The stories going round were dreadful in relation to disappearing in the bog! The land from here was either water or thick forest, there was no choice except that!

They decided to stay overnight here and make the trek to Brandon in the morning, the camp here was huge! Nobody had ever seen the like before. Nearly all the Norman force in and around Cambridge based at little Burwell didn't quite seem possible!

Up at first light, the whole group began to move off, the water spread as far as Mildenhall, so they decided to go around to the east of the settlement, crossing the river Lark as they went. The forest was really thick, the low growth as well, so it must have been hard going for them all.

Very slow movement was not good for Williams temperament, he was in a hurry to attack the Isle, had got a very bloody nose at Willingham, he was determined not to get the same here! He wanted to get on with the job, fast! The general weather was wet so the going was heavy to begin with. This did not please William either, it appeared even the weather was against him!

Hereward had other ideas though. Nobody was going to get onto what had become his Isle, the Saxon cause depended on this. Their very own Camp of Refuge!

He was constantly being told where Williams force was at any given time, he moved troops along the edge of the Isle, to protect if needed, couldn't see the need really though, it was good practice for the troops. He would have plenty of time to do whatever was necessary if the enemy tried to get through the water as they could only do so slowly, thereby giving time for Hereward's men to get into place and repel them, push them back into the water, they could be pushed back relatively easily he was confident. Then maybe push them all the way back to France! That was the long term hope at the very least!

Chapter 96

Near Brandon—Williams Force

The forest became thicker and thicker, much harder to get through, especially if you had several thousand horses to get to a certain point just before Brandon, which was still the plan.

They passed a small group of houses, he was told this was called Eriswell, somewhat stuck in the middle of nowhere, he couldn't think why in the world they should be here, but they were, in this dense forest that gave the appearance of never ending. He was hot, tired and fed up with all this water, and flies, and blasted forest! He still had not recovered from the burning of his beloved causeway at Willingham, though it seemed an age ago. It would sting for a very long time, to be brought down by these peasants was almost too much to bear!

At last, they found the bit of land before Brandon that seemed to strike out into the fen, surrounded by seemingly millions and millions of reeds, it was very unusual. It did at least give one the idea that the land was fighting back against the water. A lot depended on just how deep the water was, if William, and his horses and men could settle into their stride on top of the reeds, the roots perhaps being strong and binding, they could hold for some way, he and enough of his men could maybe get close enough to launch an attack.

But if there were, as he suspected, areas where the bog was deep and thick, he would be very lucky to get through. The trouble was the only real way to find out was to attack and see what happened! He was not disposed to waiting around to see what his scouts suggested, they would surely have told him this was no way to progress.

So that became the plan. He was advised to send men across the fen and make sure there were no really deep places where they may well sink without trace. He cried out that he had already wasted much too much time on trying to attack these damned Saxons, he knew he would not have time to fight today, so he agreed to send in just a few men, just a little way into the fen to appease his advisors. This was a bad mistake! William knew his own mind and would resist anyone who opposed him. He was not a man to argue with.

Normans on the Attack!

They had all spent a huge amount of effort to actually get to this point, so it was decided to prepare all armaments, sharpen swords in other words, and prepare for a dawn attack. William stated they would be on the Isle by midday tomorrow, a little too casually, thought his next in command.

All was prepared for them to settle down for the night.

No Peace Allowed for the Enemy

As Hereward now knew where they were for the night, he set a group of his men on them which he would lead, the express purpose was to cause as much disruption as they could to their night's sleep, and of course to kill as many as possible, kill or be killed was still the order of the day! Or night, come to that. There was no way he was going to allow the enemy to have a good sleep before fighting, the more on edge he could put them the better.

Fighting-Attacking on Stilts

The group took some time in preparation but when ready made their way to the waters edge and through the bog and reed beds. They silently came close and prepared to attack.

Then he signalled all to move forwards, Hereward and his men came upon them through the reeds and water, on their fighting stilts, silent movement through the water, they were on top of their foe before they knew it! Nothing there one minute, lolling into slumber.

Then they were upon them, swords bringing more death to the fens, to begin with many arrows flew into their enemy and panic ensued! People running everywhere, straight into swords, a great many of them. Their eyes were stabbed by the bright light of their fires, then they could not see in the darkness and before they had acclimatised their sight they were slaughtered by Hereward's angry men. They had taken a great deal of care to get through the fen to this point in silence, to catch the enemy unawares, the stilts were superb to travel these fens in silence and speed. It was a knack and took many months of practice before becoming expert.

Hereward headed a small group of his best men, his fight was with William himself so their plan was to get their leaders group and cause it as much damage as possible, maybe even killing the man himself, that would be a coup, would it not!

Montgomerey Haggard joined Hereward's group a little late, as he was not very accomplished on stilts. He felt a need to get at these enemy as soon as possible and help provide as much of a problem as he could, we all felt this way, I am sure, ……..fight we must! As Herewards second he had much to prove! "Monty," as he had become known, was a rising star and was being promoted as a leader of men.

Two of these men cried out to Hereward to follow them, they knew where they were, quickly they followed and saw a group by themselves, this indeed seemed likely to be their target, all were dressed in such finery, all big chaps, they were fighting to one side of this group, so Hereward rushed in on the full, Montgomery had to make up a lot of ground, being a little slow on the stilts, charged in with his best men following, knocked out the first line of defence, all were now involved, no other fight mattered to Hereward. Montgomery was occupied with trying to keep Williams guard at bay along with Hereward's best fighters and what a battle that turned out to be.

The clashing swords must have been heard a huge distance away, as the sound carried in the flat lands of these fens. The rest of the world was lost to these men!

Chapter 97

A Fight with William

Hereward looked up after killing off one more of the French giants, he saw his prey and attacked. William was no slouch with a sword and he saw our mighty Hereward on the attack just in time. He defended his sword against Hereward's first thrust, what a mighty clang as their respective irons met!

William went to Hereward's left and Hereward brought his sword up again without moving, this mighty crash caught William by surprise as the logical thing for Hereward to do was move opposite the way William had done, but Hereward's blood was up and he was going to get this man once and for all, to fight like a Lion and knock him off his perch.

William was a little rattled by now but he stood his ground like the champion he was, he was not going to give in to this ruffian from the fens!

Against the light of a fire, he caught a glimpse of part of Hereward's face, he had never seen such an expression of contempt, utter hatred, he shuddered again as he realised what he was up against.

Hereward must have got a glimpse of his enemy as he threw all his weight into the next strike, he all but knocked Williams sword out of his hand, such force William had rarely encountered.

Hereward quickly pulled back his arm and sword and thrust it into Williams side, though he had thick chain mail on, it pierced it and entered Williams side. Hereward was by now ecstatic, he knew he was winning and winning well! What a rush!

William cried out something in French as he turned away and all of a sudden three other rather large enemy stood in front of their champion. There was little Hereward could do but back away a little and call some of his own men, myself included, over to help him despatch these enemy.

I had the honour of first meeting these men, tough and well trained they were, but I was mad as hell now, realising how close we were to the Norman leader, and knocked a guy's sword down and finished him quickly as did the brave men around me.

Others came right away to help us, Hereward took the man on the left, his men took on the other two, though he was built like an oak tree this enemy soldier, Hereward was much faster and stronger and dispatched him with ease. Hereward was not a very tall man, just average, so he used his size to move very fast when fighting, nearly always catching out his enemy.

In despair, Hereward looked for our enemy, William, in fact we all did. The man was not to be seen again for some time. He had evidently been carried away by his men, much to our disgust! He had obviously hurt him badly. Under the circumstances, joy was in our hearts!

Battle in the Darkness!

This battle was supposed to be a dainty morsel compared to what was going to happen tomorrow. It seemed to be a main battle was going to be fought in the dark, now.

The trouble was we were mightily outnumbered so he made the only decision he could and decided to pull his men out quickly and disappear back into the night. We had brought stilts to get us through the fen in silence rather than trying horses or walking, we were very adept at using them, we could move quickly and be lost from sight in a moment, a great advantage over the enemy.

In a short space of time, Hereward and his men were gone, the Normans could almost feel they had been in some awful dream. The trouble was, the reality was all around them, dead, groaning, and dying comrades!

What a start to their campaign, a tiring march, food and the thought of a good night's sleep had been rudely mucked up by our Saxons fighting spirit. Also, word was out that Hereward had injured their king, nobody knew how badly, but it was not a good start at all. How could Hereward and his men have got so close without the Normans knowing, they must have pondered?

They were told to rest as best they could as the fight was still planned for the morning; they would not be in fine fettle at all, as William had hoped.

Hereward's Return

Hereward and his men carried on through the fen towards the Isle knowing they had done real damage to the enemy, his plan had been to rest these men he had used tonight and get ready the rest of the men he had here to fight if needed during the daylight campaign.

He would rest and see what tomorrow brought! They had brought back quite a few injured men. They were taken to the special covered area towards Littleport where they were looked after as best they could be, it sounded awful to say, but the groaning was a little unsettling if we listened to it for too long, we did sympathize, but felt it was not good for moral or sleep in the dead of night!

Peace settled on the Isle once more and Hereward and his men got some good rest.

Fight Day on the Fens!

The next day dawned, everyone got their bows and arrows etc. together, then some food, not everyone would eat as some could not keep it down on a fighting day, others ate as though starvation faced them, good for energy, and they might just need that bit of extra food! Everyone was silent, thinking this may be their last day alive. Everyone was also very excited, having trained, and trained, for this day, many more days like this ahead, no one doubted. Everyone knew how important it was to win this fight to help the growing confidence of all the Saxon race!

When all was ready, we were informed the Normans were preparing to attack from the same point they had been at when Hereward had engaged with them last night. They had men mapping a route through the fen, and had gone out in front to make sure horses could get through, though not very well as there was not nearly enough time to check the depths of these fens and bogs.

Hereward had left men out on the fen just to see what William would do, they waited until the Norman scouts got near and unleashed a barrage of arrows into them, killing most and maiming many more, causing much bad feeling amongst the enemy, even some of the leaders doubted they could win a battle against Hereward, especially in his back yard!

Chapter 98

A Long Way From Home

They were a long way from Ely, much water and Saxon men waited for them, one to drench, the other to kill as many of them before they reached the Isle.

As the batches of reed were so thick, it was sometimes impossible to see what lay in wait behind them, William ordered his men to attack, their horses were in deep water now so the Normans were very low, just above water level, on horseback.

Target Practice!

Hereward's men were having a field day! Knocking off the Normans as soon as they appeared, or having arrows go up into the air, over the reeds and down into the enemy, it was easy, no other word for it. The only problem at this time might be that we run out of arrows to shoot, with that in mind, the defending leader gave an order for a team of his men to go and get as many as they could muster and bring them back for this battle, also to order for a great many more to be made from the moment his men asked, which was from now, thinking of the number of enemy we were facing.

Impossible Mission

More and more enemy came to die, it seemed a dreadful waste of life. It was up to William, however, maybe his chosen men were in charge as William was out of any fighting now, or could even be dead! We were ever hopeful! Someone decided to plough on with this silly idea, an impossible mission! Hereward thought that maybe these replacement leaders were trying to impress the man himself, to show they were capable of leading without him being present, however, obviously they were not up to the mark, of that there was little doubt!

William, or whoever, decided to send in one more batch of "arrow fodder" to presumable get past the men in the fen, needless to say they did not progress any more than the last batch.

They then pulled everyone left, who could still ride back to dry land to reconsider their plan, and what to try next!

Approximately, an hour later, we could hear some orders being given, rather sharply, and we could see from our high ground that most of the rest of his horses were lining up to attempt an attack, good thing the plan was a bad one, thought

Hereward, and would not succeed any more than before. There were a huge number of horses getting ready, surely some must get through, we thought.

As the first line of his horses jumped off the ground into the water, the next lined up to do the same causing an awful lot of disturbance in the fen. More and more enemy entered the water to attempt entry to our fabled Isle.

If they did get over to our land in the numbers they had, our force would be outnumbered, they really could cause us major problems!

Fire in the Fen

One of the scouts rode up to Hereward and excitedly said, 'Why don't we now set fire to the reeds, as we had done at Littleport to great effect.'

Hereward immediately thought, what a great idea, lets quickly set fire to the area around this mass of enemy. The wind was in the right direction to flow the fire straight onto the Normans from right to left.

They were the aggressor and never let that be forgotten. Though, this was not a nice way to go, they would have done the same to us had they been given the chance, as especially we were so outnumbered at the time!

No doubt about that thought Hereward, and the group of leaders including myself made encouraging comment. Let's get on with it as some of the enemy were getting closer and closer!

So, Hereward and myself, as fast as we could, sent men out quite some way from the enemy, to the sides and in front of them under the disguise of the reed beds to start fires. We should have time to get to the other side of them, thought Hereward, a total ring of fire! The wind would not be with us that side but it might add to the confusion, so let's do it!

The men were really up for this, so they went about their work with added gusto, this would teach those damned Normans to not even try and get us on our Isle.

It was not long before the arrows were sent up from the front and the sides, they were the ready signals. The far ones hadn't sent up their arrow as yet, it may be that they may have been caught. Hereward pitied them if they had, but probable it was just because it took a lot longer to get there, William, or his generals, would have placed scouts at the rear of this fight just to make sure nobody was coming up on the rear. Our men were probably trying to either get around them without being seen or were fighting them to get past.

Time went by very slowly, if they didn't get into position quickly, Williams men might be too close for the fire to be effective! Some snorting enemy horses could in fact be heard coming from the reed beds so time was of the essence!

Whatever the problem was, it was no longer a problem as three arrows went up, then the final two. We were ready! We waited until the vast majority of the Conquerors soldiers were in the water and signalled the fires to be lit.

Fires in the Fens

A little smoke showed at first at the front of the enemy, there was a big enough mass of reeds to really make a show!

It quickly caught on all along the front, smoke right through the ranks of enemy, that alone would not be nice, the sides were by now smouldering and suddenly the fires were off.

The Normans were in panic now, horses thrashing about in the water, they had tried to turn as one madly struggling mass of men and horses. They were trying to get out of the fen, the way they had come, a lot of our best bowmen had gone out after the men who were lighting the fires and were busy putting arrows into any area they thought contained the enemy, which to be honest was all the areas under the smoke, more mayhem, the usual madness, added to this, huge fire and lots and lots of water. The total area being consumed had to be seen to be believed!

Not one horse or one man came out of that area to begin with, many were perishing where they stood, or sat, the wind was with us this day, it made the fire into an inferno, after a time quite a few bolted out towards Brandon. They had got through by going straight through the flames, some were on fire, which was so tragic.

We all felt pretty bad that things had come to this, of course, we had no choice. Quite a few more were getting out of the fire at the rear, we saw nobody in fancy cloths so we didn't know if William had even gone with his men to fight. It would surely be ironic if Hereward had cut him badly enough to get him to stay in camp for this fight, time would tell! He would have had to receive treatment due to the injury he had got while fighting Hereward.

Some of our bowmen had gone around the back and began firing into the fleeing enemy, they must have thought they were out of this very one sided battle. Bad luck, they were not!

The fire was totally out of control now; it was an inferno! The heat generated must be terrible, and the speed the flames moved, aided by the wind, was incredible, no one stood a chance of riding away from them.

Hereward was considering sending out a battle group to finish off any more enemy as they broke free from the fire. Considered it and sent them off as soon as possible. We must try and wipe out these soldiers, they must be given the message to all, do not dare to show your faces in our Islands of England, here or in the country as a whole as an enemy, because you will lose!

Chapter 99

End of Our Fiery Battle

The fire swept through the lines of enemy so fast, the wind pushing it as though it wanted to finish this job and get on with another. The heat generated was incredible!

Where it was set alight first, it had already smouldered out, lots of smoke coming off the fen, this was going to be the case all around. This was the first we had seen of the devastation we had caused, body's everywhere, a great many of the horses had just madly ran through the fire and were saved as a result, which was good. Most had thrown their riders.

Hereward sent men out to see if they could find any of the leaders in the hope that William was with them, many were dead but William was not with them as far as we could tell, an awful shame that was! Having encountered him face to face, and at least injuring him, we were not in awe at all; we knew we could beat him, if and when the time arrived!

Maybe It Had and We Just Did Not Know About It?

Anybody who would like any new shields, swords, knives, bows and arrows were invited by Hereward to go and get what they felt would be of use. Scavenging, after battles, was a way of life, though it was sometimes frowned upon. Clothes were in quite high demand, those that were not too burned, that is. The jackets under the main coats were in high demand.

Burned reed beds everywhere, it was devastation and no mistake, nobody had seen anything like it. Reed beds turned into a smouldering mess, smoke everywhere, dead men and horses at every part of what had been our lovely fenland, what a waste of everything that was normal, all gone. The enemy devastated!

I have never said devastation before so many times in my life but it has left such a lasting impression on my mind that I reiterate it. It was as though a small part of our world had come to an end.

The group Hereward had sent out got into position on land outside the fen on dry ground and began riding through the reeds, this was the reeds that grew on land around the fen area to move anybody out that was hiding, quite a number were chased out and run through.

Disaster for the Enemy!

This must count as the worst result of any battle in the history of the Norman empire! Tales abounded regarding their exploits throughout the Mediterranean, the places they had taken over on their way to the fighting in the holy land, during the crusades, this was momentous and no mistake.

We were all having dreadful thoughts, regarding the terrible loss of life, though, we comforted ourselves by reminding that the Normans were the aggressors, us Saxons and the local Girvii, even the Iceni were now a peaceful bunch though there were not many pure Iceni left now, we all of us liked getting on with our lives, peace, progress and happiness were the most important parts of our existence! At least they were once!

It was difficult to see, how the enemy could pick themselves up from this disaster. If William had managed to get away, and we hoped so much that he hadn't, he would have to get virtually a new army and that may well take some time. We must continue to hit his army while, they had any soldiers left alive. All of us must make sure they got no peace! Give them no time to bring over new soldiers and no time to plan fighting us, to put them on the defensive and keep them there.

Hereward's shared ambitious planning with myself!

Hereward's and my mind were doing overtime, we thought this could be the chance we needed to get our army organised. This was the chance the people on the Isle had been waiting for, the enemy force could not possibly police the whole country now, it would give us the time we needed to organise, with or without William the Conqueror.

The group we had sent out to finish off any stragglers, the remains of the enemy that had not got away, had not been seen for some time, though nobody was concerned, as they thought all organised resistance was finished, as indeed it was, from this battle force at least.

As our Saxons had gone out over the water to scavenge all they could, we asked all to keep their eyes open for anyone in senior enemy military dress, as we needed to know just how many officers had perished, as well as William. If in fact, he had died!

They may well not be able to tell as their cloths may well be burned, as well as the bodies, things were never simple, he thought to himself, it's a hard life. Moments like this made it all worthwhile, defeating the enemy was superb, not proving William was dead was annoying.

Hereward and his men thought they could defeat anyone at this moment, so it mattered little if he was dead or not. The trouble was he was the talisman for the Norman takeover!

Time to Celebrate

Having called back all our men we could from the battle scene we congratulated everyone on this historic days' work. This was a battle nobody would ever forget, the odds had been against us and we had accomplished more than we thought possible with so few of our men lost, it was momentous!

It was time to clean up and it was definitely time for some ale and a large feast, Hereward thought, and told one of his men to go and have a word with the powers that be in the kitchens.

As the men and women began returning from the burnt area with all the things, they had taken from the dead, they told of several batches of what they thought were officer's bodies, there would be a lot spread out as they would have run if possible to escape the flames, some would doubtless have paperwork which would help establish who they were. Several of the people gave in paperwork that they had collected which might be helpful. Still no mention of anyone who could have been William.

All those who had contributed to this victory, were to come along first to drink and eat, there was just about enough covered space for all as it was raining as it often did in these parts. Hereward gave a few words of thanks to these men again, though the fire had helped us beyond measure, he said, the strength and spirit of you men had shone through.

The men Hereward had sent out to finish this fighting had returned and the leader came to speak to him, he confirmed there were quite a few enemies in the reed beds, trees, and wherever else they had found temporary sanctuary.

They had put an end to them, so for the time being, no enemy to attack. There were of course all the other camps to consider, none of them had a great deal of soldiers, and they didn't seem to have a main leader to unite them to fight. Time would tell!

Thinking again, we decided to send out another group in the morning to try and find tracks any soldier had made in getting away from the fight, we wanted to make sure all efforts were made to kill all opposition if possible. Simple wipe them from the face of the earth, beat them into leaving us, and our main island that was England, alone!

The meal went on for a lot longer than intended, ale consumption was a little higher than normal. After all, it was not every day we had the chance to almost wipe out the enemy, with so few losses to ourselves, so it carried on into the early hours.

Hereward and his officers left early, though there was not much chance of getting much sleep, due to the noise, they had much work to do the following morning.

Chapter 100

The light of the new day arrived and woke Hereward from his slumber, there was quite a lot of noise outside his room, he opened the door. A loud salute greeted him, to his surprise a pretty large group of what appeared to be his best men stood to attention claiming they needed to be off to see what had become of the remains of the dreaded Norman army.

They would be a very angry bunch by now, much would depend on which leaders had survived the fighting, and how they were organised. If, Hereward thought, I was one of them I would want to regroup as a force and make my way back to their nearest safe area as quickly as possible. These soldiers of ours job was to try and cut them off and fight them until there was no one left.

He said it was his duty to lead these men, in truth he was a fighting man, and he could not stand by and do nothing while his men were busy with exciting work! I joined the group as well for much the same reason. A prolonged rest might have been a much better idea!

We all ate and prepared to leave, some were nursing bad heads from the night before, but not many admitted it, kind of unmanly to do so!

We had some hard riding ahead, if we were going to get those stragglers. Many of the leaders left in camp tried to deter Hereward from leaving, said he was too important to risk his life, the other men were more than capable of sorting out the remaining enemy. He agreed they were, but in his usual stubborn way he said his goodbye to all and marched off at the head of this group of Saxons, towards the usual exit from the Isle.

We managed to cut some of the trek by going a slightly different way across the fens, cut off a corner of the journey. It really was a dreadful mess of charred reeds, bodies and dead horses. A very sobering trip off the Isle for us all. All of us shut our minds to this mess. Concentrated on the job in hand.

We exited the fens and spread out a little, to find if our enemy had regrouped as one. It was easy to pick up their track, it was quite wide, so quite a number had got away. What a shame, I thought, as we called all to follow our lead. We quickened the pace now, the horses seemed to be enjoying the stretch, a good workout for them!

A few groaning bodies lay by the side of the track waiting to die, pretty dreadful for everyone, they either needed helping on their way or treating to heal, we would never leave our men like this, though this situation was unusual, Normans had not suffered like this for many a year, Hereward thought, plus they were in a rush to get protection in a large group of their fellows. It was

Hereward's job to stop this happening and he intended to do just that, if at all possible!

We were still going along at a fare pace, we had sent out two scouts, it almost seemed they came back before they left, with news that there appeared to be quite a bunch around the next bend in the track. They said they seemed to be in a bit of a daze, they must have seen our scouts, but did not pay them much attention!

Hereward slowed before they reached the corner, he peered around, not bothering to get off his mount, he saw some were back on their horses and most of the rest were preparing to do likewise. They must indeed have seen our men, as they were preparing to leave, quickly if possible, one of the enemy was shouting at all the men to move.

He didn't need to spur his men on as they knew what their duty was, kill or be killed!

Our men filled the track as they stormed at these enemy at great speed, the Normans tried to get up speed to get away. They were never going to make it.

Several of the men on horseback set their sights on going out with a bang by attacking us with swords held high in defiance, they did not last long as they were cut down and wasted.

The rest managed to damage a couple of horses, never mind that, we just took a couple that were left rider less from the enemy and off we went again.

That had got the adrenalin going, we began pushing our men more now as we thought the remnant's would not be far away from enemy camps. Burwell would be the first, the camp there was large and well-guarded. The causeway was stacked with covered areas for soldiers.

We were not far off now, so after a few more miles they slowed, so Hereward could go forward and see for himself what lie ahead in relation to how many enemy there were, and were they organised to repel us at a moment's notice.

What he saw took him by surprise, the enemy had hugely increased the number of their men here, plus a number of stragglers from the battle could easily be made out. These men alone would be very angry at having so many of their brothers killed and for a Norman army to be so defeated was unnatural, their minds must be reeling to say the least. An awful lot depended on their leadership now. They must surely be bringing more and more soldiers here from other areas of southern England, however many could he call on? The arrival of these men must have been planned quite some time ago, they may even have come out of Cambridge.

I was not sure we should take them on, if our boys were beaten back or suffered badly in any way that would be a real blow for our Saxon cause.

As we watched them preparing to eat, the numbers didn't add up at all, several hundred men against our tiny group we reckoned.

We made our way back to our tiny group of fighters, told them what lay up ahead, we all agreed it would be suicidal to take them on. What else to do before returning to our Isle?

Hereward sent the scouts out to see what groups of enemy were nearby, and could be realistically taken on and defeated. We took our men into the woods so they could not be seen and settled down to wait.

The scouts returned and said the group near Bottisham appeared ready to fight, and not too many of them, they thought. There were still considerably more men there but they thought we could deal with them.

Hereward and I decided to at least go and have a look but as we got ready to leave a number of enemy came from the track from Burwell, probable to see if they could see any Saxons. This was not the whole group thankfully. They were using a lead scout, the same as we did, he saw the track in the scrub made by our horses. We should of course have been much more careful! He guessed some enemy were in the woods and quickly rode back to his relatively small group.

There didn't seem to be a huge number of them, so it looked to Hereward like a fight was about to start, perhaps the leader of these men was trying to make a name for himself. He should have gone back to the main Burwell force and joined up to fight as a whole unit, thankfully he did not.

He didn't do anything but call to attack, they came in a rush, the enemy did in fact outnumber our men. We had fought many battles with the numbers against us, and still won! So we cried out to let battle commence!

108. Attack!

Hereward gave not much thought to anything but to attack, he did stay in the trees a little as he thought that might be an advantage, he gave the order to his bowmen to knock out as many of the soldiers as they had time to, they did well. In came the Normans, a huge clashing of swords ensued, usual madness as horses reared and snorted, men fell to the ground, some were stamped on by the horses, some managed to reel away from the fight waiting for some enemy to be grounded so they could fight them!

I had what seemed like a normal fight with a couple of enemy, they came straight at me, I swerved my horse and managed to knock a sword clean out of my adversary's hand, the other horse came right at me so I was forced to aim straight at him, swords clashed. I nearly fell from my animal, pulled myself back and the first guy came at me. I managed to dispatch him quite well but by this time the other chap was about to come down on me with his sword.

I urged my horse to move very fast to one side, just out of reach, just in time, I clashed with his sword and turned as quickly as I could manage, I then tried to lull him into thinking that I was badly injured, he relaxed his sword a little, just enough time for me to go straight for the kill. Battles like this were going on all around here, alarmingly busy, this fighting!

Madness on the field of battle was changed to even more madness in these woods.

Quickly, Hereward took out not one but two men who attacked him, slashing them to his right, then his left. No time to consider anything but attack some more, so he did. He had a moment then to look around, the enemy were in some trouble, they would have been better to have got him and his men on open ground. The woods seemed a distinct advantage to us, we had knocked out a huge percentage of his force by hitting them with arrows before they could see or reach us.

He saw two of his men go down, three enemy had cornered them against a couple of large trees. He urged his mount towards them, as he neared he hit the first one with his trusty sword, he went down without a whimper, the other two turned and came towards him, quite fast.

They were excited, he imagined he could see the glint in their eyes. At having just hurt at least two Norman enemies, they thought they were looking at a third. Hereward had other ideas as he clashed with the first man, knocking his sword and arm away and damaged his other arm as he passed him. Quickly, he turned his horse and aimed for the other man, he seemed rather slow to raise his sword arm, Hereward took advantage of this and took his arm off with one clean swipe, he would be no more trouble Hereward thought.

Before he had time to turn properly, the other Norman was screaming at him at the top of his voice and about to hit him when a sword appeared from another man on horseback and ran him through. I didn't expect that, thought Hereward, but thanks anyway!

Things were still hectic, more to do, thought Hereward, so he pushed his horse yet again into this fight. Another Norman attacked, brushed him off and ran him through, and so on. There were five of the enemy left now, Hereward thought, he and I left the men to sort them out. He needed to think fast as to what to do next.

The rest of the Burwell Camp Normans would soon be looking for their friends, they would have heard the noise of our fighting. On finding them dead, they would be after us, and no mistake, we thought, so maybe a fast run back to the Isle was on the cards.

That decided, we quickly got our remaining men together and wasted no time at all in getting under way for a speedy return.

As we rounded the first bend in the track, they could hear French cries in anger at losing yet more men to their soldiers. Hereward and I quickly thought we must get under cover of the forest and make our return using the cover of this very thickly wooded area, our group of soldiers were too small to take on the remnants of Williams forces, there were hundreds of his men stationed around Burwell and they would be up for a fight, even though they were licking their wounds.

He instructed all to follow him into the darkness this woodland offered, it would without doubt slow us down but he knew enough to say this would give him and his men the best chance of keeping alive. These men had been at his side a long time, he didn't want to lose any of them, they were strong and would go to their deaths doing as he instructed, Just the sort of men you needed in a fight, especially against the dreaded Norman.

The going was slow to be sure but as they got further into the woodland the lower brush became less dense so it was easier to get along. This cheered the men, as the pace became quicker the sound from the enemy became less. Perhaps they were more than a little wary of entering the tree line, a bit like putting ones head into a noose, they could not see if we were still in the area. It clearly gave us the chance to escape so we did just that!

Hereward and I agreed the idea to travel towards a settlement that went by the name of Chippenham, then along the edge of the fen, towards Soham, passing the mere that would be on our left, follow the land until it became fen, get through towards the high and dry land of Stuntney, thus onto our Isle again! It sounded good but as Hereward said much depended on who we met between here and Stuntney.

They would have to wait and see if any enemy were either sent to Soham to see if we arrived or not, and kill them if possible, they may just run into a group of enemy anywhere. They would travel in confidence and fight if the occasion needed. They would of course make sure the group was a relatively small one to fight! Otherwise they would have to hide and or run and hide, whichever was expedient.

We all settled down around the fires as it had turned quite chilly, it began to rain gentle as well though not a great deal fell on them as they were covered by the trees.

Chapter 101

We all slept well, finished off the Boar, and broke camp at first light. I called in the scouts, they reported no noise or movement of soldiers so off we went towards Chippenham. This area had a lot denser wood, it was odd how it altered, Hereward supposed that it was down to the ground make up, though it didn't seem to look any different, no matter, he thought, now was not really the time to consider soil types, only think about matters in hand, fighting, that is what he always told his men! Too much thinking was clearly not good, a distraction that could wait!

They made their way to the edge of the wood to see if anyone was about, soldiers or locals, there was nobody so they decided to go back to the track, as it was so much quicker to travel. Nobody was sorry to leave the woods. It had made sense to keep under cover when they did but now it was time to get many more miles between us and the enemy as soon as possible.

The lead scout came back and said Chippenham was ahead, the track he assumed lead to Soham was nearby on our left, we should take it and make our way as quickly as possible. He said to Hereward that he thought we had been lucky to date but he had a feeling that the enemy were close by. He was sure that by now Soham would have unwanted guests in the shape of a band of Normans, even if they were just some scattered remnants from after the fighting they would be on the lookout for any group of Saxons soldiers. Maybe some men had been sent from Burwell to prepare to ambush our Saxons on our return to refuge on the Isle.

He said, he knew, it wasn't his place to say such things, he was probably right and Hereward said so, also thanked and agreed with him. He also said that any of his group of soldiers would always be listened too, he would be angrier if nobody said anything, he couldn't possibly be right all of the time, plus, as a scout he would expect him to be more of a thinking man than anything else. The scout took his place with the rest of our brave Saxons and felt a better man for his efforts!

We turned off towards Soham and quickened our pace, sending out another scout to lead, the woods were either side of this track, really quite close, so all the men were ready. Well almost ready, ready as you could be on horseback, to draw out their swords and fight.

The trees became much more spaced out as they neared Soham, they had clearly been cut down, great gaps appeared, with piles of timber laid out in heaps. The scout turned around and came back in haste!

He said, he did not like the look of these piles of timber, spaced out as they were, Normans could be hiding behind them. This particular scout had shown just how good he was on a number of occasions to date, so they all went off into the woods to the left of the track, dismounted, and began talking about what they should do.

They went off into the woods a little more and Hereward and Cedric decided to very silently go through the trees, get in line with the piles of timber and see what was, if anything, behind them.

It's very difficult to move around in woodland silently but they managed it quite well, they thought so at least!

They were startled to catch a glimpse of a man, not in Saxon dress, he was crouching which was suspicious, they saw movement ahead in the trees and were about to turn around when all of a sudden the world seemed to crash around them. Some of these enemy must have been deeper in the woods, so they had missed them in hiding. Hereward and Cedric only just had time to pull their swords and the enemy were on them!

Two to begin with, swords clashed, Hereward ran the first one through, as always, in brush, it was almost impossible to fight normally, they tried to move a little where it was thin bushes, but the next Normans were on them. Cedric moved to one side and knocked the next guy's sword arm with such force that it left his hand, he finished him as he drew his sword back and thrust into his chest.

Hereward was now fighting two enemies, he did have a little more space now and he used it well as he knocked away one sword and hit the other as it was thrust towards him, he went back to the nearest man and swiped towards his arm. He didn't move fast enough so Hereward thrust his sword into his arm and chest, badly injured, the man moved out of the fight, the other man threw all his weight at Hereward with his sword aimed at his chest. Hereward was much too experienced to allow this to come to anything, he moved very quickly out of the way of the blade and thrust his sword towards the oncoming enemy. The hapless fellow quickly ran onto his sword and was quickly dead!

Cedric was dealing with the last one quite well, a little bit of sword craft, and then death to the enemy! I had heard the noise of the fighting and quickly joined them with all the other men, all our swords clashing, very noisily in the close confines of these woods.

Where there was little noise there was now an awful lot of it!

A Lot of Frenchmen Shouting

They attacked full on, once they had spread out, this was a bunch of men with nothing to lose, and they looked menacing! In fact they did not just look it!

A couple of moments later the two lines of men clashed, and continued to for some time, this was a fight to the death! Hopefully the Normans, not us Saxons.

Chapter 102

Hereward's, and my, hope was that our men were a lot more experienced at fighting than the enemy, this should win the day, and that our men were very fit, they should be able to stand and fight for longer. I at least hoped this was the case, though there must surely be twice the number of enemy.

The fighting became heavier, as the Saxons gained through killing more of the French, another batch of them filled their depleted ranks, how long could we sustain enough energy, to continue this, I thought? I was fighting someone who appeared somewhat crazy, huge eyes stared at me, he fought bravely, but he did not seem quite with the rest of his fellow soldiers. He was strong as he came for me, our swords clashed, both ended pointing to the ground, he grinned at me, strangely. He tried to stab me with his small knife, I managed to leap out of the way, I aimed a kick at him, fairly knocked the breath out of him! He staggered a little, and launched himself at me again, our swords met, I hit him harder and his sword flew out of his hand altogether. He looked at me again and in an instant leapt for it, collected it, and tried again to run me through.

He did this so fast, I thought, he must have taken something, some sort of drug, perhaps! Who knows, perhaps he was having an extra bad day, what did I know?

Amusingly, I thought we had all better get some, whatever it may be as he fought madly but well, we clashed again, this time I managed to cut into his arm quite badly, he was not a happy man anymore! He stood back a little, adjusted his jacket, quite a lot of blood appeared. I attacked him, too soon for his liking, as he was not ready, I managed to cut into his arm again.

He let out a mighty cry of pain, I must have hit a nerve, or bone. He staggered badly, came at me yet again, I managed to finish him with a thrust to the neck, as it was unguarded, the man was not wearing his gorget. These things were a pain to wear but they gave good protection from most attacks. He was also not wearing his helmet, several of the enemy were not battle ready, a good thing for us.

Hereward knocked down another of the French and moved forward as another came at him for the kill, it was exhausting and even quite satisfying beating these men back, he moved out of the man's sword reach and again thrust into his chest.

A couple of our men were out of the fight, they didn't seem to have really bad wounds so we left them for the time being.

The brush area where we were fighting was more than a little trampled, it was smashed into a mess with dead bodies all around, wounded men groaning. Not for the first time, I thought that it was more than a little sad that human beings carried on in such a way. No time to think, back to work again! At this time in our life it was definitely kill or be killed, not sit back and think about what to do, and indeed when to do it!

The fighting came to a close, the last few enemies tried to run away, they were defeated but we wanted nobody to get away, so two of our men expert with their bows, Guthrum and Manton Espenson aimed, fired and missed, too many trees in the way, fired again and both met their targets. We were all so tired we couldn't have bothered to try and run and catch them so it was the only end to the encounter we could have managed.

Hereward immediately went to check the wounded. It was a lot worse than he had earlier thought, two men had passed away and four injured quite badly, plus two more lightly injured. We had two men trained a little in dressing wounds, they did the best they could. They cleaned the wounds and wrapped clean cloth around them to stop the blood flowing. This seemed to stem the flow, hopefully they would begin to heal quickly, though that may have been wishful thinking on my part.

We went back to where the horses were tied and prepared to make our way as best we could through the brush/woods, made a lot slower by trying to help the injured.

No more enemy appeared which was good. Soon, Soham appeared in the guise of small houses dotted about the lane which was opening to a large clearing in the woods.

We were reluctant to show ourselves as any of these houses might have been taken over by enemy soldiers, we went further into the woods just in case, it was not long before we reached Soham Mere, a huge expanse of water, reed bound, as was normal here!

We decided to settle here for a time, maybe a few hours, we all needed a rest and we could make sure the injured were as good as could be expected, they could be bathed if it would help, again.

We had a very good fisherman with us, his eyes lit up at the thought of catching food, Alton Endicott, was his name, Hereward and I believed he performed miracles at this time, cheered the men up with some mad comment as he went about his task.

Camp was set up a little from the water, well in the thick brush, we could hide well, even though, as usual, scouts were set up at particular points around camp. The injured were a worry, we told them we were not too far from Stuntney Island, and then home to the Isle, that cheered everyone!

Some deer were spotted nearby so we all ate well that night.

The sky became overcast quite early and it rained steadily, adding to the gloom, though we were in the woods we still became a little wet, it didn't seem worth making covering for us all, Hereward said he wanted the injured in the dry but that did not take long. Set for the night! Funny really, it made us all feel better men, making an extra effort for the injured among us.

We slept well, until one of the scouts woke Hereward to tell him of a group of men, possible enemy, were on their way towards them along the water's edge. Everybody had to be woken from their slumber, as we had to be ready to fight at a moment's notice, or not, as the case maybe!

After a few minutes, we listened and the conversation was in good English, so we rightly assumed they were Englishmen, though we didn't want to make fools of ourselves by calling out to them. We waited for them to draw near and walked out of the brush towards them, they were a little startled to begin with. Hereward did not need to tell them who we were or where they were from, Cedric and a couple of other men joined him, he asked if there were many Normans in Soham and if so where were they?

After the surprise had worn off they chatted freely, they said there were quite a number in a few alehouses they had virtually taken over, they asked about us and eventually Hereward said we were fighters off the Isle, the men got a little over excited at this. Hereward asked them to calm down, were these Normans treating the locals badly, he asked. The men folk in the place were just talking of taking them on in battle to chase them out once and for all. Hereward suggested he and his men fight them, kill or send them on their way, otherwise reprisals might be a problem, if not now, sometime in the near future, perhaps.

The Soham men talked to themselves for a while and decided that it would be much better for battle ready men from the Isle to take on the task, which made sense all round.

We all went with these men who showed us where they had billeted themselves. The day was getting under way for the town now, people were walking the streets.

Hereward and our men decided to hit them on this day, no point hanging around, they knew where they were, most of them at least.

It Would Be Interesting, Fighting House to House if Needed

He placed his men, around a particular ale house that he had been told most of the enemy inhabited. Two appeared at the back door, they were quickly dealt with, and pulled out of sight, followed by a half a dozen more, sword fighting ensued, the clashing was very loud, it was something that had become usual to all.

Hereward's and my men fairly took these enemy apart, they were simple not expecting any trouble at all from these "English fools" or normal townspeople to us. At the front Hereward and his men were busy with their bows, very soon a barrier of dead bodies lay about the street, again they had caught these soldiers at a very "lazy" moment.

They began exchanging arrows from the windows now so it was becoming more difficult to finish them easily, Hereward and I led some men to the sides of the building and entered it from there, more sword fighting came about quickly as we went from room to room, clearing it as we went. Several of our men came in the back door, cleared the back rooms and ran up the stairs.

It didn't take long before all enemy were dead, cleared out in no time at all, they must have let their guard down as life for them had become a little too easy after the fighting in the fens.

We went along the street to the next building they had taken over. Hereward and I placed our men at all doors into the establishment, and waited. Nobody appeared at first so we sent an arrow through a window. That got their attention! Soon enough they came running out of the front and back to meet the same end as their comrades. A few had the sense to stay behind the doors and began to fight back, arrows flying all over the place, not daring to show any targets to the men killing their fellow soldiers, they could not see where the danger was coming from!

Hereward approached the front of the building, he could hear his men fighting at the rear of the property, so they had got into the building before he had! Whatever next, we were a very experienced bunch of men now so sometimes the men took the initiative without us telling them what to do. This was only to be expected we supposed on commenting about it afterwards. And in truth we were glad. We had taught them well!

We crashed through the door, swords flailing all over the place, as we sought to finish this fight, Hereward felt a sting in his left arm, someone had come from behind him and caught him unawares!

He became somewhat annoyed at this, clashed with this enemy s sword and ran him through.

The building was soon cleared in much the same fashion as the last.

Two more buildings that they knew of to empty of the enemy!

The last two were on the outskirts of town, they would have to be taken together as they were next door to each other.

Chapter 103

Stuntney

These men were up and about now, a different storey than the other two places, so Hereward took half the force and Cedric took the other, I went with Cedric.

Again, they guarded the doors, any man who came out was shot with arrow first, then again we led our men to the doors and crashed in, causing a major disturbance against any enemy that was about, they were finished quickly.

As an exercise, this had proven easy, the locals were overjoyed at having their town back, the cost, a few injuries, none any real trouble though. Hereward had his arm cleaned and dressed, as did a couple of others. His injured men from the fight in the woods were brought to the rest of the Saxon soldiers and they began their trek through the water to Stuntney, then, hopefully, and at last, the Isle!

Normans on Stuntney

Hereward had hoped all enemy would have left this island by now, unfortunately this was not the case. There was a small camp the enemy had erected, with about thirty men on it, they found, much to their annoyance. They trod through the fen water, the scout had informed them of these enemy, so they tried to go around them and not be seen, that is, through the water around the island and make dry land nearer the Isle. So much fighting had about exhausted this force, moving from fight to fight as fast as we had, then running to keep clear of the enemy possible following. All very exciting and exhilarating, but definitely exhausting, at the same time. Had our training made all the difference? I had insisted on doing it, so I liked to think it had won the day! All the leaders kept up with training and tried to outdo the other groups, the result was we all became better fighters.

We managed to make dry land alright so continued on our way as silently as possible, we heard some cries from the direction of the enemy. Hell! I thought, another fight, just when we thought we were home and dry, quite literally!

Quickly, we lined up along the edge of the tree line on the island, the enemy quickly prepared themselves to fight, had they really not had enough of this?

Surely, it was time to sulk off into the forest and get some sort of peace after having been beaten as badly as they had. They must have been obeying orders, still, they must know it was over for them, at this time at least.

They began firing at us at quite a rate, they were too far away to cause any real danger, we told our men to pick off any enemy they could get a clear shot at. We knocked out quite a few, they ran back for their horses, obviously planned to get us by sword alone. I called out to the men to kill off as many on their horses as they could, then to mount our horses and attack.

This we did to great effect, we met about the middle of the island, not many of them left. What a waste of life, as we knocked them out as easily as knocking over sticks, we were in a hurry to get back to the Isle and nobody was going to stop us, even though we were tired out!

We decided to take their horses with us, might be handy sometime!

Getting back onto the Isle was made more difficult due to our injured, as we approached, a crowd of people, led by our leaders, began cheering and shouting. We all picked up considerable on hearing this, tired out, we made the last section quickly.

All managed dry land without any more problems, and cheered to be back, it was very good to return. Our horses were led to stables, the new ones too.

We went off to wash and settle down, to feel we were not being chased at this moment was great, we had won the day!

Having done what we had set out to do, what next! A bit of celebrating would not be amiss! More training in the morning to look forward to!

All had changed for us know, we had beaten back the enemy, we were strong and confident, if somewhat battle weary, we knew we could take on the best the Normans could throw at us and win. Their main force was nothing but a mess now, we knew we would confidently move forward from this time, and win! It would take us some time and an awful lot of thought and effort but we were on the right track at last!

We had to think we would suffer setbacks at times in battles and what effect that may have on us all in the long term. The enemy would be hurting now and would be thinking of ways to get back at us as we celebrated our fighting prowess.

We returned to the Isle through the deep water of the river and reeds, cold, wet muddy and tried to tend our wounds and bruises.

Plans for tomorrow could wait a little longer. They did, and what plans they were!

Book Three

We ate and rested as a group. After a time, us leaders went to our meeting hall to talk to the rest of the heads of all groups.

All were pleased of the success of our mission.

Plans were put forward now from anyone who had ideas on where to establish more groups of fighters to get them established and trained to our very high standard so we could begin again as our kingdom of Anglo-Saxon England. We must move forward quickly now to keep us all on the front foot!

Meanwhile

A rushed meeting was taking place, with all the leaders of the Normans in Cambridge.

William and his army had suffered the biggest loss in memory, his forces had been thrashed, beaten and burned by the Saxon army and fen folk. This was a massive humiliation, what was he to do?

This group of Normans was somewhat depleted in numbers now, many were dead, gloom was the order of this meeting.

Somehow William knew, he had to drive his leaders forward to regain their stomach for the fight ahead.

His closest friend said they must call for reinforcements from France, William stated he had already sent for a number of his top men to bring over a several thousand strong force of new soldiers.

This seemed to bring about some enthusiasm from all in the room, it was as though a spark had been reignited, and maybe there was hope after all!

It was agreed that a small force would be sent out from the Cambridge base to round up any men that were left in the forests, fields and indeed ditches and with the injured bring them back to safety. Every man was needed now! As they were at their weakest they could expect another visit from the Anglo-Saxon forces that is what he would do if he were in their shoes.

As Estienne Enguerrand, Roland Vauquelin, Guiscard Onfroi and Piers Roul knew the area as well as anyone they would lead this force. They set off with thirty men in a hurry to find all they could and bring them in. Spare horses were to be taken along to bring back injured men.

It was cold, wet and getting dark when they set off. The new men were not amused at being pulled out of their camp as the rain began to come down from the skies. These men had settled back into life at the protected camp near Cambridge, no more peace for them for a time at least.

The track took them past Fen Ditton and then between Horningsea and Bottisham. When they reached Swaffam they found about a dozen injured

Normans and told them in no uncertain terms to quickly make their way back to town and get treated as best they could. They were needed, fit and ready to fight, not to stay skulking in the woods where they were no good to anybody!

They did protest but Estienne gave them short shrift! He said he would make sure they were not here when he returned, he would also make sure they entered the Cambridge camp when he arrived back.

It was getting really dark, as they approached Devils Dyke near Reach, here they camped, food and rest was needed. The covers were put up and fires lit, food to cook produced from their carrier bags. The high bank provided cover from the wind, dry and warm at last!

They would spread out in the morning and try and find survivors of what had quickly become known as the great battle, victorious from the Saxons view, not so from the view of these men. They were all despondent!

Estienne left out a couple of guards during the night but they were not disturbed. The sun woke them, bright on the horizon, start to a lovely day. The grumbling of the night before was forgotten as they ate well. Estienne explained he wanted them to fan out and cover as much ground as possible of the ground between Newmarket and Burwell.

Burwell still had quite a force stationed there but he knew, some of his soldiers would be hiding amongst the force there, hoping to not get pulled back and fight yet again with Williams force. He would go and weed them out and return them to Cambridge, even if they tried to hide.

As they spread out, they found half a dozen men who were all injured, they had set up camp in a dried out ditch in some woods. They were a little careless with their fire, the smoke filtered through the trees but Roland told them to dampen it down a little and they would come back to take them back to base on their return. He left them with some clean bandages, as they had boiled some water he told them to clean the damaged parts of their bodies as best they could and hope they would not be caught by the enemy.

These men were well spread out now, Estienne reached Burwell, he was horrified at the state of some of the remnants of the Norman fighters. They were being treated a little by the men who had stayed behind from the fighting, they were the lucky ones he had no doubt. A number of their men who could ride were told in no uncertain terms to get on their animals backs and follow him. To re-join the fighting now! He bade farewell to the injured who obviously could do nothing but lay back and try and recover or simple pass away.

Dead Bodies Everywhere

The area up towards Soham was littered with Norman dead in the main, a few Saxons had fought their last fight but not many.

This is not what they joined up for thought Estienne, this is not the glory and riches he had been promised. He had seen a great many riches, land and plunder to begin with, then these battles so far ending with so many of his dear brothers being slain by the Saxons of the Heptarcy, men from the seven kingdoms in England of the Anglo-Saxons.

Several of his men came in to say there were none from the battle left in their area and just to see all these dead was demoralising to all. Just what was to become of these dead? It seemed wrong to leave them but what could they possible do. The answer was nothing.

They spread out again and began to find a few more of their heroes injured. They began to lay them across the spare horses they had brought, this was going to be a huge task to get them to safety, but try they must as they had been ordered.

A number of horses were found near Chippenham, so they collected them and roped them together so that helped as the number of injured increased.

Roland found a decent area to camp near this settlement, so they all set up for the night. Estienne set out many guards that night as they were not far from a particular area of fighting, yet another batch of dead Normans littered the ground.

As they fitfully slept, they were disturbed at about midnight by their guards. A group of roaming Saxons were about coming their way. The fit Normans were woken and made ready for a fight, they prepared in a ditch lined by some trees as their enemy could be heard not far away.

Roland could just about make out their outline against the sky, so he settled an arrow into his bow and let fly. He caught the man in his shoulder, who let out a cry of pain, the Saxons were startled and pulled their horses away, back behind some trees.

The Normans could hear them calling to each other as they thought of a plan of attack. They tied their horses and could be heard spreading out around where they thought the Normans were, Estienne called out to his men to fire at anything that moved that may be Saxon.

The Saxons seemed to know the area well, as even in the darkness they surrounded the front and sides of where the Normans were. On a call from their leader they began sending in arrow after arrow into the Norman foe.

As the Normans tried to move or they cried out in pain it seemed the Saxons increased their volume of arrows. There was a call from them and they all attacked on foot.

The Normans felled quite a few but it was soon obvious they would have to retreat and carry as many of their injured as possible with them, slowing them which gave them little time that they could ill afford if they were going to survive.

Roland and Estienne rushed about giving orders and helping men onto their horses, just twelve fit men survived this with a few injured, another bad tale to tell William. No good news whatsoever.

They still had to try and return to Cambridge in one piece, if they could avoid the Saxons though they seemed to have not bothered to chase them. Perhaps they thought that chasing them off and killing some of them was enough to put yet more fear into the Norman enemy. The story recounted to William might just be more important than that of killing them all?

Who knows, thought Estienne, but at least they were alive to tell the tale!

They pushed their mounts as fast as they dared back to the town that was Cambridge, struggling badly with their injured.

On arrival, Estienne and Roland went straight to William to tell of their narrow escape.

It was only, as he had supposed said William, the Saxons would be cock a hoop with their runaway success at this time. He had no doubt, they were drawing in more and more men to their cause each and every day, they seemed to have fighting units everywhere you travelled in and around these fens and waterways.

A section of the Devils Dyke, close to Reach.

Harvesting with a boat at Ramsey in August 1912. It could have been taken during any era.

Photo: Cambridgehire Libraries.

A picture of the reed beds anywhere in the fenland.

Digging and stacking peat to dry and burn during the cold winter months.